THE DICHOTOMY OF ANGELS

N.R. WALKER

COPYRIGHT

BLURB

Nathaniel and Chasan are no ordinary angels.

Destiny chose them to be twin flames, fated mates. But Nathaniel has avoided Chasan for nearly a thousand years.

When sent to Earth on a mission to live and work together, Nathaniel comes face-to-face with his destiny. Short-tempered, petulant, and grumpy, he hates the idea of being fated to anyone and has chosen an existence of isolation rather than spending time with the calm, kind, and serene Chasan.

But now he has no choice.

One is fire, the other is air; a true dichotomy of angels. Together they will be ignited, or they will be extinguished. This assignment will seal their fate either way.

85,000 words. A sometimes-funny, sometimes-serious story about love, destiny, and other heavenly disasters.

THE DICHOTOMY OF ANGELS

N.R. WALKER

PROLOGUE, OF SORTS

TIME WAS a human construct that held little meaning for Saint Peter. Sure, time passed over eons and millennia, much the same way it did when a life flashed before someone's eyes before their mortal clocks stopped ticking; fast and slow, both together and separate, in slow motion and all at once.

Time, in its meaningless and indispensable significance, was something he'd had a lot of, and it was something that stretched out endlessly before him. It was infinite, in both directions, and would remain so for as long as there was existence.

Which was why he sat in his office at his wits end. Dressed in his white robe with gold trim, his gray hair in long wisps, worry marred his brow. He simply couldn't let this go on for one more minute.

Wait up. Hold on. Saint Peter has an office?

Well, kind of.

If Heaven was an organization, an ethereal factory, of sorts, then yes, Saint Peter had an office. There was The Boss's office, which no one went into. Not even Saint Peter.

Like most CEOs, they oversaw the machine as a whole but had little clue how the smaller, individual parts worked. Then there was the Upper Management, which was where Saint Peter and his colleagues all worked.

The next level of Heaven was the many different divisions that made the factory work. Like the Prayers Department, which was kind of like the mail room. Then there was the Souls Division, which kept track of the souls-in and souls-out, so it was basically just accounting and general ledger stuff. There was also the HR Department, which made sure all the ranks of angels were performing duties and tasks adequately. IT, of course, took care of interdepartmental correspondence and information, and Security One kept eyes on all departments to make sure all the cogs were turning efficiently. Security Two kept eyes on the humans to make sure the world wasn't about to end. If you could picture a room full of screens like in those government spy movies where they have facial-recognition and license-plate-identification software. Well, it was like that. Just times eight billion and without the espionage.

All angels rotated throughout the different departments, keeping things fresh and motivated. However, the most popular department was the *Canes Omnes* Department, for obvious reasons. Endless fields of long grass and sunshine, it was the equivalent of Earth's Disneyland, only this was the happiest place in Heaven. All angels looked forward to their time overseeing this department the most.

The Marketing Department was in charge of ensuring the humans were convinced Heaven was worth the wait. And it was. Ordinarily.

Unless you were a soul that burned up on re-entry. No, those souls didn't enjoy an eternity of damnation too much at all. Given each human got the Heaven they deserved, not everyone's *Heaven* was pleasant. Humans had given this particular department the name of *Hell*, and it had stuck some several thousand years ago; another spot of genius by the Marketing Department, really. The Hell Department was filled with endless torment, suffering and pain, the very worst of fears realized, unimaginable horrors and excruciating nothingness. A void so black, it even absorbed the screams of the damned. But the Science Department had since figured out a way to recycle that absorbed-scream energy into a ball-projectile machine that spat out tennis balls into the fields of the *Canes Omnes* Department. It was a win-win, by all accounts.

And like all factories with staff, there were hierarchies of angels. All angels worked in order to keep the organization running effectively. They each had duties to perform and departments to oversee, and for the most part this ran smoothly.

Except for today.

Saint Peter's sigh was more of a grumble this time. *He didn't like this. He didn't like this at all.* "I knew I should have taken vacation time when I had the chance." With one more grumble for good measure, he hit the intercom to reception. "Can you please send in Nathaniel and Chasan."

A few moments later, the grand white double doors opened and two angels walked in. Nathaniel stalked in first, and he wore his rage like body armor. His short reddish-brown hair was ruffled, his reddish-brown eyes narrowed under his scowling brow. His lips were pressed together in suspicion with a tinge of anger. His wings had a reddish-brown hue, matching his whole aesthetic. It was as though he'd spent far too long staring into the flames of the Hell Department. Which, in all fairness, he probably had.

Chasan glided in behind him. His blond hair was all

loose curls, tousled as though he'd just floated in on a breeze. His eyes were a sharp blue. His wings were stark white with ice-blue at the tips. His nose was straight, his features were dainty, his smile pleasant.

If Nathaniel was fire, then Chasan was air.

There had never been two angels more different.

Though they were both angels from the same order of the same hierarchy, they were realms apart. Both served their purpose, both were on equal standing within the gates of Heaven.

But these two angels were more than that. They were an anomaly, a unique twinning of souls. A weaving of eternal light which Nathaniel had refused to accept. But the burn of twin flames couldn't be ignored forever. Peter wasn't sure how long before the flame would die out or consume them both.

Well, he surmised, he was about to find out.

"You asked to see me," Nathaniel prompted. He completely ignored Chasan, who now stood beside him, and the other higher-ranking angels at the table. Typical Nathaniel; raised chin, steely gaze directed ahead.

"Yes," Saint Peter said. There was no point in beating around the bush with this, and he needed to assert his authority here. Peter was almost certain Nathaniel could smell fear. "You're being assigned a new mission."

Nathaniel's wings bristled. "Pardon?"

"A new mission," Peter clarified. "Effective immediately."

"But—"

"It's not negotiable," Peter said, cutting off whatever argument was coming. "Highest order, priority one."

Not even Nathaniel would argue with that.

But he gave a sideways glance to Chasan, then shot a

look back at Peter. His nostrils flared. "And you're telling both of us because . . ."

"Because you're both assigned to it. It's important, and it will take both of you. The length of this mission is indeterminable at this point. It could be over quickly." Peter waved his hand. "Or it may take longer than usual."

Nathaniel raised a pointed finger in protest. "Wait just a minute—"

"There will be no waiting," Peter reiterated. He spoke with more authority. "You're both to leave, effective immediately. You will work together, and"—he stared directly at Nathaniel—"you will not complain or jeopardize this case."

Nathaniel took a deep breath and bowed his head. "As you wish." He clearly wasn't happy, but he would never defy a direct order. Peter knew this.

"As you wish," Chasan echoed, his voice neutral, sweet even. Chasan would *never* question Peter's authority.

"Michael will take you to your destination and see you are properly briefed. You will not have your powers—"

Nathaniel's head shot up, his expression stricken. "Oh, are you fucking kidding me?!"

"Thou shall not have powers!" Saint Peter said, his voice ringing loud and clear. He took a calming breath and began again, quieter this time. "Like with all missions, you will be human; you will integrate with humans until your mission is complete. You will guard the secret of our existence at all costs. Or you'll find your time will expire with the human life you assume. Am I clear?"

Nathaniel glowered.

Chasan gave a nod. "Of course."

It was standard procedure for angels to be without powers when on a human assignment, after all.

Saint Peter let out the mother of all sighs. But he softened when he looked at Nathaniel. "You will make me proud, I know you will."

Nathaniel stared right back at him, or right through him, it would seem.

Of course Nathaniel would see. "What aren't you telling me?" he asked. "Peter, just exactly what is this mission? What exactly will I be doing?"

Archangel Michael appeared out of nowhere, as he was wont to do. "We ready to go?"

"Yes," Peter replied quickly.

"Peter," Nathaniel warned. "What is this mission?"

Peter turned to Chasan. "Take care of him."

Nathaniel's mouth opened, and Saint Peter was certain an unholy tirade was about to spew forth. But Michael gave him a wink, and in a flash of light, he disappeared, taking Nathaniel and Chasan with him.

Peter sagged with relief. He looked around the room at all the faces staring back at him. "May Theliel and Achaiah watch over them now."

Though Peter knew it would take more than Love and Patience to make this work. He briefly wondered if there was any sacramental wine handy, but with a dawn of realization that it was far too late, he did all he could. He said a prayer.

Kind of.

"Heaven help us all."

CHAPTER ONE

NATHANIEL

THE TRANSFER to a human form was never easy. It felt confined and constricting, like an ill-fitting suit, and Nathaniel always hated the residual squeeze the morphing left in its wake. He shook himself out, rolling his shoulders and fisting his hands a few times until the discomforting buzz subsided.

The room Nathaniel found himself in was typical living quarters for twenty-first century humans. There was a sofa, a dining table, a kitchen, a fluffy white rug, all spacious and grand, and any human would have appreciated the apparent wealth and luxuriousness of it all. But not Nathaniel.

Human niceties weren't something he much cared for.

He did, however, notice the skyline out the window. He'd seen it in reports and videos enough to recognize it, and it was apparent the apartment was high up and well-positioned because of the view.

"New York," he grumbled.

Chasan walked to the window, inspecting the nearby

buildings and the park across the street, then turned and smiled. "This city never gets old."

Nathaniel suppressed the urge to roll his eyes. Chasan found beauty in everything. He had for thousands of years, and it had always been a burr in Nathaniel's boot. Chasan would simply smile and nothing was ever an issue. He took everything in his stride, and everything was cheery and promising. His blessed cup forever runneth over.

Nathaniel was more of a chalice-half-empty kind of angel.

Chasan and he had worked together several times over the eons, not particularly well, Nathaniel could admit. They were too different. Like night and day: Chasan was sunshine and roses; Nathaniel was darkness and thorns. If you thought angels couldn't have such vast and varied personalities, you'd be mistaken. They most certainly did. And with differing personalities came personality clashes.

And that's what this was. Between Nathaniel and Chasan. Just a clash of personalities. The tension, the push and pull, that instant irritation Nathaniel felt from being anywhere remotely near Chasan could all be explained by a difference of personalities.

At least that's what Nathaniel had convinced himself of since their last disastrous encounter. An encounter that might or might not have led Saint Peter to down most of the sacramental wine—actually, half of the heavens had taken a hit that day—so why Saint Peter had insisted they work together again now was as bold as it was stupid.

"Nathaniel?" Archangel Michael said, as though not for the first time.

Nathaniel blinked and focused. "Yes. Apologies."

"How does the human modification feel?" Michael

asked. "There can be a period of adjustment. It's been a while for you, has it not? Since you've taken human form?"

Nathaniel rolled his shoulders again, noting the absence of his wings and the tightness of his skin, and shook off the unease. "It'll pass, I'm sure." Michael's gaze darted to Chasan, then back to Nathaniel, and a smile played at the archangel's lips. Nathaniel had always liked Michael—well, he hadn't *dis*liked him, so that was always a start—but Nathaniel knew this mission was going to be a rough one. Saint Peter had been behaving oddly and wouldn't divulge any information, and that never boded well. And given he'd been partnered with Chasan . . . "Michael, what is the emergency mission we have been sent here for?"

Michael smiled at them both, then gestured toward the sofa. "Please take a seat."

Chasan sat, because of course Chasan sat. Chasan did everything he was told. Nathaniel did not. *This mission wasn't going to be good. Not good at all.* "I'd rather stand."

Michael gave Chasan a patient smile and ignored Nathaniel's petulance. With a small flick of his wrist, in a flourish of sparkles, two files appeared in his hand. "Your missions," he began, handing Chasan his file first. He held out Nathaniel's file, but Nathaniel refused to take it. Michael pursed his lips and sighed, his annoyance clear. "This mission isn't optional, Nathaniel. So quit the dramatics. We're not here to pander to you."

"Oh dear," Chasan murmured, and when Nathaniel shot him a look, he saw that Chasan was reading his file.

"Oh dear, what?" Nathaniel demanded. He held his hand out to Michael for his file now, but this time it was Michael who ignored him. Instead, Michael opened the file and read out loud. Probably because if Nathaniel wanted to act like a child, Michael would treat him like one.

"Nathaniel Angelo." Michael paused. "That's your human name, by the way."

"Angelo?" Nathaniel scoffed. "It means angel. Was the Creative Department off work that day?"

"Don't complain," Chasan said. "My surname's Bellomo. That's Italian for beautiful man."

Nathaniel rolled his eyes out loud that time. "Because of course it is."

Michael ignored both of them. "Nathaniel, age thirty-one. Youngest of three children to Christian and Mary Angelo of Bethlehem, New York."

Nathaniel blinked. "Christian and Mary of Bethlehem? Why did they stop short of calling my father Joseph? Is this someone's idea of a joke?"

Michael just kept on reading. "The Angelos are a wealthy family, which explains this apartment." He gestured to the room they were in. "So your parents weren't overly impressed when you decided that being an early childhood development teacher was your true calling—"

"Wait, wait. What?" Nathaniel asked.

Michael looked up from the file, his expression serious. "A teacher. A preschool teacher to be more specific."

"No. Nope. No. Absolutely not." Nathaniel shook his head. "Actually, the enormity of the no I must insist upon should not be underestimated."

Michael raised one archangel eyebrow. "This mission, or any sum of its parts, is not negotiable."

"A *teacher*?" Nathaniel barked. "Of infant humans?"

Michael just kept reading, as though Nathaniel's abject horror was irrelevant. "You studied at Columbia University where you met Chasan. He was also studying to be an early childhood development teacher. You dated for six years and married three years ago in front of family and friends in a beautiful ceremony at your parents' stately house." Michael waved his hand and an array of photo frames appeared on the bookcase. Not just any photos, but wedding photos.

Nathaniel and Chasan's wedding.

To each other.

Oh, mercy bless.

Nathaniel opened his mouth to protest the greatest of protests ever protested, but a burst of pain pierced his brain, and his stomach knotted painfully. The air became suddenly too thin to sustain his human form, and the world tilted ever so slightly. He swayed, put his hand to the side of his head, and groaned. "What is this?"

Michael looked him over, apparently none too concerned. "I believe that's called a headache. It's a human ailment where the blood vessels—"

"Make it stop!" Nathaniel cried.

"It's not that bad. Stop being such a baby," Michael mumbled, rolling his eyes. But blessedly, he snapped his fingers, and the biting pain in Nathaniel's head disappeared. Nathaniel swayed again and put a hand on the back of the sofa to steady himself. Michael just kept right on. "Right, so, where was I? Oh, here. Okay, so yes, you two are married. Happily, blissfully married. And you both start work the day after tomorrow at Eisenhower Learning Center, two blocks from here. The two teachers who you're both replacing had an unfortunate accident at the end of last term, so there was, most conveniently—" He cleared his throat. "—a requirement for two qualified, experienced teachers. You'll be a two-man team in charge of twenty four-year-old children."

Nathaniel couldn't believe what he was hearing. No wonder Saint Peter hadn't wanted to disclose any details. *A preschool teacher? Twenty four-year-old children?* He put his hand to his forehead. *Married?* Were human foreheads always this clammy? "I think I'll take that seat now," he whispered, then held onto the sofa as he walked around to sit, as though the floor was unsteady. He lowered himself onto the sofa. In angel form, he'd have sworn and possibly kicked the coffee table through the window by now. But this body . . . "I think there's something physically wrong with this human body. Can I get an exchange, or diagnostic check?"

"There's nothing wrong with your human body," Michael said flatly. He flipped to another page of the file. "Ah, here it is. Nathaniel, you're prone to anxiety. Which can manifest itself as headaches and nausea, elevated heart rate, general irritability, impending doom, that kind of thing."

Nathaniel blinked up at him. "Why? Why would you do that?"

"I didn't," Michael replied. "You'll have to take it up with Peter at the end of the mission. There are some clauses on page fifteen about losing powers, the ability to swear, and curbing all bouts of temper. But that was added by the Legal Department, I believe. You'll need to take it up with them too."

"Believe me, I will," Nathaniel replied. "Truly. They'll both be the first in what will be a long and distinguished list. Because, if this cruelty is supposed to be funny . . ." He put his hand to his forehead again. Now it was even wetter than before. "I just don't even know where to start. I think I'm leaking . . ."

Chasan closed the file soundlessly, his gaze fixed on Michael, brow furrowed. "And the child?"

"We have a *child?*" Nathaniel wheezed. His stomach did some awful squeezy-rolling thing, tying itself in knots and somehow making the act of breathing difficult. He made a face at Michael. "Argh, is this nausea? And my head hurts again. A child? Why?"

"Calm down," Michael said flatly, and with a snap of his fingers, Nathaniel's ailments disappeared, which was dizzying in itself. "You don't have a child."

"Oh, thank Heaven's mercy for that," Nathaniel breathed, sagging into the sofa, a little woozy, but at least the pain was gone. "And please put a stop to the anxiety. It's all rather awful, and I'm certain a human body shouldn't be hot and cold at the same time. Are we sure you can't do a swap or at least run a diagnostic check—"

"Nathaniel, stop talking." Michael put his hand up. "The child may not be *yours*, but your mission is to ensure the safety of a child in your preschool class."

In your preschool class.

Nathaniel sank lower into despair when he realized this was, indeed, actually happening. He was a preschool teacher. A teacher of underdeveloped human children. The adult in charge of a room full of four-year-olds. Where there would likely to be things like untied shoelaces, nasal discharge, and awkward questions . . . He began to feel unwell again.

He wondered what the consequences of disobeying the highest order would be. Just exactly how much worse could it be? What punishment could Saint Peter throw at him that would be worse than being a preschool teacher?

"You know," Nathaniel said, standing up. "I've overseen the Hell Department for quite some time, and I think I'll take my chances—"

"Sit down!" Michael ordered. His voice boomed with the power of Heaven.

Nathaniel sat. Well, it was more he slumped peevishly

but it was still technically sitting. He crossed his arms and pouted for good measure. At least his headache was gone.

Wait . . . nope.

There it was.

That sharp ache at his right temple. He pressed his palm to his head and squinted one eye shut. He tried to let out a string of obscenities, but none were forthcoming. "Can we at least put a stop to this cruelty? And why can't I curse?"

Michael sighed and put his hand to the side of Nathaniel's head, doing that archangel thing he could do. "Oh for the love of . . . it's a mild headache. It's not even a migraine. Stop your whining. You should have done more human missions long before now, and if you had, you'd be used to it. The cursing and temper control is like a celestial anger-management thing. You'll get used to it. Use the time to learn how to channel your anger into something less destructive." He thrust the mission file into Nathaniel's hand. "Read this. Become familiar—with all of it. No excuses. Mess this up, and overseeing the Hell Department will be the least of your worries." Michael took a step back, then nodded to Chasan. "Good luck. You'll need it." He lifted his hand, about to snap his fingers but stopped. "Oh, and get him to a CVS for some Tylenol or something. Or some Valium . . . or edibles. Or some catnip if you get desperate. If he won't take it, I suggest you do."

With a snap of his fingers, he was gone in a spark of light, leaving Nathaniel and Chasan alone. In their New York apartment. As humans. And husbands! And preschool teachers!

"Oh Heaven's mercy." Nathaniel rubbed his temples and peered at Chasan. "Did you know about this?"

"No," he replied sweetly. "Not even a whisper." He

studied Nathaniel for a moment. "I understand this isn't what you wanted."

Nathaniel groaned as the tightness in his belly returned. He pushed against it with the heel of his hand. "I really am of the opinion that there is something wrong with this human body. There seems to be a short circuit or an imbalance of some kind. It doesn't feel right at all."

Chasan stood up and walked into the kitchen. He opened a few cupboards; apparently Saint Peter's team had been grocery shopping. Chasan found a packet of salted crackers, plated a few, and filled a glass with water, then held them out to Nathaniel. "Here, have this. You could be hungry."

"Hungry?" Nathaniel was disgusted at the thought. "Human food is terrible!"

"It's not all bad. And I'm guessing you haven't had to eat human food in quite some time."

"Not for . . ." Nathaniel began but stopped himself from finishing that sentence. "No, not for a while, no."

"It's improved," Chasan said gently, sitting beside him. "Please eat. Then we need to go over our mission files, and . . ."

"And what?" Nathaniel ate a cracker, mildly surprised it wasn't completely awful. He didn't want to admit that it did make him feel a little better.

"Well, we need to go grocery shopping. There are some basics here, but we'll need more. Possibly clothes shopping, though we should take a look at the outfits they gave us. Not sure if what's been provided is suitable for teaching. We'll need to go over our profile histories to make sure we get it right. And considering you haven't been back to Earth in a while, you'll need to brush up on some world history."

Nathaniel groaned as he finished another cracker,

because the idea of shopping wasn't bad enough. "I'm a preschool teacher! I'm sure all of Heaven is looking on right now, laughing hysterically, and taking bets to see how long I last."

Chasan almost smiled, but he opened his file. "Uh, there's something else you're probably not going to like."

Nathaniel paused, a cracker halfway to his mouth. "What?"

"This gorgeous apartment," he replied. "Right on Central Park, Upper West Side. Designer furniture, ultra-modern. Luxurious, elite real estate . . ."

Nathaniel looked around at the marble tiles, the high ceilings, and yes, the view was a little impressive. "What about this apartment? What won't I like? Besides the fact it's in the human world and we're on some secret mission as teacher-husbands, and sweet Heaven's mercy—" He put his hand to his forehead. "—why do we have American accents?"

Chasan looked up from page four of his report. "Ummm, this apartment? It's all very lovely and all," he said again, making a pained face. "But it's only got one bedroom."

CHAPTER TWO

CHASAN

IT HAD BEEN a long while since Chasan had spent time with Nathaniel, but he was used to his idiosyncrasies. He was moody, prone to outbursts, prone to long periods of self-exclusion, prone to overreaction and bouts of temper, over-thinking, and prone to sulking. To put it bluntly, Nathaniel was either temperamental, difficult, argumentative, and irrational. Or he was quiet.

There was rarely any in-between.

But, Chasan knew there was more to Nathaniel underneath his prickly exterior. He'd known him long enough—longer almost than time itself—to know his brusqueness and barbed retorts were simply a defense mechanism.

Chasan knew in his heart that Nathaniel could be sweet and caring, funny, and protective. Though that had been a long time ago . . .

But Saint Peter knew that side of Nathaniel as well. He'd tolerated more attitude from Nathaniel than he had from any other angel in all the ranks of Heaven. And Chasan believed Saint Peter had chosen Nathaniel for the role of preschool teacher because he saw the good in Nathaniel.

And possibly because he wanted to see Nathaniel squirm just a teeny tiny bit. A little heavenly payback for all those centuries of insolence.

Chasan also knew why they'd been chosen *together* for this mission. They needed to bury the hatchet, so to speak. Well, Chasan didn't. But Nathaniel certainly did. And perhaps this mission wasn't so much about saving a human child, as Michael had said, but more for allowing Nathaniel the chance to finally deal with whatever had tormented him for so long.

"Oh, for the love of Mary's donkey," Nathaniel said after he struggled to swallow the water. He held out the offending glass. "What is this awful . . . ? No, wait. I think it actually came from Mary's donkey."

"New York City water," Chasan said by way of explanation.

"It never used to taste like that!"

"Probably because the last time you drank New York City water was when it was grazing land. Things have changed a little since then."

"I've been here since then," he argued—he always argued—then put the empty plate and glass on the coffee table. "Though I think we may need to obtain our water from another source because that was not pleasant. And the crackers helped, so thank you," he added, then leaned back on the sofa, his hand to his belly. "This human body is rather peculiar. I still believe there's something not quite right. Definitely an imbalance of some sort."

Chasan smiled. "Perhaps you just needed a little food to settle your stomach. It's good to know if you suffer nausea next time, you'll know what to do. Eating regularly always takes some getting used to, for me at least."

Nathaniel made a face. "Next time? I do wish there wouldn't be a next time."

"Let's not dwell," Chasan said. "We should inspect the apartment. The adjustment teams are usually efficient, but we may need to make a list of foods and any personal items we may require. Then we can go to a store. We have charge cards for any expenditures."

Nathaniel blanched. "A store? Where there are humans?"

Actually, Nathaniel looked about ready to have a full-blown panic attack. It was so palpable, Chasan swore he could feel it, so he reached over and squeezed his hand. "Breathe, Nathaniel. This is New York City. There are a lot of people. You're going to need to get used to them. And your assignment here is to teach and care for children, so perhaps some practice with human interaction is a good idea, yes?"

Nathaniel let out a breath of relief. Until he realized Chasan was still holding his hand. He shot up off the couch and paced to the window, his hand to his forehead. "Yes. Apartment inspection. Great idea. Human food and whatever else the humans are doing now. That seems like a logical thing to do. In case there's something specific these days that would be a requirement of preschool teachers."

"Such as?"

"Well, I don't know. Dueling pistols? Are they still a thing?"

Chasan almost smiled. "Not really, no."

He pondered that for a moment. "Shame."

Chasan chuckled and stood up. "Let's have a look in the kitchen first."

The adjustment teams had done a great job. The kitchen was well-stocked: both pantry and fridge were full. There was even a coffee machine. Chasan searched the cupboards. "We'll need coffee pods."

"Coffee what?"

"Pods. They use pods now. Little capsules that slot into the coffee machine. They're punctured, and hot water steeps the coffee grinds."

"Well, that seems all rather unnecessary and very sterile. Do you remember that time in Yemen with the Sufi around the campfire?" Nathaniel said with the beginning of a smile. "They roasted beans on an open flame, then ground the beans on a stone before boiling it."

"It was bitter sludge," Chasan reminded him.

"That was good coffee," Nathaniel said wistfully. "Not quite the same without the ash and sand mixed in with it."

It was also over a thousand years ago, Chasan wanted to add, but he kept that part to himself. The memory had made Nathaniel smile, so Chasan didn't dare spoil the mood. Though maybe his smile had little to do with the coffee and more to do with simpler times.

Before their lives got overly complicated.

"I can look online to see if there are any Yemeni coffee blends with ash and sand," Chasan said. "Though nowadays you're more likely to see it infused with hazelnuts or vanilla."

Nathaniel stared at him, horrified. "That is . . . that's . . ." He huffed then, his shock giving way to outrage. "That's a humanitarian barbarity."

Chasan chuckled. "Well, prepare yourself for this . . . they also have chai coffee now. They call it a dirty latte or something like that."

Nathaniel's mouth fell open. And he blinked slowly, several times, very confused. "What? That makes no sense! How is that even possible? Who is to blame for this?"

"Well—"

"Are they even aware that chai is tea? It literally means tea. That's what the word chai means. Who drinks tea-coffee? Tell me who!"

"Well, a lot of—"

"You know what? Never mind. I think it might be time for Noah to do his flood thing again. Or perhaps some locusts. We'll soon fix this nonsense. Tea-coffee. I've never heard of anything so preposterous. I'll be adding this to my report. Saint Peter needs to know this."

"I think he knows," Chasan said, still smiling. "Come on, bathroom next. Then we can have a look at the tech-bundles they've assigned us. You should probably get your-self acquainted. Those four-year-olds will probably know more than most adults, but we can't be oblivious." Chasan wasn't sure how he was going to explain how Wi-Fi or the internet worked without Nathaniel having a meltdown. Heaven was pretty high tech, but Nathaniel would need to get used to it on an earthly level.

But he actually took everything else really well. He grumbled about some of the bathroom stuff, citing human anatomy functions as grossly inconvenient, though he was very impressed with the inventions of toilet paper and toothpaste. That made Chasan smile.

"Have you really not been back to Earth in that long?"

"A few hundred years, perhaps," Nathaniel admitted quietly. "I've been busy in the Hell Department. Time is different on Earth."

Chasan went to the walk-in closet and opened the door.

It was incredibly large, split into two equal sides. Chasan's side was mostly light blues and whites, Nathaniel's was dark grays and blacks. Each side had rows of trousers, pressed business shirts, sweaters, shoes. It was boggling. "Do you like it there? In the Hell Department?"

"Yes, of course" Nathaniel replied. He didn't seem to care too much about the clothes. He saw his side of darker threads, and that was apparently enough. "It's not as bad as everyone makes out. And let's face it. The humans who find themselves there are deserving of it. Murderers and rapists, tyrants and dictators. People who drink tea-coffee. Eternal torment and pain are well-deserved."

Chasan frowned. "Doesn't it get to you after a while?"

"Not really," Nathaniel answered quickly. But then he hesitated and touched the sleeve of one sweater before he added, "Sometimes."

"Is that when you take leave in the canine department?"

Nathaniel shot him a look, clearly unaware that Chasan knew that. He swallowed hard, looked away, and avoided his gaze. "Well, yes, I . . . it's a reprieve from Hell. I never asked for it. Saint Peter insisted—"

Chasan put his hand on Nathaniel's arm. The warmth, the closeness was heady. "It's okay. I get it. I love the canine department. Everyone does."

Nathaniel scowled at the clothes hanging in pristine rows. "It's okay, I guess," Nathaniel replied, pulling his arm away from Chasan's touch.

He might say it was okay, but Chasan had it on very good authority that Nathaniel was never happier than when he was in the canine department. That he'd sit out in the fields for days and greet all dog-souls as they entered.

Not that Chasan would ever tell Nathaniel he knew that.

"Saint Peter knows what he's doing," Chasan said instead. "If he insists you put time in at a certain department, then it's for a good reason."

Nathaniel frowned and grumbled, and Chasan allowed that it was probably the most interaction Nathaniel had had in a while, so Chasan suggested they look over the tech-bundles they'd been assigned. Over the centuries, when assigned missions, they'd be given packs to help them integrate with the human society they found themselves in. A few hundred years ago, when Nathaniel was last on assignment, he'd probably been given a rudimentary rucksack, a leather-bound notepad, and perhaps some coins or gold rings he could sell.

But this was the twenty-first century.

And to his credit, the computer, phone, and iPad didn't faze Nathaniel too much. Chasan showed him the basics. "I can give you a more detailed lesson tomorrow. We should go to the store. We'll need to find something for dinner. Unless you want to cook?"

Chasan meant it as a joke, but Nathaniel nodded. His permanent scowl was in place but Chasan saw the moment of hesitation before he spoke. "I could. If you wanted me to, that is. Though I haven't had to in some time, but I can make a mean Mongolian *boodog*. Haven't had that in a while." He glanced around the living room. "Though there's no open fire and this is not a yurt, which might be a problem."

Chasan laughed as he handed Nathaniel a brand-new wallet with identification and his charge card. "Come on, this is New York. Everything we could ever need is right outside our door. And perhaps we could cook something that doesn't involve the deboning of goats."

Nathaniel shrugged. "Your call. I guess."

Chasan slid the apartment keys into his pocket and motioned toward the elevator. "Oh, we have a penthouse apartment. Elevator opens directly inside." Nathaniel wiped his hands on his thighs, and he swallowed hard as the elevator doors opened and he stepped inside. "I know this isn't easy for you," Chasan said. "We won't be out long. Just a quick trip to the store and maybe a stroll along the street to help get you acclimated."

Nathaniel scowled. "I'm not useless."

"I know you're not. But you are out of practice. You haven't been on assignment for quite some time. The world has changed."

"And you have? Done many assignments, that is? Since . . ." He shook his head, flustered. "I mean, I know you've done some, obviously, because I was there for some of them. But you've done a lot more than me, so good for you, I guess."

Chasan sighed. "I have, yes. Saint Peter thought it best if I dove straight back in after . . . I mean, yes, I've done a lot of assignments in the last thousand years."

"And did it help?"

Chasan couldn't quite read if that question was sarcastic or genuinely heartfelt. He hoped the latter. "I think so."

Nathaniel scowled again, chewing on the inside of his lip before stuffing his hands in his pockets. The elevator doors opened and they stepped out into the grand foyer. "So I just have to get back out there, right?"

"Right."

He nodded. "Just get back on the chariot, yes?"

"Well, chariots haven't been used in a while."

"Oh, that's right. Just get back on the penny-farthing."

Chasan laughed as the doorman opened the door for them, and he and Nathaniel walked out into New York City. "Something like that."

CHAPTER THREE

NATHANIEL

SWEET HEAVEN'S MERCY.

"What happened to New York City? I mean, I've seen pictures and footage, but to see it . . ."

Nathaniel had stopped the second he'd stepped outside the ground floor lobby. There were walls of buildings, impossibly tall. Automobiles and people. So many people. Everything was gray. The streets, the sidewalks, the buildings, the air.

"And what is that smell?"

Chasan laughed and pulled his arm, moving him from the path of humans barreling down the sidewalk.

"Is something on fire?" Nathaniel asked, staring after the crowds of humans. "Why are they all in such a hurry?"

"It's how the world is now," Chasan replied. "You really are out of step with this, aren't you?"

Well, Nathaniel could have sworn it was green wetlands and tribal farmland not that long ago. "Out of step? To be quite frank, I'm not certain I'm the one out of step. I thought New Amsterdam was a travesty. But this . . ." He looked upward at the sky, past the walls of brick and windows. It was dizzying. "Oh," he mumbled, swaying.

"Okay," Chasan said, steadying him with both hands. "Don't look up. Let's just take a moment to breathe."

And despite the bustle of the street, the noise, the smell, the overwhelming proximity of everything, it was the closeness of Chasan that calmed him. His hands, his touch, his voice, and Nathaniel's lungs could take in more air, his mind cleared.

Chasan had always had that effect on him.

And he knew why . . .

Which was why he took a step back. "I'm okay. Just . . . this is a lot to take in. And why you? Why did they pair us? Again? I mean, what was Saint Peter thinking? It won't end well. Like last time. He had to have known I'd object. And I do. Object, that is. And a preschool teacher? Maybe he's gone mad. Me, around small humans? This was to punish me, wasn't it? I'm being punished. Still, after all this time."

Chasan put his hand on Nathaniel's arm. "Just take a breath for me."

Nathaniel did, because even against his better judgment —and being aware of Chasan's touch—breathing did seem like a good idea. It seemed to help with the clawing panic inside his chest.

"You're not being punished," Chasan added. Worry creased his brow, and concern filled those pretty blue eyes. No, not concern. Hurt. "I'm sorry you feel that being on assignment with me is akin to a punishment. I wish . . . I wish it wasn't that way between us." He appeared conflicted, as though he had much to say but couldn't find the words. He settled on a sigh. "Are you feeling better?"

"I'm fine," Nathaniel replied. He wasn't. He was quite the opposite, in fact, and he knew Chasan could see that.

"I'm fine. Let's just concentrate on the assignment and see it done." He left the 'because the sooner we complete the stupid assignment, the sooner we can get back to our very separate lives' unsaid, though from the way Chasan flinched, he might as well have yelled it from one of the ridiculously tall buildings.

"Okay," Chasan said, pulling his hand away. Nathaniel missed it immediately. "The store is just a block or two away."

And so they walked to the store. Nathaniel avoided bumping into the humans, which wasn't easy, given there were so very many. But he did peruse the store without incident. He was actually a little impressed. Markets had improved so much with cleanliness and refrigeration. The variety was surprising too. But Chasan carried all the goods in a basket, and Nathaniel studied the whole transaction as he paid at the counter.

It wasn't exactly a hardship to study Chasan. He really was incredibly handsome. Those blond waves and pink lips, that strong jaw and kind smile . . . But Nathaniel didn't want to study him or think of him in that way. He'd spent eons avoiding it. Why would he start now?

Which led him back to his earlier question. Why would Saint Peter put them together for this assignment? Why now? After their disastrous efforts that one time . . . Granted, that was a long time ago, but still. Nathaniel had vowed to keep his distance, and by Heaven's mercy, he'd almost managed it.

Now he was stuck with him, sequestered in human form, for some indeterminate length of time. Instead of studying Chasan, he would study this assignment and see it done—the quicker the better.

"Are you ready?" Chasan said, clutching a full brown paper sack to his chest.

Nathaniel gave a nod. "I am."

They walked back toward the apartment, and Nathaniel could see past the crowds of people now. Past the constant stream of cars and cabs, even past the grayed-out buildings. There were some trees planted curbside, a human with a baby in a stroller, and another walking two golden retriever dogs headed their way.

Both dogs wagged their tails, excited to see him, and they pulled their human over toward him. "Gentlemen," Nathaniel said to the dogs, giving them a good pat.

"I'm sorry," the human said. "They don't normally do that."

"It's fine," Nathaniel said. "I have this effect on dogs."

The human managed to pull them away, and Nathaniel smiled as they went. He looked up to find Chasan trying not to smile at him. "What?"

"Nothing," he replied.

"I like dogs."

"And they like you." Chasan grinned. "It's sweet."

Nathaniel scowled. "Sweet? I'm the overseer of the Hell Department."

Chasan rolled his eyes and chuckled. "A sweet overseer of the Hell Department."

He grumbled the whole way back to their apartment, and just as they walked up the block, Chasan nodded farther down the busy street. "Look!"

Nathaniel followed Chasan's line of sight. There were more cars, more humans, more noise, more pollution. "Look at what?"

"The restaurant with the yellow sign, halfway down the block."

Nathaniel saw it and tilted his head. "Is that . . . ?"

"Mongolian," Chasan replied. "You don't have to cook the boodog you mentioned earlier. We can order it in."

"Order it in?" Nathaniel asked. "You can summon deboned goat?"

Chasan laughed and opened the door to the lobby. "It's New York. You can summon anything you like."

NATHANIEL WAS QUITE content to sit and go through his mission file while Chasan busied himself doing whatever it was Chasan did. Nathaniel was feeling much more acclimated now. He was even used to being human. His body had adjusted and his mind wasn't far behind, though immersing himself into his mission was helping.

The assignment itself was easy enough. The target was cryptic, though given Saint Peter's obscure behavior leading up to now, Nathaniel wasn't too surprised. Not all human targets were outlined in assignments, or so Nathaniel was told. Sometimes the angels had to let the human and the miracle opportunity present themselves.

That was not too uncommon. He could accept that. And he could even accept having to work alongside Chasan during the assignment. Even as husbands. It wasn't as though anyone would ever see them inside their private apartment or outside of the school classroom. All Nathaniel had to do was spend a few hours every day in a classroom.

Despite the twenty four-year-olds he had to wrangle, his earlier fear had subsided a little. Perhaps it was his adjustment to human form. He'd even seemed to get a better hold of his anxiety. He hadn't had one of those dreadful headaches in hours.

Until a very odd beeping split the silence and Nathaniel's brain at the same time. He shot to his feet. "What is that noise?"

Still smiling, Chasan breezed to the door. "It's just the delivery man."

"The delivery man? For which purpose does he make that noise?"

Chasan pressed some buttons by the elevator door and the noise thankfully ceased. "It's the security buzzer. You press this button and it allows him access to the elevator so he can deliver the food I ordered."

Nathaniel put his hand to the side of his head. "And I was doing so well without the pain in my brain."

Chasan laughed and waited for the doors to open, and a human male appeared holding a white bag. They exchanged pleasantries, and Chasan took the bag and closed the door. "Come. We can eat at the table."

The table had been set with plates and silverware and two glasses of water. Nathaniel hoped it wasn't that ghastly stuff he'd tasted before—though he didn't mention it. The food wasn't as good as he remembered from his time on the Mongolian plains all those centuries ago, but Chasan ate his meal with such pleasantness, such a kindness, it was hard not to enjoy his own.

Why even being near him like this calmed him, Nathaniel would never quite understand. He'd spent so long apart from him, avoiding him, he'd forgotten the effect Chasan had over him.

"So your assignment file?" Chasan asked. "Is that what's bothering you?"

When Nathaniel glanced over, Chasan had eaten his meal, yet Nathaniel's was barely half done.

"The children won't be so bad. You'll see," Chasan added.

"No, I'm sure it will be fine." He shrugged and tried to smile. "Though I'm not sure what Saint Peter was thinking when he put me in charge of children, to be honest. You're a much better match for this role."

"Clearly he thinks it's your time."

Nathaniel rolled his eyes. *My time for what?* "The assignment is vague, don't you think? I can understand why the target isn't disclosed, but the mission outline is basically no more than 'secure the path of the child.'"

Chasan nodded. "Sometimes that's all we need to do. Just make sure the target remains true to their destiny. A human life can change direction in an instant. Sometimes for the better, sometimes not."

"Yes, I'm aware," Nathaniel replied quietly. He pushed the food on his plate with a fork. "I was not expecting this assignment, and I'm long out of practice, so I'm not sure how successful it will be."

"You'll be fine."

The way Chasan smiled at him made Nathaniel actually believe it was true. "I will try though," Nathaniel said. "To be successful and timely. I don't want you to think I'll be deliberately negligent."

"I wouldn't think that," Chasan whispered.

"And I will try to not make your time with me too unbearable." All of a sudden, Nathaniel's stomach did that twist-and-tighten thing, and he needed to wipe his palms on his thighs. And his human lungs seemed to have shrunk. "Oh mercy bless. Is there something wrong with the air on this planet? In this apartment?" He pulled at his collar. "What exactly have they done to the atmosphere? I remember a discussion once about the industrial revolution in Europe. I thought they were fixing that? Why is it hard to breathe?"

Chasan stood up and casually walked around to Nathaniel's side of the table. He leaned against it, and with a slight curve of his lips, he put his hand to Nathaniel's shoulder. "Just breathe," he murmured.

Nathaniel breathed in deep and he could feel the pulse of calm seep through his skin from Chasan's touch. It bloomed inward, spreading warmth and a stillness as it went, and the waves of turmoil and anxiety subsided. Nathaniel hated how Chasan could do that to him, but by the mercy of Heaven, he loved it too. He hung his head, and he tried with all his human strength not to lean into Chasan's touch. So he stared at Chasan's shoes instead, because his legs, his thighs, his hips were right there . . .

"Why don't you go finish reading over your file," Chasan said after a moment. "I'll clean this up. It won't take a second. Then we can go over our files together and practice our backstories."

Nathaniel nodded, because a little distance between them was a good idea. He stood, not realizing just how close he was . . . how aligned they were . . . how devastatingly beautiful Chasan's eyes were . . . His human body reacted, buzzing, thrilling at their proximity. His skin flushed, and his . . . oh, sweet Heaven's mercy. His nether regions betrayed his angel-mind.

And just like that, his stomach was in knots, his heart rate took off, and his lungs had shrunk again. He took a step back and put his hand to his forehead, ignoring the heat pooling in areas where he was not accustomed. "Why are human bodies so prone to malfunction?" he asked. His voice failed too. It was pitched higher than normal. "How is it possible the single greatest-designed species can be wired so poorly?"

Chasan chuckled. "Still adjusting?"

"This human form is somewhat of a disaster," Nathaniel answered, taking another step back.

Though he knew all too well that it wasn't *just* the human body he was in; his angel body wasn't much better when he was around Chasan—which was why he'd avoided him for so long. Chasan knew this as well, though Nathaniel appreciated how he had the decency and good graces not to mention it.

"Here," Chasan said, handing Nathaniel his glass of water. "Probably best to stay hydrated."

"Yes, probably. Thank you," he replied, not even wanting to think about other possible medical catastrophes he could be subjected to. He took the drink and walked to the couch where he'd left his file, trying to ignore the way his human body felt so wrong, when something out the window caught his eye.

Lights. So many lights. A galaxy in its own right, both clustered and spread as far as the eye could see.

New York City at night was . . . well, it was rather beautiful. He stood there and watched it for a moment. As beautiful as a million fireflies on a meadow . . .

"Pretty, is it not?" Chasan whispered beside him after a few minutes.

Nathaniel hadn't heard him approach. He glanced back to the table to see everything had been cleaned up. He cleared his throat and turned his attention back to the view. "It is."

"Humans aren't all bad," Chasan mused. "They've come a long way."

"True. Though they have a ways to go yet." Nathaniel

sighed. "I guess I'm used to seeing the worst of them. The Hell Department gets busier every year."

"Have you considered asking for a transfer?"

"No. Actually, I requested permanent placing."

Chasan didn't reply to that, though Nathaniel didn't miss how he frowned.

"Someone has to do it, do they not?"

"Alternating placements were implemented for a reason," he murmured. "Does it not weigh you down after a time?"

Nathaniel couldn't answer that, so instead he repeated what Chasan already knew. "Saint Peter insists I do those regular rounds in the *Canes Omnes* for a break."

Chasan smiled. "That's why those two dogs were happy to see you. They recognized you."

Nathaniel nodded. "And I them. Every canine soul is a beautiful one."

"They are." Chasan smiled in the reflection of the window. "You're feeling okay now? You seem a little calmer."

Nathaniel frowned. "I am, I guess. I'm just not used to . . . interaction. Or conversation. Or anything, really. I've been on my own for a long time." He was irritated at himself for giving so much away already. "It was an isolation of my own choosing. And when this assignment is over, I'll go back to it."

Chasan's gaze shot to Nathaniel's in the reflection before he nodded and turned away. "I'm tired," he murmured. "I need to sleep. Guess this transformation took more out of me than I realized."

Nathaniel gave a nod to acknowledge what he'd said and Chasan walked away, and Nathaniel had to admit that he was tired as well. Sleeping, or even rest, wasn't something that angels had to worry about, but in human form, they required everything a human requires. Food and water, and sleep, for example.

It would take some getting used to, Nathaniel allowed. It wasn't *just* being so close to Chasan that had him so off-kilter. But he agreed with Chasan about how tiring it was. Getting some sleep was a good idea.

He followed Chasan to their sleeping quarters. He'd seen the bed earlier, and logically he knew they'd be sharing it. But seeing the bed now and Chasan walk out of the master bath . . . Oh Heaven's mercy. He was wearing blue pajama pants and a white T-shirt. "Just brushed my teeth," he said. "Bathroom's all yours."

Nathaniel nodded and ducked past Chasan into the bathroom. He closed the door and did what he needed to do. For all the advancements the humans had mastered over the last millennia, flushing toilets and toilet paper were some of the best. Same with toothbrushes and toothpaste and running water. Then he eyed the shower . . . He'd heard about how good they could be.

He stripped down and turned the water on like Chasan had shown him earlier. And sweet, sweet mercy, it felt good. The water streamed out of some wide silver spout that dropped out of the ceiling. The water cascaded over him like a heated waterfall, soothing his aching human body, and Nathaniel never wanted to get out. This was a human thing he could get used to.

But he couldn't avoid Chasan all night, and when he shut the water off and reached for the towel, he realized his error. He'd not brought his pajamas into the bathroom with him, and that meant he'd have to walk back out into the bedroom undressed.

He toweled himself, then wrapped it around his waist,

then opened the door. Chasan was sitting up in bed, reading his assignment file, the covers pulled to his waist, and the sight made Nathaniel stop. His heart rate kicked up a notch. "Oh," he breathed.

Chasan looked up and was clearly startled at seeing Nathaniel's half-naked form. His gaze raked over him, slow and thorough. His mouth opened but he closed it again, and he held up his assignment file, though Nathaniel could hear him swallow.

"Yes, I forgot my sleepwear. I do apologize."

"Ah, no apology necessary," Chasan said, lowering the file again. He flushed and blinked a few times. "It's fine. Really. I mean, it's not an issue . . . for me. Or in general, not me specifically."

Nathaniel dashed into the walk-in closet. He went to his side of clothes and found sleepwear similar to what Chasan had on, only dark gray and black, of course. The adjustment team had done well. Not normally one for fashion, though Nathaniel could appreciate the finer clothing this century afforded compared to the heavy woolen clothing he'd worn last time he was on Earth. The kind that irritated his human skin, scratched and smelled like a swine pen when wet. These clothes to sleep in were soft and silky. *Another win for the humans.*

Nathaniel walked back out, and this time, Chasan put the assignment file on his lap. "Find everything okay?"

"Oh yes, thank you. These clothes feel very good. And the shower . . ."

Chasan smiled. "The humans have done okay."

"The bed . . . " Nathaniel began, not sure what he was even trying to say.

"Is very comfortable," Chasan said.

"Could they not have arranged sleeping quarters for two?"

Chasan almost smiled. "We're supposed to be husbands. It's all part of the mission." He held up the file.

Nathaniel went to his side of the bed, pulled back the covers, and slid between the sheets. The very soft, cool, amazing sheets. He lay down, sinking perfectly into the mattress, his head on the pillow. He felt as though he was floating. "Oh my."

Chasan chuckled. "Not bad, huh?"

"For all their flaws, they've managed to master comfort." He let out a sigh. "Why do we not have these in Heaven?"

Chasan laughed. "Because our angel bodies feel no discomfort and require no rest." He put the file beside the bed and flipped a switch on the lamp, sending the room into darkness. The silence boomed off the walls, and Nathaniel was struck by just how close he was to Chasan. In bed, wearing nothing but underclothes.

Oh, mercy.

And just like that, that awful anxiety hit him hard. His heart thundered, his stomach coiled tight, the synapses in his brain were mimicking gunfire: rapid, unpredictable, and most likely lethal. He wondered if it could actually kill him . . .

"Hey," Chasan whispered. "Just breathe." Then Chasan's hand touched his, interlocking their fingers and squeezing tight.

And just like how Chasan had turned off the light, he shut down the panic inside Nathaniel too. Nathaniel breathed in deep a few long and measured times, cursing his malfunctioning human body, and he closed his eyes.

CHAPTER FOUR

CHASAN

CHASAN·REVELED in the feel of Nathaniel's hand in his. His touch, his warmth, lying next to him. His face as he slept, his closed eyelids and his long lashes, and how his lips parted just so.

To have this with him, no matter how fleeting it may be, made Chasan's heart full.

After all this time. After all they'd been through.

Nathaniel's human anxiety wasn't too unlike how he was in angel form—short-fused, antsy, nervous, introverted, grumpy—but here on Earth it manifested differently. In Heaven, Chasan would be able to give Nathaniel a peaceful, easy feeling just by being near him. On Earth, it was by touch.

Chasan wasn't complaining. In fact, he was certain Saint Peter had stipulated that deliberately. Chasan and Nathaniel had to be together. That's just how destiny worked. Except when Nathaniel refused.

He said he chose free will. None of that fated nonsense. Well, Chasan allowed, it was more complicated than that, but the bottom line was Nathaniel had said no. That was a long time ago though, and apparently Saint Peter had grown impatient.

Fated angels were rare, and their destiny wouldn't wait any longer.

So Chasan could only assume that throwing them back to Earth for a while, as husbands no less, living together and working on the same assignment, was a last-ditch effort to right a long-standing wrong.

Nathaniel had spent the better part of a millennium avoiding him, but he couldn't do that now. And Chasan knew Nathaniel's reluctance wasn't with him exactly. Chasan knew this. Nathaniel's problem was Nathaniel himself. If he'd just let himself be happy . . .

If he'd just forgive himself.

"It wasn't your fault," Chasan whispered.

Nathaniel didn't stir, so Chasan held his hand a little tighter and put their joined hands to his chest. He closed his eyes and allowed the human slumber to claim him.

CHASAN WOKE up to an empty bed. He wasn't surprised, all things considered, but he was disappointed. He wondered if Nathaniel had shot out of the room in a panic when he woke up and remembered they'd shared a bed . . .

He threw back the covers and made his way to the kitchen. Nathaniel was sitting on the couch by the window, his legs curled up underneath him, his assignment file on his lap. He looked freshly showered and dressed, so he must have been up for a while. He wore black jeans and a charcoal T-shirt, his short brown hair was neatly brushed, and he had a little bit of stubble. He looked incredible.

"Morning," Chasan said. "Sleep okay?"

Nathaniel glanced up. "Uh, yeah, I guess." He went back to reading until it seemed he remembered his manners. "And you?"

"Yes, slept very well. It's strange, isn't it? Needing to sleep?" Not really expecting a reply, he went to the kitchen and turned the coffee machine on while staring out to the city. The sun was barely up, spilling a yellow light onto silver buildings; the sky was shades of blue and pink. "Did you dream? I do find dreams fascinating. Not something we experience unless we're in human form."

He looked over at Nathaniel, who was staring at him. "Um, I don't think so. Not that I remember, at least."

Chasan gave him a smile. "Maybe tonight, then."

Nathaniel flushed and quickly looked away, back to his file. "Uh, yes. Perhaps."

Chasan thought that was a strange reaction but ignored it. "How's the reading going?"

"Oh, good," he replied, frowning at the file in front of him. "Just looking over the teacher thing. Protocols, procedures, that kind of thing. I'm sure it'll be fine." Nathaniel's gaze shot to Chasan and dropped straight to his crotch, then he shook his head and cleared his throat, his cheeks red.

Chasan looked down at himself to see what had bothered Nathaniel so much . . .

Oh.

He'd forgotten about that human bodily trait. He had quite the bulge happening in his boxers. He turned back to look out the window, secretly pleased by Nathaniel's reaction. He set about making two coffees. "You'll handle teaching just fine. But I thought today we should practice with some technology. The world is run by it nowadays. You don't want to get tripped up."

"Yes, of course," he replied. As Chasan carried the coffee over, Nathaniel had his hand to his forehead. Chasan was almost certain he wasn't perplexed about his assignment at all but about Chasan's tented pajamas.

"Here, taste this," Chasan said, handing a cup over. "It's not made by Yemeni Sufi, but it's not bad."

Nathaniel's gaze darted from the cup to Chasan's crotch, back to the cup. He blushed again and Chasan smiled. "Ah, thank you," he said, blinking a few times.

Chasan stood there for a moment, so his crotch was pretty much at face level. "You're most welcome. I'm just going to shower and get changed. Then I can make you breakfast if you'd like?"

Nathaniel nodded and sipped his coffee. His eyes widened with surprise. "Actually, this coffee's not bad."

Chasan chuckled. "Won't be long," he said, giving Nathaniel's shoulder a squeeze before heading off to the bathroom. He smiled as he sipped his coffee, then set the cup on the bathroom counter. He stripped in front of the mirror, not ashamed to admire his human body.

Not too different from his angel form, he was tall and lean, muscled in all the right places. But his morning erection hadn't waned at all. Now angels weren't sexual creatures, but humans sometimes were. Their anatomical reactions weren't something he'd ever get used to or ever tire of. His cock was hard and it felt good to touch and stroke, and it shot flares of pleasure right through him.

He turned the water on and stepped in under the spray. The warmth, the wetness, felt amazing, and he let himself indulge in the same fantasy he'd imagined for centuries. He imagined Nathaniel's mouth on him, and it was a sublime visual. The way he would suck and moan sent waves of pleasure through him. But it was imagining Nathaniel inside him that always sent him over the edge.

Every single time.

Chasan panted as his orgasm subsided, and he rested against the tiles for a beat, a lazy smile on his face. Then he quickly soaped himself and washed his hair, rinsing off just as fast. He was dried and dressed before his coffee had even had time to get cool. He drained his cup, then walked back out to where Nathaniel was.

Nathaniel did a double-take, then almost knocked his coffee cup over. So Chasan leaving his shirt unbuttoned had been a great idea.

Oh yes, Chasan rather enjoyed being human.

Don't misunderstand . . . he loved being an angel. But his time as a human wasn't *un*appreciated. Orgasms, coffee, and Nathaniel. It wasn't bad at all.

It wasn't cruel to taunt Nathaniel in such a way with a little nakedness, Chasan reasoned. Especially after he'd come out with nothing more than a towel around his waist last night. But Nathaniel had spent eons avoiding contact with him, so Chasan was merely making up for lost time. He put his cup in the sink and turned so Nathaniel could watch him do up the buttons. "Another coffee? How about a toasted bagel for breakfast?"

"Um, coffee," Nathaniel mumbled, straightening his paperwork. "Coffee would be great. I've never had a bagel, toasted or otherwise. I don't know what one even is, so I will have to take you at your word."

"It's a type of bread," Chasan said, opting for the easiest explanation.

"Ah, remember that flatbread we had in Bornholm?"

Nathaniel said, smiling. "The Vikings knew how to put on a good show."

Chasan laughed because they obviously remembered those times very differently. Perhaps a few millennia in the Hell Department changed one's perspective . . . But that was twice now that Nathaniel had recalled their times together when it came to meals they'd shared. Albeit, that was when times were better between them. Though things were okay between them now, and Chasan wanted it to stay that way.

He made more coffee and toasted the bagels, putting a plate between them at the table. "Oh, thank you," Nathaniel said. "I'm not sure I'll get used to needing to eat. But thank you."

"You're welcome," Chasan replied.

They went over their mission, discussing fictional parents and siblings, getting names and ages and occupations right. They rehearsed previous fictional jobs and locations, and of course the details about their engagement and wedding.

"Oh, that reminds me," Chasan said. He collected a small box from the assignment package. "I suppose we should get used to these."

He put the box in front of Nathaniel, who eyed it cautiously. "What is it?"

"Open it. It won't bite."

Nathaniel slowly reached for the offending box and opened it as though it were a ticking bomb. There were two silver rings inside. Simple, plain, effective.

Nathaniel looked positively horrified.

"Oh, come on now," Chasan said. "It's a human construct. It doesn't have to mean anything. It's not like we'll actually be married."

He made some high-pitched squeaking sound but apparently couldn't form words. Chasan took the rings and slid the smaller one onto the ring finger on his left hand. "See, I didn't burst into flames or anything." He held his hand out. "Give me your hand."

Nathaniel, who had paled to some degree, held out his hand. Chasan took it, paying no attention to how it felt in his own. How warm it was, how his skin felt, how he was looking up at him. Chasan slid the ring on Nathaniel's ring finger, but instead of letting his hand go, he held onto it.

"We should also get used to touching," Chasan said, his voice low. "Considering we're supposed to be newlyweds." He skimmed his thumb over the back of Nathaniel's hand, then slowly, carefully threaded their fingers. It felt so good. Such a simple token that meant more than he could explain.

Nathaniel yanked his hand away and shot to his feet. "Why must you do that?" he barked. And there it was; Nathaniel's temper of fire and wrath. He stalked off and began to pace the living room, scowling at the floor as he did. "You always push, Chasan, and try to make me fall under your spell. Well, stop it! We're here on a mission for Saint Peter, nothing more. Whatever ulterior motive you might have or wild fantasy of us being anything more than celestial associates is not going to happen."

"I'm very well aware," Chasan replied coolly. He had no intention of fueling Nathaniel's fire. He'd learned a long time ago that Nathaniel's outbursts were best left to peter out by themselves. He might rant and rave, but he'd calm down. He always did. Chasan collected the plates and cups from the table. "Have you had enough to eat?"

Nathaniel stopped pacing and glared. Then he huffed and mumbled something Chasan couldn't hear.

"Well, I'll set you up with the internet and world

history, everything you've missed over the last thousand years," Chasan said. "I'm heading out to run a few errands."

Nathaniel looked a little forlorn. From angry to lost in a few seconds . . . "Where are you going?"

Chasan smiled at him. "The thing is, Nathaniel, you don't get to rant about me trying to blindside you with affection, then in the next moment demand to know where I'm going." He took the iPad and tapped the screen. "If you must know, I'm heading out to get us some cash. We're going to need some tomorrow."

His forehead furrowed, and he frowned. "I apologize. I'm not yet accustomed to being . . . here. And around you again." Then he whispered, "It's confusing."

Chasan sighed, feeling bad. He handed the iPad to him and said, "Get comfortable, this might take a while; it's a complete history of technology and politics. Tap the triangle Play button when you're ready. If the screen goes dark, you just tap it again to bring it back up."

He nodded at the screen. "Thank you."

"I'm taking my phone with me. You remember how to call me if you need? And how to answer if I need to call you?"

Nathaniel nodded again. "I remember."

"In all likelihood I won't need to, but there might be an emergency."

His gaze shot to Chasan's. "Emergency?"

"Well, this is New York. It's not America's most dangerous city but—"

His eyes widened. "Dangerous? I should come with you . . ."

Chasan put his hand up, fighting a smile. "I'll be fine, Nathaniel."

"I know what humans are capable of," he whispered grimly. "I've seen the very worst, Chasan, I . . ."

That stopped Chasan; the way he said his name, the softness to his voice, and Chasan gave a sympathetic nod and he put a calming hand on his arm. "I know, and thank you. But I have been immersed in the human world for centuries. I'll be fine, I promise."

He grabbed his phone and keys, made sure he had his wallet, and headed out. It was a beautiful spring day. The sky was blue, the leaves were green, and flower beds were in full bloom. People were walking dogs, jogging, strolling, working. Doing things busy humans did. And as he made his way up the street, he thought he saw someone familiar watching him—well, familiar in their human form—but when he looked again, they were gone. By the time he got to the next block, he was sure of it.

He stepped in closer to the wall, out of the way, and pretended to check his phone. *Yep, definitely a familiar face.* Tall, lanky, shaggy black hair and white pale skin, he looked like the singer of a goth band the 1970s forgot. He melded into the crowd and walked past him, so Chasan zipped up behind him. "Zophiel," he said, startling him.

"Oh." Zophiel put his hand to his heart. He sagged with disappointment and shame in being caught.

"What are you doing following me? Peter got you spying on us now?"

He rolled his eyes. "He's concerned, that's all."

"You can tell him we'll be fine. I left Nathaniel to catch up on world history."

Zophiel grimaced. "Ouch." But then he shrugged. "Guess he's used to terrible things."

"Walk with me to the next block," Chasan said.

Zophiel fell into step beside him. "How's he been to live with so far? A miserable pain in the halo, no doubt?"

Chasan almost chuckled. "He's not that bad."

"You *would* say that."

Chasan did laugh at that. "No, honestly. He's been okay. Doesn't care too much about technology, but he's rather impressed with toothbrushes and flushing toilets. And coffee pods."

Zophiel laughed. "All the important things."

They crossed onto the next block. "He hasn't been on assignment for a long time," Chasan said, feeling defensive of him. "It'll take some adjusting."

"True."

"He's been sweet, and funny. Then the next minute he's glowering and snappy."

"So, he's being Nathaniel."

Chasan stopped walking. "Yes. Too long overseeing the Hell Department. It can't be good for the psyche. I'll make sure to tell Saint Peter that too."

Zophiel smiled at that. "Do you think that would change anything? Nathaniel requested it. And what Nathaniel wants, he gets. Saint Peter's always had a soft spot for him. You know that."

"Because he feels guilty. We all do."

Zophiel sighed and looked to the yellow sea of passing taxicabs. "Also true." He put his hand to Chasan's arm. "Do you think this could be it? His last chance to . . . I mean, your last shot at . . ."

Chasan frowned. "I think so, yes."

He shook his head like that was the saddest news he'd ever heard. "Would explain why he's got every available pair of wings on it—"

"Every available pair of wings on what?"

"On this case," Zophiel replied. "Watching, helping, that kind of thing."

"Does he think me that incapable?"

"Not you, old friend," Zophiel said with a smile. "But Nathaniel's the most stubborn, wallowing being that was ever created. If he doesn't want this . . ."

"I know."

Now Zophiel frowned, and Chasan imagined it matched his own. "That's why we're all on this case, man."

Chasan gave him a sad smile. "You know two dogs recognized him yesterday? They were almost as happy to see him as he was them."

"He's got a good soul."

"He does!"

Zophiel let silence fall between them and they watched a few people walk by. Then he said, "So Nathaniel . . . a preschool teacher? And there I was thinking Saint Peter didn't have a sense of humor."

Chasan side-eyed him. "Do you know anything about the child we're supposed to oversee?"

"Nope, not a thing. No name, gender, ethnicity, nothing." He held up both hands. "I promise. Not a thing. No one knows. Well, none of us mere angels do. Peter does, obviously."

"But there *is* a child?" Chasan pressed. "It's not just a ruse to have Nathaniel and me sequestered together?"

He smiled. "There is definitely a child. That much I know."

Then something occurred to Chasan. *Oh no . . .* "Please tell me the child doesn't die." *Nathaniel can't go through that again.* "No, Saint Peter wouldn't do that to him. Would he? Please, tell me if you know."

Zophiel clapped Chasan on the shoulder. "Relax. The

child lives. And will go on to do important things, apparently."

Chasan sighed with relief. "Oh, Heaven's mercy."

Zophiel gawped at him, then laughed. "Man, you sound like him already! It's been a day!"

Chasan finally smiled and nodded to the bank ahead. "I need to get some cash, and I should get back to Nathaniel. He was already worried about me venturing off alone."

"He was?" Zophiel asked, eyebrows almost at his hairline.

"Yeah, don't act so surprised."

"There's hope for you yet," he replied. "I mean, if he's worried and all, that means he cares, right?"

Chasan couldn't help but smile a little. "Perhaps." *I certainly hope so.* "But I better go. He's probably up to the 1940s in the history lesson, so I better get back there for that. Next time try a little harder not to be seen."

Zophiel rolled his eyes and disappeared into the crowd. Chasan withdrew enough cash to last them a few days and headed back to their apartment. He was rather pleased with himself; he'd spotted Zophiel and learned a thing or two about their assignment, and surely Nathaniel would be happy.

When the elevator doors opened, Chasan walked into silence. He'd half expected to hear the iPad or maybe even Nathaniel grumbling at the screen, but there was nothing.

Oh, he hadn't left, had he? He didn't venture out on his own?

"Hello?" he called out. "Nathaniel?" Panic started to set in. Nathaniel hadn't set foot on Earth for hundreds of years and he'd been in New York City for one day! Getting lost or overwhelmed was the least of his worries. Oh no, his phone was on the table . . . "Nathaniel?"

He checked the bedroom and the bathroom to find them empty. Before panic could tear him apart, Chasan raced into the kitchen, and there he was . . . He was leaning against the sink, staring out at the city. He turned slowly, his face a mask of horror and sadness.

"Nathaniel," Chasan breathed, his hand to his heart. "Oh, my word. You scared me. Are you okay? I was calling out to you." Chasan could feel a well of sadness and despair . . . Was that coming from Nathaniel?

"I don't think I'm okay," he whispered.

Chasan went to him and took his hand. "Why, what happened?"

"The world," he replied. "Humans happened."

Chasan sighed.

"What are we even trying to save?" Nathaniel shook his head. "There is so much evil, so much destruction and greed." He put his free hand to his forehead. "But the apathy, Chasan. The apathy toward such evil and greed is the worst of it all." His eyes became glassy, but they were angry tears. "Why should we save any of it? They don't care when millions die because it happens to someone else. Everyone just keeps going about their lives while millions of people die on the other side of the world. Well, I can assure you, they'll care when it's their turn."

Chasan lifted Nathaniel's hand and held it to his chest. "Yes, the world is all of those things. But there is also good. There is also light and love. And kindness. It's there, I promise. You just need to know where to look."

He shook his head. "I'm not sure of that, Chasan. How . . . how can there be anything good in this world after all they've done?"

"Come with me and I'll show you," Chasan replied, pulling him toward the door. "I want you to see it. And I can show you the school on the way. Then we can backtrack and have lunch in the park. But I want you to see, Nathaniel. I want you to see what it is we're trying to save and know it's worth it."

CHAPTER FIVE

NATHANIEL

NATHANIEL HAD to wonder if all the human pollution and chemicals had gone to Chasan's brain. All that smog and the fumes and putrid smells had done irreparable damage, Nathaniel was sure of it.

The city was still gray, it was still busy, and there were too many people in too big of a hurry and too self-absorbed to realize what was truly important.

But Chasan showed him trees and flowers, more coffee, more people laughing, one lady helping an older gentleman across the street. There were birds and squirrels and another dog that stopped to wag its tail in front of Nathaniel.

The human with the dog was confused and apologized but Nathaniel laughed, and they made their way into the park. Which was, apparently, Central Park. "I take it our apartment is one of the most sought after in town?" Nathaniel asked, considering their apartment was just across the street.

Chasan laughed. "Ah, yes."

"I don't mean to sound ungrateful," Nathaniel said, frowning. "The apartment is very nice. And by comparison, we could have found ourselves in much less favorable living quarters. I'm not being churlish."

Chasan chuckled. "I know that. I also know you'd probably prefer to be in a river hut in India or a yurt on the Mongolian plains. You'd be more comfortable there than here."

"Probably."

"But is this park not beautiful?" Chasan asked. They stood on a bridge near the pond. "The trees, the flowers, the ducks. I mean, really, look at the ducks!"

"We should save the world because of ducks?"

"Sure. The ducks, dogs, and any other innocent creature. Humans included. Like those kids who will be in our class tomorrow."

"Oh, Heaven's mercy. I forgot about that."

Chasan nudged him with his shoulder. "Shall we walk farther around? It's quite a beautiful day."

Nathaniel sighed. "I can appreciate your positive outlook in, well, everything. But in case you haven't noticed, I'm more of a glass-half-empty kind of man."

He found something particularly funny about that. "Ah yes, I'm very well aware."

Nathaniel scowled at him. "What do you mean by that? What's so funny?"

"Absolutely nothing," he replied and took Nathaniel by the elbow and began back the way they'd come. "How about we go check out our new school."

THE SCHOOL itself didn't look like a school. Nathaniel wasn't sure what he expected exactly, but it wasn't a brownstone building alongside a row of other brownstones with wrought iron handrails up the stone steps and flowers in the windows. It looked residential.

It looked expensive.

What is it with humans and money?

"It looks nice," Chasan said brightly. Everything Chasan did, he did brightly. It drove Nathaniel crazy.

"It looks like the Hell Department, only prettier. And I'm sure tomorrow when I'm subjected to such torture with those hellion-humanlings, it won't be so pretty."

Of course Chasan found that humorous too.

"I'd like to show you the Metropolitan Museum of Art," he said, his smile ever-present. "We can walk right through the park."

"The way we just came? You're just all about the sunshine, aren't you?"

He grinned. "And you're all about the gloom, aren't you?"

"Well, I was just thinking earlier that everything here is gray."

"Gray?" he cried. "Oh, Nathaniel. The sky is blue, trees are green, taxicabs are yellow. There is so much color."

Nathaniel let out a long-suffering sigh, though he had to try not to smile. He hated to admit that Chasan's ray-of-sunshine attitude didn't bother him as much as he remembered. Instead, he rolled his eyes and grumbled, but he went along with it, very willingly, and even a little graciously.

Well, as gracious as Nathaniel could be.

They made their way back through the park—Chasan insisted on a leisurely stroll—and Nathaniel was loath to admit that yes, the park was lovely, and yes, the people looked happy. The museum seemed more Nathaniel's style, although the herds of people were off-putting. "Ugh. Do they have to be here?"

"Stop your grumbling," Chasan said. "Being here is what people do. They come to appreciate art and human excellence. There are worse places we could be."

Just then, a child walked past with his finger up his nose. Worse places? "I doubt that."

Inside the museum was quieter, at least. Though there was one particular lady who spoke incredibly loud and incredibly nasally and squawked when she laughed, also incredibly loud and nasally. Nathaniel raised his hand but realized he was without his powers. "Oh, how I wish I could smite."

Chasan laughed. "And *that* is the very reason they took that power away from you. You can't just go around smiting people because they annoy you."

Nathaniel glared at him because, if this had been his Hell Department, he could do exactly that. But Chasan only seemed to find that funny. He took his arm and pulled him into another exhibit. It was a Baroque exhibition, full of old paintings and sketches in grand frames. One, in particular, caught his eye. It was of Archangel Michael. "Oh dear." He snorted rather loudly. "Does he know that's here?"

Chasan chuckled. "Don't know."

"It looks nothing like him."

"Humans don't know that."

Nathaniel rolled his eyes. He nodded to another painting, depicting a crowd of people in a Parisian street. "Why is that hanging up in here?"

"Because it's art. It's important and significant to culture and history."

"It was the early 1600s. Those were ghastly times. I swear, if you could smell those people in that painting, it wouldn't be hanging up in here."

Chasan had to cover his laugh with a cough when a dour-faced man gave him a disparaging *shush*. "Come on, this way," Chasan said, taking Nathaniel's hand and leading him toward the next exhibition.

Japan at the turn of the last millennium was much more his time. "Now this is more like it. Do you remember Kyoto in 1086? Shirakawa abdicated the throne to become a Buddhist monk." Nathaniel chuckled. "No one saw that coming, I can tell you. Much sake was drunk that night. I was sick for days." But it was then he realized that Chasan was still holding his hand. He pulled it free, missing the warmth of his touch immediately.

Chasan's smile died a little. "Maybe we should have Japanese for dinner tonight."

Nathaniel grimaced. "Hold the sake."

He nodded. "Definitely no sake before school tomorrow."

"Ugh, don't remind me."

Chasan nodded up ahead to the next exhibit. "Let's see what's next."

The next was an exhibition on the art and empires of the Sahara, which Nathaniel enjoyed immensely. But the Timeline of Art History was spectacular, and Nathaniel was certain he knew why Chasan had insisted he see it. From the rudimentary bowls and carved clay figures of women with babies to the finest, masterful gold filigree ornaments.

Chasan wanted him to see the good of mankind. Throughout the ages up to the present day, despite the horrors they were capable of, they were capable of beauty too.

"Thank you for the reminder," Nathaniel said quietly.

"What for?" He pretended like he didn't know, but his acting was terrible.

"You know what for. For reminding me there is still good here."

Eventually a smile won out. "You're welcome."

They walked through the final exhibition, one of Renaissance drawings. One, in particular, was an etching of a poor soul surrounded by what were supposed to be heavenly beings floating above and a demon following on foot close behind him. The angels were majestic, while the demon was gnarled and ghastly, and Nathaniel couldn't stop looking at it.

Chasan stood beside him and stared at the artwork and tilted his head, just so. "I think they captured my best side, don't you think? I mean, clearly I'm the second angel from the right. The handsome one, naturally."

Nathaniel even smiled. "Naturally." He looked at it a while longer, taking in every detail, every implication, every interpretation. "Do you think we should tell them?"

"Tell who?"

"The humans. People. Everyone."

"Tell them what?"

"That the devil doesn't look like that." He smiled ruefully. "That there is no devil, no evil keeper of Hell that lurks and follows and lures people to evil. That the evil humans have attributed to Satan lurks within each of them. There is darkness in everyone. For some, it's too big a beast to tame."

Chasan was quiet for a moment. "That's why we do what we do, is it not? To protect and guide and to make sure they don't succumb to the evil within. And no, we shouldn't tell them. They're better off not knowing the truth. It was decided long ago to personify the evil into a being to be fearful of. To give humans a moral and ethical line they should fear crossing, lest they lose their souls."

"And look where that got mankind. They believe that Beelzebub and Asmodeus are evil demons." Nathaniel smiled at that. "They're just two normal guys in the Hell Department. Beelzebub hosts the monthly book club meetings and we have poker nights at Asmodeus' place. They get a bad rap, those two. If anything, it's Lucifer you need to watch. Once, he followed some damned soul around singing 'Who Let the Dogs Out?' nonstop for so long the guy actually begged us to throw him in a fiery pit of lava."

Chasan laughed. "Well, did you?"

"Of course not. Lucifer just sang it louder and for longer." Nathaniel looked at him. "Do you know who did it? I never did find out."

"Who did what?"

"Who let the dogs out."

Chasan's laughter echoed off the walls, and they scored a few scathing looks from humans nearby. Nathaniel didn't really get what was so funny but Chasan grabbed his arm and led him back outside. There were still a gazillion people, but for some reason, Nathaniel didn't seem to mind. Perhaps it was his closeness to Chasan, the calmness he exuded. But when they began their walk back through the park and Chasan let go of his arm, Nathaniel was a little disappointed.

But Chasan smiled as they walked, at the people, at the squirrels, and at the sky. He was so optimistic, so cheerful, it was hard not to smile back along with him. Nathaniel was certain his own lifted spirits had much to do with just being around Chasan because he'd always had that effect on him. It was part of the reason he was so attracted to him and the main reason he'd spent most of his existence avoiding him . . .

"Oh, I almost forgot," Chasan said as they neared their side of the park. "I ran into Zophiel earlier."

"Heaven's spy?" Nathaniel raised an eyebrow. "Is he on assignment in New York as well?"

"Yes, kind of."

"Who's he spying on? Some rich old billionaire with arteries clogged by greed and gluttony?"

Chasan snorted out a laugh. "No, actually. He's watching us."

Nathaniel stopped walking. "He's what?"

"Watching us. It's not uncommon on the big assignments. And this is a big one, apparently."

Nathaniel blinked. "If they've sent Watchers . . ." He put his hand to his forehead. His heart was doing that beating-too-fast thing again. "This assignment is a catalyst event. Why have they put me in as one of the leads? Oh, this is a disaster. They're all going to watch me fail. This won't just be something they'll teach the younglings in angel-cadet training as what not to do. This will go down in celestial history as the biggest mistake Saint Peter ever made. Oh Heaven's mercy—" Was his skin leaking? He looked at the palm he'd pressed to his forehead. There was definitely moisture. "Why is my skin leaking? No one ever told me human skin leaks? Chasan, what's happening to me? Am I dissolving? Can humans actually do that?"

Chasan put both his hands on Nathaniel's shoulders, and Nathaniel didn't even mind that he stood far too close because it helped with the breathing thing. "You're not dissolving. Your skin isn't leaking. Just take a breath for me."

And Nathaniel breathed.

"It's just nervous sweating. Your skin is trying to cool you down because your heart rate is elevated." Chasan smiled reassuringly, and Nathaniel both loved and hated how much he needed it.

"If they've sent Watchers . . . Are they watching us now? Oh, this is bad."

"Look at me," Chasan whispered, his voice the sound of distant bells, a frequency that tolled just for Nathaniel. "You won't fail. You'll get through this just fine."

I failed before, Nathaniel wanted to say but didn't. He didn't have to say that out loud because Chasan knew this. He'd been there, afterward. He'd seen the aftermath.

"I um . . . I don't know," Nathaniel replied instead. "Maybe we should have a word with Saint Peter. What in Heaven was he thinking putting me on this job?"

Chasan smiled, and his blue eyes gleamed in the fading sunlight. "You're his favorite. He adores you."

Nathaniel's mouth fell open. He was . . . well, he was flabbergasted. "I am not."

Chasan laughed. "You so are his very favorite, and everyone knows it." He hooked his arm back through Nathaniel's and began walking again. "He has a total soft spot for you, and you can do no wrong in his eyes."

He scoffed, now totally affronted. "Well, that's the biggest load of festering rot I've ever heard."

Chasan put his hand to his heart. "I'm an angel. I cannot lie."

He scowled at that. That was a trait he'd learned to hate over all these centuries. "A celestial flaw, that's what that is. Something else I'll add in my report. We should be able to lie. It would be only fair."

Chasan found something about that rather amusing.

"Pretty sure that one won't even get past pre-marketing. They're pretty big on the honesty and truth policy. You know, being angels and all. Not even Saint Peter could get that one over the line for you. Angel's pet or not."

Nathaniel stopped walking. In the middle of the street, apparently, and humans driving like maniacs disapproved with a cacophony of car horns and colorful language. Nathaniel didn't care. He stared at Chasan. "Angel's pet?"

"Yes, like a teacher's pet, but you know—" He waved between them. "—angels." He laughed some more at Nathaniel's expression and dragged him off the street and toward the lobby of their apartment building. And Nathaniel only realized what Chasan had done by the time they'd gone inside . . .

He'd made him completely forget about his panic attack, and the melting-dissolving-sweating episode, and the Watchers information and the fact this assignment was a catalyst event. A catalyst event was an incident in the course of human history that marked a significant change. Not always for the better. But something huge. That he and Chasan were in charge of.

"What else did Zophiel say about the assignment?" Nathaniel asked. "About the child."

Chasan opened a bottle of water, took a mouthful, then handed it to Nathaniel. "He said the child was destined for great things."

If the child was destined for great things, that meant the child survived. Nathaniel let out a breath of relief. *Thank the heavens.* "Good. Well, that's good."

Chasan smiled warmly. "Still want Japanese for dinner? We need to get ready for tomorrow. First day and all that."

Nathaniel grimaced. "I wish I could still swear and smite things." He put his hand to his forehead. "They took all my angel powers *and* my ability to curse and smite. Totally not fair."

"It's like they're almost trying to tell you something about your behavior," Chasan said with a smirk.

Nathaniel glowered at him.

"Well," Chasan continued, amused, "I did hear about the photocopier incident in the Admin Department. How you cursed up quite a storm and smote the copier to ash."

"Well, I kicked the toner out of it first, then I smote it. It was the old copier," he explained. "You know, the one that jammed all the time?"

Chasan tilted his head. "The one in the corner with the button that sticks?"

Nathaniel nodded. "Yes!"

"I hated that photocopier."

"Everyone hated that one," Nathaniel replied. "I did everyone a favor, and all I got for my troubles was the 'that's not acceptable behavior' spiel from Saint Peter, and a week later, I'm sent on a mission to babysit twenty hellions without the ability to curse or smite. A simple thank you would have sufficed."

Chasan laughed. "Allowing you to babysit twenty hellions with the ability to curse and smite has PR catastrophe written all over it."

Nathaniel sighed petulantly. "Everything was so much less stressful when broadsword fights were still a thing."

Chasan chuckled. "You've spent far too long overseeing the Hell Department."

Nathaniel bowed his head. "Why, thank you."

He grinned, his blue eyes alight with humor. "So, *gyoza* and *akashiyaki* for dinner?"

Mmm, Japanese dumplings. "Yes, please."

Saint Peter's Office

"Status report," Saint Peter demanded as he walked in.

Metatron read the report out loud. "Nathaniel caught up on the world history that he'd missed."

Saint Peter made a face. "Ouch."

Metatron nodded. "Yep. They spent the day in the city. In Central Park. Chasan took him to the museum."

Saint Peter paled. "Was there any damage? Any security footage?"

"No. No damage."

Saint Peter did a double take. "No damage? At all? Was Nathaniel even there?"

Metatron laughed. "He sure was. He had a few anxiety attacks, one or two minor meltdowns, but Chasan helped him through it."

Saint Peter let out a huge sigh of relief. "Oh thank goodness."

"It's only been about twenty-four hours," Metatron added. "Give him time. I wouldn't expect a major incident until around the forty-eight-hour mark."

Saint Peter glared at him, and Tennin looked up from her papers and laughed. "Yeah, he hasn't started work yet. Because Nathaniel in charge of a bunch of little kids has PR incident written all over it."

Saint Peter glowered. "Give him some credit."

"Oh, Chasan spotted Zophiel," Metatron added. "Some great Watcher he turned out to be."

"He was supposed to be keeping a distance."

"Well, now they know they're being watched."

"Damn it." Saint Peter sighed. "Send in some more backup."

"Raguel's free," Jegudiel added, keeping the smirk hidden.

Saint Peter gave a nod. "Send him in. He can team up with Zophiel."

CHAPTER SIX

CHASAN

CHASAN WAS THOROUGHLY ENJOYING his time with Nathaniel. Showing him the museum, Central Park, talking, laughing . . . this was the Nathaniel he'd missed all these years. Well, Nathaniel minus his tendency to curse and smite, but still Nathaniel.

Chasan's heart knew this was it. If, at the end of this mission, Nathaniel still rejected the idea of him as a partner, then . . . well, then at least he'd know.

It was rare for angels to be fated to one another. It was called a twinning of souls, where their eternal lights were destined to be weaved as one. Nathaniel had denied it for so long, but the spark still burned in Chasan. And all the heavens knew the burn of twin flames couldn't be ignored forever.

Twinned souls could, however, be unbonded. Unentwined, disentangled, and let go. Apparently it had been done once, a long, long time ago with catastrophic repercussions. But it *was* done.

So this mission was the litmus test. Saint Peter didn't say as much, but he might as well have. It was no secret that

Nathaniel's recent behavior hadn't been great. His outbursts and his request for solitude were common knowledge among the ranks of Heaven. Not that he'd ever tell Nathaniel that.

But it was like the winds of destiny were blowing, pushing for their twinning to either be completed or broken. So it wasn't just Saint Peter who was pushing for this. Fate had waited long enough.

Maybe he could show Nathaniel it wouldn't be the end of the world if they went through with it. It wouldn't be terrible. In fact, it was supposed to be a higher level of amazing. It was rumored to be a completion like no other. Blinding and brilliant.

Maybe that's what scared Nathaniel so much?

As much as Chasan was resigned to give himself into the bond, to be one half of the twin flames, Nathaniel was opposed.

Nathaniel had a lot of baggage to work through. And this mission—putting them together, working with kids—was going to be a torch to gasoline. It would either ignite, warming the cold and lighting the dark. Or it would ignite and consume them both.

Either way, it was happening. And despite the uncertainty, Chasan was pleased.

He was particularly pleased that he got to share a bed with Nathaniel, and that Nathaniel was adorably awkward about the whole thing. He came out of the bathroom, this time having remembered to take his pajamas with him, much to Chasan's disappointment.

He slid into the bed and sighed. "I don't know if it's the mattress or the bedding," he said. "But this is very good." He lay on his back, the covers pulled up to his chest. Chasan sat against the headboard, reading on his iPad. Nathaniel was nervous again, the anxiety rolling off him in small waves, pulsing like a heartbeat.

It wasn't full-blown anxiety, but he was nervous enough for Chasan to feel it. And he could feel it. He was attuned to him, and the more time they spent together, the more attuned he became.

"I think it could be both," Chasan offered. He wasn't an expert on human beds, but it seemed a fair assessment. "Believe me when I say, I've slept on worse."

Nathaniel shot him a look. "Have you . . . ? I mean, of course. But have you . . . ?" He turned back to glare at the ceiling. "Never mind."

Was that jealousy mixed in with his anxiety?

Chasan smiled. "Have I ever shared a bed with anyone else?"

Nathaniel's jaw ticked, and his anxiousness kicked up a notch. He turned his head once more to look at Chasan. "That's not my business, and it wasn't what I was going to ask. At all." More anxiety. His breathing changed, and he clutched the covers at his chest. "It's not my concern if you've shared a bed with someone. A human, perhaps. Or maybe another angel, I don't know. Oh Heaven's mercy, please tell me it wasn't Hadraniel from the Admin Department. I've seen the way he looks at you, and it absolutely wasn't the reason I kicked and smote the photocopier. It was jammed. Again. The fact that he . . . You know what? Never mind."

Nathaniel's hands were now fists in the blankets, and Chasan dared not reach over to touch his fingers should the contact be too much for him. So he slid his foot over and rested the side of his foot against Nathaniel's, and immediately Nathaniel's breaths deepened, and he calmed.

It took him a moment to realize. "How did you . . . ?"

Chasan tapped his foot with his own. "And you didn't even notice."

Nathaniel gasped. "That's cheating."

"You're welcome," Chasan replied. He rolled onto his side to face him, keeping his foot on Nathaniel's. He smiled at him. "And no, I've never shared a bed with anyone, human or otherwise. Well, there have been a few shared floor mats in centuries gone by, but not like this."

His eyes burned. "Shared floor mats?"

It was definitely jealousy, and Chasan liked that very much. "Yes, you know. In times when lodgings weren't as accommodating as this and everyone shared rooms and cots or reed mats or dirt floors."

"Oh. Yes, of course. I didn't mean to imply—"

What Chasan wanted to say was, 'That was exactly what you meant to imply but I've never been intimate with anyone else because I'm fated to you, you big idiot,' but that wouldn't do them any good right now. Nathaniel had baggage to work through, scars that ran very deep, and this closeness he had with him right then was lovely. He didn't want to ruin the moment. So, instead, he said, "And Hadraniel from Admin doesn't look at me any such way. You're imagining things."

"I imagined no such thing, and he's lucky I smote the stupid photocopier and not him."

Chasan covered his smile with a grimace. "Mmm, lucky. Not even Saint Peter could have gotten you out of that mess if you had."

"I'm nervous about tomorrow," he blurted out in a whisper. "I don't want to fail."

Chasan did reach over to take his hand that time, and Nathaniel turned to face him. Chasan threaded their fingers and their joined hands lay atop the blankets, and when

Chasan moved his foot back an inch, Nathaniel followed it to keep the contact. "You won't fail, Nathaniel. We'll see this assignment done, and we'll see it done well. Just you wait and see."

"How do you know that? How can you say that with such conviction?"

"Faith."

"Well, the heavens and all their holy glory aren't much use to us when we're without our powers."

"No, silly. Faith in you."

Nathaniel stared at him, and Chasan could see a storm brewing in his bronze-colored eyes. He went to say something but stopped short, and instead, he pulled his hand free and rolled onto his back. "I'm tired," he mumbled. "Guess we should get some sleep . . ."

"Yes, of course," Chasan replied. He was tired as well. They'd walked quite a ways today, and he was still getting used to the human body. He reached over and flipped the lights off. Darkness filled the room, and for all the steps forward he and Nathaniel had taken, he couldn't help feel there was always one step backward.

But forward was still forward, he reminded himself. No matter how small the distance. And clutching onto his ever-positive attitude, he closed his eyes. His thoughts went straight to Nathaniel, his jealousy over the idea of Chasan bedding someone else. Then his thoughts went to bedding Nathaniel. The things they could do to one another in human form, in angel form . . . And he wondered whether Saint Peter could hear his thoughts or the mental images that were running like a film through his mind.

He bit back a laugh and sent up a silent apology. Though he wasn't entirely sorry, and he had no intention of stopping.

NATHANIEL WAS ALREADY UP and showered by the time Chasan awoke. He was mumbling in the closet about deciding what to wear. Smiling, Chasan threw back the covers and walked to the closet and leaned against the doorframe. "Can I help?"

Nathaniel spun to look at him, his gaze slipping from Chasan's face, down his body, and back up again. He held up a shirt that had seemingly offended him. "What does a preschool teacher even wear? This whole wardrobe is terrible. What the hell is this?" He grabbed an Argyle sleeveless vest off a hanger and showed Chasan, as though it had offended him too. "This is a betrayal of humanity, that's what this is."

Chasan laughed. "No it's not. You wear it over a shirt." Currently, Nathaniel was wearing only black trousers. The zipper was done up but the button was still undone. Chasan didn't mind one bit. He went in and took the vest from Nathaniel and pulled out a gray button-down shirt. "Put this on."

Nathaniel was about to object, but Chasan silenced him with a look. He grumbled instead, but he did slip the shirt on and began to do up the buttons. "Looks stupid . . . what does it matter how a preschool teacher dresses anyway? . . . doesn't have to stand that close . . . wearing his underwear, Heaven's mercy . . . can't believe I'm doing this . . ."

Chasan had to bite the inside of his lip to stop from smiling. He waited for Nathaniel to finish grumbling under his breath, and when he had the last button done up, Chasan handed him the vest. "Now put this on."

He snatched it from Chasan and grumbled some more

while he pulled it on over his head. Chasan fixed his collar and tweaked the vest a little until it sat just so. "Now, your sleeves."

He held out his hands. "What's wrong with them?"

"Roll them to your elbows."

Nathaniel's head shot up and he looked at Chasan as though he'd gone crazy. "What on earth for?"

"Just trust me." Chasan began folding the sleeves neatly until they sat just beneath his elbows. "It looks hot."

"Hot?" Nathaniel was clearly confused. "If I'll be hot, why wear the vest? Why am I adding layers? I already told you the internal diagnostics of this body don't run right."

Chasan laughed out loud this time. "You won't overheat. I meant hot as in pleasing to the eye."

Nathaniel gaped, and his cheeks flushed pink.

"Sexy, even," Chasan added with a smirk.

Nathaniel's blush deepened. "I think the internal diagnostics are definitely broken." He put his hand to his forehead. "And I'm leaking again."

Chasan took both Nathaniel's hands in his and did his best to not smile. "Take a breath for me." Nathaniel did and he calmed down. "You're gonna do just great. You look great. Very professional, and you'll fit right in." This was one of New York City's wealthiest districts, after all. They did need to look the part.

He nodded and took another deep breath. Until he seemed to notice Chasan's boxers. Or more so, how he was filling them at the front. He pulled his hands back and turned to face a row of shirts. "Oh. Um. Right then. Okay, wow."

Chasan fought a grin. "Sorry. This body likes sleeping next to you."

Nathaniel almost swallowed his tongue, and Chasan

felt bad for being so playful when Nathaniel wasn't used to it, so he put his hand on Nathaniel's shoulder, dousing him with calm. "How about you go start the coffee machine. I'll go shower and get dressed."

"Right. Coffee. Good idea," he said and ducked out of the closet.

A short while later, showered and dressed, Chasan found Nathaniel in the kitchen. Coffee was made and bread was toasting. "Something smells great," he said.

"Oh," Nathaniel startled. He'd been studying the dawn out the window. Central Park looked fresh under the soft glow of daybreak, and the city itself was taking a moment to rest after a busy night before another busy day. "Um, I don't know if I did this right," Nathaniel said, handing Chasan his coffee.

Chasan took it, noticing both of their wedding bands as their fingers brushed. It made him smile, even though a pang of longing flooded his chest.

Nathaniel grimaced and put his hand to his heart. "What was that? Is this a heart attack? Oh Heaven's mercy. Am I going to die?"

Chasan gave him a smile and rubbed his arm. "It wasn't your heart, it was mine."

That apparently was the wrong thing to say because Nathaniel's eyes almost popped out of his head. "*Yours*? Are you going to die? I can't be a preschool teacher on my own, Chasan. That has disaster written all over it."

Now Chasan chuckled. "No. I'm not going to die. You know how I can feel when you're anxious? Well, you can sense that in me too. I thought you'd remember that." Feeling each other's emotions was something Chasan wasn't prepared for. They'd spent so long apart, he'd forgotten what it was like.

Nathaniel studied him for a long moment. "I remember . . . it's just that you've never felt anxious or anything like that. What was it? Pain? It ached." He rubbed his chest.

Chasan wished, not for the first time, that he could lie to him. But he couldn't. "Yes. A type of pain. Not physical so much. More . . . emotional. It's fine. I'm fine. It was fleeting and now it's gone." He sipped his coffee. "This is good, thank you."

The toast popped and startled them both, but Nathaniel took it as an opportunity to avoid any discussion of emotions—as he always did—and he busied himself with buttering the toast.

And it wasn't that Chasan hadn't felt pain around Nathaniel, because he had. It was that Nathaniel had been so consumed by his own pain and anger he wouldn't have felt anything else.

But they ate a slice of toast each, finished their coffee, made sure they both knew their human backstories, and they walked to the school. It was early, but they had paperwork to sort out and a brief initiation to go through before the kids arrived.

Nathaniel mumbled to himself the whole way. Mostly repeating his name and credentials, and griping about how stupid this entire assignment was, and with each step they took, Nathaniel's anxiety rose.

Chasan stopped him just outside the building. "Nathaniel, you're gonna be fine. Just wait, soon enough we're going to have a room full of excited kids and it's gonna be fun and you won't have time to be nervous or worried."

Nathaniel rolled his eyes, mostly at himself, Chasan was sure. "You know, if I was in angel form right now, I'd waltz in there without a care in the world. But this human body . . . there's something wrong with it."

"You wouldn't waltz," Chasan said lightly. "In angel form, you'd stomp. There would be no waltzing."

"Exactly."

"So I'd like to remind you that you're still you. This human body isn't that different. You're still Nathaniel, overseer of the Hell Department, where you see that karma is duly served without flinching. Without remorse and without fear. Well, preschool is going to be exactly like that. There's a very good chance it's going to be crazy, unruly, chaos." Chasan poked Nathaniel in the chest. "And that is your domain. That's why Peter chose you for this mission. To be the overseer of—"

"Of underdeveloped Earthlings," Nathaniel finished. "Who ignore rules and reason, who would reign in chaos and bedlam should they be allowed."

"Exactly!" Chasan said, spurring him on.

Nathaniel nodded. "I can do this! Chaos and bedlam are my specialty! I can do this with my eyes closed!"

"Yes, you can!"

"Without the cursing and the smiting," he added thoughtfully. "But I can do this! It's just like Hell . . . but with snacks and naps."

Chasan grinned. "Yes. Snacks and naps."

"Will there really be snacks and naps?" Nathaniel asked, hope and seriousness twinkling in his bronze eyes. "Because that actually sounds pretty great."

Chasan laughed. "Snacks, maybe. Naps for the kids, yes. For us, probably not."

"Correction. Naps for you, probably not. Naps for me, fair to middling."

With Nathaniel's confidence freshly bolstered, Chasan led him toward the front door. "Okay, but we really need to work on your vocabulary. It's the twenty-first century."

They were met by Geraldine Goldstein, the school principal. She was a tall, thin woman with a long neck, her hair in a tight bun, and a beak for a nose. She wore a cardigan with feathers around the neck, and she reminded Chasan oddly of a cartoon condor. She pecked through their paperwork like it was last week's newspaper. Whatever qualifications Saint Peter had manufactured worked like a charm because Geraldine found it all very boring. Every box was checked, every *i* dotted, every *t* crossed.

"It says here," Geraldine said, reading from their paperwork, "at your last school upstate, you both embraced environments where a child can harness their inherent curiosity through rich, sensory experiences, structured and unstructured play activities that allow them to sharpen their skills of observation, communication, and discovery."

She looked up at them both expectantly. Nathaniel swallowed hard, and Chasan gave a nod, not entirely sure if this was going well or not. "Yes, that's correct."

She smiled. "That's exactly the approach we have here. I spoke to your last school, and they couldn't speak highly enough. Said the parents thought you were angels."

Chasan almost choked, and surprisingly, it was Nathaniel who recovered first. "We totally are. Angels, that is."

"And a married, teaching couple," Geraldine went on. "I will admit, I had my doubts, but everyone speaks so highly of you, how you work together, and how you complement each other in the classroom. And our current preschool teachers had that terrible accident during spring break, so finding two with such short notice was a blessing."

"That's us," Nathaniel said. "Angels and blessings."

Oh my . . . he was enjoying this?

She gave a spiel on her school, how it ranged from ages

two to five, and how its esteemed reputation was built on distinction and the highest levels of care, and how the parents—who paid obscene amounts of money in school fees—expected nothing short of excellence. "All parents have been informed of your position in the school, and I would expect a few to have some questions this morning. I assume you have no issue with that."

"That's perfectly fine," Chasan replied, even though it sounded somewhat like a thinly veiled threat. "I would hope they take their child's education and well-being seriously."

"Oh yes, believe me. They do." Finally, she gave them a very quick tour of the school, showed them to the staff break room, then lastly their classroom. By this time, other teachers and admin staff had arrived, and it wasn't long after that the first kids began to filter in through the hallways. Geraldine said she'd be back before class started and left them alone.

The classroom was just like Chasan would have imagined it. There were a few small tables and even smaller chairs, learning tables, boards with the alphabet and numbers, books, toys, reading nooks with beanbags, and several areas for play. A long counter ran under the windows with a sink and tubs of crafts underneath. Everything was brightly colored, labeled, and neatly stacked in its place.

"It doesn't look much like Hell," Nathaniel mumbled. "Smells a bit like it though. Minus the brimstone, that is. But there's definitely a faint odor of disinfectant and bleach." He shrugged one shoulder when Chasan stared at him. "What? It's Hell. There's screaming, urinating, and vomiting. We need to be sanitary too."

Chasan sighed happily. "You handled Geraldine really

well," he said. He leaned his backside against the desk at the front of the room.

He shrugged. "Oh, she was easy. I deal with the likes of people like her, but a thousand times worse, all day long."

"I can't believe they added commentary to our backgrounds that parents at our old school called us angels," Chasan added with a sigh. "Pretty sure someone in HR needs a vacation. Can you add that to the list of things to tell Peter?"

Nathaniel smiled just as the door opened and the first child walked in. It was a small boy with black hair to his ears, a robot shirt, and a dinosaur backpack. He eyed them both cautiously as he put his backpack on a hook. Chasan gave him a bright smile. "Hello!"

"My mom said not to talk to strangers," the boy said.

"Well," Chasan replied, putting his hand to his chest. "I'm Mr. Bellomo, and I'm one of your new teachers."

The kid smiled back. It was part of Chasan's natural charm and pleasant looks that humans trusted him. "I'm Cole," the boy said.

"This is Mr. Angelo," Chasan added, gesturing to Nathaniel. But when Chasan chanced a look at Nathaniel, he found him staring right back at him. "What?" he asked with a don't-scare-the-child smile.

"I think I just figured out who in the admin section gave us our last names," he murmured. He had rage in his eyes. "Hadraniel. He's basically calling you a beautiful man . . . to your face. I think I need to pay him a little visit when we get done."

Chasan nudged him with his elbow. "We can discuss this later," he hissed, while smiling at the new people walking in. And more people, and more. Both kids and their parents who, as Geraldine had said they would, wanted to meet the new teachers.

Chasan was surprised at how well Nathaniel adapted. He shook hands and greeted moms and dads and crouched down to greet kids at their eye level. He did it so well, Chasan had to wonder if Nathaniel was playing a role here or if this was the real him. Under the bristles and the gruff armor, was he really this sweet man who made timid four-year-olds smile?

Chasan was pretty sure he knew the answer.

There was a wonderful man underneath that body armor. He had just been hidden away for far, far too many years.

It didn't take long before the room was quite crowded. Some parents were chatting with Chasan or Nathaniel. Some were being given a guided tour of painted artworks on the wall or pipe cleaner caterpillars on a shelf, fashioned by their child. Some parents stood off to the side in quiet conversation . . .

"Oh yes, the blond one. He's very attractive. He has a wedding ring, but he still might want some side action," one woman said to her friend. They might have whispered it, all nudgy and giggly, and they even said it in Russian. But the thing about angels is that they have great hearing, and they can speak every language.

Every. Single. One.

"The ring he wears belongs to me," Nathaniel said back to them. He said it with a smile, but there was enough bite to it. He also said it in fluent Russian. He held up his own left hand and spoke in Russian again. "See? I have one to match."

Their faces were priceless.

So was Geraldine's. She'd walked in at the right

moment. "Oh, Mr. Angelo, you speak English and Russian?" Geraldine asked. "That's fabulous!"

"Ah, yes," he replied in English. "And some Italian and Spanish."

It wasn't like he could admit he spoke every language under the sun. Even some that hadn't been spoken in centuries.

Geraldine and some of the parents all *ooohed* and *ahhhed*, smiling among each other at the news of having a bilingual teacher. Well, except for the two Russian women who looked a few shades of mortified. But for such a multicultural city, this was clearly a good thing.

Chasan really hadn't had time to dissect what Nathaniel had said. That the ring Chasan wore belonged to him, or that Chasan belonged to him? And just moments before that, he'd threatened to go have a little chat with Hadraniel for calling Chasan beautiful.

He was being jealous and possessive. Which was a good sign that perhaps he was coming to terms with their shared destiny. Or perhaps it was a not-so-great sign of the kickback that would no doubt be coming when Nathaniel resisted his destiny.

Again.

Thankfully, Chasan didn't have time to dwell. Geraldine made official introductions to their audience, and Chasan was grateful for the pretentious, expensive clothes and backstories because this audience would have expected nothing less. Saint Peter, or his team at least, knew what they were doing. They knew what humans expected, wished for, thought.

There was a thorough mix of ethnicities, and that always made Chasan smile. One thing was certain over the millennia the world had definitely become a lot smaller.

Sure, humans had their downfalls, but essentially, they were good.

He had to believe that.

Otherwise, what was it all for?

Nathaniel oozed charm and manners, and whereas he might have had a few anxious moments this morning, his confidence was a little surprising. But Chasan reminding him that this was no different than overseeing the Hell Department had clicked with Nathaniel, and it really was no surprise that he was so good at running Hell.

He had these parents eating out of the palm of his hand.

And when the parents left and the children all gathered on the circular rug, sitting cross-legged with their wide-eyed innocence, it was Chasan who became nervous.

Nathaniel clutched at his stomach and shot a look at Chasan. "That's not me."

"No, it's me," he replied quietly, still smiling for the children.

Nathaniel put his hand on Chasan's forearm, and he was met with a rush of calm.

Wow. Is that what it felt like when I did it to him?

"Okay, class," Nathaniel said, taking charge. "We're going to play the name-game."

And so they did. Each child took turns to announce their name and to make it fun, Nathaniel asked them which animal they'd like to be. "I'll start," he said. "My name is Mr. Angelo, and I want to be a fire-breathing dragon!" He put his arms out as though he was flying, and roared imaginary fire.

River chose a cat who could sleep all day, Johanna chose a butterfly who would smell flowers all day, and Ahmed chose a dinosaur who could stomp. James wanted to be a lizard like his brother's pet lizard, Ling wanted to be a tiger who could roar, and Finn wanted to be a horse who could run really fast. Cole chose a puppy who could play all day. And so it went on. It was a good way to get the kids to open up and to feel comfortable, and it helped with learning names. And it helped Chasan relax.

He was so grateful for Nathaniel.

After they'd done the rounds, Chasan clapped his hands and was about to change their activity, trying to regain some control, but Nathaniel said, "Excuse me, Mr. Bellomo. What about you? You didn't get a turn."

The kids laughed and eagerly waited for him to answer. He couldn't help but smile. "My name is Mr. Bellomo," Chasan said. "And if I could choose to be any animal, I would want to be an eagle. I would fly up really high and see all of the world." Then he changed his mind. "Or a dolphin so I could swim in the ocean. Or a giraffe so I could see up really high. Or a monkey so I could swing from the trees, or a zebra so I could be all stripy."

The kids laughed, getting more excited with each addition. Johanna spoke up. "You can only pick one!"

Chasan grinned. "Then I pick a chameleon so I can change colors whenever I want!"

"That's not even a real animal," Theo proclaimed. "Animals can't change color!"

"Yes they can," Holly said. "I rode on a pink pony once. They colored it pink."

Chasan laughed and took the classroom iPad and brought up photos and then a video of a chameleon changing colors. The kids loved it, and they spent a few minutes learning about its diet and habitat, and Chasan asked the class if they wanted to learn about a new animal every day, and the response was a very loud, very excited yes.

It got easier after that.

Chasan settled in, his nervousness long forgotten as they continued their planned lesson. It was the beginning of spring, so using that as inspiration, they pulled out paper and yarn and glue and made some birds and flowers and sheep. They figured out the first letter sound on *sun* and *dirt* and *garden* and tried to identify all the letters in each word. They counted flowers and added bees, and they sang and danced to the rain song on the iPads.

When the bell rang for lunch, Geraldine stuck her head in the door as the kids were filing out. "How are you settling in? I can see lots of smiling faces."

"It's been great," Chasan answered.

"Please join us for lunch in the staff break room," she said before disappearing.

Nathaniel let his head fall back and groaned quietly. "This is worse than Hell."

"You're brilliant with them," Chasan said. "You really took charge, so thank you."

He cast Chasan a strange look. "Did you assume me to be incompetent?"

"Not at all. I just wasn't expecting to freeze like I did."

"What were you nervous for?" he asked incredulously. "You're not nervous about anything."

Chasan could have laughed at that because he most certainly had been. "I just felt pressured. And I don't want to fail either. And . . ."

"And what?"

"And if you think I don't get nervous or have fears, then . . ." He shrugged sadly. "Maybe you don't know me as well as you think you do." He walked to the door. "Come on. Or Geraldine will think we're rude."

Nathaniel was caught off guard, clearly. But he ducked his head and walked out.

While the school itself was small compared to most, there was a lot of staff. From admin to assistants, aides, and occupational and speech therapists, and parent coordinators, the lunchroom was quite busy. Geraldine asked for everyone's attention when Chasan and Nathaniel walked in. She made introductions, telling the room a very brief history, and everyone seemed pleasant enough. Most were curious but polite, and some were bright-eyed and a little too keen for information.

One lady by the name of Cheryl-Anne, who had blonde curly hair and eyes that seemed impossibly round and possibly too big for her head, pounced on them first. "Oh my goodness, you two are adorable! And I bet all those kiddies in your class think so too! I thought I heard singing and laughing coming from your room earlier, and I can tell you as an early childhood music teacher there is no happier sound! Happy kids give me a happy heart!"

She was so bubbly and loud and so horrifyingly full of goodness that Nathaniel took a step back from her. Chasan almost laughed at him but hid his smile as he pulled out a chair for him, then one for himself. "Thank you, Cheryl-Anne," Chasan said. "Those kids are just a joy to teach."

She put her hand to her heart and cooed like a drunk pigeon, and Nathaniel began to cough. Chasan wasn't entirely sure if his coughing fit was fake or not, but Chasan patted him on the back and someone else handed over an unopened bottle of water. But Cheryl-Anne was called away, and Nathaniel's cough miraculously disappeared.

"What is wrong with her?" he asked, quiet enough that no one else could hear. "Is that a new kind of malevolence?"

Chasan chuckled. "You can handle sociopathic mass

murderers but not a little bright and bubbly woman like Cheryl-Anne?"

"Believe me when I say it's ones like her you have to watch. She's the bodies-in-the-basement type, let me tell you."

Another woman sat next to Nathaniel. She wore denim pants and a moss-green sweater. She had a wrap thing around her hair, a nose ring, and a kind smile. "Don't let her bother you," she whispered. "She's a bit crazy. She's the music coordinator, but I think her metronome ticks to a different tempo, if you get what I mean."

Nathaniel smiled at that. "Thank you for the warning."

She smiled right back. "My name's Gian, by the way."

"Nathaniel," he replied.

"Chasan."

"Everyone else here is okay," Gian went on. She looked at Nathaniel, then Chasan. "So, four-year-olds, huh?"

"Yeah, great age," Chasan said, hoping it would be enough. "And you?"

"I'm the three-year-olds' teacher. Nothing like a gaggle of threes to keep you on your toes. Makes the Fete Day lots of fun."

"The what?" Nathaniel asked.

"The Fete Day? It's a big family day in Central Park this semester. As soon as the weather warms up. There's face painting and food stalls, and each class puts on a show for everyone to watch. All the parents and grandparents, aunts and uncles come. It's a big day and a lot of fun. Unless you're in charge of the two-year-olds. Then it gets crazy."

Nathaniel squeaked.

"Puts on a show?" Chasan repeated.

"Geraldine didn't tell you?"

"Uh, no."

Neither did Saint Peter. I bet he knew . . .

Gian took one look at Nathaniel's face and she tried not to smile. "Not a fan of singing and dancing in front of everyone?"

He shook his head, seemingly incapable of words.

"We'll be fine," Chasan said. "We'll come up with the best idea yet."

When it was time to go back to the classroom, Nathaniel walked in first. Thankfully, the room was still empty. "A fete day," he whisper-hissed. "I thought she meant fate. As in a f-*a*-t-e day, and I began to get excited, but she said fete. With an e. And there'll be singing and dancing. In public. In front of people. A lot of people, Chasan. This is a disaster. I bet Saint Peter knew about this. I bet they're all watching right now, laughing hysterically. Where are the Watchers? The ones sent to spy on us. I bet if you listened really carefully, you could hear them laughing too."

"Nathaniel," Chasan murmured. He stepped in real close and put his hand to Nathaniel's chest. "Breathe for me."

Nathaniel inhaled deeply and he hung his head on the exhale. He was calmer already, but he was a lot more petulant. "A play! Like a musical or something else equally horrifying. This is the type of malarkey HR tries to pull in the Hell Department."

Chasan chuckled. "We'll be fine. We may not even still be here by then."

"Oh, we'll totally still be here. Saint Peter is exacting revenge on me, remember?"

"If we are still here when it's on, we'll make it fun. It doesn't have to be a form of torture."

Nathaniel cocked his head, confused. "Torture is fun.

Singing and dancing are not."

Chasan rolled his eyes as he smiled. "You don't fool me, Nathaniel. I've seen how you interacted with these kids today. You're not a villain."

Now he scowled and huffed out a disgruntled breath. At least he wasn't anxious. "My reputation will be ruined. In tatters, I tell you."

Just then, the door opened and a line of kids trickled in. They were dragging their feet, shoulders slumped, and looking tired, so Chasan had the kids lie down on the floor mats. Some kids napped, some kids just had quiet time.

Nathaniel was looking as though he could lie on the floor and have a nap too, but Chasan didn't say that. Instead, he made a 'this week' board, adding pictures and words of what they'd learned. He added a picture of a chameleon and the word 'spring' and every day they could add new pictures and words. It would be interactive and visual, and when the kids woke up and regrouped on the floor, they were excited about all the things they could add.

But the bell couldn't have rung soon enough, and when the last child was collected, both Chasan and Nathaniel slumped in their chairs.

"Heaven's mercy," Nathaniel mumbled, scrubbing his hands over his face. "I've had better days in Hell."

Chasan chuckled tiredly. "It wasn't as bad as I expected. And you were great today."

He rolled his eyes and groaned. "Don't you dare tell anyone that. I have some kind of reputation to protect."

Chasan laughed, but wow, he was tired. "I'm thinking early dinner and bed."

"I'm thinking of never getting out of a steaming hot shower."

Chasan could almost feel how good that sounded.

"Mmm, that sounds good." He stood up and held out his hand to Nathaniel. Reluctantly, he took the offer, and Chasan pulled him to his feet, just as Geraldine opened the door.

"I see everyone survived their first day," she said, meaning it as a joke, obviously.

"Because I'm not allowed to smite anybody," Nathaniel mumbled.

Thankfully she didn't hear. "You're more than welcome to stay until the older classes finish and do some lesson planning if you wish," she said.

"Thank you, but we're heading home. We can discuss and amend our lesson plans over dinner," Chasan said, adding his charming smile. "The joys of working with your husband."

She laughed that off and bid them goodnight with a promise/threat to see them bright and early.

"I don't think she's the type to have bodies in her basement," Nathaniel said. "But I'm almost certain she's thought about it."

Chasan clapped him on the back. "Let's go home."

The walk home was nice enough, save his tired human legs, but as soon as they walked into their apartment, they both slumped on the couch. Nathaniel turned his head slowly to look at him. "Can we summon dinner again?"

Chasan laughed, but he pulled out his phone and summoned Italian food. Nathaniel showered while they waited for the delivery person, and Chasan began lesson planning. They ate their dinner and Chasan left Nathaniel to add some final touches to the lesson plan while he took a long, hot shower.

Only when he came out, Nathaniel was sound asleep on the couch with the iPad held to his chest. The sight made Chasan's human heart skip a beat. "Hey," Chasan whispered, waking him with a gentle shake. "Let's go to bed."

Nathaniel sat up, bleary-eyed and a little confused. He studied Chasan's full form, from his bare feet to his sleep boxers and tight T-shirt, before he caught himself. "Mmm."

Exhausted, they climbed into bed. Chasan was even too tired to read. "I've done manual labor in human form that wasn't as tiring as today," Chasan said, half-joking, half not.

Nathaniel rolled onto his side, facing him. He slow blinked, almost asleep. Chasan was expecting some jibe back or some remark about Hell and torture. Instead, he frowned. "Which child do you think it is? Which child are we here to protect?"

CHAPTER SEVEN

NATHANIEL

TEACHING GOT EASIER. The next few days were busy and tiring, but they got easier. The underdeveloped hellions weren't actually that bad. Some of them were even . . . cute.

Though Nathaniel would vehemently deny ever admitting that.

Just as he wouldn't admit that spending time with Chasan wasn't all that bad either. Hearing him laugh or even the sound of his voice made him . . . happy. Falling asleep next to him, sleeping in a bed beside him, waking up before him, and watching him unbidden . . . how his pink lips would part just so, how his Cupid's bow was perfect, how his eyelashes fanned down toward his cheeks. His soft breaths, his pale skin that looked so soft and warm, his cheeks tinted pink . . .

Yeah, that wasn't terrible at all.

Though it did absurd things to Nathaniel's human body. Which was why he needed to be up and showered before Chasan. Even if it meant he was duly responsible for starting the coffee and making toast. That was a small sacrifice compared to letting Chasan see just how much he enjoyed sharing a bed with him.

Not that Chasan had any qualms whatsoever about parading around in his sleeping shorts with a rather proud bulge when he first awoke. He didn't mind at all. In fact, Nathaniel was certain that Chasan wanted him to see it. Otherwise, why would he choose to come out to the kitchen all sleep rumpled and totally *not* adorable at all? What was the point of that if not to parade his human physique in front of Nathaniel?

What was it with sleeping that did this to the human male anatomy? Were all human males subject to such torture? Waking up with tented boxers was horrifying.

Not to mention how absurdly good it felt.

Nathaniel would also never admit to how tempted he was to perhaps feign sleep and move a little closer to where Chasan still lay asleep. Or even pretend to outstretch his arm and lay it over Chasan's chest. Or his hip.

Sweet Heaven's mercy, his hip.

The hot showers weren't terrible either. And Nathaniel was rather taken with toast. Such a simple pleasure, long forgotten. Whoever took it upon themselves to look at bread and decide to cook it a second time and add butter was perhaps a genius.

All in all, the first few days of their assignment had gone swimmingly, and Nathaniel had adjusted to his human body . . . well, as much as one could, given his body's inclination to do the anxiety-shutdown horror show, or the everyday occurrence of *mane lignum*, or whatever Chasan had called it. That didn't make much sense to Nathaniel, because he thought Latin was dead, but Chasan assured him some words still existed today. And Chasan was much more competent in the twenty-first century than Nathaniel, so he dared not argue.

And surprisingly, or not surprisingly at all, Nathaniel had finally adjusted to spending time with Chasan. He'd adjusted to being around him, he'd adjusted to how his human heart reacted when they accidentally brushed hands, he'd adjusted to how his skin would flush at the worst possible times, and he'd adjusted to the ring on his finger that told the world they were sworn to each other.

He could even consider admitting that maybe, just maybe, they didn't have a clash of personalities. It wasn't their differences that made Nathaniel so antsy around him. It wasn't that Chasan irritated him in any way. But Nathaniel didn't want to admit that. Not yet.

He hadn't adjusted *that* much. He could adjust to many things. But adjusting to the rare angel-twisted-fate that he and Chasan had was something he just wasn't ready for.

He didn't want it. At least that's what his foolish pride kept telling his gullible heart.

Personally, he'd found it easier to adjust to being human and adjust to being a preschool teacher. Even adjusting to the twenty-first century hadn't been so bad. People were fundamentally the same. Mostly caring and empathetic, but not always. Everything just moved faster these days. Everything came with an expectation of now, now, now.

The twenty four-year-olds in his class were no exception.

And no, they had no idea which child was *the one*. When it was said the child was destined for something great, of human significance, that could mean a great many things. It didn't have to be someone with genius intelligence who would find the cure for cancer. It could be someone who wrote poetry that saved a life, or someone who worked as a janitor who found someone's lost insulin, or a bus driver who safely drove kids to school every day of the year for forty years. Maybe one of the kids would rescue animals. Or maybe one of them would run an orphanage in some far-off country, saving many lives . . .

"It could be any of them," Chasan had replied that night in bed. "Being destined for great things is a broad and subjective statement. Milo's very articulate for his age, Julian is very kind. Ahmed is extremely bright. Holly can read at a third-grade level. Marlow is just the happiest soul in the room. They each have a gift for something."

"Mmm," Nathaniel had agreed sleepily.

Chasan smiled, all cute and snuggly in bed across from him. "But not all heroes wear capes," he said. "That's what they say these days."

Nathaniel slow blinked. "I thought capes went out of fashion in the 1500s. And I don't recall any heroes wearing them. They were usually worn by pompous aristocracy who couldn't do up a button without a servant."

Chasan chuckled and sighed. He yawned, clearly as tired as Nathaniel felt. "It's a saying. Like 'not all angels have wings.'"

It was Nathaniel's turn to sigh. "Now, *that* I understand. I miss my wings."

Chasan smiled, but he didn't say that he missed his wings as well. Nathaniel assumed, after so many missions, that perhaps Chasan was used to being human.

"I also miss my ability to swear and to smite things," Nathaniel added.

"Of course you do." Chasan laughed again, but he closed his eyes and they stayed that way. "Goodnight, Nathaniel. Sweet dreams."

"Goodnight," he echoed. He didn't say the sweet

dreams part because it wasn't a Nathaniel thing to say. But he wanted to say it. And he wanted to reach out and touch the side of Chasan's face.

But he couldn't.

Sweet dreams, he thought instead. Chasan deserved the sweetest of dreams, and if wishes were horses, beggars would indeed ride. Nathaniel's dreams these last few nights had been of Chasan, of stars and hearts and every single thing Nathaniel both wanted and detested. And knowing his dreams would be of Chasan again tonight, he closed his eyes.

Because as much as he didn't want to dream of him, he didn't want to not dream of him either.

FRIDAY PUT a skip in everyone's step. The kids had had a busy week but were excited for the weekend, and so was Nathaniel. No work, no school, no kids for two whole days. He had no intention of seeing another human being—except Chasan—from Friday afternoon until Monday morning. Only six hours to go . . .

He helped the kids finish the weekly activity board. This week they'd learned about springtime, and they'd planted seeds on cotton balls, and they were taking turns watering them. No seeds had sprouted yet, but that didn't stop them from checking every other minute. They'd learned about a different animal every day, and words like flower and bird and kitten and puppy. They got to choose which weather symbols matched the day outside, and every child got to contribute and change the pictures. It was a lot of fun and was a great way for the kids to start their day.

Chasan was very good at the structured learning ideas,

and all Nathaniel had to do was go along with it. And as the day went on, as the kids settled into some free-play time, Nathaniel leaned against the teacher's desk and looked over the class. Chasan soon joined him. "There's no way to know, is there?" Nathaniel asked him quietly.

Chasan didn't need to clarify. "No. We won't know until it happens."

"Yeah, but until *what* happens?" Nathaniel mumbled. "It'd help if we knew."

"We can't force it or it could change the course of destiny."

"You sound like Saint Peter." Nathaniel scowled. "If we have to suffer this for another month just to have some random talk about fire safety for Jacob to realize he wants to be a fireman, and then he goes on to save people in a burning building, then can't we just tell him now and be done with it? I could be back in the Hell Department before lunchtime, swearing and smiting to my heart's content, and you could be off doing whatever it is you've been doing for the last thousand years."

Chasan smiled and bumped Nathaniel's shoulder with his. "You can't fool me. You're enjoying this. You just refuse to admit it."

"That is so ridiculously untrue."

"I can see how much you get out of it." Chasan smiled at the kids who were all busy with one thing or another. "You're good at it. You might want to be careful or Saint Peter will put you back on active mission duty."

Nathaniel gasped in horror. A few of the kids looked up, but he waved them off. He leaned in close to Chasan and spoke through gritted teeth. "I will smite every photocopier in every department if he even thinks about suggesting that."

Chasan covered his laugh with a cough. "You might want to add that to your report."

"I will, don't you worry." Nathaniel nodded, determined. "Paragraph one. In bold. And italics. And underlined."

Chasan smiled that charming and disarming smile that Nathaniel hated. And he hated the way Chasan smelled too. Was it really necessary to smell so good? It was distracting and mesmerizing like some kind of attraction potion.

Nathaniel couldn't remember Chasan's scent affecting him in such a way before. Maybe his body's olfactory senses were broken or short-circuiting as well.

Twenty-first-century humans were weird, and Nathaniel couldn't wait for the weekend. Two days of blessed isolation sounded like paradise. And as he all but fell into his chair in the staff break room at lunch, he could almost hear what his weekend promised: silence, the space, the very real absence of another single human being. Just him and Chasan. They could have food summoned. Chasan had even said they could summon groceries nowadays. He wouldn't need to leave the apartment at all.

"That sounds amazing, doesn't it, Nathaniel?"

Chasan's hand on his knee startled him, along with the discernible glare to let Nathaniel know he knew he hadn't been listening.

"Sorry, what was that?" he asked, aiming for a pleasant smile. He had no idea if he pulled it off.

"Gian was just saying there's a food festival in the park," Chasan said. "It runs all day tomorrow. Everyone's going. Most of New York goes. It's a huge deal. We should go!"

"Oh, excellent," Nathaniel said flatly. It was, in fact, not excellent. It was the very opposite of excellent. His plans for no human interaction were being thwarted. "But I—"

"We'd love to go!" Chasan spoke over him.

Gian grinned, and they made plans to meet up beforehand and all go together.

Nathaniel would rather spend a few millennia in the Hell Department, but he could tell by Chasan's enthusiasm there was no getting out of it.

Heaven's mercy, give me strength.

But by the time school was over, Nathaniel was too tired to even argue. He was washing paintbrushes in the too-low sink and his back was beginning to ache. "I can't believe you said we'd go to that food festival tomorrow. I was looking forward to a weekend where I didn't have to see another human being."

Chasan smiled as he finished straightening the chairs and tables. "Most families will be there," he said. "I figure it will give us more insight into the family dynamics and home situations. Plus, seeing them outside of the classroom has to be beneficial to the mission, right?"

Nathaniel hated how he hadn't thought of that. "Yeah, I guess you're right."

"And there's food from all over the world. How bad could it be?"

"Well, I don't know about bad. But authentic, no. I can't picture them setting up a Mongolian yurt and deboning goats in Central Park," he replied. "But one can hope."

Chasan laughed. "One can hope."

Nathaniel finished cleaning the last paintbrush and put his hand to his lower back and stretched. "This human body definitely needs a recalibration. It's a disaster."

Chasan put the last toy away. "I was going to suggest maybe going out for dinner, but if you're all peopled out, how about I make dinner instead? You can have a hot shower and we can watch a movie? How does that sound?"

Nathaniel groaned. "Like the best thing ever."

A quiet knock sounded at the door, and Gian poked her head in. "You guys done for the day?"

"Yessssss," Nathaniel drawled out. "Thank the heavens." Even though he wouldn't be thanking the heavens. In fact, he *blamed* the heavens, but this was not the time nor the place for that conversation.

"Been a week, huh?" she asked with a smile. "Thought you guys did great. Even Geraldine's impressed."

"Thanks," Chasan said.

"Any plans for tonight?" she pressed. "We sometimes head out for a few drinks, if you're interested. I could see what everyone else's up to?"

Nathaniel shot Chasan a horrified please-save-me look, and Chasan smiled. "Thank you for the offer, but we have plans."

"Anything exciting?"

Heaven's mercy! When did polite conversation become an inquisition?

"Well, if you must know," Chasan said, acting all coy. Well, Nathaniel *thought* he was acting. "It's my turn to run Nathaniel a bath and cook dinner. We were going to watch a movie—"

"Oh my gosh, you guys do that?" she cried, her voice three pitches higher. She put her hand to her heart. "That's the sweetest thing I've ever heard. And there I was thinking love was dead."

Then to Nathaniel's abject horror, she winked at him. Actually winked. "Then I'll see you two lovebirds at the food festival tomorrow."

Lovebirds?

The room tilted and the air went all weird again, but Chasan seemed to realize . . . Maybe it was the way Nathaniel was now holding the paintbrush like a sword, coupled with his inability to breathe. Chasan put his hand on Nathaniel's lower back, and calm permeated through him. "See you then," Chasan said, ever so casually.

Gian waved and cheerfully walked out the door, and Nathaniel finally breathed. "Oh my word." He panted a bit and put his hand to his forehead. He could feel a headache coming on. "She called us lovebirds."

"Yes, I heard." Chasan took the paintbrush. "I should probably take that before you impale someone, or yourself."

"I miss broadswords," Nathaniel said. "And the ability to swear. I could have dropped some wonderfully creative linguistics just now. Instead, I'm stuck sounding like an English professor with an American accent. It's all rather absurd."

Chasan laughed and put the paintbrush away. "Let's go home. To our lovebird nest."

Nathaniel shot him a well-aimed glare. "Can you not?"

He simply grinned. "We're husbands, remember? We need to act like it."

"Yes, I remember. It's on my list of complaints to write to Peter about."

Chasan held the door open for him. "Of course it is."

Nathaniel flipped the lights off. "Along with the swearing and smiting, or lack thereof. And this accent."

Chasan smiled as Nathaniel brushed past him into the hall. "I'm sure it's quite the list."

"And human feet."

That earned him a strange look. "Human feet?"

"I don't recall them aching before. And my back.

What's up with human bodies these days? Saint Peter should be made aware."

"He should," Chasan said, not even trying to hide his smile. "But there is one thing a husband could do for that."

Nathaniel stopped walking. "Pardon?"

"I can massage your feet."

Nathaniel was horrified. "You'll do no such thing!" The idea of someone, something, anything touching his feet was ghastly.

"Oh, really?" Chasan said, smirking. "We'll see."

"Yes, we will," Nathaniel replied, determined. He pursed his lips and looked down his nose. "We will see, indeed."

Well, later that night—after Nathaniel's hot shower and after Chasan cooked an amazing pasta dish—they took to the couch to watch a movie. Now Nathaniel wasn't at all used to couch etiquette, or movies, for that matter. But Chasan chose some film Nathaniel couldn't even remember the name of, because when Chasan suggested Nathaniel get comfortable and put his feet up, he did.

Right by Chasan, in fact. And when Chasan grabbed Nathaniel's foot and dug his thumb into the sole, Nathaniel was . . .

"Please don't," he began.

Oh, sweet Heaven's mercy.

"Oh my word. That is . . . that is disturbingly good." He groaned without shame, and he ignored the look Chasan gave him. "Don't you dare say *I told you so.*"

Chasan chuckled. "Wouldn't dream of it."

Nathaniel tried not to make obscene noises, but apparently biting back a groan made Chasan blush even more than if he'd been vocal about it. "I do apologize," Nathaniel murmured. "It's just that it feels so good. Please don't stop."

Chasan tapped Nathaniel's other shin. "This one's turn." Then he worked his magic on that foot, and Nathaniel couldn't help but wonder just how talented those hands might be at other things. He was clearly well-practiced . . .

Nathaniel sat up rather awkwardly, given his feet were in Chasan's lap. "Where did you learn to do this? I mean, on whom? Have you massaged the feet of many men before?"

All those traitorous words were out before he could stop them.

Chasan stared at him, his fingers stilled.

"I mean, that would be perfectly fine," Nathaniel said quickly, as though the words tasted sour, because it would actually not be perfectly fine. He pulled his feet back and scooted up on the sofa, putting some distance between them. "And completely understandable, given the years since . . . I mean, you've been on countless missions, it stands to reason there've been other men . . . other men's feet." He cleared his throat. "There's probably been a thousand men, given it's been longer . . . or maybe two thousand men. I've lost track of years, and you've been human more times than Saint Peter can count. And you're allowed to do whatever you choose," he said, almost a wheeze. "It's not like we're betrothed or anything. Not officially, or not at all, really." He shot to his feet. "Right then. I'll be heading to bed. I'm very tired. But thank you for dinner. It was really very delicious. And the foot massage was . . ." He put his hand to his head again. There was definitely a headache coming on. That nauseous feeling was starting to swirl in his belly. "It would appear I need to add incoherent rambling to my list of physical ailments this human body endures. Along with headaches and anxiety. Sweet Heaven's mercy."

He stood there, out of words, and feeling very much the fool. He realized then, somewhat belatedly, that Chasan hadn't tried to calm him down. He simply sat on the sofa, staring at nothing, frowning.

Having said far too much, Nathaniel turned and went straight to bed. Leaving the lights off, he crawled into bed, and he considered pulling the covers over his head to hide but decided the overseer of the Hell Department was beyond hiding under the blankets, so he faced the wall instead.

An eternity later, Chasan came in. He used the bathroom, then silently slid into the bed, staying as far away as possible. And after the longest time, when Nathaniel was sure his heart would expire, Chasan spoke. "There's never been anyone else. No human, no angel, not in all the years past. How can there be when my soul is entwined with yours?"

There was such sadness in Chasan's voice that it physically squeezed Nathaniel's heart. Hearing those words, hearing them from him, ripped open old wounds. He wasn't ready for this conversation. He hadn't been ready all those centuries ago; he wasn't ready now.

In insisting on a life of solitude for all this time, he'd condemned Chasan to the same. Without consulting him, without care or consideration of what that meant for him. He'd been so consumed with his own misery, he hadn't really thought about what that meant for Chasan.

An eternal existence of loneliness.

Nathaniel wanted isolation and loneliness, Chasan didn't. But Nathaniel never gave Chasan an option.

Nathaniel rolled over, not knowing what to say or even where to begin. But Chasan had his back to him. Nathaniel wanted to reach out, he wanted to say something . . . but he wasn't brave enough.

So he frowned into the darkness, and although both of them had the ability to ease each other's pain, neither of them did.

CHAPTER EIGHT

CHASAN

CHASAN BARELY SLEPT. He was up and out of bed before Nathaniel, which was a first. Nathaniel was curled into an inconspicuous ball, sound asleep. And Chasan might have thought the sleeping-Nathaniel looked adorable, peaceful even.

But the awake-Nathaniel was a mess.

He was hot, then cold, close, then distant. He behaved like he wanted to finally be with Chasan, then shut down and acted like he could never entertain the idea. He would be jealous, then catch himself and pretend he couldn't have cared less. Chasan felt like a yoyo on a string.

It was tiring.

But he had to hold out hope that Nathaniel would get past this.

And it was the flickers of the old Nathaniel, the little snippets of the *real* Nathaniel that kept his hope alive.

Well, that and the fact he had no choice. He was fated to Nathaniel, in whichever capacity he would have him.

Was that cruel?

The fate itself wasn't cruel. The fact that Nathaniel didn't want him was the very cruelest.

Chasan was showered and on his second cup of coffee, staring out the window overlooking Central Park, when Nathaniel appeared. "Oh, morning. Sleep okay?"

"Hmm," he grunted, walking straight to the coffee machine. He fixed himself a mug, wearing only his pajamas. Plaid gray sleep shorts and a black tee, his hair stuck out in every direction, his stubble finished the look. He had somehow managed to squint and scowl at the same time, looking adorably irritated until he took his first sip. Then he sighed and walked over to where Chasan stood by the tall window. He saw the gathering crowds through the trees and tents and marquees, food stalls, all being set up. He sagged. "Mary's donkey. I forgot about the food thing."

"It might be fun," Chasan offered.

Nathaniel made a face as though he found the word fun offensive. He nodded toward the park. "It's awfully people-y out there. Humans. Lots of them."

"This is New York. That tends to be a thing that happens."

He grumbled into his coffee mug. "I can't wait until this is over. And I can go back to the Hell Department, and when the malignant bags of slime and sludge need a good smiting, I can give them what they deserve."

"What is it with you and smiting?"

"Ever smite someone?"

"No, can't say I have."

He sipped his coffee. "Highly recommended. Very therapeutic."

"See, I don't work in any departments that require me to smite anything. I can imagine the Hell Department has quite a lot."

"Ah, yes. Murderers. People who mistreat animals. I do like to hear them scream."

Chasan stared at him, trying to determine if that was supposed to be a joke or not.

"Just kidding," Nathaniel said, smiling behind his coffee. "Since we installed the screaminator—you know, the thing that absorbs the screams of the damned and turns them into tennis balls for the Canes Omnes Department? We call that the screaminator. Well, since they installed that, we don't hear the screams anymore. It's much better for morale, if I'm being honest. The evil humans walk around kind of like that Edvard Munch painting."

Chasan laughed. Clearly Nathaniel's coffee was kicking in. "Toast or bagel for breakfast? Or I can do eggs if you'd prefer," Chasan said as he walked back into the kitchen.

"Uh, bagel would be fine, thank you." He peered down at the crowd below. "Do you think they'll have haggis at this food fair?"

"I sincerely hope not," Chasan replied from the kitchen.

"Ah, it wasn't that bad. The Scots were a good bunch. And the Saxons. And the Vikings."

"Anyone with a broadsword, right?"

"Exactly," he said, coming over to lean against the kitchen counter, mug in hand. "Those were the days."

Chasan couldn't help but laugh and shake his head. He spread some cream cheese on the toasted bagel and handed the plate to Nathaniel before he took care of his own. But while Nathaniel was there, and in particular after Chasan's restless night, he needed to bring up a subject Nathaniel had avoided for an age. Nathaniel was in a good mood, and that was very likely to change, but Chasan couldn't put this off any longer. He'd put it off for long enough.

They needed to clear the air.

"So," Chasan began, picking at his bagel. "We need to talk."

"About what?" he asked, oblivious. "It's my turn to cook tonight. I was thinking—"

"No, Nathaniel," Chasan interrupted. "We need to talk about us."

"About our fake human wedding, or about . . ." Nathaniel's words died off and the color drained from his face. "Oh."

"It's been long enough, and I think we need to clear the air. At least talk about what happened."

"No thanks."

"It was a different world back then, and—"

"I'd rather not do this."

"It wasn't anyone's fault." Chasan forged on regardless. "It wasn't *your* fault."

Nathaniel put the plate down with a clang, effectively putting an abrupt stop to the conversation. "I said no. I don't want to talk about it. Not now. Not then. Not ever. I told you to leave me alone about it when it happened, and I'm telling you again now, Chasan. Drop it."

"Nathaniel," Chasan whispered. "You and I have to get past this."

And that, apparently, was pushing it too far.

"There is no you and I," he snapped, taking a step backward. "There never has been. I told you and Saint Peter, I don't want it. So I don't need to get past anything. *You* do."

He turned and disappeared down the hall. Then a door slammed, and a moment later, the shower started.

Damn it, Chasan. Damn it, damn it, damn it.

They were almost getting somewhere.

One step forward, two steps back. Such was his entire relationship with Nathaniel.

He put his hands on the counter and let his head hang down, at a complete loss about what to do. Should he follow Nathaniel into the bathroom and make him talk?

Just then, his phone buzzed in his pocket. Frowning, he fished it out and read the message on the screen. It was from Zophiel.

You can't make him do anything.

Chasan sighed.

Incoming in three, two, one . . .

The elevator doors opened. Zophiel and Raguel, another Watcher, stood there smiling. "Morning," Zophiel said brightly.

Chasan sighed and stood aside, letting them in. "Nathaniel's in the shower."

"We know," Zophiel replied.

Oh. Of course. They were Watchers. They saw everything.

"You tried to get him to open up," Raguel said.

"And he shut me down." Chasan sighed again. "He won't talk about it. We were finally getting along okay until I opened my big fat mouth."

"You were right to question him," Zophiel said. "He needs to talk about it. The sooner the better."

"But I can't make him do anything," Chasan said, holding up his phone with the text as Exhibit A. "You said so."

"Well, of course you can't. He's as stubborn as a mule."

"He's worse than a mule," Chasan grumbled. "I don't even know why I'm bothering. It's been so long now. If time can't get him to see reason and change his mind, then nothing will."

"You know why you're bothering," Zophiel said gently. "You're meant to be together."

Chasan pointed his thumb toward the bathroom and whisper-hissed. "Tell that to him."

Raguel stepped forward, his face serious, his voice sure. "He is so in love with you he doesn't know how to deal with it."

Chasan was certain Raguel had lost his mind. "In love . . . ? Have you lost your faculties?"

Raguel smiled. "Chasan, he has much to overcome. It won't be easy, but it will be worth it."

Chasan counted on his fingers. "He's stubborn, pigheaded, and not to mention, difficult. He's indecisive and oddly jealous over me as though he doesn't want me, but he doesn't want anyone else to have me either. And he leaves his wet towels on the floor. What kind of heathen does that?"

Zophiel chuckled. "You sound like you've been married for a thousand years already."

"That's not funny," Chasan replied. "He wants to smite everything."

"He has some anger issues," Raguel added.

Chasan stared at him. "Some? Just *some*?"

"His anger is directed at himself," Zophiel said quietly. "He doesn't think he deserves you. He doesn't feel worthy. And he's scared witless of failing you again."

Those words hit Chasan hard, right in the solar plexus. "He is worthy. And he won't fail . . ."

"We know that," Raguel offered. "But he thinks the only way to not fail again is to never try again."

"Well, that's . . ." Chasan was floored. And frustrated

and mad, but mostly he was saddened. "Well, that's just awful."

"He's been lost for a long time. Peter had hoped that he'd deal with this on his own, after a time, but that hasn't happened," Raguel said. "But he's here to find himself."

"Well," Zophiel added. "It's more that he has to come back to himself. And the one thing that can do that, that can help him find his way back, is you. He's tethered to you, Chasan. Whether he likes it or not."

Chasan sighed again just as the bedroom door flew open and a towel-wearing Nathaniel appeared. He was still wet, his hair dripping, water beaded on his well-sculpted body. "What's wro—" He stopped when he saw the two other angels in the living room. He swallowed hard and tightened his towel. "Oh. Sorry." He cleared his throat and eyed both of them with contempt. "I could feel Chasan's distress. Now I see why. What do you two want?" He didn't wait for a reply. "Are you okay, Chasan?"

"Yeah, I'm fine," Chasan replied. And he was. But this was part of his problem. This was part of the hot/cold ebb and flow that was Nathaniel. He could say hurtful things and stomp off, then come bursting into the room the moment he felt that Chasan needed him.

Nathaniel stood there, water pooling on the tiles at his feet, not taking his eyes off Chasan. He could obviously feel that something had upset Chasan, and he very likely knew he was the reason, but what could he say? That he was sorry for a thousand years of hurt? That he would finally accept that they were fated?

Of course he couldn't.

Instead, he turned to Zophiel. "So . . . to what do we owe the pleasure of your company? I thought you were supposed to be watching from"—he waved his hand out yonder—"afar."

"We're here for the food festival," Zophiel replied smoothly. "I mean, who doesn't love good food?"

"That's utter hogwash," Nathaniel shot back. "You can click your fingers and be in any country on the planet for an authentic meal."

Raguel gasped. "Hogwash?"

"I can't swear. It's disgraceful," Nathaniel said, his hands on his hips. "The overseer of the Hell Department should be entitled to drop the effest of eff bombs ever dropped, wherever and whenever he so chooses. But no, I try to curse and it comes out like I'm at an eighteenth-century tea party."

Chasan, Zophiel, and Raguel all tried not to smile, but Raguel choked on a bubble of laughter.

"It's not funny!" Nathaniel snapped, and in his attempt to huff and stalk off, he lost his footing on the wet tiles and proceeded to do a twenty-second-long MC Hammer imper-sonation dance-off in the hallway. He put one hand on the towel at his waist, and one hand on the wall to regain his balance. He took a breath in and let it out slowly, looked at his audience, and spoke with an unusually calm and quiet tone. "My desire to swear and to smite you all into oblivion is really high right now."

He shuffled into the bedroom, and as soon as Nathaniel had slammed the door behind him, Zophiel and Raguel both burst out laughing. Chasan was surprised they'd held it in for that long because it was rather funny, but he couldn't help but feel sorry for Nathaniel. "Leave him alone," he said. "He hasn't been human in a long time."

Zophiel gave him an apologetic look. Raguel had to wipe away a tear. "Sorry."

Chasan sighed and ran his hand through his hair. "I'll go check on him," Chasan said, quietly excusing himself, but he stopped when he got to the door. *May as well make the most of them.* "Oh, if you two still have your powers, please make yourselves useful and wave your housekeeping fingers at the kitchen and the laundry hamper, thanks."

He found Nathaniel in the huge walk-in closet. He had black jeans on and was pulling on a black tee-shirt, and Chasan could only guess that his choice of color matched his mood. "You okay?" he asked gently.

"Yes, why wouldn't I be?" he replied. He plonked himself onto the plush padded seat and angrily unfolded a pair of socks. "Are they still here?"

"Yes."

"Still laughing?"

"No." Chasan frowned at that. "I put them to good use. At least we won't have to worry about doing laundry."

He rolled his eyes, then set about pulling on his socks. "Well, at least that's something."

"I can ask them to disappear if you'd prefer," Chasan offered.

Nathaniel seemed to consider that for a moment, then pulled on one of his black leather boots. "What's the point? They're watching anyway. At least if they're here, we know where they are."

"True."

He tried to pull on his second boot, but his foot wouldn't comply and he was too angry and his frustration was almost at breaking point. He grumbled and fussed, still unable to get the boot on, and Chasan could feel the pent up rage rolling off him. Chasan went to him and put his hand on Nathaniel's shoulder, sending a wave of calm through him. "You're okay," Chasan whispered.

Nathaniel almost sagged with relief. He let his head drop, and Chasan could feel the tenseness of his shoulder, so he gave it a squeeze. "I'm sorry," Nathaniel murmured.

Chasan was so stunned, he didn't know what to say.

"I'm sorry about what I said earlier. I hurt you, and I didn't mean to do that," Nathaniel continued. "What I mean is, I *did* mean to hurt you, that is. That's why I said it; to make you stop. To hurt you before you hurt me. But I don't *want* to hurt you, Chasan. I really don't. That doesn't make sense. I'm sorry. I'm just so angry all the time."

Wow.

Just wow.

Chasan was speechless. This was monumental. This was a huge step forward, and he was stunned into silence. But he had to say something.

"I don't want to hurt you either."

Nathaniel let out a long breath, leaning slightly into Chasan's touch. "You could never hurt me. I know that."

"It's okay to be angry," Chasan offered. "You're allowed to be angry. But you don't have to be alone, and you can talk to me about anything. I'll always be here for you."

He groaned quietly, then shucked away from Chasan's hand and yanked his boot on. "Yeah, well. Let's do this peopling thing. Get it over and done with."

Chasan took a step back, giving him the space he clearly desired. "Yep. Let's do this."

Nathaniel got to his feet, and for a few beats of Chasan's heart, they stood and stared at each other. Nathaniel was the first to look away. "I better grab a coat," he mumbled, turning his attention to the row of coats and sweaters. He chose a gray coat, and Chasan had to wonder if that was because his mood had lightened a little from the angry, all-black attire before Chasan had spoken to him. Happy this conversation hadn't been a total disaster, Chasan walked to the door, but Nathaniel stopped him. "Wait."

Chasan turned to find Nathaniel anxiously looking at Chasan's clothes and shifting from foot to foot. He was nervous. "What's up?"

"Well, the weather's so weird right now." He made a face. "And it could be warm in the sun, but then it can turn rather cold without warning, and it might make sense if you take a coat too. If you want to, that is? I'm totally not suggesting a coat because I care. I don't want you getting sick or anything. These human bodies are fragile. And if you get sick, that means I have to work by myself, and that'd be terrible. For everyone involved, really. And if you made me sick, I'd be utterly miserable to be around, so it's really in your best interest to perhaps consider a coat." He sighed. "Please."

Chasan smiled at him. Nathaniel showing he cared by pretending he didn't really care was kind of cute. And very Nathaniel. "Good idea. Can't have me making you sick, can we?" Just imagining Nathaniel with a human head cold made Chasan want to leave the country. But, to keep Nathaniel happy, he chose a jacket and folded it over his arm. "You ready?"

"Not at all, but sure, why not."

"I promise it won't be bad. If it's terrible or too people-y for too long for you, we can leave."

He gave a nod and a grateful smile. "Thank you."

"You're welcome, Nathaniel."

He finally smiled, so Chasan opened the door to find Zophiel and Raguel sitting on the sofa, each reading a newspaper that had somehow magically appeared. "Oh, you two done nattering on in there?" Raguel asked. "Not that we were listening."

They both folded the newspapers into halves, then quarters, and as magically as they'd appeared, both newspapers disappeared in a small burst of sparkles.

"How come you two get to keep your powers?" Nathaniel asked from beside Chasan.

"Because, unlike you, darling, we wouldn't set the world on fire just to watch it burn," Raguel said brightly.

Nathaniel rolled his eyes. "Whatever."

Chasan chuckled. "Well, shall we go see what this fair city has to offer today."

"Yes, we shall," Zophiel replied. "Oh, and your kitchen's clean and your laundry's done."

"Thank you," Chasan said, and he meant it. He really was grateful.

"Yes, it must have been so strenuous," Nathaniel mumbled. "Having angel powers and all. What did you have to do? Twitch your nose or wave your hand? Must have been exhausting. Do you need a nap?"

Zophiel and Raguel found it amusing. Mostly. They rode the elevator in awkward silence, and as they walked into the foyer, Raguel said, ever so casually, "Oh, Chasan. I ran into Hadraniel from Admin."

Nathaniel gave him a death stare.

Raguel smirked. "He asked how you were doing."

Nathaniel growled.

"Wanted to know when you'd be back. I think he misses you."

Nathaniel snapped. He stopped walking; his jaw was clenched. "Well, how about you tell Hadraniel to mind his own business. What Chasan does or doesn't do is none of his concern."

Chasan pulled on Nathaniel's arm, not bothered in the slightest. "Ignore him. He's just trying to get a reaction out of you." Chasan shot a grinning Raguel a look. "Leave him alone."

Zophiel laughed as they walked out onto the sidewalk. "Oh, I forgot how much fun this was."

"I hate you both," Nathaniel said. "And so you both know, I'm adding this to my report. And just because I am without the ability to swear or smite you both to ash, doesn't mean I am without the ability or the desire to kick the ever-loving stuffing out of you."

"Ever-loving stuffing?" Raguel asked.

"I can't swear," Nathaniel said through clenched teeth. "But if you'd care to find me a piece of paper and crayons, I can draw you a picture. Then once done I'm explaining the drawing to you, you can fold it up neatly, then shove it right up your—"

"Okay, stop," Chasan said. He still had Nathaniel's hand, so he pulled him in close, their fronts almost touching. "Ignore him. They're just antagonizing you to get a reaction."

Nathaniel frowned and mumbled, "He's being a jerk."

"Yes, he is." Then Chasan turned to face them but Raguel in particular. "And I said enough. Intentionally antagonize him again, and *I* will kick the ever-loving shit out of you."

They both gasped, but it was Nathaniel who spoke. "You can swear?"

Chasan had to think . . . "Did I swear?"

"You said 'shit,'" Zophiel replied, still clearly stunned.

Now Nathaniel gasped. "You can swear too? Oh man, I've been short-changed here. This is ridiculous. I'm most definitely being punished." Then his gaze lingered on Chasan's lips, then back to his eyes. "Say it again," he murmured huskily.

"You want me to swear?" Chasan whispered, unable to look away. He felt a little faint.

Nathaniel swallowed hard. "Yes."

"Shit," Chasan whispered.

The corner of Nathaniel's lips curled upward, his eyes darkened. "Threaten him again. What you said you'd do to him, say that again."

"I would kick the ever-loving shit out of him if he dared make fun of you," Chasan murmured.

"Heaven's mercy," Nathaniel breathed. "So that's a thing that's new."

They were standing so close, staring at each other's lips, and Chasan wanted to kiss him more than anything he'd ever wanted. He wanted to know what it felt like, what it tasted like. How it would feel to have Nathaniel pressed against him, their arms around each other, holding, moving, kissing . . . Nathaniel licked his lips and Chasan's heart almost stopped . . .

"Oh, hi guys!" a familiar voice said, cutting through their connection like a bucket of cold water.

Chasan turned to find Gian rushing toward them, grinning, waving. "I wondered if I'd see you two here. And oh, look at you, so in love. I see how you're gazing into each other's eyes. Just melts my heart."

Chasan had never had to smite anyone or anything before in all of his years of existence, but he considered it right there for interrupting their moment. And not just him, because he could feel how irate Nathaniel was as well. So Chasan put his hand to Nathaniel's lower back, trying to pass on a calm he didn't rightly feel, and he smiled at Gian. "Good morning," he said as cheerfully as he could manage.

She grinned up at Zophiel and Raguel, wide-eyed and

expectant. "Hello, I'm Gian. I work with Chasan and Nathaniel. And you are?"

"These are friends of ours," Chasan said quickly. "Zophiel and Raguel."

"Oh," she replied. "Such exotic names. Kinda fitting, I guess. Jeez, Chasan, are all your friends supermodels?"

Nathaniel snorted, but he leaned into Chasan a little. "Only the ones we don't like."

Chasan couldn't help but laugh. "He's just kidding."

"Yes, I'm just kidding," Nathaniel said a little too cheerfully. "Actually, Zophiel and Raguel just got married. Don't they make the cutest couple?" He gave them both a pointed stare, urging them to not blow their cover.

"Oh, yes," Zophiel said, recovering first with some indistinguishable fake accent. Raguel looked as though he had something sharp stuck in his throat. Zophiel pulled him against his side. "Married just last week."

"Oh, how exciting," Gian said. "And I thought these two were lovebirds."

"Yes, they make us look tame," Nathaniel said with a wicked gleam in his eye. "They can't keep their hands off each other, kissing all the time." He stared at them, giving them a little nod.

Clearly this was payback for earlier. Nathaniel was obviously enjoying watching them squirm.

But, like all good undercover angels, Zophiel and Raguel had to play their part. Zophiel turned to Raguel—who looked terrified—slid his hand along his jaw, and lifted his face for a kiss.

Nathaniel laughed, but then Raguel turned toward Zophiel and returned the kiss. Like really returned the kiss. Zophiel was surprised for half a second until he tilted his head, and right there on the sidewalk, they made out.

"Oh, I see what you mean," Gian said, her cheeks flushed. Zophiel and Raguel made no attempt to stop kissing. In fact, their hands were beginning to wander. Gian looked up at Chasan, slightly disturbed. "They're really just going to go for it, aren't they?"

Nathaniel, stunned beyond words, was gawking, mouth open, eyes wide.

Chasan cleared his throat. "Uh, guys?" he said, interrupting them.

Zophiel and Raguel broke apart, smiling, lips wet.

Chasan pointed to Central Park across the street. "Food festival?"

"Yeah, sure," Zophiel said. Raguel licked his lips, but his eyes were still unfocused.

Chasan pulled Nathaniel away. Nathaniel managed to walk, but he glanced over his shoulder toward Zophiel and Raguel a few times. "Well, that didn't go to plan," Nathaniel whispered.

Chasan laughed. "I don't know. I'd say it went very well."

"That was supposed to be payback. What on earth just happened?"

"I'm not entirely sure. But they look happy," Chasan said, looking back over his shoulder. Zophiel and Raguel were holding hands and both had rosy cheeks and huge smiles. "Pretty sure they owe you one."

Nathaniel frowned. "Owe me one what?"

Chasan laughed. "A favor."

"Oh wow," Gian said, once they'd gotten across the street and into the park itself. "Look at all these stalls. Where did you guys want to start?"

"Is there a Mongolian yurt by any chance?" Nathaniel asked.

Gian stared, and Raguel laughed. Or maybe he was laughing at something Zophiel had whispered . . . Chasan was more horrified by the notion that Gian had implied their plans included her.

"Let's start at the beginning," Chasan said. He gave Nathaniel an exaggerated glance. "We might see some of the kids from class."

"Yes, that sounds fabulous," Zophiel piped up. He and Raguel were still holding hands and he made a point of holding them up for show, then speaking loud enough for Gian to hear. He grinned at Nathaniel. "You two haven't been married that long that you don't hold hands anymore, have you?"

"Oh," Gian said, all dreamy. "They take turns cooking dinner and running each other a bath. It's the sweetest thing ever."

Raguel's smile became a grin. "Is that right?"

Nathaniel glowered at him, but then he rolled his eyes and took Chasan's hand. It was more of a begrudging death grip than a gentle hold, but it still felt nice, and Chasan couldn't hide his smile.

Zophiel didn't miss it. "You're welcome," he said with a wink.

"I hate them both," Nathaniel whispered. "Equally and profoundly."

Chasan laughed and gave his hand a squeeze as they strolled past the first few stalls, sampled some German pretzels, Czech *palačinky*, and some Austrian cheese. There were a lot of people, but the sun was out, the breeze was cool, and it really was a beautiful day.

The fact that Nathaniel kept hold of Chasan's hand made it even more so. They'd stopped at another stall, and

Nathaniel was quite content to buy something from each. "We'll never eat all this," Chasan said.

"Yes, but Peter's paying," he replied. "If he doesn't regret sending me on this mission yet, he will when the credit department gives him the bill. And if we can't eat it, we should give it to a homeless shelter. Actually, that's a really good idea." He smiled brightly. "We should send a few hundred dollars' worth of supplies to all the homeless shelters in the city. Peter's paying, after all. And he can hardly object, right? Helping the needy and all that. To be honest, he'd probably like it. And it's not like it's real money to him. He just tracks the numbers and snaps his fingers to make it balance." He glanced over Chasan's shoulder and made a face. "Oh, would you look at them. Still going at it. They're going to get arrested."

Chasan followed his line of sight, and sure enough, Zophiel and Raguel were over by a tree, kissing passionately between laughing and being rather handsy.

Chasan went to call out, but Nathaniel stopped him. "No, don't interrupt. I want them to get arrested. *That* would be comedy. Actually, can we be the ones to summon the police? That would make it even funnier."

Chasan chuckled and considered it, but no. It wouldn't be worth it. "Imagine the paperwork."

Nathaniel huffed. "Ugh. I didn't think of that."

"I'll go tell them to behave."

"I'll get us some of whatever this is," he said, nodding to the stall they were near.

Chasan walked over to the kissing couple and cleared his throat. "Guys? Are you done?"

"Not really, no," Zophiel said. Their lips were puffy and red; their smiles were huge. "It's rather fun."

"Yes, I'm sure it is," Chasan replied. "Just so you know,

Nathaniel wanted to call the cops just to see you both arrested for lewd behavior. And I'd rather not draw the unwanted attention to us."

Raguel sighed. "If you insist. Where is he anyway?"

Chasan nodded to the stall he'd left him at, and they all turned just in time to watch Nathaniel turn around holding two small tubs with a very confused look on his face. "Oh dear," Chasan mumbled, heading back toward him with Zophiel and Raguel in tow. "What's the matter?" he asked Nathaniel when he reached him.

"It's supposed to be ice cream," he whispered. He was holding two small tubs with something that, yes, looked very much like ice cream.

"Supposed to be?"

"It's vegan," he whispered, his expression becoming horrified as he handed one tub over to Chasan. "How does one make ice cream without dairy? Now, I know I've not spent much time on the surface of late, but surely not that much has changed."

Zophiel laughed. "Taste it."

Nathaniel's mouth drew into a watery line. "Uh, I think I'd rather not. I have concerns. And many questions."

"Well, it can be soy- or almond-based. There are quite a few plant-based alternatives now," Chasan said quickly. He tasted it, and it was actually very nice. "This is good. Try it."

Nathaniel was staring at him as though he'd sprouted a second head. "Very funny, Chasan. And just how does one milk a soybean or an almond?"

Raguel burst out laughing, and Nathaniel shoved the ice cream toward him. He took it and hummed at the first taste. "Mmm, try this," he said, feeding it to Zophiel.

Nathaniel grumbled. "Plant-based ice cream. Sweet Heaven's mercy, now I've heard it all. I'll take my milk the old-fashioned way, thank you. Cows, goats, yaks, and camels."

Zophiel laughed. "Yaks and camels? You need to start doing a lot more assignments."

"Mr. Angelo?" a little voice said. "Mr. Bellomo!"

It was Austin, a small, blond boy from their class. He was with his mom and an older sibling, and oh look, they'd found Gian. "Here you all are," Gian said.

"Hey, Austin," Nathaniel said, giving him a huge smile. "Having fun?"

"Lots of fun! There are ducks and sheeps and goats, and I patted them!" He bounced on his toes. "And a pony!"

"There's a petting zoo," Austin's mom explained, probably due to the strange looks they gave Austin.

"Wait, there are goats?" Nathaniel asked. He was actually excited for goats . . .

Oh no.

"Not the boodog kind, dear," Chasan said with a smile.

Nathaniel looked at him, hopeful. "They could be."

"I'll show you!" Austin said, even more excited now. "Mom, can we please show Mr. Angelo the goats? Please?" Austin took Nathaniel's hand and started to pull him in the direction they'd come. "It's this way."

Austin's mom gave Chasan an apologetic smile. "Sorry. We won't keep him long, I promise."

"Oh that's fine," Chasan replied, smiling after them. Watching Nathaniel with the kids made his heart so happy. Though that didn't stop him from nudging Raguel in the ribs. "Go with him, or Heaven knows what'll happen."

But then Holly spotted them, running up and showing off a colorful pinwheel and some baklava. Then it was Ahmed who walked past, and the kids were most excited about seeing one of their teachers outside of school. Chasan chatted with the parents, and the kids of course, and then kids from Gian's class joined in as well. They moved out of the way of the crowds and stalls, out into a grassy spot where the kids could kick a ball and run themselves crazy while the adults stood around and chatted.

There were moms and dads and bright and happy kids who were genuinely delightful little humans. It was all a rather nice way to spend a human Saturday, and Chasan loved that for such a large city, there really was a great sense of community.

But it didn't really help in trying to determine who the target-child might be. Which child was the reason for their mission? And what would the catalyst be? Chasan knew all too well that a human life could change in an instant. Sometimes the smallest of niceties—a smile, a hello, asking someone how they are—would make all the difference. Sometimes it wasn't pulling someone from a burning building or from the path of a speeding car. Maybe there was a kid in their class who needed to hear it was okay to be whatever they wanted. Maybe some kid needed to hear that despite what a parent or society might tell them, it was okay to be true to themselves. And maybe that kid would grow up to become president or an astronaut or a scientist. Or maybe they'd become a teacher and change hundreds of lives instead of one.

Maybe Chasan and Nathaniel had to be preschool teachers for the rest of the year to set a good foundation for all twenty kids. Maybe for five years . . . Saint Peter did say this assignment could take longer than necessary. Maybe longer . . .

Heaven have mercy, Nathaniel would hate that. Working together, and working with kids, but also being on assignment with him, living as husbands, sharing a bed—

forced to spend an indeterminate amount of time together, possibly years. Oh yes, Nathaniel would most certainly be adding that to his list of complaints.

Whereas Chasan would love every minute.

"How are you finding it?" one mom asked him.

"Loving it," Chasan replied.

"Do you know how long you'll both be here?" another asked.

"We're not sure," Chasan replied.

"Well, I hope it's a while, because Alexis is so happy with you both."

Chasan gave her a warm smile. "I hope it's a long while too."

Just then, another family spotted them and walked over, joining their little circle. It was Macie and her mom and dad, pushing a stroller with a baby version of Macie. And Macie was very excited to tell Chasan something.

"Mr. Bellomo, Mr. Angelo is being really funny," Macie said, all bright eyes and wild brown curls. She'd caught the attention of all the adults who were now listening.

Nathaniel being funny?

Oh dear.

"Is he?" Chasan asked, not sure if he wanted to know. "What's he doing that's so funny?"

Her little grin widened. "He's got baby goats on him." She patted her shoulder. "They is jumping on him."

Zophiel coughed to cover his laugh. "Should I go rescue him?"

"Oh, no," Macie's mom said. "He was getting out of the pen as we were leaving."

Chasan stared at her. "He was in the pen. With the goats?"

She laughed. Like, really laughed. "Funniest thing I've

ever seen. Here, I took photos." She produced a phone and showed the screen to Chasan.

And lo and behold, there was Nathaniel sitting in straw with a baby goat on his knee. And another photo of Nathaniel leaning at an odd angle with a baby goat on his shoulder.

His face . . . caught mid-laugh, his smile, the light in his eyes, was the purest thing Chasan had ever seen. And he felt a little sad that he hadn't seen it himself.

Or that he'd never been the reason Nathaniel had smiled like that.

"Oh, that's beautiful," Chasan said. "Can you please send those to the class email?"

The photos did the rounds, everyone having a look, and Zophiel nudged Chasan's shoulder. "What's that look for?"

"Oh, it's nothing," Chasan replied quickly. "I just . . ."

"I know what you're about to say," Zophiel said. "And I can tell you, he smiles like that when he's with you. You're just too blind to see it."

Chasan shot him a look, about to argue, but Zophiel nodded over Chasan's shoulder. "Here they are now. And would you look at him? Never thought I'd see the day."

Chasan turned to see what he was talking about, and what he saw stole his breath. Nathaniel, Raguel, and Austin's mom were coming back, but Nathaniel had Austin upside down over his shoulder as they walked. Austin was laughing, Raguel and Austin's mom were smiling, but Nathaniel's face was . . . well, it was something else.

There was a peacefulness, a joy. Where he was without burden or blame, without a care in all the heavens. He was so beautiful like that.

Chasan's heart hammered, his stomach tightened, and he forgot how to breathe. Nathaniel, obviously feeling

Chasan's physical reaction, stopped and scanned the crowd for him. Their eyes locked, and Chasan knew that Nathaniel could feel him when his smile became something else. Almost shy and unguarded like he used to be, for a perfect fleeting moment, and Chasan could see the moment Nathaniel remembered he was supposed to be angry. Nathaniel frowned and set Austin back on his own two feet.

But the thing about kids is that their innocence doesn't allow for adult concerns, and no sooner had he set Austin down than he was bombarded by other kids all wanting to join in. It became a game of chase, and kids laughed and squealed, and Nathaniel pretended to be an ogre or something.

"Who even is that guy?" Zophiel asked quietly.

Chasan didn't take his eyes off Nathaniel, not wanting to miss a second. "That's who he really is. That's who he was . . . before."

Raguel came over, still smiling, and whatever he was about to say was thwarted when Zophiel gave a slight shake of his head. Instead, he shoved his hands in the back pockets of his jeans and gave Zophiel an up-and-down inspection that bordered on obscene. "I think you and I need to go somewhere more private," he said to Zophiel, smirking. "You know, those newlywed obligations Nathaniel bestowed upon us and all."

Zophiel chewed on his bottom lip, clearly tempted but unsure. "I don't think our work here is done."

Raguel nodded. "I do. Our work is so done. Actually, I think I even know which kid is the catalyst."

"Who?" Chasan asked. "Which one is it?"

Raguel grinned. "I cannot say, sworn to the highest order. You know how that is." Then he gave Zophiel another heated look and not so subtly adjusted his crotch.

"My word, I can't stop thinking about you." He pulled Zophiel in close. "These human bodies have to be good for something. How about we go find out what that is," he murmured. Then he gave Chasan a grin as he started to pull Zophiel back toward the path. "We'll be around." Zophiel laughed as he waved goodbye, but they were soon kissing again as they walked out of view.

Chasan wasn't used to feeling envy. But how could they be so physically intimate because of a stupid whim when Chasan had been deprived of it for thousands of years?

It didn't seem fair.

"Oh my goodness," one mom said, laughing and putting her hand on Chasan's arm. "Look at them. They just love him."

Chasan followed her line of sight toward where a laughing Nathaniel was being taken down to the ground by a swarm of four-year-olds. Seeing him like that made his heart both happy and a little sore. "What can I say?" Chasan replied. "He's a lovable kind of guy."

CHAPTER NINE

NATHANIEL

CHILDREN WERE HELLIONS.

Underdeveloped humanoids that giggled and squealed —with tiny little hands and fingers and button noses and chubby cheeks that were not at all cute and adorable—and they were all savage hellions. It was an evil ploy to lure in unsuspecting adults into giving them what they wanted.

Like playing chasey, and tag, and making them laugh and having a great time.

Nathaniel's human body wasn't used to that kind of energy output. By the time he fended off the last kid, he called a truce and made it back over to where Chasan was sitting on the grass with some of the other adults who had somehow avoided being mauled by a battalion of four-year-olds. Nathaniel fell into a heap on the ground beside Chasan with a groan.

"Did you survive?" one mom asked.

"No," Nathaniel replied, unable to move. "This body wasn't made for that kind of battering."

Chasan chuckled and patted Nathaniel's chest. "Here, have some of this." Chasan had one of the bags from one of the stalls opened. It had some kind of hummus that Nathaniel had chosen because it was expensive and he was trying to spend as much of Saint Peter's money as possible. He hadn't expected to actually eat it. But Chasan dipped a celery stick into it and handed it to him, and people were watching so, begrudgingly, he bit into it.

"That's actually pretty good," Nathaniel said, surprised. "We should get some more of that."

Chasan handed him a bottled water. "Yes, we should get going if we want to see more stalls." He gave him a pointed stare, which Nathaniel had no problem reading.

"Okay fine, but you're going to need to help me up. I wasn't kidding about this body."

A few of the parents laughed, but Chasan jumped to his feet and helped Nathaniel to his. While Nathaniel brushed himself down, Chasan picked up the bags of goodies, and they announced they were leaving but would see everyone bright and early on Monday morning.

Once they were back among the crowds perusing each stall, Nathaniel took Chasan's arm. He would have held his hand, but Chasan was holding bags. And not that Nathaniel would have held his hand because he liked it, but because they were supposed to be husbands. Not because he liked how it felt. Not at all. Though holding Chasan's arm wasn't exactly terrible either. "Did you really want to check out other stalls?"

"Um, if you want?"

"You sounded pretty determined to leave, that's all."

"I didn't want anyone to start asking awkward questions we couldn't answer, that's all. I already had a few while you were off playing Best Teacher Ever."

Nathaniel laughed at that. "I absolutely was not *playing* that. I'll have you know, I *am* that."

Chasan smiled and gave him a bit of a nudge. "You were great, actually."

"I know. And let me tell you, those little hellcats are evil."

He barked out a laugh. "Maybe that's why they're drawn to you, oh all and mighty powerful overseer of the Hell Department."

"I can confirm," Nathaniel said. "That there's not much difference between a class of preschool kids and the Hell Department. There's chaos and bedlam, a complete disregard of the rules, and a lot of screaming."

Chasan laughed again, and Nathaniel's heart soared at the sound. "I saw photos of you and the goats. I wish I'd been there." Nathaniel stopped walking, causing people to almost bump into them. He pulled Chasan to the side of the walkway. "What is it?" Chasan asked, concern blazing in his blue eyes. "What's wrong."

"The baby goats," he whispered, very seriously. "They're the cutest things, probably ever. I'm never eating boodog again. I can't believe I even did once. Heaven's mercy, Chasan. I've *eaten* them. When they're so cute and bouncy, with smiley faces and tiny horns and teeny little feet."

Chasan pressed his lips together as though he was trying not to smile. "Humans eat meat. It's a thing they do."

"Well." Nathaniel shrugged. "I know what I said earlier about that awful ice cream and plant-based whatever, but I think the humans might be on to something there."

He made no attempt at hiding his smile now. "Are you trying to tell me you've had a change of conscience?"

Nathaniel put his hand to his forehead. "I went along with Austin to see the goats because I had every intention of buying one and taking it to Mongolia myself if I had to. I thought, exactly how hard would it be to track down a traditional yurt and you know, have the goat deboned and barbequed." He made a face at the thought. "But baby goats have smooshy, smiley faces, Chasan. And personalities. And the littlest baby goat horns and goaty-hooves I've ever seen. I can't eat one now that I've seen that. It's horrifying."

Chasan apparently found something in that very amusing. "Well, we can have vegetarian for lunch if you'd prefer."

"And for dinner. And probably forever." Nathaniel made a hopeful face. "Well, maybe we can have some beef. Cows don't have smooshy, smiley faces, do they?"

Chasan cringed. "Well . . ."

"Oh Heaven's mercy, they do."

"Only the baby ones. The older ones, not so much."

Nathaniel couldn't believe what he was hearing. "Chasan! You can't eat the elderly cows. What kind of barbaric human are you?"

Some people walking past gave them wary glances. Chasan laughed. "Well, there's always chicken or turkey."

Nathaniel gasped. "Yes! Turkeys are evil. We can eat turkey. They don't have smooshy, smiley faces. They have bald heads and talon claw feet and whatever those awful chin things are called, I don't even know." But then . . . "Oh mercy bless, Chasan. That's not their fault." Nathaniel was starting to not feel well. He put his hand to his gut. "Oh boy. What is this?"

Chasan rubbed his shoulder. "I believe it's called an existential crisis."

He squinted and tried to get air in his lungs. "It's worse than anxiety. Make it stop."

Chasan pulled him in close, Nathaniel's forehead

pressed to his jaw, and Nathaniel was doused with calm. It permeated his every cell and he almost sagged with relief.

"Feel better?" Chasan whispered.

Nathaniel nodded. He didn't want to pull away—every part of him wanted to stay right there—but he . . . he just couldn't. He took a small step back, missing that sense of home immediately. "Thank you."

"Any time." Chasan studied him for a moment. "Did you still want to grab lunch?"

Nathaniel frowned. "I guess I could just eat hummus and celery until I die. Or until we're recalled and I never have to worry about eating human food again."

Chasan smiled. "It's not that bad. Come on. I know of just the thing." He took Nathaniel farther along the stalls and stopped at one in particular. He smiled up at the vendor. "Two vegetarian burrito bowls, please."

"Here, let me take these," Nathaniel said, taking the bags of goods they'd already bought from Chasan. "You don't have to carry everything." Nathaniel felt like a jerk for not realizing sooner.

"Thanks," Chasan replied with a smile as he took their lunch. And as they walked back to their apartment, Nathaniel realized a few things. That he was woefully unprepared, that he was utterly clueless about the human world, and that Chasan knew a lot. Which meant Chasan had spent a lot of time here, probably avoiding all the realms of Heaven because that was where Nathaniel was. He realized that he'd made Chasan feel unwelcome where he should have been the most welcome, and he realized that Chasan was even better looking in the sunlight. He paused for the cars and the wind caught his hair, but he smiled at some passerby.

"You've spent a lot of time here," Nathaniel noted, but it was more of a question.

They crossed the street. "I have, yeah."

"Was it all on assignments?"

"Mostly."

"Ever been paired up with someone before? I mean someone who's not me."

Chasan paused while the doorman greeted them; then he replied as they neared the elevator. "A few times."

"Do you like it?"

"Sure."

"Did you take all those assignments because of me?"

The doors opened and they stepped in. The doors closed and Chasan hit the top button. "Not all, but mostly, yes."

"I'm sorry I made you do that."

"Well, technically Peter made me do that, but it was the right thing to do. And I enjoy helping people."

"I never meant to make you feel like you couldn't be there. It's your home, and you were kinda pushed out because of me. I just wanted to apologize."

The elevator doors opened and Chasan gave him a tight smile. "Heaven's not my home."

Chasan stepped out of the elevator into their apartment, and Nathaniel had to scramble to follow before the doors closed on him. He had no idea what to make of that. Was Chasan implying he'd spent so much time on Earth that Heaven no longer felt like home, or was he implying that perhaps his home was someplace else?

"What does that mean? Where feels like home to you? Where have you spent so long that it feels more like home than Heaven?"

Chasan sat on the sofa and pulled the coffee table

toward him. He put their lunch down and looked up at Nathaniel. "My home is you."

And everything stopped. The world stopped spinning, but Nathaniel's mind didn't. It was dizzying and awful, and the last few thousand years were about to topple down on him . . .

"Though I'd rather not talk about that right now," Chasan said. He got up and took the bags from Nathaniel, who still hadn't moved, and he disappeared into the kitchen with them. "We've had a great day and I'd rather not ruin that. If that's okay with you."

Nathaniel tried to get his mouth to work, and it took a few turns. By the time Chasan came back out with sodas and forks, Nathaniel had finally remembered how to breathe.

"I didn't mean . . . I just meant . . . ," he tried to say. "You've been on Earth a lot. You know how to fit in, and adapt."

Chasan slowly lowered himself to the sofa, and he thought for a moment before he shrugged one shoulder. "Because the infinite space of Heaven wasn't big enough for the two of us, remember?"

Ouch.

Nathaniel swallowed hard and his mouth was suddenly very dry. Was that a human thing too? Was he evaporating? Disintegrating? Dehydrating? He tried not to panic, even though his thumping heart rate couldn't have been healthy. "I'm sorry I said that to you. Back then. I was . . . I was angry."

Chasan kept his eyes down.

"But maybe . . . maybe we could . . ." He put his hand to his forehead. He was leaking again, and his stomach felt like a bubbling cauldron. "I don't know, maybe we could . . . what I mean is . . ."

"What do you mean, Nathaniel?" Chasan snapped. He threw his fork onto the food and pushed it away.

Nathaniel had never heard him angry with anyone, over anything. Seeing it now, knowing it was directed at him, didn't help his anxiety. "Oh." He took a shaky breath. "I just thought maybe being around you isn't so bad and clearly not as horrible as my memory would have it. Which sounds wrong, and I don't mean it in a bad way. I mean it in a good way. That this hasn't been *entirely* horrible, and what I'm trying to say is that maybe Heaven is big enough for both of us, and you shouldn't have to keep doing assignments and missions just to avoid me. Which is admirable, by the way, on your behalf. Pretty dismal on mine. But you can spend as much time in Heaven as you want. Even do a shift or two in the Hell Department if you like. I won't mind. I mean, we share a bed here, and that's a kind of torture, isn't it? Well, it is for me because it's so confusing how I love it *and* hate it. Meaning, I hate that I love it and part of me loves that I hate it, and oh Heaven's mercy, the words just won't stop. I don't know if this brain is broken or the mouth. Possibly both. There is a definite misfiring of the synapses—"

Chasan put up his hand. "Stop, Nathaniel. Take a breath."

Nathaniel inhaled, and then, of course, he felt light-headed. He needed to sit, which he did, across from Chasan. "And anyway, what I'm trying to say is I'm sorry for being such a mome for so long and I hope one day you can forgive me."

Chasan stared at him for a long, insufferable moment.

"A mome? No one has said that for a long time." He almost smiled. "But I won't disagree with you."

"That I'm a fool? No, I don't suppose you would. That's fair. You won't forgive me either," Nathaniel whispered. Chasan had very obviously not touched that part of his tirade.

"There's nothing to forgive. Not on my behalf anyway. And until you're ready to start talking about what happened . . ."

"It was so long ago," Nathaniel murmured. "It must seem inconsequential to you after so many missions."

"None of them are inconsequential," Chasan replied. "Not one."

Nathaniel frowned, and when it was clear he wasn't going to say anything, Chasan did. "Okay, so here's the thing. I'm only going to say this once, then we can never talk about it again if that's what you want." Nathaniel could feel his gaze burning into him, but Nathaniel could only stare at the wall. "I didn't want to talk about it like this, but here we are. Nathaniel, you and I are entwined with a fate neither one of us chose. You know how I feel about it. I'm all in, all of me, utterly and thoroughly. But yes, your indecision—if that's what it still is, I don't even know—affects me. So, perhaps when this assignment is over, you might be so kind as to make a decision."

Nathaniel's heart felt so heavy, he wasn't sure how it didn't crush its way to the Earth's core. Or maybe that was Chasan's heart he could feel. Maybe it was both. "I never meant to hurt you."

"You say that," Chasan replied quietly. "Yet you don't seem to be able to stop."

Just then, Chasan's phone rang. He sighed heavily and

answered. "Hello?" His eyes cut to Nathaniel's. "Sure." He disconnected the call. "Zophiel's on his way up."

"Oh?"

"He's drunk."

"He's what?"

The elevator pinged and the silence of the apartment was torn in two. "Nathaniel? Where are you?"

Nathaniel frowned as he stood up. "Here. Why?"

Zophiel slunk out of the elevator as though gravity was doing strange things to his body. He was walking at an odd angle and his steps were out of sync. He held a bottle of amber liquid . . . Correction: half a bottle of amber liquid.

He pointed a finger at Nathaniel. "'S your fault."

"What's my fault?"

"Raguel got recalled."

"He what?"

"Peter said we weren't supposed to be snogging like we were. Tried to tell 'im that it was your idea." He swayed some more. "And now I miss 'im, and it's your fault."

"I didn't know," Nathaniel offered. "I'll speak to Peter and sort it out."

"Fat lot of good that'll do me now," Zophiel said. "Do you have any idea how fun it is for humans to make out?"

Nathaniel cringed. "Uh, no, actually I don't." He could feel Chasan's gaze burning into the side of his head, but he didn't dare look.

Zophiel took another swig of alcohol. "You wonder why so many of 'em do stupid things. Humans, that is. Well, I can tell ya. Snogging is a lot of fun. Did you know the male human body can—"

"Okay, I'll take that," Chasan said quickly, relieving Zophiel of the bottle. "How about you come sit down."

"Ooh, is that food?"

"Yes," Chasan replied. "Here, have mine. I'm not all that hungry."

"What is it?" Zophiel asked, taking the lid off.

"It's vegetarian because baby goats exist," Chasan said, plonking heavily onto the sofa.

Zophiel turned his head slowly to look at Nathaniel. "What?"

Nathaniel shrugged. "Baby goats."

Zophiel laughed far too loudly. "Raguel told me . . ." Then his smile died. "And now he's gone." He held his hand out for the bottle, but Chasan refused to give it to him. So Zophiel waved his hand and another full bottle appeared. Chasan rolled his eyes.

"I hate that you still have powers and I don't," Nathaniel grumbled.

"And I hate that you made m' kiss Raguel and now I can't have 'im," Zophiel replied, then took a mouthful of liquor.

"Well, I hate that you both have a bottle of liquor and I don't," Nathaniel said petulantly. And Zophiel waved his hand at Nathaniel, and a bottle appeared in Nathaniel's hand. "Oh, thanks."

"Still hate you," Zophiel mumbled sadly, eating a mouthful of food.

"And I still hate that I can't swear and smite anything." Nathaniel took a dramatic swig of his bottle and regretted it immediately. It burned in his mouth, down his throat, and it burned in his gut. He let out a roar of a breath, surprised—and mostly disappointed—when no flames billowed out. "Oh, Heaven's mercy," he wheezed, turning the bottle over in his hand. "What kind of malicious liquid is this?"

"Fireball," Chasan replied.

"Well, I hate it," Nathaniel said, then took another swig.

The second mouthful burned just like the first. "I hate it a lot."

"And I hate that Raguel got recalled." Zophiel pouted as he stabbed his fork into the burrito bowl. "And I hate that this vegetarian stuff is actually really good."

"And I hate—" Chasan stopped and made a face. "I hate . . . circumstances. Not a person or a being; I could never hate someone." His gaze darted to Nathaniel. "But I . . ."

"You what?" Nathaniel prompted.

Chasan shook his head. "But it is what it is, right?" He held up the bottle of Fireball with his gaze fixed firmly on Nathaniel. "Here's to everything that causes us pain," he announced, then took a long pull from the bottle. He grimaced a little but didn't cough or breathe fire or almost die like Nathaniel had.

Right then. Nathaniel didn't require a cartographer to draw him a map of where that was directed.

Zophiel held up his bottle and nodded toward Nathaniel and knocked back a swig. "To everything that causes us pain."

"Oh come on," Nathaniel scoffed. "I'm not responsible for everyone's pain."

They both stared. Chasan raised one eyebrow.

"Okay, wow." Nathaniel took another swig. "Fair enough. Chasan's eternal heartache I will own because, in all fairness, there's a good chance I am the cause. The fact you had your tongue down Raguel's throat is something you can thank me for, not blame me for."

"Eternal heartache," Chasan repeated. He raised his bottle to Nathaniel before taking another drink from it. "You've been wrong about a lot of things, Nathaniel, but that's not one of them."

Nathaniel winced. "Ouch."

Zophiel laughed. "You deserved that."

"You know what?" Nathaniel asked to no one in particular. He took another mouthful of his drink. "I absolutely did, that is correct."

"And there's not a good chance you're the cause," Chasan added. "You *are* the cause. There are varying factors to some degree, but one hundred percent, yes, you are the cause of my eternal heartache." He took a huge gulp of his liquor and grinned. "It feels really good to say that."

Nathaniel frowned. "I already agreed and apologized. No need to be harsh."

"Harsh?" Chasan cried. "You know what's harsh? Being a twin-flame angel, a once-in-forever thing, and the guy turns out to be a selfish ass. That's harsh." He guzzled more of his bottle. "Being ignored for a thousand years. That's harsh."

"A selfish ass?" Nathaniel scoffed.

"Yes. A selfish ass."

Zophiel shrank back in his seat. "Well, this got awkward."

Nathaniel didn't really have a rebuttal for that, so he gulped down more Fireball. "Okay, that's probably true. Selfish . . . I can see why you'd think that."

"Why I'd think that?" Chasan sat forward in his seat and pointed his finger at him. "Because you are. So you messed up one mission—no not even just you. We messed up one mission. No, no, you know what?" He shook his head. "No we didn't. A human died. Lemme tell you something, Nathaniel. That's what humans do. They die. All of them. Wanna know how many humans have died in all my years of doing assignments? All of them. That's why they're called mortals."

"This vegetarian burrito bowl is really good," Zophiel said, glancing awkwardly between them.

"Humans are supposed to die when it's their time, and it was not her time!" Nathaniel cried. "It was my mission, my job. It happened on my watch."

Chasan's ice-blue eyes softened. "It happens to everyone. There isn't an angel that it hasn't happened to. I've lost someone before too. And Zophiel. We all have."

Nathaniel shot a quick look to Zophiel, and he nodded. "Yep. 'S true."

Nathaniel glowered at them both and took an angry nip of liquor. "Well, it shouldn't have happened to me. It was pointless and stupid. She was eight."

"It was a long time ago."

"Time doesn't matter," Nathaniel shot back.

Chasan shook his head. "Time is everything. When you're told to wait. When you're told he needs space and time. Believe me, it matters." He shrugged. "How much time? A thousand years, apparently. Sure, no problem. What even is time anyway? It moves differently on Earth than it does in Heaven, so maybe you don't get how long time is. But I've done 967 assignments since then, Nathaniel. That's 967 souls, 967 humans, 967 times I've been human, waiting for you to pull your head out of your ass, and I can tell you, unequivocally, time is everything."

Nathaniel was stunned.

Zophiel too. He sat there with his mouth open, his eyes wide. "Jeez, Chasan. Tell him how you really feel."

Chasan stood up. "He knows how I really feel. He just doesn't care."

"That's not true," Nathaniel offered weakly. "I do care. I just . . ."

"Just not in the way I need you to." Chasan put the

bottle on the coffee table and walked to the elevator. "I need some air."

"Chasan, wait," Nathaniel said, trying to stand up. He stumbled, swayed, then staggered to his left. A dining chair saved his fall. "Whoa. I think there's something wrong with the gravity. Can we get a physics guy down here? Someone tell Isaac Newton that f does not equal ma." He tried to right himself, but gravity pulled him in the opposite direction. He tried to line up a straight line to Chasan, but the room tilted. "What even is this?"

Suddenly Chasan's hands were on him, holding him still, but now the room was spinning. And tilting. "I seem to be experiencing some inertial difficulties."

"There's nothing wrong with gravity or the laws of physics, Nathaniel," Chasan grumbled.

And now Chasan was tilting him the other way. He hung onto him, but his body was so heavy . . . and then Chasan began to go blurry. "Now quantum mechanics are all wrong."

Zophiel laughed from somewhere close by, and Chasan grumbled about that too. "Don't encourage him. Help me get him on the couch."

Then Zophiel had Nathaniel's other arm, and the next thing he knew, he was lying down. The ceiling turned in one direction, the walls in another, and it made Nathaniel's stomach churn. He had to cover his eyes with his arm. "Chasan, there's something fundamentally wrong with this body."

"You're drunk, Nathaniel," Chasan said.

"Drunk? I not drunk. Didn't drink tha' much."

"Yes, but that's what happens when you don't drink alcohol for a few hundred years." Chasan lifted Nathaniel's arm off his eyes and Chasan's face appeared where the ceiling should have been. "Remember Japan?"

"Not really. Up till I did *kenbu*. Then nothing."

Chasan scowled at Nathaniel. "Because you knocked yourself out." Zophiel laughed from somewhere out of Nathaniel's field of vision. Chasan dropped his arm, and it hit Nathaniel's face. Chasan grumbled about something else, then said, "We're going to get written up about this. You and Raguel making out like teenagers, the three of us drinking on the job, Nathaniel passing out. Saint Peter will have my halo for this."

Nathaniel snorted because that was funny, and he wanted to say something really witty but his stomach was doing something all on its own. "Uh, Chasan? I don't feel too good."

"Zophiel, help me get him to the bathroom."

Then Nathaniel was up and being drag-carried through the apartment. Which would have been great if everything didn't spin in slow-motion. Chasan's hands felt particularly good, and Nathaniel clung to him a little more than was completely necessary. His arm was strong, his body felt nice . . .

"You smell really good too," Nathaniel said, though his words sounded like slow-motion as well. Then he was lying on the tiled floor of the bathroom, and it was so much cooler, but he missed Chasan's body. "Lie down with me?"

Chasan's face appeared above his. "No."

That made Nathaniel smile. "The angel of air with the blondest of hair."

Chasan rolled his eyes. "You're such a child." He got a strange look on his face as though he could hear something no one else could. "Oh."

"Oh, what?" Zophiel asked.

"Nothing. Just something Raguel said at the park," Chasan said.

Nathaniel wanted to know what they were talking about and why Chasan looked so worried, but the room and his head began to spin. He closed his eyes and gave in to the vortex.

OH DEAR.

Heaven's mercy.

"Chasan," Nathaniel whispered. His head hurt in ways that just weren't right. "Chasan?"

There was only silence.

Nathaniel took stock of the room, and he wondered why the ceiling looked so far away until he realized he was lying on the floor. Maybe that was the reason his body hurt too. He sat up, his back protesting and full of cricks and knots. "Ow."

He thought he heard faint laughter, and the door opened. It was Zophiel. "Oh, you're alive."

"Barely. What the hell hit me?"

"That would be Fireball."

"It's evil."

"Says the overseer of the Hell Department."

He ignored that. "Where's Chasan?"

Zophiel nodded toward the shower. "Get showered. I'll make you coffee."

Nathaniel looked over at the shower, which was a whole six feet away. "It's so far away."

Zophiel laughed. "Chasan was right. Get showered and dressed."

Nathaniel knew something was up. "Where's Chasan?"

"He's not here." And he pulled the door shut. "Get cleaned up and dressed," he called out as he walked away. "You've got some work to do."

Work to do?

What in the heavens did that mean?

But the shower actually sounded like a great idea. Sitting up and then standing up was a feat, undressing made his head hurt, so he made the shower as hot as he could stand. It helped iron out his sore back from sleeping on a tiled floor, but it didn't do a great deal for his queasy stomach.

Ugh.

Washing his hair and brushing his teeth made him feel a fraction better, so he got dressed and went in search of Zophiel. He was standing in the kitchen holding a mug of black coffee, which he held out to Nathaniel. "For you."

"Thank you," he mumbled, taking a sip. "I feel extraordinarily bad." He looked out the window to see dawn was yet to break. "What time is it? And where is Chasan?" He didn't know if the coffee was fixing him or making him worse. "I think I need to sit down."

"Good idea."

He lowered himself onto the couch. "I think I need to eat something."

Zophiel did his magic fingers and a plate of buttered toast appeared on the coffee table.

Nathaniel managed half a piece and washed it down with coffee. "Can you do your angel thing on hangovers?"

Zophiel smiled. "And where would the fun be in that?"

Nathaniel snarled at him. "If you ever want to do a shift in the Hell Department so you can watch people suffering, just let me know."

He laughed but made no attempt to quell Nathaniel's misery. He also made no attempt at conversation.

"So, where's Chasan? And what did you mean when you said I had work to do?" Then he had a horrible realization. "Wait? How long was I asleep for? Is today Monday?"

Zophiel laughed again. "Relax, it's Sunday. It's just after four a.m. You crashed out just after lunchtime yesterday. Fireball is—"

"Four a.m.?" Nathaniel put his coffee down. "Zophiel, where is Chasan?"

"Well, that's what you need to work on."

He was too hungover for games. "Zophiel," he growled.

Zophiel raised his hands. "Calm down. I don't know where he went, exactly. But I'm going to help you find him."

Nathaniel blinked. His head was pounding, his stomach rolled. He pressed the heel of his hand to his left eye. It didn't help. "You let him go out at four o'clock in the morning, by himself, in New York City? Have you lost your mind?"

"Here," Zophiel said casually. He waved his hand, and two white pills appeared on his palm. "Headache tablets. Take them, then we can start."

Nathaniel was feeling so decidedly awful, he did what he was told. He even managed more toast and coffee.

"And anyway," Zophiel replied. "I didn't *let* him do anything. He's free to do as he pleases. And he didn't leave at four. He's been gone for hours."

Rage began to surge inside Nathaniel. An anger he hadn't felt since he'd spent time with Chasan this last week. "Zophiel, so help me. Start talking."

"I'm going to help you find him."

"Good. I'll get my keys."

"Not yet. Stay seated. We're gonna do a little exercise."

Nathaniel stared at him. "Like calisthenics?"

Zophiel looked at Nathaniel like he was an idiot. "No. An exercise as in trying something."

"Oh."

"Okay, I want you to close your eyes."

"What?"

"Just do it."

Nathaniel grumbled, but he closed his eyes.

"Breathe slowly," Zophiel said, his voice melodic. "You need to focus."

Nathaniel opened his eyes again and glared at him. "How is this finding Chasan? We should be out there looking for him!"

"Nathaniel, may the heavens help me. I now know why Chasan left. Because you'd drive anyone crazy. Even the most patient angel to ever exist."

Wait . . . what?

"What?" Nathaniel could suddenly feel every ounce of toast and coffee gurgling in his belly. "He left me?"

Zophiel inhaled deeply and closed his eyes. His tone had more bite now. "Do you want to find him or not?"

"Yes!"

"Then shut up and do what I say."

Nathaniel pouted, but he did as he'd been instructed. He closed his eyes and tried to focus.

"Think of Chasan," Zophiel said. "And feel."

He wasn't sure he was allowed to speak, but he had to be sure. "Feel what?"

"When you think of him, you feel it in your chest. Right behind your sternum. Yes?"

Nathaniel took another breath in. "Yes."

"What do you feel?"

"It burns. Not heat, but bright. It burns . . . for him. It's small but intense. A flame. I've ignored it for a long time. I tried to snuff it out."

"Concentrate on it, Nathaniel. Let it burn."

Nathaniel did. For the first time in a thousand years, he let himself feel the flame he'd tried so hard to ignore. He felt the warmth, the flicker of red fire. He fanned it and let its flames lick at his ribs and glow warmly.

"Follow it," Zophiel whispered. "Close your mind to everything else. Let it lead you to him."

Nathaniel didn't even have to try. The fire in his chest would always find its twin. They were, after all, the twin flames. Nathaniel's fire burned red, and Chasan's fire burned blue, apparently. They burned for each other.

He needed to find Chasan, and now he could. Like a beacon in the darkness, he knew exactly where he was.

"He's not far," Nathaniel said, opening his eyes.

Zophiel looked stunned. "That worked?"

"Yes, of course."

"Well, I'll be damned."

"Yes, you will if you don't hurry." Nathaniel was already up looking for his keys. "Why would you think it wouldn't work?"

"Because it's never been done before. Saint Peter told me the steps."

Nathaniel stopped. "Correction. It has been done once before."

Zophiel made a face. "Yeah, well, we've learned a lot since then."

Nathaniel didn't want to think about that right now. He pulled on his coat and hit the elevator button and stepped inside. Zophiel hurried to join him. "All right, all right. I'm coming. Hold your horses."

Nathaniel felt better now that he was determined to

find Chasan, and the fire inside him burned a little brighter. He let out a relieved breath. "He better be okay, or I'll . . ." He wasn't sure what he'd do. "Or Saint Peter will want to join some witness relocation program."

Zophiel smirked. "Could you imagine him wearing anything but the white flowing robe?"

Nathaniel didn't want to smile, but that was kind of funny. "I'd like to see him as a preschool teacher." He imitated his deep authoritarian voice. "Thou shall not wipe snot on thy sleeve! Ye small heathen."

Zophiel laughed as they walked through the lobby and out onto the sidewalk. Nathaniel turned right, and Zophiel fell into step beside him. "How do you know where he is? Like, how does it work?"

"I don't really know. It feels like a cord between us, pulling me to him." Nathaniel made a face. "It feels strange but natural. It's hard to explain."

Zophiel didn't say anything for half a block, like he was trying to figure out how to phrase something. "Do you think you'll ever get used to it?"

"No."

"In a good or bad way?" he pressed. "I mean, in a good way like exhilarating? Or a bad way like exhausting?"

"It's . . . both."

"If you could put an end to it, would you?" Zophiel asked.

Nathaniel stopped walking. "Zophiel . . ."

"Because honestly, if you really wanted it over with, you would have asked Saint Peter to sever the ties a long time ago. But you haven't. So I was just wondering . . ."

Nathaniel's heart thumped uncomfortably; his stomach twisted. "You don't know what you're talking about." He set off walking again, faster this time. He was close . . . the flame was pulling him. Almost there. "And perhaps you could mind your own business. What goes on between Chasan and me doesn't affect anyone else."

"But it does," Zophiel countered. "And you know it does. All of Heaven waits for it. As though it's out of step, holding its breath, waiting for equilibrium. Or to see what—"

"And why should that responsibility rest on my shoulders?" Nathaniel snapped. "Why does the fate of Heaven fall on us?"

"Because you were chosen for it."

Nathaniel stopped again. "And that's part of the problem. Where is our choice? How are we to know if what we feel is real or because fate made it so? If fate was fair at all, it would have chosen someone more deserving for Chasan to be fated to than me."

Zophiel's face softened. "Nathaniel . . ."

Nathaniel glanced up at the tall buildings across the street, at the stained-glass windows, at the gothic architecture of spires and turrets and gargoyles. And the big ol' cross.

Of course this is where Chasan would be.

"He's here," Nathaniel whispered. He crossed the street and took the first three steps and stopped, his hand on the large wooden door. The flame behind his sternum burned, but he tamped it down and took a step back. "I can't go in there."

Zophiel snorted. "You know the whole bubbling-holy-water thing isn't real, right? You might be the overseer of the Hell Department and you have the dark cloudy aura thing going on, but you can still go in there."

"Yes, I know the bubbling holy water isn't real," he replied. "It's just . . . he wants to be alone, clearly. So I'll give him that." Nathaniel took another step back. "I'll just wait out here."

Zophiel frowned. "Suit yourself."

"I will, thank you."

He pointed his thumb to the door. "But you're sure he's in there?"

"Certain."

Zophiel shrugged, pulled the door open, and disappeared inside. And so Nathaniel waited. At first he sat on the brick railing that framed the steps. Then he paced for a bit. Then he sat on the steps. He crossed his arms, shoved his hands in his front pockets, then his back pockets. He put his hands through his hair a hundred times.

Early dawn became early morning, and still nothing.

The flame in his ribs burned on, and he could feel Chasan was okay. A little tense, but mostly calm.

Was Chasan testing him?

Is that what this was?

It wouldn't be totally undeserved.

You have made him wait a thousand years, so you can wait another hour.

Time was, how did he put it?

Everything. He said time was everything.

He also called you a selfish ass.

Which might not be entirely untrue.

"Listen, subconscious, you're supposed to be on my side." Realizing he'd said that out loud, Nathaniel looked around to see if anyone noticed. There was one couple, but they didn't appear to think a disheveled, pacing man who was talking to himself outside a church was anything unusual, apparently.

And while I've got you, you want to know what else he said? That being ignored for a thousand years was harsh.

And being a twin-flame angel, which is a once-in-forever thing, to a guy who turns out to be a selfish ass is really rather harsh.

"Okay, you've said enough. Thanks."

So you exile yourself to Hell for a thousand years, and by doing so, inflict the same punishment on Chasan. Only difference being is that you chose yours, and in doing so, you chose Chasan's for him. What was it that you said before about having your fate decided for you?

"I said that's enough!"

That earned him a wary look from a lady who happened to be walking past. Apparently talking to one's self was okay; yelling not so much.

He put his hand to the side of his head. His headache was back and his stomach was roiling to the point he thought he might vomit when suddenly the doors opened and Chasan appeared.

"You okay?" he asked casually, more than likely knowing he wasn't.

"I think I'm having one of those existential crises again. Possibly a brain aneurism. My own subconscious hates me. My back certainly does. I can't believe you let me sleep on the floor. Then you were gone because you didn't want to see me. I had to use the flame-tracking device to find you, which is weird, just so you know—"

"The flame-tracking device?"

"Yes, you know. The eternal-twin-flame thing that links us." Nathaniel frowned. "Wait? You couldn't feel that?"

His face unreadable, Chasan shrugged and glanced up the street. "I needed a place to think, that's all."

"And you couldn't do that when I was passed out on the floor?"

"No," he replied simply. "I needed to be where you weren't."

Oh. *Oh.*

"Oh." Unease crept over Nathaniel like a hundred tiny spiders. Followed by a cold mist of realization. "Oh."

"Zophiel told me you wouldn't come in."

"Yeah, I got here and just figured you needed some time."

Chasan shook his head and chuckled without humor. "Right. Time."

"Where is Zophiel anyway?"

"He had things to take care of."

There was a distance, a cold wariness to Chasan as though maybe, just maybe, he'd finally had enough of Nathaniel's crap.

There was no panic. No rush of anxiety. No bubbling fear that everything was about to come crashing down.

Nathaniel was almost relieved.

Because that level of pain would be everything he deserved . . .

"Anyway," Chasan said, shoving his hands into his coat pockets. "There's a bodega up here, and I need breakfast." He started down the stairs.

"Chasan, wait," Nathaniel whispered. Chasan turned and waited. "Did you . . . find what you were looking for? In there?" He nodded toward the church. "Did you get the answers you were seeking?"

He stared. A thousand things flashed in those blue eyes. "Yeah. I think I did." And with that, he turned and walked away.

Saint Peter's Office

Saint Peter read the report that Malakai had handed him. Then he read it again. There'd been drinking and arguing and Chasan ended up leaving, and all of those things weren't good. But one thing was so much worse . . .

Nathaniel refused to enter a church.

Refused. Couldn't bring himself to enter, had an anxiety attack at the thought.

"Oh dear," Saint Peter whispered.

"That's not good, is it?" Ridwan asked, his expression grave.

Saint Peter shook his head. "That's not good at all."

CHAPTER TEN

CHASAN

CLARITY WAS A FUNNY THING.

It trickled in at first, then dumped like an avalanche.

Chasan had always held out hope, and now it would seem that hope was fading fast. As much as he wanted, as much as he wished otherwise, Nathaniel didn't want him.

Nathaniel didn't really understand what he'd put Chasan through all these years. He knew it hurt Chasan, and he knew Chasan wanted him . . .

But the horrible truth was, whether Nathaniel was prepared to admit it or not, he had made his choice. And he could claim he still needed more time or that he was still unsure, but his refusal, his denial, was answer enough.

Even though there had been moments of doubt, times when Chasan thought maybe, just maybe, Nathaniel might change his mind. He could be sweet and attentive, funny and caring, and he searched for Chasan whether he realized he did or not.

Somewhere, deep inside Nathaniel, he wanted Chasan. Zophiel had told Chasan that Nathaniel was in love with him—he just didn't know it.

But the truth was, Nathaniel *did* know it.

He just didn't want it.

Getting drunk and telling Nathaniel a few hard truths had felt incredible. It was freeing, and Chasan had felt empowered. He'd said things he'd wanted to say for a long, long time.

And with that empowerment came a stark revelation.

It was over.

The quest for the twin flames was finished.

Not that it ever really began.

And that wasn't even the worst part. Chasan had assumed—along with Saint Peter and everyone else in Heaven—that Nathaniel's anger and self-imposed isolation were born from the death of that sweet child all those years ago.

But Chasan realized that had just been the beginning.

There was so much to unpack, so much to get his head around, he wasn't sure where to start. So he went to the only place he could think of where he could find some peace and clarity.

He'd slipped into a pew and sat with his head bowed, his eyes closed. And spent hours coming to terms with what he had to do. Part of him had always known. All this time later, he still wasn't prepared to face the truth.

A priest eventually found him and sat beside him, patient and kind. A tall man with a cherry in his warm brown cheeks, and forgiving eyes. "You look troubled," he'd said.

"You could say that," Chasan replied.

"A burden shared is a burden halved," he added.

Chasan had smiled at him. "Thank you. But I'm not sure I'd even know where to begin." Or that the priest would believe a word of it.

The priest sat back in the pew and smiled up at the altar. "At the very beginning is usually a good start." He smiled kindly. "My name is Father James."

"My name is Chasan."

His eyes lit up. "Ah, the name of an angel."

Chasan smiled and nodded. "Ah, yeah."

"So," Father James continued. "The beginning . . ."

Chasan laughed quietly at the ridiculousness of that truth. "It seems a thousand years ago."

"Time is like that."

"It sure is." Chasan sighed. "Father, I feel uncertain of my path."

The priest nodded wisely. "But you know what's in your heart." It wasn't a question.

"I do. And I wish it wasn't so."

"The hardest hills to climb often have the better view. Perhaps this is to test your strength and you'll be better for it in the end."

"Perhaps." *That or it will kill me.*

"Is it love?" the priest asked. Chasan shot him a look and the priest smiled. "When one is so tormented, it is usually love."

Chasan fixed his gaze on the cross above the altar. "I am . . . supposed to spend my life with someone who can't be with me."

"Interesting word choice. You say can't be with you but didn't say they didn't love you."

"I think he does. Well, I know he does. But he won't allow himself to be happy. He won't admit it or give in."

The priest frowned. "What's holding him back?"

"Fear. Pride. Ego."

"Sounds like there might be more to it than that."

"There is a lot more. So much more. He . . . he's been through . . . some things. Bad things."

"Ah. So there's unresolved pain, guilt, and blame at play here too."

Chasan smiled at him. "You're good at this."

He smiled right back. "Been doing it a long time."

Chasan sighed and his heart grew heavy. "I'm just not sure how much more of myself I have to give." No, his heart wasn't getting heavy. It was getting warmer.

The flame . . . the flame in his chest was alight.

What the . . . ?

Chasan rubbed at his sternum. "We're not the only ones affected if this ends badly." He couldn't exactly say the ramifications would be biblical. "It's complicated."

"It might seem that way," the priest added kindly. "But when all the unnecessary stuff is stripped away, all that's left is what's truly important."

Someone else walked in and the priest looked up. "Can I help you?"

"I'm with him." It was Zophiel.

"Oh, are you . . . ?"

Zophiel put his hand up. "Oh, Heaven's no. He, who shall not be named, is waiting outside. Being petulant and insufferable. He knew where you were."

"He didn't come in?" Chasan asked.

Zophiel shook his head. "Nope. Gave some made-up reason."

Chasan frowned at that. How strange . . . Of all the places Nathaniel should want to walk into.

Zophiel gave a shrug and sat down beside Chasan. "He's a mess. Doesn't know what he's doing, how he feels, which way is up, nothing."

"I know," Chasan mumbled, rubbing his chest again.

The priest stood up and patted Chasan on the shoulder. "I think you know what you have to do. The only happiness you're truly responsible for is your own."

Chasan nodded but kept his head down. "Thank you, Father."

Zophiel waited for the priest to disappear before he spoke. "I got him to use the twin flame thing to find you."

"I know. I can feel it. I haven't felt it in a long time."

"When he realized you were gone, he freaked out." Zophiel sighed. "He does love you. He just doesn't know what to do with it."

"I know."

Zophiel didn't speak for a moment, but Chasan could feel him staring. "Oh wow. You're going to do it, aren't you?"

"Do what?"

"You're going to ask Saint Peter to sever the bond. To kill the twin flame."

Chasan sighed and his heart squeezed. The flame in his chest burned hot. "I'm thinking so, yes."

"That didn't sound very convincing."

"I need to finish this mission first. And I don't know if that's even possible. Saint Peter said this assignment might take a long time."

Confusion marred Zophiel's face. "Why? Don't you just have to fix some kid? Ensure their path and destiny, or however Peter phrased it."

"Yeah." Chasan swallowed. "Something Raguel said in the park got me thinking, and then Nathaniel later on."

"What did Raguel say?"

"He said he thought he knew who the child in our mission was, that they were in the park with us."

"And?"

"I agree with him."

"Well, if you know who it is, your assignment's almost done."

Chasan almost laughed. "Quite the opposite really. I'm not sure this child is helpable."

"What? All human kids are helpable."

"Exactly."

It took a second for the penny to drop. "Oh." He put his hand through his hair. The color seemed to drain from his face. "Oh, man. Really?"

"I think so, yes."

He blinked and concentrated for a second. "It makes sense."

"It does."

"Oh, holy . . ." He nodded toward the altar. "What the hell was Saint Peter thinking?"

"I don't know. But Zophiel?"

"Yeah?"

"I think I need to step down from this assignment. I'm too close. It's too personal. My judgment is clouded."

He swallowed hard. "I dunno, Chasan. If there's any angel who can do this, it's you."

"I share neither your courage nor your conviction."

"Chasan, if Peter chose you, it was for good reason."

And that's what had Chasan so conflicted. Normally he'd never question Saint Peter. Not ever. But this? This catalyst-event, code-red, world-changing *child* that needed saving . . .

Was Nathaniel.

"I don't know how to save him," Chasan admitted. "If Saint Peter thought I was enough, he was wrong."

"Want to know what I think?" Zophiel asked rhetorically. Chasan was certain Zophiel would tell him regardless.

"I think you need to figure out the real reason why he is the way he is."

"You know why. His time in Peru in 980. He was never the same after that."

"The child?"

Chasan nodded. "He blames himself."

Zophiel frowned. "Are you sure that's all he blames?"

"What do you mean?"

"Maybe you should ask him who he's really angry at."

Chasan studied him for a long moment. "You think he blames me?"

"No. Not you."

"Then why is he so angry at me? Sure, I was there but not with him, exactly. I couldn't have stopped what happened any more than he could."

"It's misdirected. He's angry, all right. But what, or who, he's angry at is something only he can answer." Then Zophiel did the strangest thing. He nodded toward the altar, toward the cross.

"You think . . . ?"

He shrugged. "I think I need to go speak to Saint Peter, not that I'm sure he'll tell me anything. But I think you're right. I'm not sure Nathaniel's ready to be saved yet." He stood up. "Oh, by the way. Nathaniel's out front talking to himself. You might want to go save him before someone calls the police."

Chasan sighed as though the weight of the world were on his shoulders. Which it kind of was. When he looked up, Zophiel was gone, and so, with a weariness he'd seldom felt, Chasan got to his feet. The flame in his chest pulled him toward the doors, to where Nathaniel was, and Chasan did his best to tamp it down. He would have to learn how to ignore it all over again, he realized. And with a sigh aimed directly at Saint Peter, Chasan walked out of the church.

Nathaniel was out front pacing and mumbling to himself, just as Zophiel had said. Chasan could feel Nathaniel's anxiety, and his whole body lit up with relief as soon as he laid eyes on Chasan.

CHASAN'S FLAME soared at the proximity of its twin. *Oh, how it burned . . .*

So close.

They were—

Correction. They *had been* so close.

But besides the twin flame, there was a swirling of emotion coming from Nathaniel. He was on edge.

"You okay?" Chasan asked as neutrally as he could manage.

Nathaniel word vomited. "I think I'm having one of those existential crises again. Possibly a brain aneurism. My own subconscious hates me. My back certainly does. I can't believe you let me sleep on the floor. Then you were gone because you didn't want to see me. I had to use the flame-tracking device to find you, which is weird, just so you know—"

"The flame-tracking device?"

"Yes, you know. The eternal-twin-flame thing that links us." Nathaniel frowned. "Wait? You couldn't feel that?"

Of course he could feel it. It beat like a second heart. Chasan couldn't bring himself to make eye contact for fear Nathaniel would see straight through him. Instead he glanced up the street. "I needed a place to think, that's all."

"And you couldn't do that when I was passed out on the floor?"

"No. I needed to be where you weren't."

The look on Nathaniel's face . . . it was realization and pain.

"Oh." Panic started to bloom out from Nathaniel, Chasan could feel it. And a tiny part of Chasan was glad. "Oh."

"Zophiel told me you wouldn't come in."

"Yeah, I got here and just figured you needed some time."

Chasan shook his head, because damn . . . Zophiel was onto something. It wasn't just the way Nathaniel's gaze darted to the church doors, it was the panic and loathing that accompanied it. "Right. Time."

Nathaniel licked his lips and raked a hand through his hair. "Where is Zophiel anyway?"

"He had things to take care of."

Nathaniel frowned, and Chasan could feel loathing coming from him . . . no, not just loathing. Self-loathing.

Oh, Nathaniel.

"Anyway," Chasan said, shoving his hands into his coat pockets, praying his resolve would hold. He wanted to break. He wanted to put his hand to Nathaniel and take away his pain, but he couldn't . . . "There's a bodega up here, and I need breakfast." He started down the stairs.

"Chasan, wait," Nathaniel whispered. Chasan turned and waited, not bearing to see the pain in his eyes. "Did you . . . find what you were looking for? In there?" He nodded toward the church. "Did you get the answers you were seeking?"

He finally met his gaze then. "Yeah. I think I did." And then Chasan did one of the hardest things he'd ever had to do. He turned and walked away.

THEY SPENT the rest of their Sunday in the apartment. It was quiet between them. Well, Nathaniel tried to engage in conversation, but it was awkward. And Nathaniel decided he'd cook their dinner, which might have even been cute if it wasn't such a disaster.

"We can just order in," Chasan suggested. His night of no sleep was catching up with him, and he was lying on the sofa while some drivel on the TV kept him awake.

"No, I can do this," Nathaniel said. He banged and clanged around in the kitchen for a few minutes, then appeared in the doorway holding an iPad and an eggplant. His eyes were comically wide. "Oh my word. I just googled this the way you showed me how. There was a tiny little picture of one, and I thought it would tell me how to best cook it. So I clicked on it." He held out the iPad, and Chasan could see a screen filled with pictures of naked men. "Why are there penises? I did not request penises!"

Chasan burst out laughing. He was too tired to hold it in. The abject horror on Nathaniel's face just made it funnier.

"Chasan, it's not funny! What has the world come to?" He looked at the iPad again, then looked a little closer. He tilted his head and raised an eyebrow. "I mean, it's not exactly terrible." He took a few more seconds to study the screen. "I mean, this guy . . ."

Chasan shot off the couch and took the iPad from him. "That's probably not a rabbit hole you want to go down."

Nathaniel squinted at him. "Rabbit hole?"

"It's a saying. Sorry." Chasan took the eggplant. "This vegetable has become synonymous with that particular part of the male anatomy . . . It's a phallic symbol on the internet. Because of its shape." He cleared his throat. "Obviously."

Nathaniel looked at the eggplant. "Then what on earth is the peach symbol that was with it?"

Oh dear.

Chasan tried not to blush. "Well, that symbol is for the . . . buttocks area. Together, they're used, typically, by gay men . . ."

"Oh," he said. Then his eyes almost bulged out of his head. "Oh." He blushed so hard even his ears went red. "Heaven's mercy." He put his hand to his forehead. "And these things are readily available for viewing on the internet?"

"Uh, yes."

He swallowed hard, but then his gaze went back to the iPad. "That's . . . interesting."

Chasan laughed and handed the iPad over. "If you want to do some more internet searching, by all means. If you're curious . . ."

He balked. "No. What? Why would I want to do that? I have no need to do that. I'm not curious at all. About that. Or about searching . . . or watching." He shoved the iPad back at Chasan, but in doing so, touched one of the thumbnails and a rather explicit video began to play. Loud moans and men grunting, skin slapping against skin filled the air.

Nathaniel started to frantically tap the screen all over. "Oh sweet Heaven's mercy and Mary's donkey make it stop!"

Chasan laughed and pressed pause, and Nathaniel sighed in the silence. "Please tell me you're going to put that in your report?" Chasan said with a chuckle.

His face was bright red by now, but he narrowed his gaze. "You're enjoying watching me suffer, aren't you?"

Chasan shrugged. "A little." He handed him back the eggplant. "I'm going to shower and make a start on lesson planning for the week. If you need a hand with dinner, just ask." Then he couldn't resist. "If you want me to find you more porn, I can do that too."

Nathaniel's mouth fell open, and Chasan laughed as he walked toward the hall. "Slice the eggplant and lightly salt it while you dice up the other ingredients. It will draw out the moisture. Helps with the bitterness too. Then blot it with a paper towel."

Nathaniel's grumbling was all he heard before he closed the door to the bedroom. It was probably poor form to tease Nathaniel, but Chasan reasoned that a teeny tiny amount of payback for a thousand years of being ignored was allowed.

The fire behind his sternum flared a little. "Oh, be quiet," he told it. "You'll get over it like you did before."

The flame burned a little hotter as if it were arguing with him. Or proving a point. Or reminding him that his connection with Nathaniel was part of him, whether he liked it or not.

And that it was starting to cause physical pain.

Chasan stood in the shower longer than he normally would. Not that he was deliberately hiding away from Nathaniel. He was exhausted, mentally and physically, and the scalding hot water did make him feel a little better.

He dressed in some pajamas, grabbed his iPad, and went back out to the living room. Lesson planning was a good distraction, though Nathaniel's frequent mumbling would make Chasan smile. He also argued with the stove, with a frying pan, and with a rice cooker. There was even a one-sided discussion with a wooden spoon.

It would have been cute if Chasan wasn't trying to put a little distance between them.

And *this* distance between them was nothing compared to what Nathaniel had imposed all those years ago. But having spent this time with him, being so close to him after so long, it felt like an impassable void.

"You okay?" Nathaniel asked. He was standing at the dining table with a plate in each hand.

Chasan realized he'd been staring out the window. He didn't know for how long . . . "I'm just really tired," Chasan said, putting his iPad on the armrest. "Sorry. Did you say something?"

"Yeah," he mumbled, looking around awkwardly. "Dinner's ready."

"Oh, thanks." Chasan stood. "Smells great."

"Actually, why don't we eat on the couch," he said, walking over. "You're beat. Sit down and I'll grab the cutlery."

He slid the plates onto the coffee table and dashed off into the kitchen. He banged around in the kitchen some more and came back holding a tray with cutlery, glasses, and sodas.

His nervousness was palpable. He sat on the sofa and laid two settings on the coffee table, ensuring Chasan had everything he might need. "Can I get you anything else?"

"Uh, no, thank you." Chasan slowly sat beside him. He inspected his plate. "Looks good. What, uh . . . what is it?"

"I found a recipe on the internet." He grimaced. "Without any more googling blunders."

Chasan chuckled. "I probably should have forewarned you."

He blushed and directed his focus on his plate. "It's a Moroccan vegetable and rice dish."

"Well, I'm impressed."

He pointed his fork to the kitchen. "There's a mess in

there that will impress you too. Remember how the dragon festival in Bhutan ended?"

"In 745?" Chasan clarified. That festival in the Buddhist village had ended up in a food fight that resembled a warzone. "The kitchen looks like that?"

Nathaniel nodded. "Well, minus the overturned carts and disheveled monks."

Chasan couldn't help but laugh. "That guy with the persimmons . . ."

Nathaniel paused, his fork almost at his mouth, and he grinned. "What a mess."

"But the mission was a success. The Buddhists and the Bons coexisted for a long time." Chasan mused. He ate a bite of the rice. "Hey, this actually isn't bad."

"You sound shocked."

"I am."

He gasped. "Well, I . . . I'm . . ."

Chasan laughed and ate another mouthful. "You just scored dinner duties this week."

Nathaniel glared at him. "That's . . . well, that's just fine. I can use a phone to summon food just as well as you can. Or text. It's a thing now, apparently."

Chasan snorted quietly. "Will there be eggplant emojis?"

Nathaniel mumbled something under his breath and shoved a mouthful of the rice into his mouth, and Chasan ate the rest of his meal with a smile. But as soon as he had a belly full of food, his exhaustion set in.

"No sleep for thirty-plus hours is catching up with me," he said. "I'm going to need to go to bed. Leave the kitchen, and I'll clean it in the morning. You cooked. It's only fair."

Nathaniel took Chasan's plate. "Don't worry about the

mess. I've got it. After all, I'm the reason you didn't sleep last night. It's the least I can do."

Chasan didn't have the energy to argue. "Don't stay up too late. School tomorrow."

Chasan had every intention of lying in bed and wallowing in his own misery for a while. He had, after all, come to the conclusion that his fated-one was never going to love him the way he needed. So yes, he was going to allow himself a dark room and solitude to bunker down with his self-pity, but as soon as his head hit the pillow, he was fast asleep.

CHASAN WOKE up with Nathaniel's arm flung across his chest. He was sprawled in the middle of the bed with his arms out, sound asleep. It was warm and heavy and right on top of the twin flame under Chasan's sternum. Chasan wondered if that was just a coincidence, or if his body subconsciously sought its twin flame.

Chasan lifted Nathaniel's hand and placed it on the bed between them, allowing himself a moment for their fingers to touch. Nathaniel turned toward him, still fast asleep, smiling.

And that was the part that tore at Chasan. Because the more he thought about it, the more the pieces fit together. He was certain the soul they had to save on this mission was Nathaniel's. That's why there were two of them assigned, and them specifically. That's why there was a team of Watchers sent to help.

The catalyst event Saint Peter had mentioned, if the mission failed, would be the broken bond of the twin flame.

It had happened once before, and the ramifications had been felt far and wide.

Maybe Heaven couldn't take a second one. Or, maybe it was destined to fail, just like the first one, because that's what twin flames did.

Maybe Nathaniel couldn't be saved. Sure as the rising sun, if Chasan told Nathaniel he was the child they needed to save, Nathaniel would dig his heels in even more.

Actually, if Nathaniel knew, the damage he'd do to Heaven would be more than a smote photocopier.

So Chasan had no choice but to continue to play along. He needed to play his part until this mission was complete, however long that took, and when it was all said and done, he would ask Saint Peter to break the bond.

If Nathaniel didn't do it first.

"We need to start a list," Chasan said as they walked to the school.

"A grocery list? Because I used all the carrots and broccoli last night."

Chasan almost smiled. "No. I meant a list of the kids in our class. We should start a small profile so we can try to narrow down the possible mission targets."

He made a face. "Oh. Yes, right. Of course. The children. Because that's why we're here. So yes, a list. Good idea."

"Perhaps we can start asking them about their families, try and gain some more background information. We can add what we learned from the kids in the park on the weekend. We met quite a few parents. Not sure what it'll tell us, but it's somewhere to start."

"Good idea. And about the park . . . well, I was thinking about what we could do for the subject board this week. All those cute animals and the baby goats ..." Nathaniel tried to act all nonchalant, but Chasan could feel his excitement. "Well, I was thinking this week we could talk about farms! It ties in with how we did spring last week. And we could learn about animals, and how farms feed the cities, ya know? I don't think people in the city give much thought about the food they see in a grocery store. You know, even bread and milk and rice and beans. So maybe the kids can learn where their food comes from."

Chasan couldn't help but smile. "I think that's a great idea."

"And we could add pictures of sheep and cows, and pictures of carrots and apples."

"No pictures of eggplants though."

Nathaniel gasped. "Absolutely not."

Chasan laughed. "Perhaps we could research a no-bake recipe and the children can all help."

He made a face. "Hmm, I don't know. There are so many allergens to consider, and have you seen where they put their fingers?" He squinted. "Not good."

Chasan chuckled as he held the door open to the school, and they were barely inside the empty staff room before Cheryl-Anne spotted them. "Good morning, boys!" she hollered.

"Oh, Heaven's mercy," Nathaniel mumbled. "I forgot she even existed."

Chasan was a much better actor. "Morning! How was your weekend?"

And so began a five-minute inundation of details about her apartment, her husband, her cat, her plants, the importance of spring cleaning, and how knitting was good for arthritis. Chasan was beginning to wonder if she ever drew breath when someone poked their head around the corner and told Cheryl-Anne she had a phone call.

Chasan and Nathaniel threw their lunch into the fridge and escaped into their classroom. "Oh boy, she can talk," Chasan whispered.

Concerned, Nathaniel pointed to his ears. "Are they bleeding?"

"Five minutes with her is more exhausting than a full day with twenty kids."

Nathaniel laughed. "Rest assured, she could get a job in the Hell Department as a tormentor. Ten minutes in and they'll be begging for forgiveness."

They hadn't even finished getting the room set up when the first kids arrived. And of course, with the kids came the parents. Some just wanted to drop in and say hello and how much fun they had at the park.

"Oh," one mom added. "And I had no idea you were married!"

Oh right. Married. The whole married-and-in-love charade was back in full effect. Chasan had forgotten about that.

The mom sighed dreamily. "And I have to say, I love that! It's important for kids to see two people who are married and happy but also working together! Not many kids get to see that, so thank you!"

This time it was Chasan who froze up, unsure how to reply, and Nathaniel who recovered first. He put his hand to Chasan's lower back and plastered a smile on his face. "Aw, thank you! But I'm lucky because he makes it so easy."

She and another mom who had joined in both swooned. "You're so cute," the second mom said. "And I just love how one of you is all light, and the other is all dark. You just complement each other so well. Like yin and yang."

Chasan smiled, because what else could he do? And Nathaniel waited for them to turn away before he murmured, "Cultural appropriation of the Chinese philosophy of dualism is a thing we need to teach, apparently."

Chasan coughed to cover his laughter, just as more kids came in. And yet more kids, and soon enough it was almost time for class to begin. The kids were excited for the week, with cheery smiles and bright eyes.

But then Marlow came in with her dad in tow. Marlow looked a little sad, and her dad gave Chasan and Nathaniel a frown. "Is something the matter?" Chasan asked him quietly as Marlow got settled in her seat.

"Our old dog Buster died yesterday. Marlow's never lived a day without him, so she's a bit sad today, but we thought the routine would help her. You know, busy minds and all that."

"I'm very sorry to hear that," Chasan said. "But you're right. Routine is important. Leave her with us and we'll make sure she has a good day."

"Thanks," he replied, then gave Marlow a kiss on the top of her head and walked out.

Marlow sat at her table. Her little chubby cheeks wobbled and her huge brown eyes got a little teary. Chasan hated how kids had to learn this lesson so young, and he had intended to carry on the morning lesson as usual, thinking the distraction would do her good.

Nathaniel obviously thought otherwise. He crouched down beside Marlow's seat. "Do you feel sad today?"

Little Marlow nodded.

"It's okay to be sad," Nathaniel said.

"Daddy said Buster did go to Heaven."

Nathaniel glanced at Chasan before turning back to Marlow. "Your daddy's right. I know that's where Buster is right now, and there are huge parks with long grass where all the dogs can run. There are couches for doggie naps and lots of balls to chase and tummy scratches."

"There is?" Marlow asked, her teary eyes wide.

Nathaniel nodded. "Most definitely."

"How do you know?"

"Because all dogs go to Heaven. And it's the happiest place you could ever imagine."

"Is there squirrels to chase?" Marlow asked. "Buster would go crazy at the squirrels."

Nathaniel nodded. "Anything he wants. Marlow, how would you like it if we all painted pictures of Buster today? We'll be talking about farms this week, and dogs live on farms, don't they?"

Marlow nodded. "Will they go on the wall?"

"They sure will. We can pin all the paintings up on the wall. I think Buster would like that."

Marlow got a little teary again, but she hopped off her chair and threw her arms around Nathaniel. "Oh," Nathaniel mumbled, his eyes almost bugging out of his head, but he patted Marlow on the shoulder. Marlow sat back in her chair, much happier now.

Nathaniel stood up, and his eyes were a little glassy.

Oh, Nathaniel . . .

Chasan gave him a moment, then took charge. "Okay boys and girls," Chasan said. "Our topic board this week is all about farms! Let's start with farm animals. Who can name an animal you might find on a farm?"

They settled on a picture of a cow for the picture board and wrote some words like milk, grass, tree, sheep, and dog. As promised, they got to paint a picture of a black dog with a red collar, and before they broke for recess, there were twenty paintings of Buster to hang up to dry—and one very happy little Marlow.

As the kids went out to play, Chasan busied himself tidying up all the paints and brushes. He didn't want to be mad at Nathaniel, but he couldn't help it.

"Was what I said to Marlow okay?" Nathaniel asked when they were alone.

"I think she really appreciated it. You made her feel better without dismissing her sadness. You're great with kids, Nathaniel. They adore you. I know you'd doubted Saint Peter's judgment when he gave you this assignment, but I think he was spot on."

He hung up the last painting to dry and frowned at Chasan. "Are you mad at me? Why are you mad at me? You've been mad at me since yesterday. Is it because I got drunk? I didn't mean to. I didn't have that much, honestly. It's just been a long time since I've touched alcohol and I forgot—"

"No, Nathaniel."

"I can feel it, Chasan. How sad you are. And angry," he whispered. He put his hand to his forehead. "Since you went to church. You've been quiet. You said you found some answers. Oh, Heaven's mercy, Chasan. What is it?"

"I did find answers. Well, I thought I did."

Nathaniel put his hand to his chest. "Ever since I re-engaged this stupid flame thing, it makes everything worse."

"Worse?"

He cringed, pushing against his sternum. "More intense."

The anxiety ballooned out of Nathaniel, and the very last thing they needed was for the kids to come back in and find Nathaniel freaking out. Chasan walked over to him and placed his hand on Nathaniel's arm. The touch felt like home, and Chasan used that to send some calm to Nathaniel. "Take a breath for me."

He did, then nodded. "I'm okay."

"Nathaniel, we do need to talk. But here and now is not the best place for this conversation."

He frowned and nodded slowly, dread mingling with his fear. "Oh. Okay. Sure. I get it."

The door opened, and Gian poked her head in. "It's Pia's birthday. She's in admin," she added when Nathaniel and Chasan both stood there, unsure of what to say or do. Then she smiled. "There's cake. Though I probably should warn you, it's a vegan cake. Different, but still cake."

Chasan put his hand on Nathaniel's shoulder, remembering their married couple façade. "Vegan is perfect."

As it turns out, gluten-free, vegan cakes are not . . . great. Well, at least, not the one Pia had made. Avocado, pureed chickpeas, and cocoa powder just didn't quite cut it. Chasan managed to swallow down his first spoonful, though Nathaniel's diplomacy and fake-smile needed some work. He almost gagged.

"Thank you so much for the cake," Chasan said, grabbing Nathaniel's arm and dragging him back to their classroom.

Nathaniel dropped his cake straight into the trash and guzzled half his bottle of water. "That's it. She's going directly to the Hell Department for that."

Chasan laughed but also dumped his cake in the garbage. "It wasn't good. But I'm not sure it's a sin worthy of eternal Hell."

"It's a blasphemy of chocolate cake."

"Is that a thing?"

"I'm sure there's a subclause somewhere."

A swarm of noisy kids came bustling through the doors and filed into their seats, and Chasan clapped Nathaniel on the back. "They're all yours."

He turned wide-eyed to him. "Where are you going?"

Chasan pointed to the teacher's desk. "Just going to get a start on that paperwork we talked about."

Nathaniel made a face as though he couldn't possibly be in charge of all the kids by himself. But he never should have doubted himself. Actually, he was better at it than Chasan was. Nathaniel would deny it until the end of time, but there was a goodness in him that drew the kids in. Chasan had always been able to see it.

The only person who couldn't see it was Nathaniel.

Chasan sat at the desk and started making a list of all the kids in their class. It was simply a ruse—given their mission was to save Nathaniel, not some kid, and therefore a mostly pointless exercise—it did give Nathaniel the spotlight with the kids.

So maybe it wasn't so pointless after all. If saving Nathaniel from himself was the ultimate goal, then perhaps having him be the one to teach, help, and laugh with the kids should have been what Chasan did from the start.

Still keeping with the farm theme, Nathaniel found some cotton balls in the craft supplies and they cut out some sheep shapes and glued the cotton on. Then they played counting games by sorting animals with two or four feet, and then they practiced some writing with animal sounds.

Watching Nathaniel as he stood at the front of the class mooing and baaing was adorable.

And pure torture.

It made Chasan's heart ache. Nathaniel shot him curious glances every now and then, and Chasan knew he'd have to explain his emotions to him when they got home.

Maybe his role in this assignment would be over sooner than he thought. With Zophiel missing in action, Chasan wondered how he would get word up to the powers that be that he wanted out.

"Saint Peter," he whispered to himself. "If you can hear me, I sure hope you know what you're doing."

Two seconds later, the door opened and Geraldine walked in. "Hello, class," she said cheerily, giving a nod to Chasan and Nathaniel. "Today you have a very special guest. You've been learning about farms, is that right?"

The class gave a loud *yes*, their excitement building.

Geraldine waved her hand at the door, and in walked Zophiel. Only he wasn't wearing his usual expensive suits. He was dressed in faded coveralls, a flannel shirt, complete with a sun hat and a sprig of straw hanging out of his mouth. He looked like he'd mugged a scarecrow. . . who was holding a big box that was. . . chirping?

"Hello, boys and girls," he said, laying on a thick Southern accent. "My friends Mr. Bellomo and Mr. Angelo here asked me to come along today. And I have a special surprise for y'all."

Oh dear . . .

Zophiel grinned. "But y'all need to sit in a circle first. Can y'all do that for me?"

When the kids started moving, Chasan used the excited ruckus to whisper-hiss at Zophiel. "What are you doing here?"

"An intervention," he hissed right back.

Nathaniel was on his other side. "An intervention of what?"

Zophiel gave a very pointed nod to Chasan. "Ask him."

Chasan smiled for appearances and spoke through clenched teeth. "It couldn't have waited?"

"Apparently not. You asked for Saint Peter; he sent me."

Nathaniel turned to Chasan and whispered, "You asked for Saint Peter?"

Chasan was suddenly aware that the children were being quiet, which made the noise coming from the box Zophiel was holding seem louder. "Why is that box chirping?"

"Because that's what chickens do."

"Oh Heaven's mercy," Chasan and Nathaniel said in unison.

Zophiel grinned, then turned around to where the class was sitting on the floor in a circle, waiting. "Look here at how good these youngsters are behavin'," Zophiel said. He stepped into the circle and set the box on the floor. "Now, who here knows how to be gentle?"

Twenty kids put their hands up, bouncing with excitement.

"Excuse me, teachers," Zophiel said to Chasan and Nathaniel. "We're gonna need all hands on deck here. These baby chickens need some special lookin' after."

He opened the box and scooped up six baby chicks, and Nathaniel and Chasan helped ensure they were passed around gently and carefully. Farmer Zophiel seemed to be enjoying this far more than he should have. "Now, we must be gentle and hold them like they're precious." He looked at Chasan. "It doesn't matter if we're mad or sad, we must still be gentle. Like all helpless critters, they need us to be kind and to look after them, even if you don't want to."

He wasn't talking about the baby chicks.

"How can they grow and get their feathers and wings if we don't try our hardest?" Farmer Zophiel said.

Chasan rolled his eyes, but Nathaniel cocked his head. Then he shot Chasan a look, clearly realizing there was more to this than he knew. But the kids and the baby chicks were the focus of attention until the buzzer went for lunch. All the kids had to wash their hands and it felt like an eternity until the last kid left the room for lunch.

And that left Zophiel, Chasan, and Nathaniel in the room alone. With all the baby chicks securely back in the box, Nathaniel crossed his arms. "Would either of you like to tell me what's going on?"

"Chasan here sent up a message to Saint Peter," Zophiel said with a shrug. He'd thankfully dropped the accent. "And I was put on a rush-response."

"I didn't realize I was on speed dial," Chasan countered. "I'd barely got the words out before you walked in."

Nathaniel turned to Chasan. "You sent Peter a message today? Like just before he got here?"

Chasan sighed. "I just asked for some guidance, that's all. I didn't expect an answer."

"You seem to be seeking answers a lot lately," Nathaniel replied. He was hurt and defensive.

"Because this assignment isn't going so well," Chasan said. "But that's something better left to discuss when we get home."

Zophiel sighed and picked up the box of baby chicks. "I need to get these guys back. You guys need to sort out your shit." Then he looked directly at Chasan. "You heard what I said." Then he turned to Nathaniel. He went to say something, but in the end, he settled on a sigh. And then he was gone.

Chasan let his head fall back and groaned. "Dammit."

"What was that all about?" Nathaniel asked. "And I still can't believe you both get to swear. That's so not fair."

"Because if you were still allowed to swear, you'd have dropped a hundred f-bombs in front of the children by now." It was the truth and they both knew it.

Nathaniel glared at him. "What did he mean this was an intervention? And what did you ask Saint Peter for guidance for?"

"Nathaniel . . ."

"If we're supposed to be working together on this, you need to tell me." His jaw bulged, his eyes hardened. "I can feel what you feel, Chasan. You can't lie to me."

"I asked him if I was the right angel for this job."

Nathaniel's whole face changed. His defiance was gone, and in its place was hurt and doubt and insecurity. "What? Why? Am I . . ."

"Are you what?"

"Am I that difficult to be around?"

"Yes," Chasan answered honestly. His answer stung Nathaniel and, in turn, stung Chasan just the same. "Difficult for me, at least. And I just wondered if the friction between us was putting the assignment at risk."

"The friction . . . ? Because of the twin-flame thing?"

Chasan nodded. "Because I'm not unaffected by it." He swallowed hard. "As much as I wish it otherwise. And it's impacting my job." He glanced toward the door. "We really shouldn't be talking about this here."

Nathaniel stared at the floor for a long moment. His anxiety was pulsing, but it was swallowed up by a swirl of adrenaline, fear, and reluctance. "Uh, yeah, sure," he mumbled. "Of course."

"We better get to the lunchroom before someone comes looking," Chasan whispered. "Time to put on the happily married couple façade."

Nathaniel winced. "Yes, of course."

And for the rest of the afternoon, they played their parts. The kids had some quiet time on their floor mats, some napped, some didn't. Nathaniel busied himself cleaning up while Chasan completed his list of kids' names and what few details they knew of them.

When quiet time was over and everything was put away, Nathaniel announced it was Mila's turn to water the seeds they'd 'planted' the week before. She leaned up on the shelf below the windowsill and squealed. In a split second, Nathaniel raced across the room and grabbed her, lifting her away from the window.

But Mila just laughed and pointed back to the little tubs of cotton balls and seeds. "Look! They did grow!"

Nathaniel put her back down, and while all the other kids came running over to look, he stepped away and put his hand to his heart. "Oh, sweet Heaven's mercy," he panted. His panic and adrenaline were piqued, so Chasan went to him and put his hand on Nathaniel's back. He was bent over, still trying to catch his breath, and he looked up at Chasan. "I thought she was in trouble."

Chasan tried to smile for him, but seeing Nathaniel's panicked reaction to a little girl's squeal just tore him up inside. "I know. She's fine. Just breathe."

He nodded quickly and stood to his full height. "Wow. My heart."

Chasan studied him for a second. The color had drained from his face, and he looked ill with worry. "You okay?"

"Yeah."

"Mr. Angelo, Mr. Bellomo, look!" the kids cried.

Atop the beds of cotton, each of the little seeds had sprouted, and tiny green stalks were unfurling toward the sunshine. It was such a simple truth that life would always find a way toward the light.

"I just need a second," Nathaniel said, excusing himself. He left the room and Chasan took charge, easily showing the kids how neat it was that last week's fun topic of spring had carried over to this week's topic of farms. It had been Nathaniel's idea, and it had been a good one.

He was gone for a while, but when he came back in, he seemed to have regrouped. "You okay?"

He nodded, but Chasan could feel the unease he tried to tamp down. He was definitely rattled.

But soon enough it was home time, and the kids left in dribs and drabs as their parents came to collect them. When Marlow's dad arrived, he walked in nervously, clearly wondering what kind of day Marlow had had.

"Daddy, look!" Marlow cried, leading him by the hand to the wall of doggy portraits. "Everyone did paint a Buster. Look!"

Her dad scanned the wall. There were twenty paintings of a black dog with a red collar on green grass. All of them done with the painting finesse of four-year-olds, so they were more Picasso than Monet, but it was the thought that counted.

"Oh, wow," Marlow's dad mumbled, his hand to his mouth. "That's incredible."

"Mr. Angelo said we could do it and that Buster is happy in Heaven with grass and his very own couch for naps."

Marlow's dad shot Nathaniel a very kind, much-appreciated look. "Thank you."

He simply smiled back. "You're very welcome."

Then Ella's mom came in and she and Nathaniel spoke very briefly in Russian. Then Diego's dad came in and he and Nathaniel conversed in Spanish.

Every single person left that room with a smile.

Except for Chasan and Nathaniel.

They were going home to have a conversation that had been a long time coming.

A thousand years long.

They walked home in silence, and Chasan got angrier and more frustrated with each step. When they were inside their apartment, Chasan headed straight for the kitchen and Nathaniel threw his gear on the sofa.

"Can I ask you something?" Nathaniel asked. He came to lean against the kitchen counter, his arms crossed.

Chasan took some bags of vegetables out of the fridge, plonked them in the sink, and turned to face him. "Sure."

"Why are you so mad at me?"

"Mad?"

"I can feel the anger, Chasan," he said softly. He put his hand to his chest. "It's sharp and biting. And heavy." He shrugged. "I thought I did okay with the kids today."

"That's just it," Chasan shot back at him. "You did great. Everything you did was perfect."

"And that made you angry with me?"

"I'm not angry at you. I'm angry at myself. I *want* to be angry at you. So bad I can taste it. But you—" Chasan waved his hand at him. "—make it incredibly hard to be angry at you."

He made a face. "I don't know what you mean. You want to be angry at me?"

"Yes. I want to be pissed at you. I *should* be pissed at you. I should want to rage and break furniture and smite photocopiers like you. But I can't. I want to be mad at you, Nathaniel. I want to hate you." He turned back to the window, leaned on the counter, and dropped his head. "But I just can't."

Confusion and hurt billowed out from Nathaniel, and

that made Chasan feel even worse. But Nathaniel needed to know how he made Chasan feel.

"I um . . ." Nathaniel started, but then stopped. "I can see that. You should be mad at me. Or hate me, even. That's fair. It would make things easier."

"I could never hate you," Chasan admitted. "Believe me. I've tried."

"I've been selfish," he whispered. "All this time."

"You have." Chasan looked at him then. "You gave little regard to what your actions meant for me."

Nathaniel looked away then. His regret and sorrow and wounded pride hit Chasan like a wave.

"And I wanted to be angry at you, but then today you just had to go and be so perfect . . ." Chasan swallowed hard. "Do you have any idea how hard it is to hate you?"

Nathaniel gave a humorless laugh. "No, actually. I'm kind of an expert on that topic."

"And that's the problem." Chasan shrugged. "You can't ever forgive yourself for something that was not your fault."

He turned away but Chasan could see his jaw bulge.

"But you don't see how brilliant you were with Marlow today. She was terribly sad, unable to put words to how she felt, but you allowed her to express her grief. And then what happened with Mila at the window."

His gaze whipped to Chasan's before he looked away again. "I thought she was in trouble. That's all."

"That's not all, Nathaniel. She squealed, and your first reaction was to protect her. If it had been a legitimate threat, you would have saved her."

He gave Chasan a dirty look. "Of course I would have."

"Exactly. That's my point." Chasan sighed. This had been a long, long day already. "I know we need to talk about what Zophiel said. And what happened today. But I think we need to talk about what happened with Mila first."

"There's nothing else to say."

"Her squealing triggered something in you, and we both know it. You went so pale I thought you were going to pass out."

"Chasan," he mumbled low and laced with warning.

"It reminded you of what happened in Peru all those years ago."

He glared at Chasan, his eyes wild. "And I told you I don't want to talk about that. Why can't you just leave it alone?"

"Because you need to deal with it. You've never dealt with it, and it's a weight you've carried for far too long."

Nathaniel closed his fist and banged the marble countertop. "Shut up, Chasan. You don't know what you're talking about."

Chasan went to Nathaniel and scooped him up in a hug. Nathaniel was surprised at first and tried to pull away, but Chasan held him tight. The fire in Chasan's chest ignited, and he was sure Nathaniel's had to have done the same. "I know that there was nothing you could have done to save her."

"Chasan, let go of me."

Chasan held him tighter. "I know you did everything you could."

He tried to pull away again. "Chasan."

"I need you to know you're forgiven. No one blames you."

He stopped struggling. Whether he'd given up or the calm Chasan was giving him helped, Chasan wasn't sure. Nathaniel never moved to hug him back, but Chasan didn't mind.

"I know you're angry, and that's okay. But you don't have to carry the weight of guilt anymore," Chasan whispered.

Nathaniel was quiet, unresponsive, as though maybe if he stayed still and quiet long enough, Chasan would eventually give up. Chasan relaxed his arms. "I'm going to let you go now, okay?"

Nathaniel gave no reply, but Chasan could feel his emotions: anger, pain, guilt, but there was also relief and a little gratitude, and that was enough for Chasan.

He pulled back and kept his hands on Nathaniel's arms. Nathaniel looked down at the floor between them. "Why don't you go have a soak in the tub?" Chasan suggested. "I'll make us dinner. How does Indian curried vegetables sound? A dhal of some kind."

Nathaniel kept his head down and stepped back. "Uh, whatever," he whispered so low Chasan barely heard him. Nathaniel turned and walked into their bedroom, the door closing softly behind him, leaving Chasan alone in the silence.

The fire in his chest burned.

DINNER WAS QUIET AND AWKWARD. The distance between them felt like every one of the thousand years that had passed since what happened in Peru.

Nathaniel barely ate anything, preferring to push the food around the plate with his fork. Chasan's appetite wasn't much better.

Chasan was unsure if the melancholy he felt was his own or Nathaniel's echoed back to him. He couldn't discern the difference; their emotions bled into each other's.

They never spoke while they ate. They never spoke while they cleaned up. It was awful and draining. Exhausted, Chasan went to bed early, though sleep eluded him. He'd hoped to be asleep by the time Nathaniel came in, but there was no such luck. Chasan faced the wall but he had no doubt Nathaniel knew he was awake.

Nathaniel sat on the edge of the bed and didn't say anything for a long time. He just sat there . . . His emotions were in turmoil, a flurry of fear and guilt. Chasan rolled over to face him and was just about to ask if he was okay when Nathaniel spoke.

"I begged him not to do it," Nathaniel whispered. "I told him it would make no difference. No difference at all. I told him the moon god didn't want him to do it." He let out a shaky breath. "He wouldn't listen."

"Oh, Nathaniel."

"So then I asked Saint Peter to speak to Shi, the moon god, herself. To beg her to please put an end to the suffering. No one had to die. Accept the shells and the tin and copper instead. But she wouldn't listen to him." He shook his head. "What kind of god takes the blood of children as an offering?"

Chasan scooted over so he could rub Nathaniel's back. "I'm so sorry."

"Qispi died at the hand of her own father. He cut out her heart while it still beat in her chest. She screamed, Chasan. Like you can't imagine."

No, Chasan couldn't imagine. He'd been in Peru at the time, but he hadn't been in the same village. Though he'd seen Nathaniel afterward, how wrecked he was. How Saint Peter was overcome with guilt and responsibility . . .

"Did her life make it rain? Did her blood, did her heart

make it rain? Of course it didn't. More died by the hands of their own than the drought ever killed."

"It was a long time ago," Chasan offered. "The world is different now. Humans are different."

Nathaniel looked over his shoulder at Chasan, his face etched with pain in the dark room. "Is it though? Humans still kill for their gods, only now they sacrifice other people's children and not their own. They call it war, but it is still murder."

Chasan wasn't sure what to say to that. Because as much as he saw the good in people, Nathaniel wasn't exactly wrong.

Nathaniel shook his head. "It was the same in China two thousand years ago. And in Rome, Egypt, the Celts, the Aztecs. It didn't matter to which god or for what purpose. Where are those gods now? Where are their shame and guilt? They sit in their golden shrines while we do their dirty work." He choked back tears. "The blood of the innocents is on our hands, Chasan."

"You couldn't have done anything else," Chasan whispered.

He put his hand to his chest; tears spilled down his cheeks. "I could have tried harder. I could have taken her away. I could have done something."

But he couldn't have, Chasan knew that. Nathaniel did too . . .

"They're all the same, Chasan," he said, not even trying to hide his tears. "Every god, every deity, every religion. I hate them. I hate how they sit so far removed while the people suffer. While *we* suffer."

Chasan sat up, grabbed Nathaniel around the shoulders, and pulled him down in a crushing hug. And Nathaniel let himself be held as he cried. The flame in

Chasan's chest swelled and grew warm, as though it could feel its twin so close, as though it was trying to meld together through their ribs. Chasan gave Nathaniel all the calm and peace he could muster, all the acceptance and forgiveness too.

And Nathaniel clung to Chasan as he sobbed, though as his tears dried up, his grip on Chasan never loosened. He fell asleep, just like that. With his face buried in Chasan's neck, his breath warm on his skin, Nathaniel's body the perfect fit to his.

They had never been this close, this intimate. This personal. Every cell in Chasan's body sang; every fiber was alive and thrumming. He was holding Nathaniel, comforting him, their arms around each other, their legs entwined. A thousand years had come down to this. Chasan had never felt so pure, so aligned. So right.

That was how they fell asleep, and that was exactly how they woke up.

It took a moment for Chasan to realize why he felt so warm, and why he felt so peaceful and well-rested. Why he felt so aroused.

Then Nathaniel stirred, and it startled Chasan, which in turn startled Nathaniel. They broke apart with a start.

Chasan wondered what kind of reaction he was going to get from Nathaniel. They'd had a breakthrough last night, as fraught as it was, as hard as it was. But Chasan didn't expect things between them to be fixed overnight.

He had, however, hoped things might have moved forward. But he had seemingly forgotten who he was fated to.

"Oh, Heaven's mercy," Nathaniel mumbled, his expression stricken before he rolled off the bed and disappeared into the bathroom.

So the more things changed, the more they stayed the same.

"Morning," he called out to the empty room.

He could feel the anxiety billowing out from behind the bathroom door, and with a heavy sigh, he got out of bed and went in search of coffee.

CHAPTER ELEVEN

NATHANIEL

THIS WAS NOT how it was supposed to go.

You were not supposed to blather on like a blubbering idiot. And you were not supposed to fall asleep in his arms. You weren't supposed to know how amazing that felt.

And you most definitely weren't supposed to wake up with a throbbing dick.

Oh, how Nathaniel hated this human body. If it wasn't trying to kill him with anxiety or headaches, it was doing stupidly embarrassing things to his privates.

The last thing he needed was for Chasan to see.

Chasan . . .

Being in Chasan's arms last night was the single most bestest thing to ever happen to Nathaniel, in all his years. Ever.

Finally talking about what happened in Peru, and finally admitting that he has issues with upper management had felt as though a weight had been lifted from his shoulders. And he'd wept, actual human tears.

He wondered if that was why he felt so good. It was supposed to be cathartic. Or so he'd heard.

Or maybe he felt so good because Chasan had held him all night.

His privates throbbed again at the mere thought, the memory, of being pressed against him. He gave his dick a squeeze, which hurt but also hurt in a way that felt good. So he did it again. And it hurt even better.

He palmed it, and that shot fireworks through his body. He had to lean against the bathroom counter so he didn't fall over.

Heaven's mercy.

So he gripped it instead, and oh Heaven's mercy indeed. Lights danced behind his eyes and his body started to move without his brain's permission, grinding out some sensual dance.

His hips moved, seeking human pleasure he'd never allowed himself before. And when he looked down, he saw the flushed head of his cock slide in and out of his fist.

A strange drawing down sensation made him feel as though he was hurtling toward some precipice . . . and he wanted more. He wanted to launch himself over the edge of it. It felt so incredibly good.

Then a thought occurred to him as he looked down at his engorged dick. How was he supposed to go to work with this?

"Nathaniel? You okay in there?" Chasan asked from the other side of the door.

Nathaniel almost leaped out of his skin! In fact, he was so startled, he jumped in fright and swung around so fast, he whacked his erection on the bathroom cabinet. Doubled over in pain, he made some strange squeaking-groan sound. It took a second before he could even speak. "Yeah, yeah." His voice was strained and high. "It's fine. Won't be long."

He hurried to turn on the water in the shower, and he

remembered some old wives' tale about cold water, so he opted for the coldest shower he could stand. Which also made it the quickest.

It did get rid of his problem. Well, if it was the cold water, the pain of penile abuse, or a combination of both, Nathaniel wasn't sure. And although he was thankful, he couldn't honestly recommend either.

He dried off and wrapped the towel around his waist. He was cold now after a freezing shower and just needed to get dressed. In his rush to get into the closet, he collided with Chasan.

"Whoa," Chasan said, holding onto him for balance. Chasan's smile faltered. "Oh, you're cold."

Nathaniel took a step back away from his touch. He gripped his towel to protect his modesty, and he got the sinking feeling that Chasan could tell what he'd been doing in the shower before . . . "Uh, yeah. Need to get dressed."

Chasan nodded slowly, sadly. "Okay."

Nathaniel ducked into the closet and absolutely did not hide in a row of sweaters. And he was not mumbling to himself or banging his head against the underwear shelving when Chasan spoke.

"You sure you're all right?"

He shot backward, his hand to his heart. "Oh, grand mercy."

"I didn't mean to startle you." Was Chasan trying not to smile? Or was that a grimace of awkward concern?

"I'm fine!" Nathaniel snapped at him. Chasan flinched, and that made Nathaniel feel awful. "I'm fine," he tried again, gentler this time. "Honestly, I'm fine. Thank you for asking."

Chasan gave no more than a nod before he walked out

and into the bathroom. Nathaniel heard the door lock, then the shower started, and he sighed the mother of all sighs.

He got dressed, into the blackest clothes he had, and went to the kitchen for coffee only to find Chasan had already made him one. And that made him feel even worse.

Chasan and his patience and kindness, his tolerance and forgiveness . . . it drove Nathaniel crazy. It would be easier if Chasan hated him.

Then Nathaniel wouldn't feel so guilty.

Well, even more guilty.

Chasan was too pure for him. He was the epitome of perfection, and Nathaniel was . . . not.

Nathaniel didn't want to hurt Chasan. He really didn't. Neither of them asked for the fated-souls thing. It was thrust upon them, putting them both in a situation they couldn't get out of without inflicting pain on the other.

The only other fated souls to ever exist had ended badly, and look at what had happened to them. The whole situation was impossible.

Nathaniel sighed just as Chasan came back out. "Everything okay?"

"Yeah, sure. Uh, thanks for the coffee," Nathaniel added. "And thank you for last night. I haven't talked about . . . Peru in a long time. I feel better for telling you, so thank you. It's given me a lot to think about."

"You're welcome," he said, popping some bread into the toaster. He took out a plate, and Nathaniel could feel his apprehension. Nathaniel didn't want to rehash the conversation again, but he knew Chasan was about to mention it. "So, um . . . you shot out of bed this morning. Everything okay?"

That was not what he was expecting. "Oh, sure. I just . . . needed to use the bathroom." Not technically a lie.

Chasan seemed to know it wasn't exactly the truth either. "Right. Want some toast? We need to get to school."

"No, I'm fine, thank you." The truth was he didn't have much of an appetite. "I'll just go finish getting dressed."

They walked to school without saying much. Chasan's smile was tight, and there was a steady stream of unease coming from him. Even as the kids arrived and during the day, there was a nagging weight that came from Chasan.

He didn't like it. He didn't like it at all.

And the next day it was no better. And the day after that it was worse.

Nathaniel knew what would fix it. If he gave into the twin-flame bond, Chasan's troubled heart would be healed. Nathaniel knew he was the cause, yet he couldn't seem to bring himself to commit.

He liked Chasan. He really did. Maybe it was more than like. Maybe that was something he wasn't ready to unpack just yet. But this time with him had been amazing. Why couldn't they just enjoy this for a bit without the added pressure of eternity?

Though apparently avoiding any chance of conversation wasn't how Chasan operated. On Thursday after work, they'd walked into their apartment and Nathaniel was about to offer to cook dinner when Chasan put his keys on the dining table and dropped a bombshell. "What scares you the most about the twin-flame bond?"

Nathaniel was completely thrown off guard. "What?"

"Clearly having a fated soul with me scares you. I want to know why?"

He didn't say that I didn't want it. He didn't say it angered me or was unfair. He said it scared me . . .

"I don't know if it scares me," Nathaniel offered poorly.

"Bullshit."

Nathaniel blinked, Chasan's curse word—and this forthright conversation—stunned him. "Pardon?"

"It scares you witless. You're not pissed off that your choice was removed. You're scared."

"Okay, first, wow. And second, that's incorrect."

Chasan sighed as though he'd been pushed one step too far. "Well, what is it? I'm kind of at the point, Nathaniel, where I don't know what else I can do. You seem to carry on like it doesn't even exist, as though it doesn't bother you one bit and you never even think of it." He put his hand to his heart. "Where it's in my every waking thought."

"I do think of it," Nathaniel replied. "But I try not to. I don't know . . . I wasn't prepared for this conversation."

"You've had a thousand years."

Nathaniel cringed. "I just don't know . . . It didn't work out for the other two fated souls, did it? Maybe what happened to them will happen to us."

Chasan rolled his eyes. "They were different. One angel, one human. But I have to tell you, Nathaniel, the more I think about it, we're not that different at all."

"How so?"

"Uriel decided he knew what was best. He removed Icarus' choice, and Icarus did the only thing he could think of to prove himself worthy. There are parallels between them and us, don't you think?"

"Uriel had tried to protect him."

"No, he removed Icarus' choice."

"He was giving him the choice. And Icarus chose wrong."

Uriel, the angel of the sun, had told the human Icarus their fated hearts wouldn't end well and had refused him, leaving him on Earth alone. Poor Icarus had died trying to reach him, and his death had killed them both.

Chasan's face fell, and he was quiet for a long moment. Eventually he nodded, as though he'd realized something only he was privy to. He took a step back. "I understand. I get it. We will never agree on this."

"I don't think so either," Nathaniel murmured. It wasn't what he wanted to say, but it was the truth.

The heartache rolling out of Chasan was crippling. It was so intense, Nathaniel couldn't think straight. "Chasan . . ."

He took another step back. "I'm not feeling great. I might just go lie down or . . ." He swallowed. "I don't think I'll be eating tonight."

"Are you sure?" Nathaniel tried to reach out for him. He didn't know how else to fix this.

Chasan put his hand up. "Don't touch me."

Oh.

Nathaniel felt like he'd been slapped. "Oh. Okay. Sure. Um. Well, if you're not feeling well, then yeah . . ." He had no idea what to say to that, but Chasan was already walking away. "Um, if you need anything . . ."

Chasan disappeared into their room and closed the door behind him. Nathaniel stood there, dumbfounded. *What on earth just happened?*

Chasan didn't come back out of their room. At first, Nathaniel was shocked, then he was hurt, then he was angry, and then he was indignant. He was also profoundly sorry, and hours later when Nathaniel finally worked up the courage to open the door, the bedroom was completely dark. Nathaniel could make out Chasan's form in the bed. He was facing the wall, and given there were deep and measured breaths and a discernible lack of emotions rolling off him, Nathaniel assumed he was asleep.

He changed into his sleepwear, but when he came back

to the bed, he couldn't bring himself to get into it. What if he woke Chasan? What if Chasan didn't want him to sleep next to him? He'd said not to touch him, and he did say he wasn't feeling well.

The couch it is then.

That decided, Nathaniel also decided that first thing tomorrow, he'd apologize to Chasan. He was sorry for a lot of things, but most of all he was sorry for hurting him.

For all the things Nathaniel hated about himself, he hated that the most.

THE COUCH WAS NOT comfortable to sleep on. Nathaniel lay awake most of the night, thinking and over-thinking every little thing, and he finally dozed off sometime around three in the morning.

He woke up to the smell of coffee and the feeling of being watched. When he opened his eyes, the first thing he saw was Zophiel's ugly mug grinning down at him. "Wakey, wakey, hand off snakey."

Nathaniel groaned. His back and hips protested as he tried to move. "Ow."

"Come on, lazybones. Or you'll be late for work." Zophiel held out a coffee cup. "You're gonna need this by the look of it."

"Where's Chasan?" Nathaniel tried to sit up but it hurt so much he could barely manage it. He let out a yelp. "Oh, Heaven's mercy. This body is broken. What on earth happened to my back?"

"You slept on the couch, that's what happened."

He managed to sit up, and keeping his hands on his

lower back, he tried to stretch it. But then his neck cricked. "Oh my word! My neck. Ow, ow."

"Quit your whining," Zophiel said. He offered the coffee again. "Here, drink this."

"Where's Chasan?"

"Shower."

Nathaniel sagged with relief. At least he was still in the apartment. He sipped the coffee and grimaced at how much everything ached. "Do I need to know what you're doing here? And just so you know, this couch needs to be burned."

Zophiel sat down opposite him. "Nathaniel, I don't have much time while Chasan's indisposed, so listen up."

Oh dear. Conversations such as these never ended particularly well.

"I would say that you and Chasan need to sort your shit out, but honestly, it's you. You need to sort your shit out."

Nathaniel sipped his coffee, surprisingly used to being forced to have conversations he didn't want to have. "Okay, so first, I hate that you can still swear and I can't. Like, I hate it. It really milks my yak that you and Chasan can swear and I can't."

"Milks your yak?"

"Do you have something against yaks?"

"No. Do you have something against Chasan?"

"What? No. Of course not." Nathaniel studied him for a moment. "What are you doing here?"

"He asked me to come."

"To speak to me?"

"No," Zophiel replied. "Don't flatter yourself. It's not all about you."

"Okay, wow. I think you need a refresher course on effective bedside manner."

"Look, if you could pull your head out of your ass for a second, that'd be great."

"And maybe you should also do a refresher course on how not to be a bag of penises."

"Let me ask you something," Zophiel said, unperturbed. "Do you think Chasan's gonna be around forever?"

"What kind of question is that?"

"A valid one. Just answer it."

"Yes, he'll be around forever. Angels are immortal. That's how immortality works."

His smile turned rueful, and he shook his head. "Oh boy."

"What's that supposed to mean?"

Just then, the bedroom door opened and Chasan walked out, putting an end to Nathaniel and Zophiel's conversation. Chasan managed a small smile, and any hope Nathaniel had that they'd wake up to a fresh start was dashed.

"Coffee?" Chasan asked as he walked through to the kitchen.

Nathaniel stood up, and every bone and every muscle in his body protested. "Oh sweet mercy bless," he cried, putting his hand to his back. "This couch," he said to Zophiel, pointing to the offending furniture. "Smite it. Smite it real good." He tried to stand to his full height, but his back hurt. "Argh. What even is this? How can this back not work properly?"

Chasan looked unimpressed over his coffee cup. "That's what you get for sleeping on the couch."

"You looked so peaceful and I didn't want to disturb you." *And I'm a coward.* "And you didn't want to see me, and I thought I was doing the right thing." *And not forgetting that I'm a coward.*

Chasan stared at him for a full few long seconds before he sighed. "A hot shower will help you." Then Chasan did some weird, silent eye contact with Zophiel, and Nathaniel took his cue to leave them to have the conversation they were obviously going to have about him.

The shower helped his muscles and it did make his back feel better; the anxiety in his belly, not so much. Or maybe it was Chasan's anxiety . . . It was getting hard to tell them apart.

Despite his better judgment, he got out of the shower, dressed for work, and walked back out to the kitchen. He needed to say something to Chasan. He just had no idea what or where to begin.

He didn't have to.

He walked out to find the apartment empty. Chasan and Zophiel were already gone. "Hello? Chasan?"

No answer.

So yep, already gone. Nathaniel tried not to panic. He tried not to crumple to the ground in a pile of anxious goo. He was breathing hard, and his forehead was leaking again. His stomach twisted awfully, and he remembered Chasan saying a dry cracker might make him feel better . . . He went to the pantry and rummaged around for the crackers, though it felt and tasted like old cardboard in his mouth. He couldn't even swallow it, so he grabbed a bottle of water from the fridge and he forced down a mouthful.

This was bad.

Chasan leaving him was bad.

He went in search of his phone so he could check the time, and he saw he had a message. It was from Chasan.

Gone to the store before school. See you there.

Relief dropped on Nathaniel like a ton of bricks. It was so staggering, he needed to sit down. He pulled out a dining chair and slumped into it.

He hasn't left you.

He should have. But he didn't. He just went to the store.

Pull yourself together, Nathaniel.

He should have left you.

"But he didn't," Nathaniel said to the empty room. To himself. "He'll be at school."

So get your stupid self to school.

Does my own brain have to hate me too?

Nathaniel, stop stalling and get yourself to school.

"Okay, okay, I'm going." He snatched up his keys and pocketed his phone. "This body hates me already and now my brain does too. Awesome."

But he got himself to school without incident and he almost raced into their classroom to see Chasan. How could he have missed him this much? He'd only not seen him for an hour, but he did miss him. And he needed to see him. He needed to feel that calm that only Chasan could provide. And it wasn't just Nathaniel who needed Chasan; the fire in his chest needed him too.

But the room was empty. There was no sign of him. The lights were still off.

The flame behind his sternum billowed, searching for its mate.

The door behind him opened and Nathaniel spun around, expecting to see him, ready for the rush of calm that would follow.

But it wasn't Chasan.

It was Ahmed, then Holly, followed by Austin . . . and more kids, and their parents of course. Nathaniel needed to get hold of himself. He needed to pull himself up by the bootstraps and deal with this assignment. He was the overseer of the Hell Department. There wasn't anything he couldn't do. Right?

He'd managed to survive centuries without Chasan. Why did the last hour feel longer than that?

He welcomed the kids and the moms and dads, but every time the door opened, he caught himself glancing, hoping for Chasan.

It wasn't until the buzzer was just about to go off that he came in. In typical Chasan form: his hair windswept, his cheeks pink, like he'd just floated in on a breeze. He had his arms full of bags, stocked with craft supplies and boxes of tissues. "Sorry, I'm late," he said. He didn't seem too sorry.

But their class began and the day went on like every other. Chasan was all smiles for the kids, though he barely uttered a word to Nathaniel. He barely even looked at him.

When the buzzer went for lunch, Geraldine poked her head in the door. "Mr. Bellomo, we've got you for playground duty."

"Ah yes," he said, like he'd requested it.

Like he'd specifically asked to be removed from Nathaniel's company.

"Need me to help?" Nathaniel asked, unsure of what to do without him.

"No thanks," Geraldine answered, and Chasan slipped out of the room without even a glance in his direction.

Nathaniel looked around the now empty classroom, wondering what on earth he was supposed to do with himself . . .

The idea of being sequestered with Cheryl-Anne made him shudder. Gian was nice though, but he couldn't guarantee she'd be in there. His lunch was in the fridge, but he wasn't even hungry. At all.

So he sat at his desk in the classroom and pretended to be doing notes. But he spent the entire time wondering what on earth was going on.

What was Chasan doing? Why was he avoiding him?

Because you're a selfish ass.

Nathaniel sighed at himself. "Ouch."

It's true and you know it. Did you really think he was going to wait forever? Did you really expect him to be your doormat for eternity? You treat him like shit, Nathaniel.

Wait a minute . . . that was a curse word. Nathaniel couldn't swear.

"Zophiel is that you?" Nathaniel asked quietly. "Are you somehow in my head?"

The door opened and the kids filed through with the usual tired faces they had after lunch. It was quiet time for the kids, and maybe that would give Nathaniel and Chasan a chance to talk . . .

Nathaniel knew they needed to talk. And he needed to apologize. It was Friday. They'd have all weekend to talk and clear the air.

But Chasan never came in after all the kids. Geraldine did. "I've just borrowed Mr. Bellomo for the afternoon," she said. Her cardigan with the fluffy trim really completed her condor-look. "I needed some help with something, and I've arranged an aide to assist you for the afternoon."

She didn't really give Nathaniel an option, and neither had Chasan.

So Nathaniel did what he was good at. When the kids were having quiet time, he went through all of Chasan's craft supplies that he'd bought from the store that morning, and given the subject of the week was farming, they had a wonderful afternoon making cardboard chickens with crepe paper feathers, and he cut four eggs for each one, and they practiced counting and subtracting, and then they colored them in and learned some chicken song.

The kids had a great time, and each one left for the day as happy as could be, proudly showing off their artwork and doing the hand movements to the song they'd learned. Nathaniel waved them all off with a smile, but he felt hollowed out inside.

Chasan never came back, even after the last child had gone.

Maybe, just maybe he'd had enough of Nathaniel's ambivalence. Nathaniel couldn't blame him exactly, but it still stung to be on the receiving end. Which was a taste of his own medicine, really, considering everything he'd put Chasan through.

But Nathaniel would talk to Chasan when he got home, and they'd sort something out. They had to. It was how they operated.

Nathaniel was a dick, and Chasan was kind and understanding. That's how they'd been for a thousand years. But then Zophiel's words came back to him . . .

Did you really think he was going to wait forever? Did you really expect him to be your doormat for eternity? You treat him like shit, Nathaniel.

Chasan would be at home when he got there, right? That was where his flame-tracking device was leading him. Home. Nathaniel knew that's where Chasan was. He just needed some time, that's all.

Right?

Nathaniel would get home and they'd talk it out and everything would be fine, right?

The flame in his chest burned hot as though the answer was no.

Nathaniel walked a little faster on the way home, and

he might have been closer to a run on the last block. The doorman gave him a nice smile, and Nathaniel thumped the elevator button, out of patience.

He needed to see Chasan like he needed air. The fire under his ribs was making it harder to breathe. It could have been the running that did that, but Nathaniel was pretty sure it was the twin flame.

The elevator took forever, but when the doors opened, he rushed out and saw Chasan and almost sagged with relief. He was sitting on the sofa with Zophiel, but he didn't look up. Zophiel did though. "You're puffing. Did you run?" he asked with a smirk.

"It was a brisk walk," Nathaniel panted. He wiped his brow. "And it's not sweat. This body leaks. It's dysfunctional." He inhaled deeply and went to Chasan and sat beside him. Chasan didn't look at him, and the emotions rolling off him were awful. "Something's wrong? What's wrong?"

Nathaniel reached for Chasan's hand, but he pulled it away. "Nathaniel," he whispered. "I've made some decisions."

"That I make excellent cardboard chickens? Because we totally knocked it out of the park this afternoon, no thanks to you," he replied, which didn't exactly come out the way he meant it. "I mean, not that I'm not thanking you, but you left me alone. I had no choice but to step up and be the best preschool teacher on the planet. And I'm going to be honest, if we're looking at the chicken-making skills of these kids to determine which one is going to do amazing things, I think we can rule out Theo. Because his chicken looked like it'd played a round of *cuju*. As the ball. Not saying artistic skills aren't a vital—"

"Nathaniel," Chasan interrupted sharply.

Nathaniel sucked in some air. "Sorry. You're making me nervous."

Chasan stared at his hands wringing in his lap. "I've asked to be removed from the mission."

"You've what?" Nathaniel asked stupidly. "I didn't quite catch that. It sounded like you said you asked to be removed from the mission."

He glanced at Nathaniel before looking away again. He gave a nod. "That's correct."

Nathaniel's mind scrambled, and his anxiety splintered in all directions. "No. No, that's not correct. If this has to do with the chicken comment, I was just joking. I mean, I can't do this whole thing by myself. One afternoon was okay, but Chasan, I can't do the whole thing!"

Chasan stood up and walked to the window, putting some distance between them. "Nathaniel," he said, barely audible. "I'm not just asking out of the mission. I'm going to ask Peter to sever the bond between us."

"You're what?"

"I can't do this anymore. I thought this assignment might change something, and I foolishly believed for one brief moment that you might want to actually be with me. But you don't. That's very clear to me now. I can't put my heart through it again, Nathaniel. To be unwanted . . . is the hardest part."

"What? That's not true!"

Chasan turned and met his gaze. "Isn't it? Which part?"

Nathaniel couldn't speak. Chasan looked so defeated. So heartbroken. The burning in Nathaniel's chest roared.

"I thought we were getting somewhere," Chasan whispered. "The other night when you told me what happened in Peru. I thought we . . ." He raised his chin, his eyes glassy. "I thought maybe that would be the turning point. But it wasn't. We're no closer, and the fact is, Nathaniel, you just don't want this."

"This?"

"Us. To be bonded with me. What you said yesterday about Uriel and Icarus . . . I realized we will never see eye to eye on . . . what we are."

Nathaniel tried to speak. He tried to say that he did, but the words wouldn't come. Neither would air. He needed to breathe, but he couldn't.

The flames beneath his ribs stole his oxygen, and if Chasan would just touch him and tell him to breathe, he'd be okay.

But he didn't.

He turned away, and that was when Nathaniel saw that Archangel Michael was now standing by the wall. How long had he been there? Had Chasan asked him to come?

Oh, Heaven's mercy, he was really leaving.

Chasan didn't even turn around. He just kept his head down, and Michael frowned deeply before giving Nathaniel a pitiful look. He reached out and took Chasan's arm, and in a flash of light, they were gone.

Nathaniel shot up off the couch as if he could somehow stop Chasan from leaving, but it was too late. He ached all over, and the fire inside him blazed and burned. The world stopped turning. Everything went dark and silent. His lungs squeezed to the point of pain.

Everything was wrong.

Then Zophiel was there, close and concerned. "Nathaniel, breathe."

Nathaniel gasped in air, but it wasn't enough. Chasan was gone.

"Come with me," Zophiel said, holding his arm and leading him to the sofa. "Take a seat." Nathaniel moved woodenly, his head hurt, his heart burned. Zophiel helped him to the sofa, and he kept his hand on Nathaniel's arm. He watched him for a long moment. "It's not getting any better, is it? Breathing? The pain?"

Nathaniel shook his head. Was Zophiel trying to send him some calm like Chasan could? It wasn't working.

"When the bond is broken, it should get better," he said. "We think. We don't know. It'll either get better or exponentially worse. It could kill you. We don't know for sure."

Nathaniel shook his head quickly, his breath rapid. "No."

"No to dying?" Zophiel pressed. "Or no to not knowing?"

"No," he tried again. "No to breaking the bond."

Zophiel sighed. "Nathaniel . . ."

"I don't want him to leave me." Then his eyes were burning too, and a tear escaped down his cheek. "I need him."

"You need him, or you want him?"

"Both."

He grimaced. "Yeah, no. No, you don't."

"Yes I do!"

He sighed. "Nathaniel, I'm gonna tell you straight. You've had a thousand years, and you didn't want him or the bond in all that time. You treated him like shit, Nathaniel. Like a doormat. You strung him along, too scared to commit, too scared to cut ties."

"I was scared," Nathaniel whispered; another tear rolled down his face. "I still am. Petrified, actually. I thought I hated the idea of not being able to choose, but that's not true. He's everything I need. He's more than I need."

"You're still lying to yourself."

"No I'm not." Nathaniel shook his head, but Zophiel

remained stoic. "I can't lie. I don't know what you mean. You have to tell Chasan to give me another chance. Please."

Zophiel ignored that. "Why the change of heart now?"

"Because I was unsure before. But now I'm not."

"You told him *yesterday* you didn't want the twin flame."

"I was scared."

"Of what?"

"Of him!"

"Scared of Chasan? The most placid angel in all of Heaven?"

"The most perfect angel," Nathaniel corrected him. "Don't you see? He's perfect. Without fault. He is pure light. And I . . ."

"And you, what?"

"And I . . . He deserves better. He should be fated to someone that isn't broken." Nathaniel sobbed out a breath. "Someone better than me."

Zophiel stared at him and clapped his shoulder. "There it is."

"What?" Nathaniel snapped, wiping his face. "That's what you wanted me to say? That he deserves better than me? Because every angel in Heaven could have told you that."

"And why should Chasan give you another chance? Haven't you put him through enough?"

"I have, yes. And I'm so very sorry for that. But maybe if I just talk to him. Maybe he'll forgive me. If I could just see him. Please."

"He doesn't need to forgive you, Nathaniel, because he doesn't blame you. You need to forgive yourself."

"I'm trying. I've had a lot to think about and it hasn't been easy. I'm trying to let some things go while holding onto others. It's hard. And I'm still angry at all the gods who sit on their thrones and who've lost touch with their people. I thought if I lost myself in the Hell Department, I could vent and redirect my anger to those who deserve it. But I'm so used to being alone, and I haven't been human in a long time. My time here with Chasan has been the best thing for me. And I've wasted so much time. I don't want to waste another minute, and the fire in my chest is burning hot." Nathaniel put his hand to his forehead. "Zophiel, please. Something's happening. It's not good."

Zophiel sighed. "Right. But you listen to me. If Chasan says no, then that's the end of it. No means no. And if he decides to make *you* suffer for a thousand years, you will agree to it without complaint."

"I will."

He rolled his eyes. "Though we all know damn well he won't make you suffer because he's Chasan. You, on the other hand . . ."

"I know," Nathaniel said. Zophiel was so close to agreeing . . . "I know. I've been an insufferable ass." *Harsh, but not untrue.* "And he deserves better. But I want to make him happy. I want to hear him laugh and see his smile. Have you seen how blue his eyes are when he smiles? And he smells like . . . like home. And I just want—"

"Okay, okay," Zophiel said, shaking his head. "Shut up and hold on."

"You know, you're really rather bossy—"

And in a flurry of light and sparks, they were gone.

CHAPTER TWELVE

CHASAN

CHASAN FOUND himself walking into Saint Peter's office with Archangel Michael. Everyone was there; it was a full board meeting. Though Chasan couldn't look anyone in the eye.

He felt like a failure.

He was a failure.

"Chasan?" Saint Peter asked, getting to his feet.

Chasan kept his head down. "I concede defeat."

Saint Peter sighed heavily and let his head drop. "Nathaniel."

Chasan didn't need to answer that. "Tell me, this assignment, the soul we were trying to save was Nathaniel, wasn't it? He was the mission."

Saint Peter sighed again, which was all the answer Chasan needed.

Chasan's hands were fists at his side. "You should have told me!"

Metatron stood up at the large table. "It was a decision we all agreed to. To keep you out of the loop; we thought it was for the best."

Chasan stared at her. "Then you're all to blame. I never understood Nathaniel's skepticism of this office. I thought maybe he was paranoid, but he's not. I'm beginning to see it now."

"That's not fair," Saint Peter said.

Chasan almost laughed. "No, what's not fair is being sent in blind to an assignment that directly affects us both. *That's* not fair."

"We'd hoped you'd find a way on your own," Saint Peter said gently. "That once Nathaniel spent time with you, he'd see more clearly."

"Well, he didn't. I can't fix him. He doesn't . . ." Chasan's voice croaked. "He doesn't want me."

Saint Peter looked forsaken, his whole frame deflated. "What can I do? Tell me, and I'll see it done."

"I want you to break the twinning of souls," Chasan whispered. "I can't bear it any longer."

Someone gasped, someone else murmured something Chasan couldn't hear, but Saint Peter put his hand up. "Quiet, please."

The room fell silent.

"Chasan, what you're asking has never been done. Not intentionally, anyway."

"But it's possible," he countered.

Saint Peter scrubbed a hand over his face. "We're going to need to resort to the Manual." He pressed the intercom button. "Please bring in the Manual."

"The Heavenly Instruction Manual?" a voice clarified.

"That's the one."

A moment later, an office clerk wheeled in a large trolley with a book on it that was almost the size of a small car. It was old—like, really old—bound in ancient palm leaves, browned with age, and smelled of dust.

"We really should get this digitalized," Peter grumbled. He turned the cover to the index, scrolling down with his finger as he read. "Ah, here it is. Twinned souls and other fated catastrophes." He looked at Chasan and grimaced. "Sorry. Appendix 364 subclause 2c. Page five thousand and . . . Oooh boy, we're gonna need some help to open the book up that far down." Several other admin angels began gently lifting pages, being careful of the binding. "The subclauses were added after Uriel and Icarus. But I must warn you, Chasan, we might not find the answers you're after. While what happened to Uriel and Icarus' bonding was tragic, your situations are not the same. Icarus was human. Your bond is between two angels. We have no way to know with certainty, if the bond is broken, how it will affect you."

Chasan bowed his head, and he tried not to feel so disheartened. "I understand."

"Do you?" Peter asked. "If the fire is extinguished, it could be a clean break, or it could send you both mad. It might even kill you both. I just don't know."

Chasan gave a solemn nod. "Staying fated to him and feeling the sting of his rejection bears a similar fate."

One of the admin angels waved their hand at the now-opened book. The page was papyrus. The writing was in a language that even pre-dated Sumerian. With a heavy sigh, Saint Peter gave a nod. "As you wish." And he leaned over the huge book and began to read.

"The twin flame is the ethereal bonding of two souls . . ." He began to mumble as he read quickly down the page. "In two humans—no . . ." He scanned some more. "One angel, one human. See the Uriel and Icarus subclause 3e. No . . ." He mumbled as he scanned farther down. "Ah, between two angels. Here it is."

And just then, the air crackled and sparked, and two angels took shape in the room. Zophiel appeared with a stylish flourish. And Nathaniel with a clatter. His wings shot out, dark umber, ethereal and glorious, but one knocked over Tennin's pen holder. "Oh my," Nathaniel said, shuffling his wings back in and rushing to pick up the pens. Every pair of eyes were on him. "Sorry. Forgot to account for my span. Wasn't expecting that. Sorry."

Chasan couldn't believe his eyes. The flame in his chest grew hot.

Saint Peter clearly couldn't believe his ears. "Oh my? Did Nathaniel just say 'oh my'?"

Nathaniel spun around to face Saint Peter at the head of the room first, then his eyes landed on Chasan, and Nathaniel visibly sighed with relief. His hand went to his chest, and Chasan knew he was feeling the fire there.

"Chasan," Nathaniel said, breathless. "I'm sorry. For everything. Please don't have the bond broken just yet. Hear me out first. Please."

Chasan's eyes welled with tears, his lips in a heartbroken frown. He shook his head. "I can't, Nathaniel. I can't do this anymore." He tried to swallow. "I've hung on long enough."

Nathaniel shook his head. "Just listen first. Then if you decide you still want to leave me, I won't object." He made a face. "Okay, well, I'll probably still object, but I won't stop you."

Chasan sighed. "You shouldn't have come. It'll only make it harder."

Saint Peter was frowning. "Nathaniel, we're reading up on how to extinguish the fire."

Nathaniel's gaze went to the huge book. "What? No. No, that's not . . ."

"That's not what?" Chasan glared at him.

"That's not what I want."

Chasan couldn't believe this . . . "Bullshit, Nathaniel. For a thousand years I've waited while you denied me, denied not just your own fate, but mine. And I'm done. I can't take it any longer. I shouldn't have to. You shouldn't want me to. But you've strung me along for eons, and it's cruel, Nathaniel. It's a cruelty like no other. And I'm done."

"Chasan . . ." Nathaniel whispered.

Saint Peter turned to Chasan. "Are you sure this is what you want?"

"This isn't what I want at all," Chasan whispered. His heart was broken, his voice thick with emotion. "What I want is to complete the bond, to live my truth and seal my fate. But clearly that's never going to happen." Then a single tear rolled down Chasan's cheek. "Extinguish the twin flames, and take my heart too. I've no need for it. I don't want it. I want to be rid of this ache, of this longing. This pain. I don't know who I am without it." He hung his head, his wings, and cried.

And sorrow detonated through Heaven, something only seen once before. A fallout, far-reaching and heavy.

Angels should never weep.

"Oh, Chasan," Saint Peter said, putting his hand to Chasan's shoulder. "I'm sorry it came to this."

"What?" Nathaniel asked. "Came to what?" He looked at Chasan, at his tears. He was stricken. "Chasan, please don't cry. I can't stand it. I . . ."

"You've done enough, Nathaniel," Saint Peter said with an unfeeling glance.

He shook his head, and panic began to creep over him. "Wait, just wait. A second, I don't . . . Chasan . . ."

"The bond between you will be broken," Saint Peter

said, his voice solemn. "I had hoped . . . I thought it would be different between you, both being angels. But it seems false hope beckons false dreams."

"Chasan," Nathaniel tried again, panicky. Had he somehow brought his human anxiety into his angel form?

"You're getting what you want," Chasan whispered.

"No." He swallowed hard. "Just wait. Please. I need a second here."

"You've had a thousand years."

"But this isn't the end. It can't be." He shook his head, frantic. "I can't . . . I don't . . ."

Chasan put his head down. His wings hung low, as if they, and as if everything, weighed too much.

Nathaniel crossed the room and put his hands to Chasan's cheek. "I know now. It's taken me this long, and I'm sorry. But now I know what I want, what I need. And that's you." He shook his head quickly. "Chasan, please. I know I wronged you. Zophiel told me some pretty harsh truths."

Chasan didn't dare believe it. He glanced to Zophiel, and Zophiel put his hands up in defense, then he nodded to Nathaniel. "Nathaniel, tell Chasan what you told me."

Nathaniel's eyes never left Chasan. "I'm an insufferable ass."

Someone in the room laughed, someone else coughed. Chasan almost smiled despite his mood.

"It's true," Nathaniel continued. "I am. And I'm sorry for everything. For how I treated you. There is no excuse. I can only apologize, and promise to do better."

Chasan shook his head. "What are you saying?"

"I'm saying I don't want you to break the bond. I want to be with you, if you'll have me. If your answer is no, then I will accept that." He swallowed hard. "I'm a mess, and I have more issues than *Reader's Digest*. But I want to be better, and I want to be with you."

The fire soared in his chest, licking up his throat and down to his belly. It was consuming him, and it was marvelous. Chasan dared to hope . . .

Nathaniel thumbed Chasan's cheekbone. "I was a fool to deny you before. I was a fool to not speak to you sooner. I have a lot to learn and a lot to deal with."

Someone at the table mumbled something, but Chasan didn't catch who it was. Nathaniel turned to their audience of upper management. "Something I have also learned that involves you lot," Nathaniel told them. "You sit up here while your people suffer. You need to spend some more time down there getting your hands dirty. Playing deities from a distance is a terrible management plan."

"I beg your pardon," Barachiel said, affronted. "How dare you?"

"How dare *you*!" Nathaniel shot back at him.

They all sat stunned, and Saint Peter spluttered. "Nathaniel . . ."

"That includes you, Peter. You too. All of you," Nathaniel added, pointing around the room. "The world's a mess. But there is good down there too. It's worth saving. But you can't do that from here. You need to be part of it. Chasan reminded me of that."

Chasan smiled and stepped closer. "You're being serious."

"I am, Chasan. I mean it. I can't be without you. You make me want to be better and *do* better. You make me happy, and you make the fire right here feel alive." He put his hand to his sternum. "I want this, and I want to be yours. But you have to know, Chasan, it's not going to be easy. I'm . . . insufferable. As you know. I'll try to be everything you need, even though I am in pieces. I don't know what I can offer you, but what's left of me is yours."

Chasan's eyes welled with tears. "Oh, Nathaniel."

He cupped Chasan's face and made him look at him. "Please. I don't want us to end. I don't . . ."

"You never wanted me for so long."

"I told myself I didn't . . . because I took you for granted, which is the worst, I know. But to imagine a life without you . . . I can't face forever without you." He turned to Saint Peter. "Complete the bond. Make it real, please. Whatever it takes. I'm in. I want it."

"Nathaniel," Chasan whispered. "I don't want your pity. I can't bear it."

"It's not pity. I've been a fool."

Chasan wanted to believe him. But he needed to know . . . "Why now? What changed? I need to know, because this can't be undone."

"For the longest time, my choice was removed. I never asked for it. I know you didn't either, and fate chose us. And we got on well, but then Peru happened, and it occurred to me that I was responsible for you. I couldn't make you happy, and what happened proved that. How can I be responsible for making you complete when I'm not? But now I realize I'm not just responsible for your happiness, I'm responsible for your misery, and if I can do anything to stop it, I will. I can't bear the pain. Seeing you in pain kills me. I want you to be happy and to be loved, and I want to be the one to give you that. I want to try. I have to try." He leaned his forehead to Chasan's. "You were always there. I thought you'd be waiting for me forever. I took you for granted for all these years, and now the thought of not having you there . . . I'm such a fool. I can't face forever without you. I'm sorry. I'm so sorry. I'll spend eternity trying to make you happy, Chasan. If you can forgive me."

Chasan met his gaze, searching for doubt, for any hidden reservations. "You mean that?"

"Please don't leave me. Please don't break the bond. Please. I'll understand if you still want to, because I've been so horrible to you. I know you're getting the raw end of the deal because I get you, and you're perfect. And you get me, which is unfortunate for you because I'm such an idiot."

Chasan smiled. "You are an idiot. But you're *my* idiot."

Nathaniel put his hands to Chasan's face. "I want to do this. I want to be yours, the twin flames or whatever it is. I just want to be yours." He bit his lip. "How do we make it real?"

Saint Peter cleared his throat. They both looked at him. "Are you both absolutely sure?"

Nathaniel squinted at him. "I'm sorry, were you not listening just now?"

Chasan snorted. "Yes, we're sure."

"One hundred percent," Nathaniel added. "How do we complete the bond? Is there a ceremony?"

Saint Peter leaned over the huge book, pointing to one particular part. "Uh, it says here you just need to kiss. That's it."

"That's it?" Nathaniel asked. "Just kiss? You mean to say this whole complicated fated-angel, entwined-souls thing could be sealed with just a kiss?"

Saint Peter raised an eyebrow. "Ever kissed anyone before?"

"Well, no," Nathaniel mumbled. "But I was expecting some fancy ceremony or something . . ."

"Are you stalling?" Saint Peter asked.

"What?" Nathaniel asked, pretending to not understand. "I'm not stalling. I'm just . . . Ugh. I've never kissed anyone, and I wasn't planning on an audience for my first time."

Saint Peter crossed his arms and raised an eyebrow. "You're stalling."

Chasan laughed and slid his hand along Nathaniel's jaw, and he licked his lips. "Yes?"

Nathaniel nodded, and his eyelids fluttered closed as Chasan ever so slowly leaned in and ghosted his lips across Nathaniel's. Nathaniel gasped and Chasan smiled, and then he pressed their lips together in a proper kiss.

White light, blinding and pure, exploded outwards, and Chasan's and Nathaniel's wings went out and entwined. They held each other, their mouths joined, and they shot upwards, spinning and flying in a flurry of light and levity.

And landed with a soft thud on their bed in their New York apartment. They were back in human form, their arms around each other, legs entwined, and their bodies aligned.

The fire in Chasan's chest roared, and he smiled. "I'd like very much to kiss you again."

Nathaniel grabbed Chasan's face and brought their mouths together, open, and when their tongues met, Chasan groaned and Nathaniel gasped. Chasan tilted his head and deepened their kiss, holding Nathaniel tighter. His fingers skimmed under his shirt at his back, and Nathaniel shivered, so Chasan did it again. He let his hand crawl up under the fabric, feeling his skin, his spine, his shoulders.

With a grunt, Nathaniel rolled Chasan onto his back and pressed his weight onto him. Chasan's legs fell open and he rolled his hands down over Nathaniel's ass, their arousal evident and hard between them.

Nathaniel groaned, their kiss faltering. "Oh, Heaven's mercy."

Chasan laughed breathlessly. "I think I can see what humans have made a fuss about all these years."

Nathaniel kissed him again. "I've been such a fool. We could have been doing this for a thousand years."

Chasan met his gaze. He saw only truth and adoration in his bronze and amber eyes. "We have thousands more."

"I've never done anything like this," Nathaniel whispered.

"Me either," Chasan admitted. "We'll find our way through it together. We have time." He pulled him in for another kiss. Slower this time, deeper, but no less passionate.

They rocked their hips. They held each other tight and found a rhythm all their own. The pressure in Chasan's body grew and they were heading toward a pleasurable end. Chasan slipped his hand between them and rubbed it against Nathaniel's cock through his pants.

Nathaniel shuddered and gasped. His eyelids fluttered. "Oh. Oh."

So Chasan deviously shoved his hand under the waistband. It was awkward and there wasn't much give in the fabric, but he wrapped his fingers around Nathaniel's cock the best he could.

He was rock hard and silken. And so, so hot.

Nathaniel was apparently incapable of kissing through it. He pressed his forehead to Chasan's and thrust. His eyes were closed until Chasan pumped his fist. His eyes shot open, dark and demanding, his lips wet and swollen. His cock pulsed in Chasan's grip, and he came.

In all his years, in Heaven or on Earth, Chasan had never witnessed a more beautiful sight.

Nathaniel arched and cried out in pure, unadulterated bliss. His eyes rolled back into his head, and warm, wetness covered Chasan's hand.

Oh, Heaven's mercy indeed. The sight of him, the sounds he made, the scent of his sex.

Chasan was so close to the edge.

But then a final shudder wracked Nathaniel's body and he thrust against Chasan at just the right angle, with just the right friction . . . and Chasan saw stars as ecstasy exploded inside him.

He bucked under Nathaniel and gripped his ass, pulling him hard against his groin. Right where he wanted him, needed him, and Chasan came.

He'd never known a pleasure like it. His body felt alight with liquid fire, and if he wasn't sure he was a human on Earth, he could have sworn he'd ascended.

When his world righted itself, Nathaniel was staring down at him, his face full of wonder. He kissed Chasan, soft and lingering. "We are so going to do that again."

Chasan chuckled and rolled them onto their sides, kissing him with smiling lips. "We should shower."

"We should."

"Together."

Nathaniel's eyes lit up. "Is that a thing?"

"Oh yes. It's a thing."

"Both of us in the shower at the same time, naked?"

"That's generally how showers work."

Nathaniel growled at him playfully. "Sarcasm does not become you."

Chasan laughed and rolled off the bed and peeled his shirt off as he walked to the bathroom. "You can stay there fully dressed if you want," he teased. "But I'll be in here, naked as naked can be." He stopped at the door. "And wet. Naked and wet."

Nathaniel scrambled off the bed, and Chasan laughed as he walked in. He threw his shirt in the hamper, turned the water on to get hot, then he pulled his boots off. He began to pull his jeans down when he noticed Nathaniel had stopped, his hand at his shirt as though he'd lost all train of thought.

"You okay there?"

"Oh," he said slowly. "I'm so much better than okay."

Chasan could feel some nervousness coming from him, which was probably natural, given this was all so new. He pulled his jeans and briefs off and then his socks, standing there completely naked. And then, because Nathaniel was now gaping and because he could, Chasan leaned over and kissed him. "Are you okay with being naked right now? We don't have to shower together if you're not ready for that."

He blinked and snapped out of whatever trance he was in, and he hurried to pull his shirt off over his head. "I'm so ready."

Smiling, Chasan walked into the shower and washed the stickiness away, and then he shoved his head under. When he opened his eyes, Nathaniel was absolutely naked and glorious, standing right in front of him.

"I meant what I said before," he said. "In Peter's office. I meant every word. I will probably drive you crazy, and I will undoubtedly do stuff that makes you mad. But it's not because I want to upset you. It's because I'm clueless."

Chasan took his hand and pulled him in under the stream of water, flush against his body. Chasan held him close as he kissed him, soft and slow. "Don't speak of my twin flame that way."

"Mm," Nathaniel hummed dreamily. He opened his

eyes slowly; water beaded on his lashes. "I was talking about myself."

Chasan chuckled. "I know. But, still. Stop putting yourself down. You're not clueless, you're not broken, Nathaniel. You are perfect."

He blushed but looked away, very clearly not agreeing.

"Hey," Chasan soothed, lifting Nathaniel's chin so he'd meet his gaze. "You're perfect, Nathaniel."

"No I'm not," he whispered. "But I want to try to be. For you."

Chasan kissed him with smiling lips. "You already are. Just as you are. And if I have to spend the next thousand years proving it to you, then that's what I'll do."

Nathaniel studied him for a moment as the steam swirled around them. "I don't know what I ever did to deserve you."

"I could say the same about you."

"And you'd be lying."

Chasan smirked. "Angels cannot lie."

Nathaniel skimmed his hands down Chasan's back, over his ass, and back up to his waist. "Your body does not lie."

Chasan laughed and grinded against him, their erections pressed deliciously firm between them. "Neither does yours." Spurred on, he pushed Nathaniel against the tiles and kissed him hard. He pinned his hands above his head and Nathaniel gasped, his cock pulsed against Chasan's.

Chasan groaned and grinned as he kissed him, and they kissed for ages, making up for lost time. He was so turned on, everything he'd always wanted was in his arms right that second. He let his hands drop to Nathaniel's face, pressed their foreheads together, and tried to catch his breath.

His body felt electric, charged with desire and a need

for more. The flame in his chest danced. "I want to do everything to you, with you. I want to learn every inch of your body, I want to taste you—"

Nathaniel groaned and his cock pulsed again. "Oh sweet mercy, I think your words might kill me," he murmured. "My knees feel funny. Why do my knees feel weird? Like wobbly or something. Is that normal?"

Chasan laughed, and reaching over, he shut the water off and reached for a towel. "Come on."

"No, wait! Where are you going? I liked it in here with you very much."

Chasan threw a towel to him. "If you're lying on the bed while I put your dick in my mouth, then you can't fall over."

Nathaniel's breath left him in a rush, and he wobbled but leaned back against the tiles. "Oh. Yes. Lying down. Good idea. And Chasan?"

Chasan paused from drying himself. "Yes?"

"You should probably wait until I'm already lying down before you say things like that to me." He dabbed the towel to his forehead. "My legs feel somewhat gelatinous, and my head is fuzzy."

Chasan laughed and walked back into the shower. "Stay there." He used his own towel to dry Nathaniel. He was tempted to simply drop to his knees right there, but if Nathaniel was already like Jell-O, lying down was probably a good idea. Chasan dried him roughly, and when he patted down Nathaniel's legs, he dabbed the soft towel to Nathaniel's balls.

Nathaniel's eyes closed and he licked his lips, and Chasan couldn't resist . . . "Now turn around and I'll do your back."

Nathaniel whimpered but managed to turn and face the wall. He put his palms to the tile, his forehead too, his feet spread wide. Chasan wiped him down, rubbing slow and thoroughly, making a show of it. Only this time, he followed each swipe of the towel with a soft kiss. His nape, his shoulder, his spine, his ribs, his ass.

By the time Chasan was done, Nathaniel could barely stand. Chasan turned him around and took in the glorious sight of him. His eyes were dark and wanting, his lips parted with desire. His cock was engorged and liquid beaded at the tip.

Chasan really wanted to taste it.

He dropped the towel, took Nathaniel's hand, and led him to the bed. "Lie down."

Nathaniel sat and quickly scooted up until his head was on the pillow, and then his eyes drew down Chasan's body. "Oh my."

Chasan gave his hard cock a stroke. "This is what you do to me. You turn me on."

Nathaniel swallowed visibly and nodded. "You're so beautiful," he whispered.

Chasan put one knee on the bed, then the other, and he crawled up between Nathaniel's legs. He kissed each thigh before pausing at his prize. "May I taste you?"

Nathaniel put his hand to his forehead. "Well, I'm pretty sure I'll expire if you do. And almost certain I will if you don't. Chasan, please."

Chasan wrapped his fingers around the base of Nathaniel's dick, marveling in the heat of it, how hard it was, and how it would pulse and jerk in his touch. He leaned down and inhaled that scent of him. It made his own cock throb. "I've never done this before, so apologies," he said, then licked the frenulum.

Nathaniel's whole body jerked, so Chasan did it again, licking more of his shaft this time. He worked his way up to the head and finally tasted his sweet and salty reward. "Mmm," he hummed at the taste.

Then he opened his lips and sucked him into his mouth. Nathaniel's back arched. "Oh!"

So Chasan did it again, pulling back a little, then sucking down a bit more. It was strange to be finally doing this, but it felt so right. And it was a powerful thing to know he could command Nathaniel's entire body with his touch.

Chasan sucked the tip and pumped his hand around the base. Nathaniel fisted the sheets at his side and made a strangled whining sound.

Chasan pulled off and pumped him some more, watching as Nathaniel's engorged cock spilled onto his belly. Watching his face, his whole body contorted with pleasure as he came.

Knowing he'd done that to him was a potent and arousing thing. His own cock reminded him painfully of its lack of attention. He climbed a little farther up Nathaniel's body and knelt, his cock pointing at the mess on Nathaniel's belly. Chasan took Nathaniel's hand and, linking their fingers, wrapped their joined hand around Chasan's erection.

A few pumps were all it took and he came too, painting stripes on Nathaniel's skin. He collapsed onto Nathaniel, smearing their mess between them. But Chasan didn't care. In fact, he liked the smell of their sex.

Nathaniel wrapped his arms around Chasan and kissed his neck. "That was the best thing I've ever seen."

Chasan chuckled but couldn't lift his head just yet. "Now it's me who's gelatinous."

Nathaniel laughed, and eventually their breathing returned to normal, and the room stopped spinning for Chasan. He propped his head on his hand so he could look

Nathaniel in the eye. "We're going to need another shower."

"I don't mind. I'm rather fond of human showers."

He was so handsome, and Chasan still couldn't hardly believe that this was real. After all this time, here they were. "I'm not dreaming, am I?" he asked. "This did happen?"

Nathaniel blushed a little. "If you're dreaming, then so am I."

Chasan put a hand over Nathaniel's heart. "You can feel the fire here?"

He nodded. "Yes."

"Mine burns for you."

Nathaniel's pupils dilated, his nostrils flared. "As mine does for you." He swallowed hard and scanned Chasan's face. "I tried to deny it for so long. It never went away, but I guess I learned how to ignore it for all those years. It's always been a part of me though."

"Same." Chasan kissed him softly. "Does yours feel different now?"

Nathaniel closed his eyes and he inhaled deeply. "Not really different. It does feel better or deeper. I think that's just because our chests are so close."

"Hmm, maybe." Chasan ran his nose along Nathaniel's jaw, simply because he could. "I just expected something crazy to happen. Or change. I don't know. Now that we've stopped fighting it." He kissed the soft skin just under Nathaniel's ear, and he writhed in response.

"Oh wow," he breathed. "These human bodies are something else." He craned his neck to give Chasan more room. "Why does that . . . oh my word. Why does that feel so good?"

Chasan's cock began to harden again, and he rolled his hips seeking more friction. Nathaniel surprised him by rolling them over so he was on top. His eyes were dark and playful, his lips parted. Chasan spread his legs wide and lifted his knees toward his chest. It felt so natural and it aligned them in ways he couldn't have imagined.

Nathaniel grunted as he devoured Chasan in a kiss. Passion blazed between them, and they rocked and rubbed against one another, their tongues entwined, their arms wrapped around each other tight. Chasan could only imagine what it would be like to have Nathaniel inside him, how good it would feel, how complete it would make them.

He could picture it, and he wanted it so bad. "Nathaniel, I . . ."

Nathaniel pulled back and took both their cocks in his hand. Their lengths pressed together, one slide, one pump was all it took.

They collapsed in a sweaty, sated heap and showered again. It seemed now, once they'd started, they couldn't bring themselves to stop. Sometime later that evening, they did manage to nap, where Nathaniel fell asleep with his head on Chasan's chest. They woke later, ignoring their sexual needs long enough to pull on some boxers and find some fruit and crackers in the kitchen. Again, Nathaniel pressed himself right up against Chasan, his face fitting perfectly in the crook of Chasan's neck. "I think this spot right here," he murmured, "was made just for me."

Chasan laughed as he rubbed Nathaniel's back, reveling in the sheer simple wonders of a hug. "I'm sure of it. And I'm glad we have the weekend, because I don't want you to be anywhere else."

"The weekend?" Nathaniel asked. He pulled back to look Chasan in the eye. "Do you mean we have to go back to work on Monday? Is our assignment not over?"

He shook his head. "It can't be. Because we're still here. If it was over, we'd be in Heaven right now."

Nathaniel frowned and snuggled back into his spot against Chasan's neck. "Well, this feels a lot like Heaven to me."

Chasan kissed the side of his head. "Me too."

But Chasan had to wonder . . . if the assignment wasn't over, then what was the assignment? Because Nathaniel had finally accepted his fate. He wanted the twinned souls, he'd asked for it.

So if that wasn't the assignment, what on earth was? If Nathaniel was the soul they had to save, what else did they have to do?

Saint Peter's Office

"Oh, this isn't good." Pravuil looked up from the huge Manual. The angel fixed their glasses and searched the room for Saint Peter and found him in a cheerful conversation of self-congratulations with Zophiel, Barachiel and Ridwan. "Ah, guys?"

"Yes?" Saint Peter replied, mildly irritated at the interruption. "What is it now?"

"There's a subclause to the subclause," Pravuil said, pointing to the page they'd been reading. Everyone else had gone on about their business once Chasan and Nathaniel had disappeared, but Pravuil had thought something wasn't right. As the record keeper of Heaven, they'd done a lot of reading. Not the whole of the Manual per se, because it was long and all rather tedious, but they'd read enough to know something was amiss. "And another subclause."

"In regards to?" Ridwan asked.

"To the twin flame."

Saint Peter frowned. "What do you mean a subclause to the subclause to the subclause?"

"Well, I thought I remembered seeing something about when the process is complete, though it was many, many years ago, and I couldn't quite remember the specific details. My early Sumerian isn't up to what it used to be. I really should take a refresher course—"

"Pravuil," Peter snapped. "The point, please."

"Oh. Yes, well . . . the bond between Nathaniel and Chasan isn't complete."

Saint Peter blinked. "What?"

"As per subclause chain to the subsection Appendix 364 subclause 2c, it says there will be an affirmation throughout Heaven when the bond is complete. It's quite a big deal in the angel world, as we all know, but it says here . . ." They pointed to the paragraph in particular. "'The skies will be alight with stars and all of Heaven will rejoice. There will be celebration and pause for the rejoining of the twinned souls.'" They looked up at Peter, Zophiel, Ridwan and Barachiel. "And that didn't happen."

Ridwan shrugged. "We rejoiced."

Barachiel nodded. "We did. But it wasn't a—" He used finger quotes. "—a 'celebration.'"

Saint Peter rubbed his temples. "Oh boy."

Pravuil rolled their eyes and continued with their findings. "So, when I realized the bond didn't actually take place, I followed the thread of subclauses, and it turns out that each of the twinned souls must be complete and whole at the time of the bonding or it will not work." They turned back to the book. "It says here, and I quote, though I'm actually paraphrasing because early Sumerian is lost a little in translation, so I'm not *literally* quoting—"

"Pravuil!" Saint Peter boomed. "Focus."

"Right, yes. Focus. Okay," they began again, "'As the twin souls were split into two equal parts, completion cannot exist in part, for the whole being must be present. If the chosen souls are of the heavenly realm, completion will not occur until each soul in its entirety can be rejoined with its twin.'"

"What . . . ?" Saint Peter squinted. "What does an incomplete soul even mean? And which one of them is incomplete?"

Everyone in the room answered in unison. "Nathaniel."

Saint Peter sighed the heavenliest of sighs. "But we came so far! He came so far."

"Not far enough, apparently," Pravuil said. "But wait, there's more." They pointed to a particular line in the book. "'An incomplete soul must renew.'"

"Renew?" Barachiel asked. "What does that mean?"

"To begin again," Ridwan replied solemnly.

"Oh no," Zophiel whispered.

Saint Peter shook his head. "We should have read the fine print."

"Yes, you should have," Pravuil said.

"They were always too different," Hadraniel chimed in, pessimist to the end. "One is air, the other fire. They'll share the same fate as Uriel and Icarus."

"No," Saint Peter said. "It is their contradictions that forge their strength. They are meant to be. I know it."

"I believe so too," Zophiel agreed. "I've seen how they are together. Two equal and opposite halves."

"Almost equal," Ridwan corrected. "Except for the incomplete soul part, apparently."

Pravuil nodded and turned the page of the book and read the next paragraph. "It says here 'A twinned soul, once renewed, can evolve back to its divinity, returning to the perfected being. Two entities as one, one soul as two entities, forever entwined, never to part again. For it is the completed soul that binds them, born of the same fate, yet their differences which sets them apart will bring them back together. For that, therein, lies the true dichotomy of angels.'"

Saint Peter scrubbed his hand over his face. "I should have taken that holiday."

"So how do we renew a soul?" Zophiel asked Pravuil.

Pravuil looked at the book and shrugged. "It doesn't say."

"How can it not say?" Zophiel cried. "It's the Manual, for crying out loud."

"I don't know!" Pravuil replied. "I haven't gotten that far!"

"Well, keep reading," Saint Peter said. "Zophiel, you're back on duty. Back to Earth with you. Keep an eye on both Nathaniel and Chasan, every second."

Zophiel grimaced. "Every second? Are you sure? Because right now they're busy doing things they don't want an audience for. If you get my meaning."

Saint Peter made a face. "Wear earplugs. They have those noise-canceling things nowadays."

"It's an important mission," Zophiel hedged. "Perhaps I should have backup . . ."

"Yes, yes, good idea," Saint Peter said, waving him off. "Pick someone to go with you. Hurry."

Zophiel grinned. "Raguel."

Saint Peter stopped and sagged. "I walked right into that, didn't I?"

Everyone nodded, and Zophiel grinned. "Excellent." He got to the big double doors, turned, and gave Peter two finger-guns and a wink. "I'll be off then." He walked out, and just before the doors closed, he popped his head back in. "Oh, quick question . . . Do I tell Chasan and Nathaniel what's going on or no?"

Saint Peter looked at all the other heavenly faces, who in turn, looked at everyone else. They shrugged, and Saint Peter sagged into his chair, defeated. "Um . . ."

"It didn't end well for Icarus," Ridwan said. "We told them, and look how that ended."

"That was different. Icarus was human," Barachiel countered.

Saint Peter rubbed his temples, and finally he looked at Zophiel. "No. Don't tell them. Their hearts will show them the way. But Zophiel," he added seriously, "take Zacharael and Abraxos with you as well. I have a feeling you're going to need all the help you can get."

With a nod, Zophiel went on his way, and when the room fell silent, all eyes turned to Saint Peter. He wasn't sure what to tell them . . . "If this ends badly, Icarus launching himself into the sun will seem like a walk in the park."

CHAPTER THIRTEEN

NATHANIEL

THE WEEKEND PASSED in a blur of orgasms, naps, and the occasional bite to eat. Oh, and more showers than were environmentally sustainable, but they did shower together, which Nathaniel reasoned made it okay.

They never stepped foot outside their apartment. They summoned their weekly groceries and even managed to put on some clothes when they were delivered. But they were both so driven mad with lust, they couldn't keep their hands off each other.

And Nathaniel really did fit against Chasan and into the crook of his neck. That wasn't an exaggeration. When he leaned against him or lay on top of Chasan, he slotted right in there like a puzzle piece. And their sexual awakening was getting a little more adventurous each time. Although Nathaniel found out he could orgasm just from being kissed and having his nipples tweaked.

That had surprised them both.

Well, mostly it surprised Nathaniel, but Chasan thought it was an awesome party trick.

"I'll find your party trick. I know you've got one,"

Nathaniel warned, rolling Chasan onto his back. They'd managed to get the groceries put away but somehow managed to get naked in bed again. Chasan had joked, wondering if Nathaniel had any more party tricks . . .

"Mm," Chasan's grin was salacious. "I think you're on the right track."

"You like it when I'm in charge."

"Very much."

Nathaniel looked between them, and yes, Chasan was turned on. "I can see that."

"I want to try something," Chasan murmured. "If you don't want to, that's completely fine. We can leave it for now. No pressure either way."

Nathaniel was more concerned that Chasan was blushing rather than the words he was saying. "Tell me what it is."

"I want you to . . ." Chasan finished with an embarrassed laugh. "I want you inside me. And I want you to finish inside me. I want to feel that . . . with you."

Nathaniel could feel his eyes getting wider, and his cheeks heated. "Oh." He pulled back so he was on his haunches, between Chasan's spread thighs. They were both very naked. Nathaniel was used to nakedness with him now; there was no shame or shyness. "Oh."

"I thought perhaps we could watch some videos online," Chasan suggested. "I've never done it before, obviously. But I've watched a lot of videos . . ." His mouth drew down. "The internet has been a great source of information and tutorials on a lot of things, and I've been around humans a lot and I've seen them do all kinds of things, but I've never experienced it." He gave Nathaniel a sad smile. "And I want to experience it with you."

Chasan lay before him, vulnerable in his honesty.

Nathaniel hadn't really thought of doing what Chasan was suggesting. He'd spent most of his existence avoiding everything, and here Chasan was, admitting to wanting such things but being denied for so long because of Nathaniel's selfishness.

He wouldn't deny him of anything, ever again.

He leaned over him and kissed him with smiling lips. "I can't promise I'll be any good at it or know what I'm supposed to do, but I'm willing to try."

"Only if you want to."

"I want to," he replied, kissing him again. "Did you mention videos?"

Chasan rolled off the bed so fast, Nathaniel fell onto the mattress. *Okay then, Chasan reeeeally wants this.* Nathaniel repositioned himself, careful of his now-permanently hardened dick.

Chasan reappeared with the iPad. "So there are a few sites. But there's this one." He slid back into bed and Nathaniel got comfortable in his spot, which was snuggled into Chasan's side, his head pressed into that perfect space under Chasan's jaw. Chasan put his arm around Nathaniel's shoulder and pressed play on the screen.

And, oh sweet Heaven's mercy.

"They're doing that on the screen?" Nathaniel asked. "In front of other people? And it's on the internet for the whole world to see?"

Chasan laughed. "Sure is. There are millions of videos."

"Oh my word," Nathaniel breathed. He was embarrassed, a little horrified, and a lot turned on. "What is he doing to him?"

"Ah, that's called rimming. We don't have to try that just yet." Chasan fast-forwarded the clip. Nathaniel wanted to ask how on earth Chasan knew that, but then one of the men was now bent over the side of a bed and the other man with a very large penis stood behind him. He poured a liquid over his huge cock and smeared it while he stroked himself, then applied it to the man's ass.

"That's lubrication," Chasan explained before Nathaniel could ask.

Nathaniel knew what lubrication was. For machinery, at least, but he figured the mechanics were the same.

Then the man pushed a fingertip inside the sprawled man's ass, then after a few thrusts, he added another. "It helps the man . . . receive," Chasan said. The man receiving was doing an awful lot of moaning, so Nathaniel could only assume it felt good.

But he was so turned on, he doubted his ability to speak to ask that question.

And then, the very well-endowed man aligned his cock and pushed in. He gripped the other man's hips and slid all the way in, both groaning. The look of pleasure on both men's faces was so overwhelming Nathaniel had to look away. He leaned up so he could see Chasan's face. "And you said there are a million of these?"

He smiled and nodded. "Probably more."

"Oh my word."

He turned back to the groaning sounds on the screen. They were picking up pace, their tempo getting faster and faster with each thrust until the man bent over the bed came so hard he screamed. The man behind him followed quickly, grunting like an animal as he did.

And then, like some kind of torture, the next video began to play all on its own. There was no lead up to this one, no kissing or talking, just one man on his back with his legs around his ears while another man lay over the top of him, and there was a close up of where he was buried inside him, sliding in and out and then pulsing as he came.

Nathaniel pushed the iPad away and Chasan, blessedly, hit pause. "Everything okay?"

"Just need a second," he whispered tensely. He feared if he even moved another muscle, his body would betray him. As it was, his cock felt as though it could burst.

Chasan seemed to clue in. His smile widened. "You liked it?" Nathaniel couldn't answer, but he didn't have to. Chasan curled into Nathaniel's side and fisted his straining cock. He'd barely got his hand around him before Nathaniel came. But this time Chasan didn't just leave it at that.

He licked his hand clean.

Nathaniel laughed and covered his face with his hands. "Oh my word. Just, oh. Have mercy, I still can't swear. I really want to say a whole lot of swear words right now."

"Want me to say them for you?" Chasan asked.

Nathaniel laughed again. "No! It turns me on. It's the last thing I need right now."

Chasan burst out laughing and ran his hand down his chest toward his groin. He was still rock hard. "I don't think this is going away anytime soon."

Nathaniel rolled on top of him and decided on licking his way down, from Chasan's mouth, to his jaw, his collarbone, his nipples and his navel, to where his cock lay across to his hip. "I think we should definitely watch more videos, and we totally need to summon some of that lube stuff, but right now I can help you with this." He licked Chasan's length from base to tip, humming as he did.

"I already did," Chasan bit out, writhing.

Nathaniel stopped and peered up at him. "You did what?"

Chasan nodded. "Lube. I put it in the bathroom when you were putting the vegetables in the crisper. Nathaniel, please don't stop." He raised his hips as though Nathaniel needed a reminder.

Grinning, he leaped off the bed and ducked into the bathroom.

"So help me, Nathaniel, get back out here and finish what you started. Or I'll . . . I'll finish myself and you can watch."

Nathaniel stood in the doorway, leaning against the doorframe. He held up a huge bottle of lube. "They don't come any smaller?" Seriously, it was industrial-sized.

Chasan froze. "What are you doing?"

Nathaniel crawled up the bed and knelt between Chasan's legs. "Practicing."

"Holy shit," Chasan whispered.

Nathaniel tilted his head. "I'm starting to take the fact you can still swear, yet I cannot, a little personally."

Nathaniel did as the guy in the video had done. He squirted a decent amount onto his hand, but instead of smearing it all over his own erection, he did it to Chasan's. It made everything instantly slick, and Chasan almost bucked off the bed. "Oh holy fu—"

Nathaniel smirked. "Say it."

Chasan groaned, so Nathaniel rubbed his slippery fingers under Chasan's balls and across his hole. "Say it."

"Fuck," Chasan whispered, and Nathaniel pushed the tip of his finger inside him.

Chasan's eyes went wide, his thighs fell open, and he lifted his ass off the bed. So Nathaniel did it again, and again and again, until his finger was all the way in. The way Chasan's body reacted was mesmerizing and like nothing Nathaniel had seen before.

Granted, his experience had been limited to the last forty-eight hours, give or take. But Chasan's orgasm obliterated him, like none before it had. He was left trembling and incoherent, as if he'd been electrocuted, and Nathaniel might have had grave concerns for his welfare if it wasn't for the stunned grin on his face.

Nathaniel leaned up and looked closely in his eyes. "You okay in there?"

Chasan replied with a high-pitched keening sound.

"Can you blink?"

Chasan's eyes finally came into focus, and he chuckled. "Oh my sweet mercy bless."

Nathaniel sagged with relief. "I thought I broke you."

Chasan writhed as though he could only now just begin to feel his body. "You can break me like that anytime you like."

Nathaniel laughed before he kissed him. "We need to shower again. And we should probably eat and check what time it is. I have no clue what day it even is, to be honest."

Chasan rolled onto his side, still smiling dreamily. "I don't know either."

"Can you move just yet?"

"Mmm," he hummed happily. "Not sure."

Nathaniel leaned down and kissed his temple. "You look so beautiful. I'm loath to leave you right now when you look so thoroughly spent, but I should run you a shower." He stood up, but somewhere in the bedroom, a phone rang.

Nathaniel found the offending noise under a pile of discarded trousers. It was Chasan's phone, still ringing but no caller ID. "That doesn't bode well," he said, handing the phone to Chasan.

He made no attempt to get up. He just pressed the speaker button. "Hello?"

"Get up and put some clothes on," Zophiel said.

"Are we expecting you?" Chasan asked with a smile.

"Incoming, three minutes."

"Give us five. Better yet, make it ten." Chasan ended the call. He rolled out of bed and stretched. He was a mess: glistening with lube and come, his cock hung half-hard, his bed-hair was all frizzy at the back, and his grin was adorable.

Nathaniel could only assume he looked much the same. "Shower?"

"We probably should."

"Is ten minutes long enough?"

Chasan's phone beeped with a message from Zophiel. Chasan read it out loud. "'Just bloody shower. And please be dressed.'"

Nathaniel snorted. "How does he know?" Then a horrifying thought occurred. "Oh, please don't say he can see us when we . . . while we're . . . oh my—"

"No, he can't," Chasan said, walking into the bathroom. "He's just assuming. And he's not wrong. We better be quick."

Nathaniel followed him. "Do you know what he wants?"

Chasan turned the water on. "Not a clue. But we're going to find out."

Nine minutes later, they were cleaned up and dressed, wearing suitable attire for company anyway, which was a whole lot more than they'd worn all weekend, when a crackle of energy sounded in the living room followed by a shower of sparkles before Zophiel and Raguel appeared out of thin air.

Nathaniel would never get used to it. He put his hand

to his heart. "Can you guys not use the elevator? At least it dings."

"Nice to see you again too," Zophiel said with a smirk. Then he looked around the apartment with a displeased expression. "Oh have mercy, what is that smell?"

"Smells like a brothel," Raguel said. Then he laughed. "Remember that brothel in Belarus, 1742?"

Zophiel laughed. "I remember. That guy with the—" He motioned to his head. "And he used the—" Then he motioned to his groin. "Oh, that was the funniest."

Nathaniel cleared his throat. "Uh, guys. The little trip down memory lane is great. Thanks for taking us with you, even though we didn't ask."

Zophiel eyed Nathaniel for a long moment. "You're looking a lot . . . less stressed, than the last time I saw you. Explains the smell of sex."

Chasan came and stood beside Nathaniel, and Nathaniel wormed his way into his spot against Chasan's neck and gave Zophiel a smile. "I am. For which I owe you one. For your help," Nathaniel said. "For kicking me in the ass when I needed it most."

Zophiel grinned. "You are very welcome."

"And I see you two are back together," Chasan added. "Is that allowed now?"

Zophiel and Raguel exchanged coy smiles. "I might have backed Saint Peter into a corner," Zophiel said.

"A little entrapment now and again reminds him who's actually in charge," Raguel added.

"Indeed," Nathaniel agreed. "Wish I'd been there to see it."

"And not that I'm not grateful for the visit . . . " Chasan hedged. "But the reason you're here is . . . ?"

"Yeah, Chasan and I have a lot of catching up to do,"

Nathaniel said. He made a point of looking at them both. "I'm sure you know what I mean. Though I could draw you a picture if you'd like. Or I could show you some links. You know, they have these sites nowadays on the internet—"

Zophiel put his hand up. "Yep. We know."

"So," Chasan intervened. "You spoke to Saint Peter and now you're here."

Zophiel gave Chasan a serious look. "Your assignment's not over."

Nathaniel could feel Chasan's alarm at that news. He pulled back enough so he could see his face. "What's the matter? You said that before. You guessed that our assignment wasn't finished."

Chasan put a hand to Nathaniel's face. "I know. I just . . . hearing him confirm it made it real. That's all."

Nathaniel snuggled back into his spot against Chasan and looked at Zophiel and Raguel. "What else did Saint Peter say? Did he tell you why our mission wasn't over exactly?"

"How do you know it's not over?"

Nathaniel smiled at him. "Because we're still here."

Zophiel ignored that, apparently stunned at the transformation of Nathaniel, and instead shook his head with amused disbelief. "I can't believe you right now. Cuddling into Chasan like that, being all cute and shit. The dark overseer of the Hell Department being all cute and loved up."

"I can't help it," Nathaniel said. "My body is physically drawn to his, like a magnet. And see this spot right here?" He pulled back and gestured to Chasan's chest and neck. "I fit in there, like it was made just for me."

"Because it was made just for you," Raguel said.

"Oh yeah," Nathaniel said with a laugh. "Good point."

"How's the flame thing now?" Zophiel asked, motioning a circle on his chest.

"It's fine," Nathaniel replied. "All good and under control."

Zophiel's gaze darted to Raguel, and Nathaniel was about to question that when Chasan spoke. "Ah, you didn't answer his question," he said. "Nathaniel asked if Peter said anything else about our mission."

"Oh, well, would you look at that," Zophiel said, looking at his wrist. Where there was no watch. "We must be going."

"Zophiel," Chasan barked.

"We must be off," he answered, taking Raguel's arm. "We have some catching up to do of our own. I'm sure you understand. Not enough time to draw a picture though, sorry."

And with another spray of those ridiculous sparkles, they were gone.

Chasan sighed, and Nathaniel looked up at him and rubbed his back. "We'll be fine, Chase. We'll nail this. You just watch."

"Did you just call me Chase?"

Nathaniel froze. "Um, I don't know. Did I?"

"You did." His smile became a grin. "I like it."

"Oh, well, I'm glad. Because that could have gotten awkward."

Chasan pulled Nathaniel's face in for a kiss. "Do you think we'll be fine? Or were you just saying that to make me feel better?"

"I mean it," Nathaniel said. "It sounds corny, and it's highly likely that it's because this human body has had an indecent amount of oxytocin and vasopressin. But I think you and me, together, we can do anything."

Chasan laughed at that. "You're kinda great, you know that?"

"Don't tell anyone. Or my reputation as the dark overseer of the Hell Department will be ruined for eternity."

He hummed happily and let out a contented sigh. "You hungry? I'm starving."

"Yep." It was dark outside, but Nathaniel had no clue about the actual time. "How about we summon some food, and you can tell me about the 967 assignments you did all alone when I was being a selfish jerk."

"I wasn't always alone," he countered.

"If you tell me Hadraniel was with you, even once, I'm going to pluck out his wing feathers."

Chasan laughed. "Awww," he said, all cutesy. "I was wondering where my angel with the anger-management issues was, but there you are!" He kissed Nathaniel soundly, still smiling. "And I seem to recall you declining any offer to attend assignments with me, so who I actually spent time with isn't really any of your concern."

Nathaniel gasped, duly offended. "How can you say that?"

Chasan laughed. "Because it's the truth, my dear. But before you burst a blood vessel or go track Hadraniel down and pluck out his feathers, no, I didn't spend time with him. Not even once."

Nathaniel sighed with relief, followed swiftly by panic. "Then who? You said you weren't always alone."

"Well, there was Rabdos and Adoni a few times. Mostly I worked on my own."

"Rabdos and Adoni," Nathaniel mused. "They're okay, I guess."

"And what about you?"

"I was always alone," Nathaniel answered. "By request.

Though the assignments I did were few and far between. I certainly didn't do 967 of them. There was one in Japan, same time as you, to keep the Dynasties from a bloodbath. And in Iceland with the Vikings. I really liked them," he said, remembering fondly. "And of course, Mongolia. You were there for that one. And England and France in the 1600s." Nathaniel made a face. "You were there for all of those."

He smiled. "I was."

"All of my assignments involved you, but none of yours involved me."

"Because Peter asked if I wanted to be assigned with you. I said yes each time. You said no. I think eventually he stopped asking you."

Nathaniel frowned; remorse and guilt flooded in. "I'm sorry I was such an ass to you."

"You've already apologized, and I've already accepted that apology, so you can stop feeling bad." Chasan pulled Nathaniel in tight. "You weren't ready then, and that's okay."

Nathaniel settled back into his spot. "So you think Peter did that deliberately," Nathaniel surmised. "Pairing us together those few times, even though I was an ass. And he did it again this time as some last-ditch effort?"

"I think that's exactly what he did. I think they needed the twin flame to happen. It was always supposed to balance some heavenly ledger, wasn't it?"

"Supposedly."

"Nathaniel, can I tell you something? I don't want you to get upset or angry."

He pulled back and frowned. Dread seeped into his belly. "Well, that sounds ominous."

"It's nothing bad." He put a hand to Nathaniel's face

and combed his fingers through Nathaniel's hair. "I thought the assignment was you."

"You what?"

"I thought the mission was you. We had to save a soul. I thought that was you. But here we are," he said, kissing Nathaniel's cheek. "The twin-flame bond is complete, but the assignment isn't finished, which means I was wrong. The mission wasn't you. It can't have been."

"Me?" Nathaniel didn't know whether he was more hurt or offended. Or mad. "What's that supposed to mean?"

Chasan tightened his hold on him when Nathaniel tried to pull away. "Listen, please. I just thought the mission was to get you to see me, the real me, and that what binds us is more than what fate decided for us. I thought that was the mission. To help you see yourself better. So you could see that you deserve to be happy."

"I was happy . . ." Nathaniel shrugged. "Mostly. Kind of. Okay, not really, but I was fine."

"You were fine. And so was the photocopier that you smote. And the other trail of destruction. A broken door, a trash can that you dropkicked across the admin office."

Nathaniel glared at him. "Your point?"

"My point is, my sweet angel," he said, giving Nathaniel a quick kiss, "is that the mission can't have been you. It must be one of the kids."

Nathaniel remembered something. "But when you said you were leaving . . . you said you couldn't be the one to fix me. What did you mean by that?"

"I thought you were the assignment, and I felt like I wasn't getting anywhere. Actually, I thought if anything, I was pushing you in the opposite direction. Because you're so stubborn, if I pushed a little, you pushed a whole lot back."

Nathaniel scowled at him. "I'm not stubborn."

Chasan laughed. "Okay, says the man who refused to budge for a thousand years. You redefine stubborn."

Nathaniel couldn't believe it! He also couldn't argue, but that wasn't the point.

"You're cute when you pout," Chasan said, smiling. He nudged Nathaniel's nose with his, which made Nathaniel's heart do crazy things. "But we should eat something." Chasan checked his phone. "Oh wow. It's nine-thirty. We've lost the entire weekend. What do you feel like?"

"I feel stubborn, apparently."

Chasan laughed again. "Well, what would stubborn like to eat?"

He shrugged, still pouty. "Something vegetarian that isn't awful."

Chasan took Nathaniel's face in both hands and kissed him, long and deep, until Nathaniel was breathless and a little woozy. Probably to make him forget about the stubborn comment and the whole reasoning that Nathaniel was the assignment because of his own stupidity thing. It didn't work, but it wasn't a terrible attempt.

"If you want to make me forget, I think we need to be naked," Nathaniel mused.

Chasan chuckled. "Thanks for the heads up." He took his phone and scrolled for a second. "I'll order dinner. How about you have a look at our class plan for the week. You'll need to think of another topic for the subject board."

Thirty minutes later, they were eating vegetarian pizza, which might just have been the best thing Nathaniel had ever eaten. Once Chasan had proved to him on the internet that vegetarian cheese was so a thing, he really enjoyed it. And they made their weekly plan for the students and talked about craft ideas and games, when all of a sudden, Nathaniel couldn't keep his eyes open.

"Oh my," he said, nodding off. "What's happening to me? Did you drug me? I think I've been drugged?"

Chasan laughed and pulled him to his feet. "It's known as a carb-coma. You'll be fine. You just need some sleep. We've been pretty . . . active . . . all weekend."

Nathaniel smiled, rather enjoying the feel of Chasan against him right now. But wow, he was all of a sudden ridiculously tired.

They put their plates in the sink, brushed their teeth, stripped off, and climbed into bed. They didn't have sex, but they did kiss and cuddle. And although Nathaniel would vehemently deny it if asked, he thought that was almost just as good.

———

"CLASS, this week's subject board is . . ." Nathaniel looked at the twenty pairs of excited eyes. "Under the ocean!"

They hung blue streamers from the ceiling and had a great time making cardboard fish and crepe-paper octopuses and seaweed, and by the end of the day, the entire room looked like an aquarium.

Nathaniel would also vehemently deny his love of crafting with the kids if anyone ever asked. He could argue that it encouraged fine motor skills, and counting skills, shape recognition, and letter recognition.

But he really just loved seeing the kids' faces light up when they were involved in each step. When the crepe-paper streamers hung from the ceiling and they pretended to be fish, when they got to learn about octopuses and count all the legs.

It was so fulfilling to watch them learn. How they responded, and how he and Chasan were making a difference. It might not be catalyst-event level difference, but they were helping these kids learn.

Nathaniel wasn't sure what the mission could be. He knew Zophiel hadn't told them all he knew, and Saint Peter could be shady when he had to be.

One thing Nathaniel was sure of though . . . He fully intended to have a little chat with Saint Peter when this was all over. He would sit down with the big fella, and all the other directors if need be, and tell them what he thought.

That their management strategies needed some work. And their treatment or even acknowledgment of post-traumatic stress disorder was severely lacking. They had no ongoing plans for the ramifications of angels having to deal with human tragedies.

Nathaniel had a lot of things he wanted to get off his chest to Saint Peter about the powers that be. It was well overdue, and now he had something to fight for—now that he had Chasan—he knew there were no more excuses.

When the last child was gone, and Nathaniel and Chasan were tidying up, the door opened and Gian poked her head in. She took one look at the streamers and fish hanging from the ceiling. "Oh wow."

Chasan smiled at her. "That was pretty much the same reaction of every parent that came to collect their kid."

"It's fabulous," she said. "You know, you two are starting to make the rest of us look bad."

"What can we say?" Nathaniel gloated a little. "We're angels."

Chasan almost choked on a laugh. "He's kidding. The kids love it."

"I can see why," she added. "Say, have you thought any more on what your class is doing for the concert?"

The concert?

"It *is* next week."

Next week?!

Nathaniel shot Chasan a panicked look, and he thankfully recovered a lot quicker. "Almost ready. It is a spring theme, right?"

"Yep. Well, it can kinda be whatever you want, really. No one polices it. It's always a fun day," she said. "Well, I better let you guys get back to it. See you tomorrow!"

Nathaniel waited until she'd gone. "Chasan? A concert? Singing and dancing? Next week? Oh Heaven's mercy. We weren't supposed to still be here for that."

"It'll be fine," he said calmly. "Just you wait and see. We can figure it out tonight over dinner."

"I had other plans for you tonight," Nathaniel admitted. "Legitimate, actual plans. And believe me, it involved watching videos on the internet, but not the ones that include singing and dancing." Then he leaned in and very seriously whispered, "Do you know how long it's been since we've been naked? It's seriously been close to eight hours."

He laughed. "I'm sure we can do both. And anyway, I already have the perfect song in mind, and it matches our ocean theme. The kids'll love it."

"I don't have to sing it, though. Do I?" Nathaniel was horrified at the thought.

"That depends."

"On what?"

Chasan glanced at the door, ensuring they were alone, then whispered, "How many times you make me come tonight."

Nathaniel's brain short-circuited. He blinked, his heart

almost exploded, and his cock . . . well, that was not appropriate for their classroom. He snatched up Chasan's hand. "We're leaving, like right now. I'm not even opposed to running home. Can you run in those shoes?" He flicked off the lights and dragged Chasan to the door. "Don't make eye contact with anyone."

Chasan laughed all the way home.

CHAPTER FOURTEEN

CHASAN

CHASAN HAD BARELY STEPPED out of the elevator when Nathaniel grabbed him and kissed him so hard, he stumbled backward onto the dining table. Or Nathaniel pushed him in that direction deliberately; Chasan wasn't sure. He was beyond caring.

All that mattered in that moment was Nathaniel. His body, his hands, his tongue. Chasan lay on the table, his legs spread, Nathaniel standing between them, both still fully dressed. Nathaniel was applying the most delicious pressure, rutting and grinding, kissing hard and desperately.

After being around each other all day but not allowed to touch, this was everything he needed. Chasan's erection was almost painful, in the very best of ways, confined in his trousers and pressed hard between them, rubbing along Nathaniel's while Nathaniel drove his tongue into Chasan's mouth.

Nathaniel came first, and Chasan a moment after. Still dressed, cocks untouched. That's how desperate and aroused they were. How aroused they *still* were.

Nathaniel was panting, but he smiled lazily. "That's one."

Chasan laughed and Nathaniel stood to his full height. He took Chasan's right foot and pulled off his shoe, then he did the left. He undid Chasan's belt, his trousers, then he began to unbutton his shirt.

They were a sticky mess and they did need to get out of these soiled clothes, but out here? On the dining table? Chasan was just about to suggest they take it elsewhere when Nathaniel undid his pants and his still-hard cock sprang free.

He was suddenly warm all over, and a new desire licked at the base of his spine. "Oh, yes please," Chasan whispered.

Nathaniel chuckled, but his eyes were dark, his lips swollen. He looked more like the overseer of Hell than he ever had, just without his burned-umber wings, of course. But he had bad intentions written all over him, and Chasan's back arched with want. His cock jerked in response, and heat spread through him like wildfire.

"I know what you want," Nathaniel whispered. He pulled at the legs of Chasan's trousers until they came off. "And I'm going to give it to you."

Chasan was wearing nothing but underpants, an open shirt, and socks. Spread out before Nathaniel, he felt exposed and sexy, and the way Nathaniel looked over him, Chasan felt desired and wanted.

"Anywhere you want me," Chasan murmured. He was so turned on, Nathaniel could have him on the floor and he wouldn't mind. In fact . . .

"In bed," Nathaniel replied, his voice husky and rough. He helped Chasan to his feet, then led him to their bedroom. Nathaniel slid his hands over Chasan's chest and peeled his shirt off, kissing along his collarbone up to his shoulder.

Chasan's patience was at breaking point. He pulled at Nathaniel's shirt, tossing it to the floor, then began to undo his trousers. "You're far too overdressed."

"I can feel how eager you are," Nathaniel murmured. "You really want this."

"I do," Chasan replied. He undressed, went to the bed, and threw the bottle of lube onto the mattress, then crawled on after it. He lay on his back, his knees bent, and reached down to fondle his balls and the delicate skin behind them.

Nathaniel watched, frozen to the spot for a few seconds before snapping out of his daze. He pulled his boots off, then threw off his clothes in a hurry. "I was trying to take it slow," he said, putting a knee on the bed.

Chasan was tempted to say he'd waited long enough but didn't want to ruin the moment. So, instead he opted for, "If you don't get over here right now, I'll start without you." He picked up the bottle of lube.

Nathaniel snatched it out of his hand. "You'll do no such thing." He kneeled between Chasan's legs and slicked his fingers, then added the cool liquid to Chasan's ass. Chasan moaned and Nathaniel leaned over him, resting his weight on one hand while the other hand began to rub and probe.

"Oh mercy, take me," Chasan groaned. He was writhing, desperate for more.

Nathaniel crushed his lips to Chasan's, and his finger delved inside him. Chasan gasped into his mouth and Nathaniel smiled. "I plan to take you," he murmured gruffly. "To have you, to make you mine."

"I'm already yours," Chasan replied. The flame in his

chest roared in response. His whole body was afire. "Nathaniel. I want you inside me."

Nathaniel pulled his finger out and smeared more lube on his cock. "Um," he began. "You have a lot of expectation about this, which implies my ability should match. And I'd just like to add a disclaimer here, that I don't expect to last—"

"Nathaniel, shut up and fuck me."

Nathaniel's eyes went wide. Then he huffed, as if horribly offended. "I still can't believe you can swear but I cannot. That is so not fair."

Chasan grabbed the lube and flipped the lid. "Fine. I'll do this myself."

Nathaniel pounced on him, pinning his hands to the mattress. "No you won't."

Chasan wrapped his legs around Nathaniel's hips, but with a firm grip behind Chasan's knees, Nathaniel eased his legs up to his chest. He positioned himself and pressed the head of his cock against Chasan's waiting ass. And he kissed Chasan as he slid inside him, slow and tender.

And Chasan was lost for words, lost to everything but Nathaniel. He thought he might split apart or shatter into a thousand pieces with the intensity of it, but Nathaniel held him together.

Nathaniel's brown-and-amber eyes searched Chasan's as Chasan's body took every inch. The fire in Chasan's chest burned blue and bright, and after Chasan relaxed, Nathaniel began to move inside him. Pleasure made itself known, and Chasan moaned as his body took over.

Nathaniel held him, caressed and kissed him, gentle and thorough.

He made love to him.

This act of intimacy was like nothing he could have

imagined. Having Nathaniel inside him, giving himself to him, was liberating. He felt free, as if he had his wings again. As if their twin flames burned as one.

And Nathaniel began to tremble and his kiss stuttered, and his thrusts were harder and deeper.

This was it . . . Chasan was about to take all of him.

Chasan took Nathaniel's face in his hands and Nathaniel's eyes opened. His eyes were liquid and fire, and he came inside him.

Nathaniel thrust hard, his cock surging and spilling deep in Chasan, and Chasan was lost to the wonder of it.

It was everything he thought it would be.

Nathaniel was everything he knew he would be.

As they lay in their bed, sated and content, Nathaniel rubbed circles on Chasan's back. He would kiss the side of his head every so often. "Are you certain you're okay?" he asked.

Again.

"Yes, I'm certain," Chasan answered. Again. Then he laughed. "You wiped the evidence of just how okay I felt off my belly, remember?"

Nathaniel chuckled and tightened his arms around him. "It was amazing," he whispered. "Thank you, Chase. For everything."

Chasan kissed Nathaniel's chest. "Thank you too."

They were quiet then, simply relishing the moment. Chasan had wondered if their twin flames would change after what they'd just done, or during even. Perhaps intensify or join in some way, but they didn't. Chasan's flame was still as it always was, still blue, still wonderful, but still as it always was.

What their lovemaking *did* was make Nathaniel cuddle and snuggle more, laugh more and hold hands and kiss. Over the next few days, Chasan was sure of one thing.

Nathaniel was actually smitten with him.

Fated, sure. Twin flames, yes. But this was smitten. Like, falling in love with him.

Chasan had loved Nathaniel for a thousand years, only now that love was cemented, forever a part of him. Though it was different for Nathaniel. For all that time, Nathaniel had denied himself that love, and it seemed now he was finally letting himself fall.

He held Chasan's hand as they walked to and from work, he laughed more than Chasan could remember hearing, he talked more. He just wanted to be closer: in class, in the kitchen, on the sofa, in bed.

It was beautiful.

And a few times over the next few days, Chasan caught himself and had to remind himself that they were on assignment. He wanted this pretend life to be real, that they were married and living in New York City, working as teachers of some pretty incredible kids.

Just before the buzzer went off on Friday afternoon, they were wrapping up their ocean-themed week with the song "Octopus's Garden" when Gian popped her head in. She called Chasan over. "It's the last Friday of the month."

"Yes, it is," Chasan replied, wondering why she would point that out.

She laughed. "That means it's payday! And we all go out for dinner on payday. Just to Pho Sure. It's a Vietnamese place just around the corner. It's cheap and really good food, a lot of fun. We eat early and we're home early." Her big eyes gazed up at him expectantly. "We'd love it if you could join us."

Chasan looked over to where Nathaniel was pretending

to be an octopus, singing in a conga line of twenty little octopuses. His heart swelled and he got those crazy butterflies in his belly.

"Oh stop it," Gian whispered, swatting his arm. "Could you two be any more in love? Ugh, and I thought true love was dead. You put my love life to shame," she said. "We'll see you at Pho Sure when you get there."

"We'll be home early?" Chasan asked. He really just wanted to cozy up on the couch and watch a movie with Nathaniel.

"Promise." She grinned victoriously as she raced off.

And now Chasan had the joy of telling Nathaniel . . . This was not going to go over well. As they were tidying up, and as the last few kids were leaving, Nathaniel put a chair up beside him and he let out a long sigh. "I'm glad it's the weekend. Can't wait to get home. We have two whole days where clothes are optional."

"Uh, about that. I might have agreed that we'd join the other teachers for dinner."

Nathaniel stared at him, holding up a tiny desk chair in midair. "You what?"

"It'll be quick and fun, apparently."

"I had other plans for quick and fun," he countered. "Well, fun, at least. I'm working on the quick part. I just need practice. Hence the plans. And two days of naked practice."

Chasan laughed, helping Nathaniel with the chair. "We still have two days, and you can practice all you like. But I said we'd go."

Nathaniel sighed. "I should take notes for the Hell Department. Because that's what this will be. Absolute torture."

"It won't be that bad."

"If I have to sit next to Cheryl-Anne, we're swapping seats. Just so you know."

Chasan laughed. "Deal."

He pulled a blue streamer down. "At least in Hell I can swear at people."

"Yes, but they deserve it."

"So does Cheryl-Anne. And Pia for that hideously awful chocolate cake. Or a few days in purgatory at least."

Chasan laughed again and squeezed Nathaniel's hand. "That is true."

Nathaniel sighed, then reached up and pulled down another streamer. "I wish these could stay up. The kids love them."

"The ocean-themed week was a great idea. Maybe next week can be jungle week and we can hang green streamers with birds and monkeys instead of fish."

His face lit up. "Oh, that's a great idea. And we can make tiger masks from paper plates. I should order some more craft supplies. On Saint Peter's credit card, of course."

"Oh, yeah. Gian said we apparently got paid today."

Nathaniel made a face as he pulled down another streamer. "We should give the money to the needy. Heaven knows there are people in this city who could use it."

Chasan's flame grew warm. Nathaniel's kindness had that effect on him. "I think that's a great idea."

"Don't look at me like that," Nathaniel said. "Just because I have a reputation as a cold-hearted ass doesn't mean I actually am one."

"Oh, believe me. I know you're not. You're the biggest softy there is."

Nathaniel glowered for a moment. "Well, when we get back to Heaven, you'll have to keep up the charade. Can't have everyone in the Hell Department knowing the truth, now can we?"

Chasan laughed again. "Your secret is safe with me."

They finished pulling down the blue streamers and just before they were ready to leave,

"Oh, I almost forgot," Nathaniel said. He went to the windowsill and poured more water into each of the seedling pots. "These little guys will need more water for the weekend."

Chasan's heart grew a little bit bigger. "How could anyone think you're cold-hearted?"

"Because I pretended you didn't exist for a thousand years. Sent myself to the Hell Department to avoid facing my responsibilities. Hurt you in the process. Possibly did it because it would hurt you. Because I blamed you for a lot of stuff that was never your fault. Because it was easier to blame you than me. Found myself actually enjoying the Hell Department because watching people suffer made me feel better." Nathaniel shrugged. "You know. The usual."

Chasan couldn't help but laugh. "Or you did it to save someone else from doing it. Or because you felt you deserved to suffer right along with them. And you'd spend hours in the Canine Department, making sure every doggy soul got equal pets and belly rubs."

Nathaniel gasped. "I did not. Who told you that?"

"Everyone knows that."

He was stunned. "My reputation will be ruined. And I mean, I did give all the dogs equal pets and belly rubs. But not because I'm a nice person. I did it because they're the purest souls ever, and they deserve belly scratches. Even from cold-hearted jerks like me."

"Mm-hmm. So cold." Chasan rolled his eyes and held the door open. "Come on, or we'll be late."

Nathaniel pouted as he walked out. "Stop smiling. I can't be mad at you when you're being cute."

They walked outside into the warm spring evening. The light was pretty, the tree-lined street looked idyllic. "It's actually really nice out," Chasan noted.

Nathaniel slipped his hand around Chasan's as they began their walk toward the restaurant. "It is. You know what? This whole being human thing isn't too bad."

"I could get used to this," Chasan agreed. "We probably should talk about what'll happen when this assignment's finished."

Nathaniel stopped walking. "What do you mean?" An explosion of anxiety billowed out from him. "What are you saying?"

"Nothing bad," Chasan quickly reassured him, squeezing his hand. "Just whether we'll do more missions together, or if you want to go back to your department and I'll go back to doing solo assignments. I mean, we don't know what the rules are, and we haven't discussed anything about our future."

"Together," he said quickly. "Whatever we do, we do together. Right? Isn't that what you want? Oh mercy, is that not what you want? Chasan, I don't know if I want you to do solo assignments. What if something were to happen to you?" He put his hand to his stomach. "I don't know if I can even be apart from you now. Is that normal? What even is normal? There's never been an us before. How are we supposed to know what's normal?"

"Hey," Chasan murmured. "Just breathe, Nathaniel." He sent a wave of calm to him and watched as he relaxed. "That's why we need to talk about it. I don't want to be apart from you either. And yeah, whatever we do, we do together. Okay?"

Nathaniel nodded and managed half a smile. "Yeah. Okay."

"We'll need to ask Peter where we go from here. What it means for us, and—"

Nathaniel's anxiety rolled out of him again, though this time it was tinged with anger. "What if Peter makes us go on separate assignments? What if they make us work in different departments? Chasan, seriously, one smited photocopier will be the least of their worries, I can promise you that."

"They wouldn't," Chasan said assuredly. "Peter would never. He's been trying to get this twin-flame thing to happen for millennia. There's no way he'd jeopardize it. And believe me," Chasan added, "if he tries, I'll be right by your side raising unholy Hell so the lava pits in the Hell Department will seem like a theme park. We'll smite the place till only ashes remain."

Nathaniel smiled. "You know how to sweet-talk me."

Chasan laughed and kissed him. "We better get moving or they'll think we're not coming."

"Oh, right. Dinner with our esteemed colleagues. Speaking of Hell," Nathaniel mumbled.

But dinner wasn't that bad at all. And Chasan would guess that Nathaniel even enjoyed himself. When they'd walked into the restaurant, he saw Gian and grabbed her by the arm. "You have to protect me," he said to her with the utmost seriousness. "You have to sit on one side of me, Chase on the other. Because if I have to sit next to Cheryl-Anne and I'm forced to endure small talk at those decibels, my eardrums will explode and I'll die. Or my brain will sever its own cerebral cortex. Like seppuku but for brains. Either way, it's fatal and there'll be a lot of blood. Such a mess."

She just laughed. "I'm so glad you're not overdramatic or anything."

"I know, right?" He relaxed immediately. Chasan could only laugh.

Their group had a long rectangular table booked, so they sat at the end with Nathaniel in the middle of them. It was probably just as well, Chasan reasoned, because the last thing Nathaniel needed was to be overwhelmed with questions, spiking his anxiety, and him threatening to smite someone.

Chasan had been engaged in polite conversation with the two first grade teachers on his left, and when there was a brief pause, he caught the end of Nathaniel's conversation.

"Yes, we married at his parents' house upstate three years ago." Nathaniel had his hand on the table and subconsciously spun his wedding ring with his thumb.

"And how do you find living and working together?" The woman opposite asked. Chasan was certain she was one of the admin staff. "I know my husband would drive me crazy if we worked together."

"Oh, it's the best part," Nathaniel said. "Chasan makes it easy, though. He's kind of great."

She swooned and her gaze cut to Chasan. "You're both so in love," she said, her hand to her heart.

Nathaniel shot Chasan a look, obviously having no clue that Chasan had heard what he'd said, and he blushed and let out a nervous breath. Chasan could feel his anxiety, but there was something else there too. Was it honesty?

Chasan slid his arm around Nathaniel's chair and gave him a bit of a nudge. "Are you telling lies about me?"

"Oh, nothing of the sort," Gian replied. "He's just reminding us all that our respective partners need to up their game."

The lady opposite nodded. "Yeah, and kick their ass to the curb if they don't."

Everyone laughed it off, but Nathaniel didn't. He put his hand on Chasan's knee and shifted his glass of water one-quarter turn on the table. "Don't take it for granted," Nathaniel said quietly, but his tone was serious. "You might think you have all the time in the world, then because you left it too late, they might be ready to walk away." Nathaniel met Chasan's gaze before shrugging. "And you might not be as lucky as me."

"Wait," Gian said, her eyes wide. "He wanted to date you and you made him wait? For how long?"

Nathaniel sighed. "Oh, about a thousand years."

They laughed, and Chasan pulled Nathaniel closer so he could kiss the side of his head. "It was more like nine hundred and ninety-eight," he said, and they laughed again.

"So now I have to spend eternity making up for it," Nathaniel said. He looked over at Chasan then, and he might have said it to play along, but there was honesty in his eyes. "But he's the best thing to ever happen to me," he said, reverently. The others did that swoon thing again, and Chasan's flame burned so bright he was surprised they couldn't actually see it. Blushing scarlet, Nathaniel turned back to their little audience. "So anyway, to answer your earlier question. Yes, living and working with him is kinda great."

Chasan was speechless. The change in Nathaniel was astonishing. Though it wasn't even a change. It was that he was finally letting his walls down and finally accepting love.

Chasan could have cried, and he probably would have if they weren't in public. "Pretty sure I'm the lucky one," Chasan managed to say. And when the conversation eventually moved on, Chasan leaned in and whispered, "I think we should leave."

He gave a small nod, and they put some cash on the table and wished everyone a wonderful weekend. When they got outside, Nathaniel held out his hand and Chasan was quick to take it. The night was still early and not even completely dark. The spring air was lovely.

"You know what?" Nathaniel asked. "I think we should go for a walk."

"You do? I thought you'd be eager to get home, and you know . . ."

He laughed. "Well yeah, of course. But we have all weekend, and it's nice out. I thought we could just walk the long way home, maybe take in the lights in the park."

"Why, Nathaniel," Chasan said, pulling him close, "are you being romantic?"

He pouted. "Or if you're going to tease me, we can just go straight home."

Chasan laughed and kissed him before taking his hand and leading him in the opposite way they'd come. It really wouldn't take that long, and he was right. The park would be so pretty at this time of night.

"I just want to enjoy this," he said after a little while. "Don't worry, I have every intention of enjoying later on as well, but this is nice too."

Romantic walks, holding hands in the New York City twilight . . . "It sure is."

They walked for half a block and Nathaniel squeezed Chasan's hand as they walked. He smiled happily to himself, and Chasan just had to say something. "You're being particularly cute tonight."

Nathaniel laughed. "This is going to sound weird, and —" He glanced over his shoulder. "I know Zophiel and

Raguel will probably hear this and my reputation will be in tatters, but . . ." He shrugged. "I'm happy."

Chasan stopped walking and pulled Nathaniel in for a kiss. "You deserve to be happy."

He rolled his eyes but his smile was genuine. "It's ridiculous. But I feel . . . happy. For the first time in a really long time. And I know you're the reason, Chase. And I'm just really grateful you didn't quit on me."

"I'm just glad too. And can I tell you something without you freaking out?"

He made a face. "I can't guarantee that. And if you think there's an actual chance of me freaking out, then the odds aren't good. Even before you've said anything, it's already not looking great."

Chasan laughed. "You want to know what I think it is? Why you're happy and that giddiness in your belly that I can feel you feel?" Chasan cupped his jaw. "I think you're in love."

Nathaniel slow blinked as though his world had stopped turning. "You think what?"

"I think you're in love," Chasan repeated. "With me."

Nathaniel stared at him, frozen. Then he made some disbelieving scoffing sound and tried to pull away, but Chasan held him tight. "And that's amazing, Nathaniel, because I'm in love with you."

He floundered for a moment, then let out a huff. Excitement and fear bloomed out of him. "You are?"

"Yes. I love you, and I have loved you since the dawn of time."

Nathaniel's eyes grew glassy, but he laughed. "Really?"

Chasan nodded. "And you want to know what else I think? I think you've loved me for that long too, but you just couldn't admit it."

He scoffed. "Is that right?"

"Yep."

"Now you're talking nonsense," Nathaniel said, but his grin was wide. "Utter malarkey."

Chasan didn't need to argue. He knew he was right. They both knew it, but Chasan didn't want to push his luck. He put his arm around Nathaniel and they began walking again. "Oh look! It's the bodega. And speaking of happiness, I feel like a treat."

They crossed the street and Chasan headed straight for the candy aisle. Knowing there was no way Nathaniel would've tried any of them, Chasan grabbed a few different varieties. Admittedly, it had been a while since he'd had candy, so he grabbed a few more.

"Are we giving them to every child in our school?" Nathaniel asked, looking in Chasan's basket. Chasan laughed. "No, and you can thank me later."

Nathaniel got an odd expression on his face. "That gives me an idea."

"What? Thanking me later? I have every intention of letting you thank me later."

Nathaniel glanced around in case someone might have heard. "No," he hissed. "That's not what I meant."

"What did you mean then?"

"You said it was our payday earlier."

"Yep."

"So I want to take out how much I got paid and give it away. It's not like we need it. We don't pay rent, we have Peter's credit cards for everything. It makes sense."

Chasan smiled slowly. "I think that's a great idea."

He grinned. "And what's Peter gonna say? That we shouldn't help the less fortunate? Isn't that like the company motto or something?"

Chasan laughed. "Something like that."

"Excellent." He clapped his hands together. "Where's the local countinghouse?"

Chasan burst out laughing. "Oh, my love, you're so funny." When Chasan realized Nathaniel wasn't trying to be funny, he led him toward the ATM. "Countinghouses haven't been a thing for a long time. Here, I'll show you how to use it."

In no time, Nathaniel had withdrawn his entire wage, which he folded into a great wad and shoved it in his pocket.

"Zophiel and Raguel are probably cursing you right now," Chasan said with a laugh.

"Why?"

"The security risk you pose carrying that much cash."

"Oh. Then we best get rid of it quick."

"Good idea," Chasan agreed. He paid for his candy and they headed outside again. The night had grown darker, and Chasan took Nathaniel's hand and led him up a familiar street. "I know the perfect place."

It was the church on West Seventy-First Street where he'd gone before. That very kind priest had taken the time to speak to him, and it felt like a good place to help out. "In here," Chasan said, taking the stairs to the front doors, which he held open for Nathaniel.

But Nathaniel slowed going up the steps and stopped before he got to the doors. "Um, that's okay," he said quickly. "Maybe not this one."

"What?" Chasan wasn't sure he heard him right. "Not this one?"

"Well, no. Maybe a homeless shelter, or surely there are some less fortunate folks looking to sleep in the park tonight. I'm sure they could use it more than here."

Chasan frowned, but he stepped out of the doorway and let the door close. "Nathaniel," he whispered. To be honest, he was a little lost for words. He remembered then that Nathaniel had also refused to come into the church when he was here before. Even Zophiel had commented about it . . .

Now, a lot of folks didn't like churches or any place of worship for a whole bunch of reasons. But an angel?

"Nathaniel, my love," Chasan said. "What's wrong?"

"No, nothing's wrong, exactly. The church is fine, but I —" He put his hand to his forehead, and his anxiety skyrocketed. "I'm just not sure . . ."

Chasan went to him and took his hand. "Why won't you go inside?"

Nathaniel looked to the front of the church. "They used to have donation boxes. Whatever happened to that?"

"People stole them."

"They stole from a church?"

"Why won't you come in? We can choose any church, temple, synagogue, mosque, if you'd prefer. You know the denomination doesn't make any difference."

"I know that."

"Then why?"

"Because I don't want to."

"Okay. But why won't you really?"

"Because I . . . I don't . . ." He shook his head. "I don't believe . . ." He swallowed hard. "I just don't believe that I . . . Here," he said, taking out his wad of cash and shoving it in Chasan's hand. "You take it in. Please. Just get rid of it. They'll know what to do with it. I'll take your bag of candy and wait out here." He took the bag from Chasan and left Chasan holding the cash. He was so stunned, he dumbly did as Nathaniel had asked.

"Can I help you?" the priest said as Chasan walked in. It was the same priest as before. Father James . . . "Ah, I remember you. Is everything all right? You look a little lost."

"Uh." Chasan stopped and had to think. What the hell had just happened? "Yeah, sure, I'm okay. It's just . . ." He shook his head, realizing this poor man must think Chasan was crazy. He collected himself and started again. "I came in to give a donation, that's all. Is there a box or an envelope?"

"Oh, yes," Father James said. "Come this way."

He led him to an old wooden box that was built into the wall and locked with a large padlock. It had a small slot, and Chasan had to unfold the money and feed it through. Father James couldn't hide his surprise. Chasan realized a little belatedly how this whole transaction must have looked. "It's good money, I promise. We have the means, and we're able to share it."

Father James smiled, perhaps seeing the goodness in him. "Then I thank you."

Chasan gave a small bow of his head. "It's a privilege and an honor."

"You were troubled last time you were here," Father said before Chasan could turn and leave. "I trust everything worked itself out. You said there was a man who couldn't be with you?"

"Oh yes. My," Chasan said, remembering his role here. "My husband. He's . . . he's outside, actually. He refused to come in."

The priest gave a nod. "Wouldn't be the first."

"Father, he's . . ." Chasan thought how he should phrase this. "He's a child of faith. We both are. And this is so unexpected, him refusing to come into a church . . . I'm a little stunned."

How could an angel take issue with a house of worship?

"Would you like me to talk to him?" Father James asked kindly.

Chasan sighed, knowing just how well Nathaniel would react to that. "No, it's okay. I guess I'm just a little shocked. I'll talk to him. But he did want you to have the donation to give to the less fortunate."

He gave an appreciative nod. "Tell him I said thank you."

"I will." Chasan meant to step back, he meant to leave, but he found himself rooted to the spot.

Father James seemed familiar with this because he spoke with all the patience under the sun. "I have seen this before," he said. "When someone who once found comfort in their faith no longer does. Sometimes their path is clear, and that's okay. Not everyone needs to attend a church to be a child of faith. But if you're concerned, if you think something has happened to change his view, you might want to ask him what his issue is. Ask him why he's angry at the heavens." Father James smiled. "No god above can fix a problem if he doesn't know a problem exists."

Chasan saw two figures in the shadows of the vestry, cloaked and hidden in the dark. But still familiar enough for him to know who it was.

Leliel and Ahura.

Chasan took a step back now. His need to get back to Nathaniel was a physical one. "Thank you," Chasan said, still walking backward toward the front doors. He wouldn't take his eyes off where the other two angels had gone.

What the hell were they doing there? And why were they watching Chasan?

Father James was frowning as Chasan got to the door and turned around, disappearing outside. Nathaniel was standing at the top of the steps, and he visibly relaxed as soon as he laid eyes on Chasan. "I thought you must have . . ." He frowned. "What's wrong? Chase, what happened?"

Chasan briefly considered trying to lie, but Nathaniel took his hand, concern etching his brow. "I'm not sure."

"Was it about the money?"

"No, he said to say thank you."

"But?"

"But . . . I don't know. Something he said." Chasan put his arm around Nathaniel and sighed. This was not a conversation he wanted to have out in the street, in front of a church no less. "Let's go home."

"Sure," Nathaniel said easily. "Then you can tell me the truth." Nathaniel gave him a squeeze.

"And you can too," Chasan said, pulling Nathaniel against him as they walked.

"About what?"

"About why you won't go into the church. Is it that church in particular? Because this is New York. We can find you any house of worship you want."

Nathaniel didn't speak for a block, and Chasan was beginning to wonder if he would at all when eventually, he said, "It's not just that church."

Chasan kissed the side of his head, a sign of thanks for his honesty. "I didn't think it was."

That was all he said for the rest of the walk, but Chasan didn't mind. At least he'd said that much, and even admitting that was more than the Nathaniel of just a few weeks ago would have ever admitted. It was a definite step forward for him.

THE ELEVATOR DOORS opened and it was so good to be home. It had been a good week, but long, and even though it was barely eight on a Friday night, Chasan was weary.

Yes, Nathaniel had come a long way, but one thing remained, a constant thought in the back of Chasan's mind. Like a drip of water, seemingly harmless on its own, but slowly filling up.

The assignment was still on.

Two angels were watching from the shadows. And not just any two angels, but Leliel and Ahura. The angel of night and Heaven's watcher. Saint Peter's versions of covert ops.

And Nathaniel had refused to step foot inside a church. Twice. Chasan couldn't help but think these two things were a coincidence.

Now, he just had to find out the real reason why.

CHAPTER FIFTEEN

NATHANIEL

NATHANIEL KNEW Chasan was going to ask about why he wouldn't go inside the church. Maybe he just should have sucked it up and gone inside to avoid the subject, but when it came down to actually walking in . . . he couldn't do it.

So yeah, Nathaniel was very aware this conversation was going to happen.

And he wouldn't deny his reasons to Chasan. Not now, not after everything he'd already put him through. Chasan had told him earlier that night that he loved him, and Nathaniel's heart had almost beat right out of his chest. The fire in his ribs burned glorious red, and when Chasan had been so bold to suggest that Nathaniel loved him back, Nathaniel had been too damn happy to deny it.

He did love him.

And yes, part of him always had. Even though he'd tried to fight it, he'd tried to deny it, it was there.

So no, Nathaniel would give him the cold, honest truth. And in return, Chasan could tell Nathaniel what had really bothered him when he'd left the church.

Chasan threw his keys and phone onto the sofa and pulled Nathaniel down with him when he sat. He held his hands and looked him right in the eye. "You know I won't ever judge you, and whatever you tell me stays between us," Chasan said seriously. "I love you, Nathaniel, and that won't change, ever. But I need to know why you won't go into a church."

Nathaniel smiled at the *I love you*, but in the end, he sighed. "It's nothing critical, really. Granted, it *is* something I probably should work on. You know, given I'm an angel and all."

"Probably, yes."

"Will you tell me why, when you came out of the church a cloud of worry came out the door with you?"

Chasan's brows furrowed for a second. "Yes. I think these two things could be related, but I'm not sure."

Now it was Nathaniel's turn to frown. "Someone was in the church?"

Chasan gave a nod. "I can't be absolutely certain, but . . ."

"But you're certain."

Chasan grimaced. "You first. Then I'll tell you."

"Well," Nathaniel said, not really sure where to begin. "I don't know how I feel about it all, if I'm being completely honest." He wanted to put his hand through his hair but didn't want to let go of Chasan's hand. He was torn. "Ugh."

"How you feel about what?" Chasan pressed cautiously. As though . . .

"Not about us," Nathaniel said quickly. "That I'm certain of. For the first time in forever, I am certain of that."

Chasan smiled. "Then what?"

"Saint Peter, the whole hierarchy, upper management,

religious sham." His own words surprised him; saying that out loud felt as great as it did awful.

Chasan stared, then he blinked. He opened his mouth, promptly closed it again. "Sham?"

"Yes, it means fake."

"I know what it means." He shook his head. "I'm just not sure I . . . agree."

Nathaniel felt a sharp pang of hurt. "I didn't think you'd understand."

Chasan squeezed Nathaniel's hands. "Then help me understand. Explain why you feel this way. I'm not saying the way you feel is wrong. It's valid. The way you feel *is* valid. I just need you to tell me. Help me understand."

Nathaniel shrugged. "I just hate how removed they are. It makes me so angry! I know I avoided coming to Earth for a long time. But I oversee Hell. I see every day how much they're failing the humans. They sit up there and think reading reports and statistics and strategies and having think-tanks is working. But it's not. They have no clue. They never have. They have angels who do all the dirty work for them, and we file reports, and upper management calls it a win." He growled in frustration. "It's not a win. People die. Kids, little kids, Chase. And do you think all the gods even care?"

"They all die," Chasan murmured. "That's what humans do. You can't save them from that. You can't change that. Mortality is . . ."

"Brutal."

"Yes. But that's what also makes it beautiful."

Nathaniel shook his head. "I can't do that. I can't be like you and see the world that way."

"No one ever expects you to be like me. The way you see the world is uniquely you. Don't change a thing."

He groaned. "You have a perfect answer for everything."

"No I don't. I've just spent a lot of years with humans. I've lived a thousand lifetimes. I've learned that nothing is constant. Nothing with humans is forever. Not even for angels."

"What doesn't last forever for us?" Nathaniel asked. "Immortality rules a lot out on that one."

"The stars," he replied. "Not even the stars last forever, my love. They die too. New ones are born, the cycle goes on."

Nathaniel frowned at their joined hands. "They need to walk among the humans, spend some time down here. All of them, regardless of title or rank. They should see the ramifications of what they cause. The wars that are fought in their name, the families torn apart, the children and babies who are murdered in the name of whatever god . . ." Nathaniel choked up. His eyes burned with tears. "They should meet the child who was sacrificed to her father's god for the price of rain. They should have seen the light in her eyes fade when she learned of her fate."

"Oh, Nathaniel," Chasan said, pulling him into his arms. "My love."

He let his tears fall. "Why do they get to sit up there with their wings and halos while their loyal subjects suffer? It's not right, Chase. It's not fair."

"I remember now," he said gently. "When you followed me back to Heaven to stop me from breaking the bond. You told Peter he should be doing more work on the ground. I should have realized there was more to that."

"I'm just not sure I believe in it anymore," Nathaniel finally admitted. He sat up then and met Chasan's gaze. "I don't know what that means for me as an angel. I can't imagine it will go over too well, and that will invariably affect you now too." He shrugged again. "What's the procedure for when an angel loses their faith? I'm sure there's a subclause for that subclause somewhere."

Chasan put his fingers to Nathaniel's chin and lifted his face for a soft kiss. "We tell upper management they need to reassess their strategic planning because it's not functional anymore. They need to see the world firsthand, not read about it in reports." He smiled. "You didn't lose your faith, my love. They lost it. And we'll be sure to tell them they need to earn it back."

Nathaniel's eyes welled with tears. "You mean that?"

Chasan nodded. "Of course I do. Because you know what? You're right. It's about time they put some feet on the ground once in a while." He cupped Nathaniel's face and kissed him again.

"I don't know what I did to deserve you."

Chasan nudged his nose to Nathaniel's. "You were just you."

Although they were on the sofa and it wasn't the most comfortable place for it, Nathaniel snuggled into his spot against Chasan's neck, and he was soon wrapped up in two strong arms. "Thank you."

"You're so very welcome."

Nathaniel sighed, and he was so comfortable and safe, he could have closed his eyes and fallen asleep. But then he remembered. "Oh. Your turn now," he said, sitting up. "You have to tell me who you saw in the church."

Chasan began with, "I can't be absolutely certain."

"But you saw what you saw."

He nodded. "I saw Leliel and Ahura."

Nathaniel had to think for a second. "Angels? Peter's angels? Aren't they like secret service or something?"

Chasan gave a slight nod. "Last I heard."

"What were they doing in the church?"

"I don't know. They were off the side of the altar, in the dark. It was hard to see them clearly, but when I was talking to the priest, I saw them watching me."

Anger rolled down Nathaniel's spine. "Watching you? Oh, let me tell you, they better not have been." He stood up and rolled his shoulders. "Let's go back there right now. I'd like to have a little chat with Leliel."

Chasan stood as well, but he took Nathaniel's hand and sent a wave of calm through him. "Stop. They'll be long gone by now."

He seethed. "What aren't they telling us?"

"I don't know. But I have to wonder . . . I thought you were the assignment, and now I'm thinking, maybe it's us?"

"But why? We did the twin-flame thing! Heaven can get off our case now and leave us alone." He was still angry, but he no longer wanted to rearrange Leliel's halo. Well, he probably would if he saw Leliel right now, but he didn't want to track him down to do it. "Can we call Zophiel? He might know more."

"I'm sure he knows more than he's letting on," Chasan said, pulling out his phone. He dialed just as the elevator dinged and the doors opened.

Zophiel and Raguel stepped out. "No need to call, we're already here."

Nathaniel groaned. "Can you hear everything we do?"

"Yes," Raguel answered with a wink.

Nathaniel was horrified. "Oh, for the love of—"

"Zophiel," Chasan said, standing up. "Why were Leliel and Ahura watching us?"

Zophiel's smile faded. "What? What do you mean they're watching *you*?"

"When I went into the church on West Seventy-First Street, they were there. I swear it was them."

Zophiel shot Raguel a quizzical look, but Raguel shrugged. "I know nothing."

"Peter never mentioned them," Zophiel said sincerely. "He never mentioned another team. He told me to choose one other angel to come with me and Zachareal and Abraxos as backup, but that's it."

"What else did he say?" Chasan pressed.

"About what?" Zophiel asked.

Nathaniel took a step closer. "Stop with the games, Zophiel. The only reason Leliel would watch Chasan was if something was wrong. I'm sick of being kept in the dark on this. I think it's about time we paid Saint Peter another visit. I'm done with the lies and the subterfuge."

"Look." Zophiel put his hands up. "You know I can't divulge information I'm sworn to keep secret. You know that."

Chasan stood beside Nathaniel, a united front. "So tell us what you can."

Zophiel whispered, "And if Leliel and Ahura are listening?"

Nathaniel put his hands out and yelled, "Then let them hear me. Come show your faces."

They waited for a moment. Nothing happened, not that Nathaniel expected it to.

Zophiel sighed. "I was told not to say anything. Actually, it was an order. I wish I could, but I can't."

"Who gave the order?" Chasan asked.

Zophiel rolled his eyes, but Nathaniel didn't need him to answer. He already knew. "Saint Peter." He turned to Chasan. "See what I mean?"

He gave a nod. "I'm really beginning to, yes."

"See what?" Zophiel asked, looking back and forth between them.

"Nothing," Nathaniel replied. "Tell me, are you two going back any time soon, or do you have to stick around until this assignment is over?"

"Until it's over," Zophiel answered. "And look, guys. I wish I could help. I really like you both, and I don't know what other shit is going down. But we're on your side, okay?"

Nathaniel wasn't all that placated, but Chasan gave a nod. "Thank you," he said. "And thank you for coming to speak to us. We do feel very alone out here, so knowing you're close by is a comfort."

"We're never far away, okay?" Raguel offered.

Nathaniel huffed. "We have no clue what we're supposed to be doing. We were given no details, no specifics." He looked to Chasan and said, "We have each other, and that's it."

"Maybe that's part of their plan," Raguel said. He put both hands up, palms forward. "Now I don't know any specifics. I'm just here for Zophiel. But it seems to me that maybe throwing you together and leaving you to sort every-thing out is part of their master plan. And it's not a terrible plan," he said, smiling. "I mean, you're together. No matter what else they get you to do, you do it together. And at least they won't separate you like they did to us."

That deflated Nathaniel's anger a little. "True, and I am grateful for being with Chasan. Though honestly, if anyone tried to separate us now, I'd part them from their wings."

Zophiel and Raguel both stared, unsure if Nathaniel was being serious, but Chasan laughed. "And I would help you do it, my love," Chasan added.

"Okay, so on that note," Zophiel said, all but dragging

Raguel with him back to the elevator. "You two have a good night. Though I know you will." He cleared his throat. "Uh, because we've had to surveil you guys all week."

"It'll be a great night," Raguel said with a laugh, as they stepped into the elevator. He poked his head out. "And I want to thank you both for the . . . mood it puts us in."

Nathaniel picked up the closest thing he could reach and threw it at the elevator doors, but they closed just in the nick of time. He realized a little too late that he'd opted to launch the iPad, and not only did it dent the wall, but it fell to the floor in pieces, the screen shattered.

"You have no idea how much I want to swear right now," he mumbled.

And then, to make matters worse, the iPad reappeared on the table, spinning with sparkles, the screen brand-new. The dent in the wall magically fixed. No, not magically. Angelically.

Chasan's phone beeped with a message from Zophiel. "You're welcome."

"I hate him," Nathaniel grumbled.

"No you don't," Chasan said, his voice light and sweet.

Nathaniel sighed. No he didn't. Well, he didn't hate Zophiel *much*. "I hate that he still has his powers, and he can still swear. The fact he can and I can't is some ripe old cow patties right there."

Chasan laughed. "You mean bullshit?"

He groaned. "The fact you can swear and choose not to is a travesty."

Chasan pulled Nathaniel in for a kiss. Nathaniel slid his arms around Chasan's waist and relished the feeling of serenity he got from Chasan's touch. "You know what I'm thinking?" Chasan asked.

"That the real travesty is I wasn't fast enough with

throwing the iPad. I need to work on my reflexes. And my aim. I hit the wall instead of the elevator."

Chasan chuckled. "Nope. What I was thinking is that it's been a long week and it's been a long day, and I'm ready for a perfect night."

"A perfect night?"

"Yep. I'm thinking we should run a bath for the both of us, we should get naked, and we should go to bed. We don't need to go anywhere tomorrow, and I'm thinking we should stay in bed all day. Maybe watch some movies, or maybe not leave our bed until Monday morning. Whatever the mission is supposed to be can wait until Monday."

"Mmm," Nathaniel hummed, and he enjoyed the warm thrill that ran down his spine. "Yes please." Then he remembered something. "Oh, and don't forget your bag of candy."

Chasan grinned. "Even better. You know what would be perfect to eat while we're in the bath?" he asked. He let go of Nathaniel and rifled through the huge bag of candy, pulling out a yellow packet victoriously. "Peanut M&M's."

He grabbed Nathaniel's hand and dragged him toward the bathroom, and ten minutes later, Nathaniel could confirm this was indeed the perfect night. He could also confirm that peanut M&M's were the best thing since . . . well, actually, since they learned how to refine sugar and emulsify chocolate from cocoa beans. But the history of confectionary aside, Nathaniel was impressed.

The bathtub was huge enough for Nathaniel to lay with his back to Chasan's front, bubbly water lapping up to their chests. Chasan had his arm around Nathaniel and fed M&M's to him, and Nathaniel loved every second of it.

He had no idea love could be like this.

Just the simple, complete joy of being with someone.

They went to bed and made love, and they fell asleep in

each other's arms. Chasan made good on his promise to stay in bed all day Saturday. They only ventured out of their bedroom to shower and eat or summon more takeout, or to cuddle on the couch and watch TV, and then to make out on the couch, which became sex on the couch, which led to more sex in bed.

Sunday started out much the same way, and while Chasan took a nap, Nathaniel cut up some fruit. He bounced on the bed to wake Chasan up, then proceeded to hand-feed pieces to him. Nathaniel was very well aware that Chasan was eyeing him weirdly, probably wondering what had gotten into him. When Nathaniel slid the empty plate onto the bedside table, their kisses were sticky but sweet. Nathaniel straddled him, though it wasn't sexual. Nathaniel was sure they'd had as many orgasms as human bodies would allow. For a few hours at least.

"Let's go do something," he suggested. "Outside."

"Outside?"

"Yep. It's Sunday afternoon, the sun is out, and the park is full of people, and there are dogs and ducks. Let's go for a walk," Nathaniel suggested. Then he made a face. "Oh, can you walk? Do you feel okay?"

Chasan burst out laughing. "Yes, I can walk. I feel great. Actually, better than great. Very limber and pliable, if I'm being honest."

Nathaniel snorted out a laugh and kissed up Chasan's back. "Then let's go out and enjoy the last of the sunshine before work next week."

Chasan rolled over, smiling. "You're in a good mood."

"Are you kidding me? I'm in the best mood of my life. I have you, and I've had two days of amazing sex. Oh," he said, kissing the center of Chasan's chest. "And I have you."

Chasan held up two fingers. "You said me twice."

"Some things bear repeating." He rolled off the bed with more energy than seemed possible. But he felt so good. He was just truly happy and it had been soooo long since he'd been without burden. "Shower time. And we should grab something else to eat while we're out for dinner later." He stopped at the door. "Come on, lazybones."

Chasan called out to him. "If I stay in bed, will you come back and join me?"

Smiling, Nathaniel turned the shower on. "Nope. I'll just be in this shower, naked and wet, all by myself then."

Chasan grumbled but soon joined him. Nathaniel washed Chasan's hair for him and laughed when Chasan got suds in his eye. Then they wrestled over the loofah, and Chasan laughed when Nathaniel almost slipped. Naked, soapy wrestling made its way onto Nathaniel's will-try-again list and they were still both smiling like crazy kids in love as they stepped into the elevator to go downstairs.

Chasan fixed Nathaniel's collar and gave him a smiley kiss. "I could get very used to seeing you this happy all the time."

"Well, that's good. Because there's a pretty good chance I will be. If it's just you and me. My mood tends to be a touch choleric when other people are involved."

Chasan chuckled at that. "Do you think when this assignment's over they'll let us just go and do our thing?"

"Pretty sure they won't get a say in it," Nathaniel replied. The doors opened and he took Chasan's hand as they walked through the lobby and out into the warm spring day.

They walked directly across the road and into Central Park. There were people on bikes, people jogging, walking, laughing. The sky was blue, the entire park was green, flowers were in bloom. It was the definition of a perfect day.

Another dog spotted Nathaniel and pulled on her leash so hard, the human holding it had to let go. The pit bull mix was brown and white and wore a pink collar, and she barreled toward Nathaniel and was wagging her tail and doing happy leaps, and he knelt down to give her the petting she deserved. "Hey, beautiful girl. I know your face."

She licked his cheek, still wagging and doing her happy trot, just as the human owner got there. "Oh gosh, I'm so sorry. I don't know what got into her. She never does this, I'm really sorry." Then the owner took the leash. "Daisy, what on earth has gotten into you?"

"I have that effect on dogs," Nathaniel said. "Not her fault at all." He knelt back down and put his hands on Daisy's face. "You need to go back with your momma. I'll see you again soon enough, pretty angel."

The woman probably thought that was a weird thing to say, and from the way she pulled Daisy away, that was exactly what she thought. But Nathaniel didn't care.

Chasan laughed as he pulled him along the path. "You're incredible."

"What? I can't help it if dogs recognize me."

"They don't just recognize you. They love you."

Nathaniel sighed. "Well, apparently I'm a lovable guy."

"Yes, you are."

They walked to the first pond and stood on the bridge for a while. Then they walked to the lake so they could find a spot to sit and watch the ducks. Nathaniel leaned against Chasan as they enjoyed the sun, and Nathaniel could never remember being happier. He was even struck by how wondrous the world was and how good life was.

"You know," he said. "I feel as though I have a lot to catch up on."

Chasan kissed the side of his head. "Catch up on what?"

"Life on Earth. I mean, look at those butterflies by the reeds. I can't ever remember noticing those before."

Chasan chuckled warmly in his ear. "I think you're just seeing the world through new eyes."

Nathaniel sat up and turned to face him. He took Chasan's hand. "That's true. I am. And I still think there needs to be some major changes to upper management and how the company is run. And I do love my work in the Hell Department and in the Canine Division . . ."

Chasan frowned. "Why do I feel there's a but coming?"

Nathaniel threaded their fingers and smiled at him. "But I think I want to stay human for a while."

CHAPTER SIXTEEN

CHASAN

"HUMAN?" Chasan didn't mean to squawk the word, but that's what he did.

Nathaniel laughed again. "I think so. With you, of course. I mean, this is kind of great, isn't it? And I know not every assignment is going to be in some ritzy apartment with a great job. But I figure if I'm with you, then it's all good with me."

"You want to do more assignments?"

"Yep. I guess I shouldn't just show up back in Peter's office and demand they all do missions when I haven't done them either." He shrugged and gave that cute smile that Chasan couldn't get enough of. "So until they sort out the mess they've created, and until there are some major changes in management structure and placement, I don't want to be a part of it. I'd rather be down here, with you."

Chasan wasn't sure what to say to that.

"Is that okay?" Nathaniel asked. "Because, honestly, Chase, I'll be wherever you are. If you want to go back for a while, then that's what we'll do."

Chasan smiled at how Nathaniel now considered them as a *we* instead of separate people. "I'll do as many missions with you as you want. Like you said, it doesn't matter where we are, as long as we're together."

Nathaniel sighed happily and spun back around, this time laying down his head on Chasan's thigh. Chasan ran his fingers through Nathaniel's hair and he closed his eyes at the touch. "I'm getting used to this human body," he said. "I don't feel anxious as much, which I'm pretty sure is thanks to you."

Chasan stopped stroking his hair. "Or it could just be that you finally began talking about stuff and how you feel."

He opened his eyes and met Chasan's gaze. "Or it could be you."

"Or it could be—"

"Or it could be you!" he said again, louder this time.

Chasan chuckled. "Or it could be me."

Nathaniel smiled and closed his eyes again. He looked so happy, so peaceful, Chasan played with the hair at his temples, eliciting a warm hum from Nathaniel. "I could stay like this forever," he murmured.

And just then, another dog—a schnauzer this time—came bounding over and launched itself at Nathaniel. It was jumping all over him, licking him and butt-wiggling, and Nathaniel, surprised at first, was soon petting him.

"Buddy! Buddy, what the heck are you doing?" A guy came running over, a horrified expression on his face. "I'm so sorry! I'm so sorry!" He grabbed Buddy and reclipped his leash.

Nathaniel sat up. "Nah, it's okay. I have this effect on dogs." He grinned at Buddy and gave his forehead a ruffle. "Look at you! You're the goodest boy."

The guy pulled Buddy away, apologizing nonstop. And when Chasan looked around, he saw a few other dogs looking over. "Okay, I think we should leave."

"What, why?"

He nodded toward the other dogs. "Let's go for a walk."

"Yeah, probably a good idea." He jumped to his feet and pulled Chasan to his.

Chasan laughed as they headed up over the next bridge. "Those dogs just love you!"

"I greet them, play with them," he replied. "Dogs have the best souls. And it's a downright shame they don't live as long as people."

Chasan let go of Nathaniel's hand so he could put his arm around his shoulder. His heart swelled with love. "You are amazing."

They kept strolling, managing to avoid any more dogs, just taking their time. If Nathaniel felt like he'd missed out on a lot, then taking time to appreciate every little thing seemed like a great idea.

Then seeing Times Square in the early evening light seemed like a good idea. It wasn't a long walk, and it allowed Nathaniel to take in parts of the city he hadn't seen. He took in the hustle and bustle and lights of Times Square with wide-eyed wonder; something just two weeks ago Chasan was certain Nathaniel wouldn't have coped with.

But he could tell Nathaniel had had enough of the crowds because he was trying to dodge people and his anxiety was on the rise. "How about we head toward home and find somewhere quieter for an early dinner?"

"Yes please," he said, clearly relieved.

"Come on, this way." Chasan led him along Seventh Avenue, and they began a slow walk toward the park, toward home. People were rushing home, or rushing out, or just rushing. But not them. They took their time, looking at buildings and trees, at the cars and cabs.

"Do you ever get the urge to tell them to slow down?" Nathaniel asked. "Does every city move this fast?"

Chasan chuckled. "No, New York is different. It's not the busiest, but it's one of them. I'll take you to Tokyo or Mumbai."

"I'd like that. When this is over, you can take me anywhere you like."

"Well, depending what Head Office says, sure."

Nathaniel laughed. "Like a holiday. Do you think they have some tropical island somewhere? With just a cabin and nothing and no one for miles and miles?"

"A holiday?"

"Well, it's more of a honeymoon, don't you think?"

Chasan stopped walking; his heart almost stopped beating. "A honeymoon?"

"Well, yeah." Nathaniel blushed, but he held up his left hand. "We have the rings to prove it. And we did just technically swear our twin flames to each other. That's kind of the same thing. Only better."

"Only better, indeed." Chasan put his arm around Nathaniel's shoulder and they started walking again. "How about we go straight home? We can summon some dinner. I've had enough people and would much rather be at home with you."

"Sounds good to me."

And they were almost home . . . just two blocks shy. "Oh hey, it's the bodega," Nathaniel said. "We should get some paper plates for our tiger masks for class."

"Can't we get them tomorrow?"

"It's right there," he said. "And they have peanut M&M's!"

Chasan rolled his eyes. "Okay, okay."

The bodega itself had several aisles of groceries; the back wall was fridges of sodas and milk. They'd only made it as far as the first aisle when a small but familiar face appeared.

"Mr. Angelo!" Marlow said, waving. "Mr. Bellomo!"

"Hey you," Nathaniel replied, smiling at her. He looked up for Marlow's mom and she was grabbing a carton of milk.

"Hi," Marlow's mom said, giving them a smile.

"Did you have a good weekend?" Nathaniel asked them both.

Marlow nodded. "Mom and Dad said we can start looking for a new dog. A rescue one from the pound."

"Next month," her mom said like she'd said that a hundred times. She smiled at Nathaniel and Chasan. "We thought a few weeks would help."

"I think that's a great idea," Nathaniel said.

"Mr. Angelo," Marlow said, taking Nathaniel's hand, "Mom said I could get a treat! Help me choose!"

Nathaniel went willingly. "Well, I happen to know that peanut M&M's are the best candy ever."

Marlow's mom smiled at Chasan. "My name's Tammy, by the way. Thank you for how you guys handled the death of our old dog. Phil, my husband, said you were brilliant with Marlow, and she's dealt with it really well."

"Ah, that was all Nathaniel," Chasan replied. "He's a natural."

"All the kids love him," she added.

"Yep, kids and dogs. They seek him out." Chasan's line

of sight went to Nathaniel, where he and Marlow were at the counter trying to decide which candy Marlow wanted.

Leliel appeared, wearing a gray suit, and ever so casually walked over to Nathaniel. He made eye contact with Chasan but took something out of his inside breast pocket and slid it into Nathaniel's shirt.

Nathaniel turned to face him, but with a pat on Nathaniel's chest and a quick glance back to Chasan, Leliel was gone.

Tammy was still talking, looking in the direction of Marlow and Nathaniel, and she never batted an eyelid. *Could she not see Leliel just now?*

Chasan looked around the store. The clerk was oblivious. No one seemed to notice him . . .

No human, anyway.

Nathaniel's gaze met Chasan's. They were an aisle apart, not a word spoken, but they both knew.

This was it.

"Chasan," Tammy said. "What's wrong?"

He grabbed her arm. "We need to leave."

But it was too late.

Because just then, two guys walked in, each of them holding a handgun. One hit the emergency door lock, the other yelled, "Get on the floor, now! Everyone get on the floor!"

Someone screamed, someone cried out in fear. Chasan pulled Tammy to the floor with him. Nathaniel scooped up Marlow and slid to the floor at the end of the aisle.

"Holy shit," Tammy cried. "Marlow!"

"Nathaniel has her," Chasan said, holding her back.

"Everyone stay down!" the guy with the gun yelled. "Stay down and shut the fuck up. Everyone put their hands on their head. Now!" Everyone did. Someone at the back of the store sobbed.

The second man walked up along the front of the aisles. "No one speaks, no one moves, and no one gets hurt."

Chasan could feel Nathaniel's fear. It swirled with his own, thick and tinged with something else.

Acknowledgment and acceptance.

Oh no, no, no.

Chasan shook his head, but Nathaniel simply looked at him. Tammy was crying beside him; she had her hands on her head, but her whole body was trembling. Chasan wanted to put his arm around her but didn't dare take his hands from his head. His human heart beat way too fast; his blood pounded in his ears.

Nathaniel's eyes were wide with fear but he kept Marlow tucked into his side, half behind him, shielding her eyes and hiding her from the bad guys, protecting her.

The gunmen had the cashier empty the cash drawer, but this wasn't just about the money. If it was, they wouldn't have locked the doors. They would've taken the money already and been long gone.

No, this was about something else.

"Get comfortable," the first gunman said. "You're gonna be here a while."

The first police siren arrived, then another. Tires screeched outside.

And then Marlow began to cry. Nathaniel took one hand off his head to put around her. "Shhh," he urged her. "It's okay."

The gunman came into the aisle and, seeing it was just a child, groaned. "Shut the kid up."

"She's scared," Nathaniel said. "She can't help it. You could let her go."

"No one leaves!" The gunman yelled at his friend, something about plans and timing and how he said they should have waited until it was fully dark, but he stalked out of the aisle.

Chasan met Nathaniel's gaze, and he tried to convey a warning with his eyes not to draw attention to himself. Chasan could feel how Nathaniel's fear had ramped up, and he had no doubt Nathaniel could feel his. Beneath his hammering heart, the fire in his chest roared.

"This is the NYPD," a male voice on a bullhorn said. "Come out with your hands up." He called the two men by name, which meant they were well-known to them, and as that was happening, Nathaniel took his hand off his head.

He slowly reached into his shirt and pulled out what Leliel had given him. Chasan still couldn't see exactly what it was. It looked silver, but it was thin, a bit larger in size than a playing card. Leliel had put it over Nathaniel's heart, and now Nathaniel very carefully put it in Marlow's vest. Whatever it was, Leliel had given it to protect him. And he'd just given it away.

Chasan shook his head, but Nathaniel smiled. "This is it," he whispered. "This is why we're here."

"No it's not," Chasan hissed back at him. He shook his head again, and his twin flame grew scorching hot. *Nathaniel, no . . .*

The gunman came back. "I said shut up! Not a word!"

Nathaniel pulled Marlow in closer, protectively, shielding her from harm. "Let her go. She's just a child. Let the child and her mother go. They don't need to be here."

"Nathaniel," Chasan hissed. "Shut up."

The police were blaring on the bullhorn again, and the two gunmen started arguing; tensions were high, and things were escalating badly. The first gunman began to pace, ranting about how they were targets and needed better shielding.

The second gunman stomped into the aisle and held a gun to Nathaniel's head, but reached down and grabbed Marlow's arm. "We have shields," he said. Marlow screamed as he pulled her up and Tammy cried out, but Nathaniel got to his feet. He grabbed Marlow and yanked her out of the man's grasp. He put her behind him, putting himself between them.

"Take me," Nathaniel said. "Leave the child alone."

The gunman pointed his pistol directly at Nathaniel's head. "Do you have a death wish, asshole?"

"No. But the little girl is innocent," he replied. His voice was calm and neutral. "I won't have you sacrifice her for your god. If you want someone, take me."

"The only place I'll take you to is Hell," the man sneered.

"Believe me, I will see you there," Nathaniel growled. Then he let go of Marlow and she ran to Chasan and Tammy. Tammy wrapped her up in her arms and Marlow made a keening sound, terrified out of her mind.

Chasan couldn't take his eyes off Nathaniel.

"Get on your knees, asshole," the man said, his gun pressed to Nathaniel's forehead. Chasan's heart was in his throat, but all he could feel from Nathaniel was calm.

He was in front of the counter now, on his knees, and his hands on his head. The police would most definitely be able to see him, but the two armed men stalked like caged tigers.

The first one was now ranting, mumbling to himself how this was a bad idea.

The second one was calmer, more in control and in charge, but still agitated. He talked about their plan and how they'd come too far for it to end now. Chasan couldn't see the glass doors at the front, but the men began to yell for whoever it was on the outside to move away from the doors.

Then there was a large bang, like someone was hitting something metal from the outside, but Chasan couldn't see what was going on.

He couldn't take his eyes off Nathaniel.

Nathaniel was watching the doors, his hands still planted on his head. There was another bang, as though the police were trying to break into something . . .

"They're busting open the fuse box. They're gonna open the doors. Marty, they're gonna open the doors," the first guy said, panicking.

Marty put the gun to Nathaniel's head. "Open the doors and he dies!"

Then someone's phone rang, loud and startling, and the first gunman spun around. Someone at the back of the store wailed. Marty yelled over the top of it all, and the police bullhorn boomed more orders into an already tense room.

The first gunman screamed for quiet and he fired two shots into the ceiling. It was deafening and frightening, and Chasan flinched at the noise as Marlow screamed. But then the police smashed through the doors and the two gunmen turned and fired.

Everything was so loud, until it wasn't.

Everything seemed to be falling in on the world, until it wasn't.

Nathaniel was caught in the crossfire, brave and valiant, alive.

Until he wasn't.

Then everything went quiet. The world stopped turning. Chasan's world stopped cold. In that very moment, all sound and color ceased to exist.

Police broke through, guns drawn, yelling. People were screaming and running, Marlow and Tammy were crying, but for Chasan, there was only silence.

Silence, slow-motion. Drained of color, empty.

Nathaniel lay on the linoleum floor. Slumped but twisted as though the bullets had made him dance. His open, unseeing eyes stared straight at Chasan. Darkness pooled out from underneath him.

Chasan tried to think. He tried to move. There was nothing.

People rushed past him, between them, yet Chasan couldn't take his eyes from Nathaniel. How, for that split second, he looked peaceful in the chaos, how his hand was on the floor, his fingers curled just so. Then sound and movement hit Chasan like a sledgehammer, everything coming at him so fast and loud, and he scrambled across the floor toward him. Touching his face, the dark stains on his shirt, the hole in his chest.

He begged him, he pleaded. "No, no, no. Please, Nathaniel. Not now. Not ever. We were supposed to have forever."

But Nathaniel's unseeing eyes stared straight past him.

Chasan sobbed and pulled Nathaniel's lifeless body into his arms. It was never supposed to be like this. Chasan sobbed and screamed, but he made no sound. He clung to Nathaniel, and he saw then, the light in his eyes was gone.

Paramedics knelt beside them and Chasan watched as one of them looked to the other and shook their head.

There were more flashing lights and more police cars arrived en masse. Officers came to Chasan, asking him, "Sir? Sir? Are you okay?"

But he couldn't answer them. Because he was not okay.

Nathaniel was dead.

And like a fault line across Chasan's chest, something cracked inside him. A discernible snap, and somewhere behind his ribs, a tiny flame burst into life.

He sucked in a breath and the flame burned a little brighter.

It was warm and beckoning, like a lighthouse in a storm. The flame grew bigger, a blue fire within him, burning white-hot and gaining power. He could feel the flames lick all the way down his arms to his hands, and Chasan knew what he had to do.

He stood up, he stepped away from Nathaniel and the paramedics, and he walked out. Officers tried to stop him, but whatever they saw in his eyes made them step back. And he walked out of the store, out of the chaos, and with each step, the fire burned.

Zophiel was beside him and Raguel. Then Leliel and Ahura. Not to stop him but to go with him. To surround him, to protect him. They formed an arrow as they ate up the sidewalk, and without a word between them, they knew where Chasan was headed.

The church on West Seventy-First Street.

Chasan pushed the front doors open with a power no human had seen. Father James was standing in the aisle, alarmed and cautious. He looked down at Chasan's blood-stained hands, the blood on his shirt. "Can I help you?"

Chasan stepped inside the holy ground, and the fire within him soared. Blue fire glowed, and right there, in front of this human, Chasan's wings expanded from his shoulders.

Father James gasped and did the sign of the cross. He looked on with wonder and righteous fear. Chasan had probably broken every rule, but he did not care.

No, Chasan didn't care at all. He burned.

He was wrath and fury. He was rage personified, and he burned brighter as he walked down the aisle toward the altar. He held his hands out. "By the power of Heaven!" he roared. The stained-glass windows shook. "Michael and Peter, hear me."

His words echoed off the walls, followed by silence. Deafening, unanswered silence.

Chasan's fire raged and he roared, "Hear me now or so help me, I will burn the world to the ground!"

Michael appeared at the altar in a flash of light, wings and all. Father James gasped again, but Michael took one look at Zophiel and Raguel, at their grave faces, then he turned to Chasan. He saw the blood, the horror, and who was missing.

"Oh no," he whispered. And with no regard for poor Father James or the three police officers who had followed them into the church or how they would explain what they were about to see, Michael simply lifted his hand and snapped his fingers, and in a shower of sparks, all the angels were gone.

CHASAN FOUND himself in Saint Peter's office. Saint Peter was grave-faced. Everyone was. Ridwan, Barachiel, Tennin, all had their heads down, and Peter stood up when he saw Chasan.

Chasan was burning blue fire, his wings, his chest, and his fingers aflame with rage and grief, and everyone was shocked when they saw him.

Saint Peter put his hand up. "Chasan."

"You!" Chasan roared as he leaped in a blur of blue fire and knocked Saint Peter to the ground. The heavens cracked with the sound of impact, tables flew apart, and angels scattered away. Chasan held Saint Peter's robe, his hands fists of rage. "You took him from me! You give him to me only to take him away! You knew, and you didn't stop it!"

Michael and Zophiel pulled Chasan back, and Krishna helped Saint Peter to his feet. But Chasan was too angry, he was seething rage and heartbreak, and the energy of emotion coiled up tight in his chest as they restrained him. It coiled tighter and tighter until he couldn't stand it and he let it explode out of him.

Michael and Zophiel flew backward from the impact, and Chasan roared again with the power. No one had seen this kind of power, this kind of rage before.

Other angels appeared beside Saint Peter, ready to defend him, but he put his hand up to call for calm. "I didn't take him, Chasan. He still belongs to you." He swallowed hard; his hair flopped messily down onto his forehead. He was pale; his hands trembled. "You feel different, don't you? More powerful. Chasan, stop and feel it."

Chasan's wings flicked out and his hands were claws. He shook with a power he had never known. What Saint Peter was saying made sense, because he did feel different. He felt powerful and mighty, but he couldn't get his mind in order. He was too struck by grief and rage. "Nathaniel . . ."

"Nathaniel's fine."

"I held his lifeless body, his unseeing eyes," Chasan whispered harshly. He looked down at himself. "I am covered in his blood!"

"The blood of his human body," Saint Peter replied. "He's fine, Chasan."

"I watched him die!"

"Feel the power in your blood," Saint Peter said calmly. "Feel the fire in your chest. He's not dead."

Chasan shook his head and rolled his shoulders. His wings extended to their full breadth. They felt stronger, bigger. He did feel different. He felt as though he had lightning and thunder in his bones. Like he could cause havoc with just a flick of his hand. "What is this?"

"It's the twinning of souls," Saint Peter said. "You can't be apart now."

Blue fire crackled in his chest. *Nathaniel.* "Where is he?"

"Gabriel's bringing him in," Saint Peter replied.

What? Gabriel?

"He's been in to see The Boss. Time works differently here, you know that," Saint Peter said. "Chasan, believe me. I would never dare part you now. It would split the heavens apart."

Chasan shook his head. "No. *I* would split the heavens apart. Where is he? Where is Nathaniel?"

Just then the double doors opened, and there stood Gabriel, all regal-like with his white-and-gold wings, though he looked somewhat bewildered. For behind him stood another angel. He wore black and his wings were burnt umber with blackened tips. Where Chasan was blue and white, Nathaniel was red and orange fire, aflame with power and glory, and he was magnificent.

Nathaniel.

The relief Chasan felt stole the breath from his lungs, and Nathaniel grinned. Nathaniel flew in to collect Chasan in a crushing hug, their arms and wings wrapping around the other, and they were consumed in a bruising kiss. But something else happened. Something even more amazing, more unique . . . Their internal fires—Chasan's blue,

Nathaniel's red—spiraled and intertwined above their heads.

Their souls entwined, the twin flames merged as one. A flash of light and the sound of harps boomed around them. Bliss and contentment, love and understanding detonated throughout all of Heaven. It was a first, a one and only for all of time.

"Amazing," Gabriel whispered.

Everyone around them was clearly in awe of what they were witnessing, their gazes fixed above them. So Nathaniel and Chasan looked up too and saw the joining of their eternal flames. Chasan laughed, and Nathaniel kissed him. The flames burst higher, sparks danced down on the room.

"Wonderful," Ridwan said with a laugh.

"And you had your doubts," Tien said to Saint Peter.

"Air and fire. The perfect dichotomy," he murmured, disbelievingly.

Chasan put his hands to Nathaniel's face. "I thought I lost you."

"Never," Nathaniel replied. "Never again. There is nothing on Heaven or Earth that can separate us now."

"What happened?" Chasan asked, both to Nathaniel and Saint Peter.

"He needed to reset his soul," Saint Peter said. "He saved that child today."

"There was nothing wrong with his soul!" Chasan said. His fire surged with his words.

"Hey," Nathaniel whispered. "Take a breath for me."

Chasan calmed immediately, and Nathaniel laughed at how the tables had turned.

"There's nothing wrong with your soul," Chasan murmured, nudging his forehead to Nathaniel's temple. "There never was."

"I feel renewed, Chase," he whispered. "Not just my soul, but my faith. I spoke to The Boss."

"You did?" *No one speaks to The Boss!*

"Sure did. We cleared a few things up." He grinned but studied Chasan's face, the blood on his shirt. "Oh, Chase. I'm sorry you had to go through that. That must have been terrifying for you."

Chasan nodded, overwhelmed with relief and love. He didn't want to think about watching Nathaniel get shot. "You told me you loved me."

"I do," he whispered. "I love you, Chasan."

Nathaniel pulled Chasan tight against him, feeling every valley and plane of muscle and strength. Their angel bodies felt everything so much more intensely. But Chasan pulled back. "I'm covered in blood . . ."

Nathaniel grinned, and with a snap of his fingers, Chasan's shirt disappeared. "Oh, how I've missed my powers."

Chasan didn't care that he was half-naked in Saint Peter's office in front of half of Heaven. He laughed. "I never want to lose you again," Chasan murmured before kissing him with very little regard for their audience.

Someone cleared their throat. Anael held up her hands in surrender. "Yeah, okay guys. I may be the angel of passion. But for the record, that's not me. That's all them."

"Maybe we should take this elsewhere." Nathaniel smiled against Chasan's lips.

Chasan kept Nathaniel tight in his arms and grinned. "Wait!" Nathaniel said, looking at Saint Peter. He held up his left hand. "The wedding ring. I'm keeping it. And Chasan's keeping his."

Saint Peter opened his mouth but decided on a shrug. Chasan laughed, and with an explosion of energy and light, they shot upwards through the ceiling like magic, their wings working in tandem. As one.

"DON'T BREAK ANYTHING!" Saint Peter called out after them. He sighed happily, in what he was sure felt like a proud-dad moment.

Zophiel laughed. "They're gonna break a lot of things." Then he put his hands on his hips. "And just so you know, what just happened down there on Earth was not cool." He pointed his finger at the hierarchy. "That was bloody disgraceful, that's what that was. Not to mention the terror that little girl just witnessed. And how are all those kids gonna cope with losing their favorite teachers? Did you ever stop to think about that?"

"We can organize a recon team," Leliel replied. "We can send in replicas; the kids won't even know."

"That little girl will know!" Zophiel said. "She just watched him die!"

"The new Nathaniel will just wear an arm sling and we can make everyone think it wasn't as bad as it was," Saint Peter said, floundering a little. "Wave a little angel dust and they'll be none the wiser."

"That's not good enough," Zophiel said. "Nathaniel was right. This whole office is a sham. You all need to start walking the walk and putting in some time down there."

Saint Peter looked about ready to object, but Gabriel spoke. "Ah, that's what Nathaniel and The Boss were just discussing. It's happening, effective immediately. Well," he corrected. "As soon as the memo goes out. All members of the hierarchy will be doing time on Earth in missions and assignments. Nathaniel said you all sit up here too far removed and you need to start spending time with the humans, and The Boss agreed."

The room erupted into discourse, and Zophiel and Raguel backed out of the office, laughing as they went. The vastness of Heaven had a golden glow, and somewhere off in the distance, Nathaniel and Chasan's laughter echoed through the clouds.

EPILOGUE

NATHANIEL

THE HELL DEPARTMENT had a pleasant vibe, Nathaniel admitted. Well, it wasn't pleasant for the inhabitants. At all. But he and Chasan ran the whole show now, and working conditions for the other angels had improved greatly. In fact, conditions had improved for all angels in all departments since his little meeting with The Boss. He never really spoke of what happened in The Boss's office. He'd told Chasan, of course, but it was their secret to keep.

But when it was all said and done, funnily enough it was the Hell Department where Chasan had wanted to work, so that's where they went. Zophiel and Raguel came by all the time, and they joined in on cards nights and movie nights. Beelzebub wanted to have poetry nights, and although Nathaniel would have rather poked his own eye out, he went along with it. Because that's what good managers did. They listened to their team.

Lucifer suggested karaoke sessions, and Nathaniel almost drew the line because Heaven's mercy no, but Chasan had said he thought it was a great idea. And so Hell had a karaoke machine now too. Which, Nathaniel thought, was kind of fitting.

He'd even managed to curb his tendencies to smite everything. It had taken some time, and he did still smite whatever he thought deserved it, but at least now he thought about it before doing it.

Like when the guy who had shot Nathaniel in the bodega finally arrived at the Hell Department, the old Nathaniel would have perhaps played with him as a cat does a mouse. In fact, Chasan wanted to.

But it was Nathaniel who showed restraint. Sure, he made the guy's afterlife exceedingly unpleasant, but he didn't just smite him for smite's sake.

Though this little disclaimer didn't include the religious politician who decided to use his entrance to the Hell Department as a pulpit for denouncing gay people. Nathaniel fucked him up without a second glance.

Small steps.

But his life was better now than he ever could have expected. He was happier, yes, but it was more than that. He was content and complete and confident in his and Chasan's love.

Heaven basked in their union. There was less discourse, less tension. There was an equilibrium now in all things. All levels of management did their part, but the twinning of souls, as the prophets had said, would empower the heavens.

Nathaniel was certain Saint Peter never imagined that meant he'd have to slum it doing assignments on Earth, but equality and equity in all its forms boosted the heavens in unprecedented ways.

Nathaniel was smiling happily as he overlooked his department when Chasan came up behind him, wrapped his arms around him, and kissed the back of his neck. "Are you ready? We have an assignment to wrap up."

They had another special assignment on Earth. Though this one was more of a revisit. "Is it that time already?" Nathaniel asked. "Time on Earth moves so differently as it does in Heaven. It can't have been that long already."

Chasan nodded. "It's been twenty-two years."

It didn't feel like that long at all. "Okay wow. But yes, I'm ready."

THE HOSPITAL WAS BUSY, like all emergency departments in all hospitals in New York City were. They slipped into the room unnoticed where the young woman was sitting on a sofa. She had her head in her hands, exhausted. She'd just come off a thirty-something-hour shift and had managed a few hours' sleep on the doctors' break room sofa. She was also wondering if she'd made the right choice.

Studying medicine, becoming a doctor was more taxing than she'd bargained for. She didn't know if she was cut out for this level of work and stress. She was so sleep-deprived, she didn't know what she was thinking.

"Doctor Marlow Brown?"

She looked up at them, then looked again. "Uh, can I help you?"

"Do you remember us?" Chasan asked. His smile was charming and his tone was melodic.

Marlow looked at them in turn, then shook her head. "It can't be."

"It is," Nathaniel said. "Mr. Angelo and Mr. Bellomo."

She shook her head again and got to her feet. She wasn't

scared. She was fascinated. "How? You haven't aged a day. You still look exactly the same!"

Chasan laughed, and the sound rang like distant bells. "Do you believe in angels?"

She gawped. "No way . . ." She stared, then squinted her eyes shut before staring again as if she couldn't believe what she was seeing. "And you," she said to Nathaniel. "What happened in the bodega . . . You got shot and recovered. What happened was all kind of vague, and the doctors said that what the brain doesn't let you remember is to protect you. And you both taught the class until the end of the year as if everything was fine. But in my dreams, I saw you die. And it was real. I was just a kid, but I knew what I saw. My memories weren't wrong. I saw you die, and it changed my life. You died right there. I saw it. I saw the blood. No one believed me when I said you'd died."

"Yes, I did."

She squinted. "So you did die?"

"Yes, I did."

"So you being here right now . . . ? You're ghosts?"

"Nope. Angels."

"Angels, yeah right." She was cautious and wary, her voice had a tremble. But she believed. "Where are your wings? Don't angels have wings?"

Chasan extended his wings as easy as exhaling. Marlow sank back in her seat; her eyes went comically wide. Nathaniel was glad they were in a hospital, because guessing from her expression, her elevated heart rate and blood-drained face she should probably seek medical treatment.

Nathaniel sat beside her. "We were on a mission."

She stared. "Like the Blues Brothers?"

"Who?" Nathaniel asked.

"Yes," Chasan replied.

Nathaniel didn't know who the Blues Brothers were. "Our mission involved you," he continued. "Indirectly."

Chasan smiled at her. "You were destined to do great things."

"I was?"

"You *are*," Nathaniel corrected.

"Great things? Like what?"

"This afternoon, you're going to meet a sick little girl."

"And that is my great destiny? To save one girl? Guys, I'm a doctor. Shouldn't I save hundreds of people?"

Chasan nodded. "And you will. But this girl is special, and *she* will go on to do amazing things in the science field. She's going to invent a water-making device that will shape how the world uses freshwater."

"So she's some little genius and she's going to come in here incredibly ill and I need to save her?" Marlow blanched. "So, no pressure." Then she put her hand to her forehead. "Oh man. What if . . . what if I get it wrong? I'm barely out of med school! This can't be on my shoulders."

"We don't get to choose our fate," Nathaniel said. "Remember when I put that metal card in your vest? In the bodega?"

Marlow nodded. "I still have it. It sits on my bookcase. People ask me what it is, but I haven't got a clue."

"It's an artifact from the Chimú people in Peru. A small tin plate lined with titanium dioxide to make it very strong. It was given to me by a little girl a long time ago, as an offering to the rain god. Another angel gave it to me that day in the bodega, but it wasn't meant for me. You needed to survive that day, not me, so I gave it to you."

"It's so smooth like it's been worn down, but it's strangely beautiful."

"She would rub it when she prayed for rain," Nathaniel explained. "It once had an impression of the rain god, but it wore down." Nathaniel smiled, and he held out his hand, palm up. In a small flurry of sparkles, the small tin card-sized plate appeared on his hand. "This is it."

Marlow nodded, looking at it. "You took it from my place just now?"

Nathaniel gave her a nudge. "Yep. It's time to pass it on."

"I have to give it to this little girl?"

Nathaniel nodded. "Yes. Well, you have to diagnose her chronic myeloid leukemia first. Rare in kids her age, but treatable if detected early. Her parents will bring her in because she's been sick, just as a precaution. But you'll run a blood test just to be sure. I'm certain you know what to look for." He winked at her. "She'll stay in the hospital for a while, and you'll become great friends. She comes from a farm upstate, and they're experiencing drought at the moment, and while most people pray for rain, she wants to *make* it rain. Give her this. And tell her Qispi would want her to have it. It will plant the seed in her mind."

"Was that her name? The little girl in Peru? Qispi?"

"Yes. It means *free*." Nathaniel gave Marlow a sad smile. "Passing this on from one girl who died for rain to another girl who will invent a way to make water . . ." He shrugged. "In a way, it's gone full circle."

"It only took a thousand years," Chasan said.

Nathaniel smiled up at him. "And a very patient angel."

Chasan grinned. "And one who was incredibly stubborn and pigheaded," he added. "But we got there in the end."

Marlow turned the silver plate over in her hand, and she

looked at Nathaniel. "Why can't you just give it to her and tell her? Why involve me at all?"

"Because twenty-two years ago, when you were just four years old, you helped save me," Nathaniel replied.

Chasan added, "And because twenty minutes ago, you were considering quitting, and you have a lot of lives to save yet."

"And we could all use a little divine intervention every now and then," Nathaniel added.

Marlow sat quietly for a while, just staring at the silver plate and shaking her head every now and then. Nathaniel and Chasan gave her the silence she needed to get her head around everything they'd just told her.

"So you're angels?" she said, clearly back at the beginning.

"Yes."

Now her analytical mind was taking over. "So that makes you, what? Christian? Or Jewish? Or . . ."

Chasan laughed. "Just between us, there are no separate denomination of faith. Heaven is whatever you deserve it to be."

Marlow stared, then laughed. "Well, shit. There are gonna be some bitterly surprised people when they die."

Nathaniel laughed. "No kidding. Boy, I could tell you some stories."

Chasan chuckled. "But you won't."

Nathaniel grumbled. "Stupid rules."

Marlow was quiet again for a bit, then a confused look crossed her face. "So, if you did die in the bodega that day, who the heck taught us for the rest of the year? Because you were there with an arm sling for a while, and everything just carried on as normal."

"Replacements who took on our appearance with some

angel magic. They took over our human lives, basically, lived in our apartment, did our jobs, and pretended to be us." Nathaniel smiled. "Their names are Zophiel and Raguel. Great guys, and they loved every second."

He laughed every time he remembered watching Zophiel and Raguel on every screen in the Security Two offices. They had twenty four-year-olds on stage, singing and dancing to the "Octopus's Garden." Zophiel, who was pretending to be Chasan, then morphed the song into "Yellow Submarine," and kids were dressed up as octopuses and jellyfish and sharks, and Raguel, who was pretending to be Nathaniel, was the yellow submarine. The kids forgot the words and where they were supposed to be on stage and the whole thing descended into chaos.

But the audience roared with laughter and applause and they got a standing ovation. The whole thing went viral on the internet, and Nathaniel couldn't even mock them for it because it was such a brilliant disaster.

"I became a doctor because of what happened to you," Marlow said quietly. "It changed my life."

"And now you get to change the course of the world," Nathaniel said. "When you meet this little girl this afternoon, that's what you'll do."

"With help from you," she countered. "I wouldn't have known what to do if you hadn't told me."

Chasan smiled at her. "Consider it your own divine intervention."

Nathaniel stood up. "We should get going. You have a busy afternoon coming up."

Marlow stood as well. "Will I see you again?"

"We'll be around," Nathaniel murmured. "Oh, and Marlow?"

"Yeah?"

"Buster said to say hi."

Her eyes welled with tears. "Oh. Is he . . . ?" Then her eyes went wide. "I'd forgotten about that! You told me he was in Heaven! With his own sofa to sleep on!"

Nathaniel grinned at her. "I'll give him a pat for you."

A happy tear escaped down her cheek as she nodded just as Nathaniel snapped his fingers, leaving a shower of sparkles in their wake.

They arrived in a vast open field of long grass, blue skies, and fluffy white clouds. There were trees for shade and the sound of a creek nearby, and it was utterly serene. A dog came bounding up to them, black in color with a red collar. "Buster!" Nathaniel said, dropping to his knee to give Buster a well-deserved pat. "She's doing just fine, buddy."

He wagged his tail and smiled before bounding off in the long grass. Chasan put his wing around Nathaniel and pulled him close. Nathaniel's wing slotted in under Chasan's, and both of them sighed at the contact. Nathaniel still thrilled at his touch, and he would never, never take him for granted again. "So, I was thinking maybe we should do another assignment . . ."

Chasan laughed. "I was quite enjoying the Hell Department. It's fun. And the occasional session over here with the dogs is great." Chasan kissed the side of Nathaniel's head. "But I'm always up for another assignment. As long as we go together."

"Always. Do you really think Peter would dare separate us?"

Chasan laughed again. "Nope."

"So what do you think? Another mission as human husbands?"

Chasan turned and lifted Nathaniel's chin so he could kiss him. "Absolutely. Where to this time, my love?"

"It doesn't matter." Then Nathaniel thought about it some more. "No, wait. Somewhere that has baby goats."

Chasan's whole body shook as he laughed. "Excellent. Let's go see the Ops Department and ask if they have any assignments that require baby-goat herders."

Nathaniel grinned and their twin flames joined, entwining and dancing in the breeze. "Or," he suggested. "Maybe we could put in a submission to the Planning Department to set up a baby-goat department like the canine department; then we could just stay here in Heaven forever."

Chasan laughed, his eyes glinting with delight. "I love that idea."

Nathaniel frowned . . . "But then that wouldn't be fair to the baby cows, would it? Or even the older cows, because ageism is discrimination too. But then we'd have to let the older goats in as well, and what about the horses and llamas, and the yaks . . ." He put his hand to his forehead. "Oh, what about the yaks?"

Chasan kissed him quiet with smiling lips. "I love you, Nathaniel."

"I love you too," Nathaniel replied. Then he reached up and knocked Chasan's halo until it sat crooked. "Oh dear," he said. "We better go fix that."

Chasan pulled him even closer with a chuckle. "Oh no!" he cried. "Now you'll have to get me naked to realign my halo."

Nathaniel grinned, a wicked gleam in his eye. "I'm counting on it."

Saint Peter's Office

Saint Peter finally sat in his chair and rubbed the sole of his foot. His sandals weren't cutting it on those human assignments. He'd just gotten back and was totally exhausted; his feet were killing him.

"What's the latest?" he asked.

Barachiel looked up from his latest report. "Well, they completed the mission with Marlow. The silver plate has been given to the child who is now healing well, apparently."

"Good, good."

Barachiel made a face. "And Nathaniel wants to implement a Baby-Goat Department."

"A what?"

"A Baby-Goat Department."

Saint Peter was aghast. "Why?"

Barachiel read the line from this report. "Because, and I quote, 'They have smooshy faces and tiny baby-goat horns and tiny goat feet.'"

Saint Peter sighed and let his foot fall to the floor. "And where is Nathaniel right now?"

"Ah," Anael said as she fanned her face. "I wouldn't be interrupting them for a while."

Saint Peter gawped at her. "They're still going at it?"

"They haven't stopped," she replied. "Well, barely. They have brief intermissions . . ."

He squeezed the bridge of his nose. "Oh Heaven's mercy." Everyone in the room stared at him, or more to the point, they stared at his use of Nathaniel's catchphrase. "Well, at least Nathaniel's stopped smiting things," Saint Peter said, trying to be hopeful.

"True," they all agreed.

"So," Saint Peter hedged. "Their next human assignment?"

"Probably won't be for a while," Ridwan said.

"A few decades, centuries," Lailah offered. "Who knows?"

Saint Peter nodded slowly. "Probably just as well."

"The Legal Department's happy," Lailah added.

Saint Peter sighed again. "And everyone else's assignments are going well, I hope?"

Everyone nodded, though only half of the directors were there at present. The rest were on assignments. Barachiel slid his clipboard toward Saint Peter. "Productivity is up by thirty percent."

Then a loud crash rang off in the distance, followed by Nathaniel and Chasan's laughter pealing through the heavens. It sounded like they'd just broken another bed or possibly another house . . . Someone snorted, and Saint Peter reached over slowly and pressed the reception intercom button. "Can we get maintenance on that, please?"

"Already on it," they replied.

Everyone tried not to smile, but Lailah couldn't help but laugh. Saint Peter smiled as well because to see Nathaniel truly happy made his heart full. Then he clapped his hands together. "All right, everyone, back to work."

THE END

ABOUT THE AUTHOR

N.R. Walker is an Australian author, who loves her genre of gay romance. She loves writing and spends far too much time doing it, but wouldn't have it any other way.

She is many things: a mother, a wife, a sister, a writer. She has pretty, pretty boys who live in her head, who don't let her sleep at night unless she gives them life with words.

She likes it when they do dirty, dirty things... but likes it even more when they fall in love.

She used to think having people in her head talking to her was weird, until one day she happened across other writers who told her it was normal.

She's been writing ever since...

The Spencer Cohen Series, Book One

The Spencer Cohen Series, Book Two

The Spencer Cohen Series, Book Three

The Spencer Cohen Series, Yanni's Story

Blood & Milk

The Weight Of It All

A Very Henry Christmas (The Weight of It All 1.5)

Perfect Catch

Switched

Imago

Imagines

Red Dirt Heart Imago

On Davis Row

Finders Keepers

Evolved

Galaxies and Oceans

Private Charter

Nova Praetorian

A Soldier's Wish

Upside Down

The Hate You Drink

Sir

Tallowwood

Titles in Audio:

Cronin's Key

Cronin's Key II

Cronin's Key III

Red Dirt Heart

Red Dirt Heart 2

Red Dirt Heart 3

Red Dirt Heart 4

The Weight Of It All

Switched

Point of No Return

Breaking Point

Starting Point

Spencer Cohen Book One

Spencer Cohen Book Two

Spencer Cohen Book Three

Yanni's Story

On Davis Row

Evolved

Elements of Retrofit

Clarity of Lines

Sense of Place

Blind Faith

Through These Eyes

Blindside

Finders Keepers

Galaxies and Oceans

Nova Praetorian

Upside Down

Free Reads:

Sixty Five Hours

Learning to Feel

His Grandfather's Watch (And The Story of Billy and Hale)

The Twelfth of Never (Blind Faith 3.5)

Twelve Days of Christmas (Sixty Five Hours Christmas)

Best of Both Worlds

Translated Titles:

Fiducia Cieca (Italian translation of Blind Faith)

Attraverso Questi Occhi (Italian translation of Through These Eyes)

Preso alla Sprovvista (Italian translation of Blindside)

Il giorno del Mai (Italian translation of Blind Faith 3.5)

Cuore di Terra Rossa (Italian translation of Red Dirt Heart)

Cuore di Terra Rossa 2 (Italian translation of Red Dirt Heart 2)

Cuore di Terra Rossa 3 (Italian translation of Red Dirt Heart 3)

Cuore di Terra Rossa 4 (Italian translation of Red Dirt Heart 4)

Natale di terra rossa (Red dirt Christmas)

Intervento di Retrofit (Italian translation of Elements of Retrofit)

A Chiare Linee (Italian translation of Clarity of Lines)

Spencer Cohen 1 Serie: Spencer Cohen

Spencer Cohen 2 Serie: Spencer Cohen

Spencer Cohen 3 Serie: Spencer Cohen

Punto di non Ritorno (Italian translation of Point of No Return)

Punto di Rottura (Italian translation of Breaking Point)

Imago (Italian translation of Imago)

Il desiderio di un soldato (Italian translation of A Soldier's Wish)

Confiance Aveugle (French translation of Blind Faith)

A travers ces yeux: Confiance Aveugle 2 (French translation of Through These Eyes)

Aveugle: Confiance Aveugle 3 (French translation of Blindside)

À Jamais (French translation of Blind Faith 3.5)

Cronin's Key (French translation)

Cronin's Key II (French translation)

Au Coeur de Sutton Station (French translation of Red Dirt Heart)

Partir ou rester (French translation of Red Dirt Heart 2)

Faire Face (French translation of Red Dirt Heart 3)

Trouver sa Place (French translation of Red Dirt Heart 4)

Rote Erde (German translation of Red Dirt Heart)

Rote Erde 2 (German translation of Red Dirt Heart 2)

Vier Pfoten und ein bisschen Zufall (German translation of

THE DICHOTOMY OF ANGELS